MW00849647

The Importance of Sons

CHRONICLES OF THE HOUSE OF VALOIS

KEIRA MORGAN

FRENCH RENAISSANCE FICTION

DEDICATION

I dedicate this book to two men:

Oscar Humberto Lopez Valdez,
my marvellous husband,
who brings me joy each day of my life.

and

Matthew Reginald Morgan Brown,
my beloved son,
who died too young.

Copyright © 2022, by Keira Morgan

The Importance of Sons

Keira Morgan

www.keiramorgan.com

keira@keiramorgan.com

Published by French Renaissance Fiction/

Fiction de la Renaissance française

Arundel, QC, CA

613 804-4710

ISBN 978-1-7773974-3-2 (ebook) June 2022

ISBN 978-1-7773974-2-5 (paper) June 2022

Cover design by Jenny Q at Historical Fiction Book Covers.

Cover created from the painting in the public domain available under the Creative Commons license: *Portrait of Eleanor of Toledo with her son Giovanni de' Medici, by Agnolo Bronzino, 1544/1545*

ALL RIGHTS RESERVED

No part of this publication may be reproduced, stored in a retrieval system or transmitted in any form or by any means, electronic, mechanical, photocopying, recording, scanning, or otherwise except as permitted under Section 107 or 108 of the 1976 International Copyright Act, without the prior written permission except in brief quotations in critical articles and reviews.

This is a work of fiction. All characters, organizations, and events portrayed in this novel are either the products of the author's imagination or are used fictionally.

Author's Notes:

- Canadian English is used throughout this book.
- Lyon, the French spelling of the city spelled Lyons in English, is used through this book.
- Names and titles present challenges to authors. First, royalty and nobility have many titles, all of which they use as names. Second, as they change their status, from a count to a duke for example, their titles change. To keep it simple, I generally ignore this change for minor characters. For my main characters I cannot, since it is important for the story. So, when Duchess Anne changes from duchess to queen it is not an error, it is an important increase in her status. **If you become confused, check back to the list of principal characters.**
- I provide endnotes and a glossary of terms for the words I expect to be less well known.

Character List

Main Characters (ages in 1492)

(15) Anne, Duchess of Brittany, Queen of France (1476-1514)

(16) Louise, Countess d'Angoulême (1476-1531)

(22) King Charles VIII of France (1470-1498)

(33) Count Charles (**Carlo**) d'Angoulême (1458-1496) — Louise's husband. [She calls him **Carlo** to make it easier for readers]

(29) Duke Louis d'Orléans, First Prince of the Blood and Dauphin (1462-1515)

(31) Mme Antoinette de Polignac (c.1460-?)—Louise's principal lady-in-waiting and Count Charles's mistress

(70) Countess Marguerite d'Angoulême (1422-1496), Count Charles's mother, daughter of Viscount Alain IX de Rohan (c.1422-1496) and half-sister of Jean I, Viscount de Rohan (1450-1516)—Louise's mother-in-law

(31) Madame la Grande, Duchess Anne de Bourbon (1461-1522), Regent for her brother, mother of Suzanne.

(12) Michelle de Saubonne, (c.1479-1549)—joins the story in Lyon in 1494 [changed her actual birthdate from 1485 for story requirements]

(59) **Joanne** [Jeanne] de Laval, Queen of NAPLES (1433-1498)—close friend and relation of Anne [changed her name from Jeanne to **Joanne** to make it easier for readers]

(28) Duchess Jeanne d'Orléans (1464-1505)—Duke Louis's detested wife, sister to King Charles and Madame la Grande

(54) Duke Pierre de Bourbon (1438-1503)—Madame la Grande's husband, co-regent and father of Suzanne.

(0) Charles Orland, dauphin (1492-1496)—first son of Anne and King Charles

(-2) François d'Angoulême, (1494-1547)—son of Louise and Count Charles.

(76) Friar Francis de Paule (1416-1507)—Holy Hermit of the Minims (a Franciscan order)

Minor characters

(?) Bishop Michel Guibé (?-1502) Bishop of Rennes (1482 - 1502)—He crowned Anne of Brittany duchess on 10 February 1489 in the cathedral of Rennes and married her on 19 December 1490 to Maximilian, king of the Romans.

(51) Cardinal Guillaume Briçonnet (1445–1514)–Bishop de Saint-Malo, later a French Cardinal and statesman,

(44) Count François de Dunois (1447-1491)—Dies on flight from Brittany

(?) Count Wolfgang de Polhaim (n.d.)—King Maximilian's representative in Rennes, Brittany

(33) King Maximilian of the Romans, later Holy Roman Emperor (1459-1519)—Anne's first husband

(45) Marshal Jean IV de Rieux, (1447-1518)–Anne's *Gouverneur* [1] appointed by the late Duke François II de Montfort, leader of the Breton Army

(8) Marguerite d'Autriche, daughter of King Maximilian (1480-1530)— first wife of Charles VIII, Louise's cousin and later sister-in-law

(15) Pernette de Montauban, daughter of Baron Philippe de Montauban (n. d.)—principal lady-in-waiting to Anne when she first arrives in France §

(11) Anne de Rohan, daughter of Viscount Jean I de Rohan, (c.1480-?)—demoiselle in Louise's household

(9) Marie de Rohan, daughter of Viscount Jean I de Rohan, (c.1482–?)—demoiselle in Anne's household

(0) Marguerite d'Angoulême (aka Margot) (1492-1549)–daughter of Louise and Count Charles

(41) Baron Pierre de Rohan, known as Marshal de Gié (1451-1513)

(47) Etienne de Vesc, first gentleman of the Bedchamber (1445-1501)—father figure to Charles from birth, Charles's favourite

(?) Mme de Bussières—*Gouvernante,*[2] to Charles-Orland (n.d)

(49) Jean de Châlons, Prince d'Orange, Governor of Brittany, Anne's first cousin and closest male relative (1443-1503)—Anne's heir should she die without children

(?) Mme Charlotte de Vesc, wife of Etienne de Vesc (n. d.)—lady-in-waiting in Anne's court §

(46) Baron Philippe de Montauban, Anne's Chancellor of Brittany (1445-1514)

(22) Catherine de Brézé, Granddaughter of Louis XI (c.1470-?)—lady-in-waiting to Queen Anne

(24) Octavien de Saint-Gelais, Bishop d'Angoulême (1468-1502)

(27) Jean de Saint-Gelais, Grand Chamberlain to Count and Countess d'Angoulême (c.1465-?)

(31) Père André de La Vigne (1470?-1526)–Secretary to Anne of Brittany and French poet

(59) Pope Innocent–Giovanni Battista Cibo (1432-1492)–from Genoa, elevated as Innocent VIII, 1484 to 1492

(60) Pope Alexander VI–Rodrigo Borgia (1431-1503)–from Aragon, elevated as Alexander VI, 1492 to 1503

(?) M. Desmon, Charles's physician, (n. d.)

(?) Père Pierre Le Pennec–almoner in the service of Marshal de Rieux, (n.d.)

Ladies and Gentlemen of the courts
A peasant family outside Chinon §
The Breton Guard [100 men]
? = unknown
n. d. = no dates
§ = fictional character

1 Gouverneur/nante—the Governor/ness of the royal children, recruited from the high nobility, oversees the education of the children of the royal couple, including the Dauphin. He or she is sometimes assisted by deputy governors. While the girls remained attached to the Queen's House, it was customary for princes raised by female governors until they were seven to "pass to men" at that age (the age of reason at the time).

2 Gouverneur/nante—the Governor/ness of the royal children, recruited from the high nobility, oversees the education of the children of the royal couple, including the Dauphin. He or she is sometimes assisted by deputy governors. While the girls remained attached to the Queen's House, it was customary for princes raised by female governors until they were seven to "pass to men" at that age (the age of reason at the time).

CHAPTER 1

Fleeing the Scene

A Forest outside Rennes, 20 November 1491

"If only I'd been a boy!" Duchess Anne raged. "None of this would have happened if I had been a boy." She flung an arm out wide, at the drizzle, the forest surrounding them, their armed entourage, and the fallen man who lay crumpled, just off the path, on the frosty forest floor.

The fifteen-year-old Duchess of Brittany and Duke Louis d'Orléans stood over the body of their dead companion. He had been riding beside Duke Louis as they fled Anne's besieged capital of Rennes when he groaned once and slipped sideways from his sturdy horse. By the time Anne and Duke Louis reined in and circled back, he lay with his eyes wide and sightless, facing the sullen skies. Louis had seen enough death on the battlefield to know his lifelong comrade was dead, but he knelt to feel for a pulse to hide the tears that sprang to his eyes.

Anne dropped from her horse to kneel beside him. "Another of my men sacrificed to this terrible war. Why, Lord? When we have already lost too many." Her voice shook. Then she tightened her lips. She must not give way.

Waiting until he could control the tremor in his voice, Louis said, "François's death could have happened at any time, Duchess Anne. His heart was weak, and he was no longer young." He rose, peering through the trees, as he considered how to deal with this catastrophe.

Anne did not argue. She had blurted the first words that came to her. It was unlike her. Their problems were much too urgent for girlish tears and childish tantrums. Only cool heads and quick thinking would serve now.

The duke decided. "We must tie him to his mount and bring him with us. We do not know how long our lead is and have no time to waste." When Anne nodded, he said, "I will go for his groom." He turned away, looked up at the sky, and sent for the captain of the guard. Then he ordered the company to stay close to their mounts and make no noise.

Anne informed them of the tragedy and walked among them to calm their first shocked fears. It was her duty. Afterwards, standing beside the fallen body of her cousin, she shivered in the chilly wind that rustled the trees. It added another level of discomfort to their long day on horseback.

They had started in the dark before Prime[1]and a short time past she had heard, faintly in the distance, church bells ringing for Sext.[2] She calculated. They had been riding for close to eight hours. Louis had told her the journey to Châteaubriant near the border of Brittany would take at least sixteen hours—if nothing went wrong. She hoped this would not become the disaster that disrupted their careful plans.

A wave of guilt washed over her. Her trusted councillor had just died, and she was blaming him for the inconvenience! What kind of ingrate was she? She added it to the list of sins to confess and said a prayer for his departed soul as she waited with what patience she could muster. Yet they must get to the Château that evening before anyone in Rennes except her Privy Councillors knew she had flown. Certainly, before Count de Polhaim, her husband's envoy—she *should* say her former husband's envoy—discovered she was gone.

She shivered again, this time with fear of the German landsknechts[3] who might even now be on their trail. When he had been an ally, before they married, her now-ex-husband King Maximilian had sent 3,000 German landsknechts to fight with her army against the French. She narrowed her eyes, thinking about him. A promising man he had proven to be. For he had not sent the money to pay them, although he promised, and promised, and promised. Nor had he come himself to save her and Brittany from defeat.

She forced herself to relive the night two weeks ago that had crystallized every painful decision of the previous four months—to surrender to the hated French, to annul her marriage to Maximilian, and to agree to marry the king of detested France.

Maximilian's German troops had broken into the stores of ale meant to last the town for weeks, got themselves totally cupshot, rioted and then run wild through the streets of Rennes. After breaking into all the alehouses, and raping any woman unfortunate enough to be in the street, they beat and stabbed the townsmen who dared to oppose them. They were a wild, vicious lot.

The captain of her troops in Rennes, had been forced to call up every armed man in the town to regain control and force the rioters back to their barracks. Many lay dead among the townsfolk and her loyal men. Then Count de Polhaim had dared demand reparations for the Germans lost. The rampage had validated her intention to annul her marriage and flee.

Gazing down on the dead count, who so recently had saved her last remaining stronghold, Anne blinked back tears but there was no time to mourn. Besides, she must not give way before this company, who were risking their lives to help her run for France and another unwelcome marriage. They were a small company, with more armed men than courtiers and servants, and she was one of only four women in the entire one-hundred-strong party.

Duke Louis rode up with his fallen comrade's groom and recaptured horse. Its saddle had been removed and a double layer of blankets thrown over its back. Since they had little choice, the duke and groom rolled the body into a sheet, tossed it over the back of the mount, and tied his hands to his feet to keep the corpse affixed. Within moments, the body was secured, and then the groom guided the edgy steed further back into the party.

Anne scrambled to the back of her own mount without help to keep from thinking about this rough treatment of her cousin's body. She was glad she was wearing boy's clothing. So, too, were her gouvernante, her principal lady-in-waiting, and her maid, for Anne had deemed it safer if all four travelled in male attire. She watched Duke Louis pull his helmet over his tousled brown hair, already streaked with grey, and vault effortlessly into his saddle. His leather cuirass was creased and worn with use. Despite his lack of care for his clothing, he was an attractive man, because of his great interest in the people around him.

In a voice accustomed to shouting orders in the heat of battle, he commanded the company to mount up. With Duchess Anne at his side, he urged them to a brisk walk and they continued their journey south-east by the shortest route out of Brittany.

Once the troop had settled into a steady rhythm, Duke Louis glanced sidelong at the young duchess. Dressed as a boy, small and slender for her years, she looked like a child of ten. But behind those large hazel eyes and flawless complexion lay a mind as sharp as a dagger and an iron will. She was as immovable as those giant granite boulders rooted into the rocky soil along the coast of Brittany that had stood there for longer than time itself.

It was a long ride for a young and fragile female. Especially one with a diseased hip that left her with one short leg and a noticeable limp. "How do you go on, Duchess Anne?" he asked.

She looked surprised. "Well. Why do you ask? About Cousin François, you mean? Do you think I take it as a bad omen? I do, of course. But nothing about this journey into France pleases me, as you know."

Louis hid the smile that leapt to his lips. He should not be surprised. He had never heard her complain about being tired. She might look fragile, but she was as sturdy as the bedrock that formed the spine of her duchy. He recollected Anne's anguished outburst in the moment after their cousin's demise. "What makes you think things would have been different if you had been a boy?"

Anne's lips hardened into a thin line. "No one would have tried to bully me into marriage. That is a start."

Louis almost interrupted, but he had learned patience the past three years in his sister-in-law's prison, so he waited.

"Neither of my gouverneurs would have rebelled because I would have been a *proper* heir. Of course, they would have tried to make me a good match, but they would not have thought they could rule *for* me, because I was a *boy*! And they would think I was still *too young* to marry." The bitterness dripped from her voice, as caustic as lye. She paused long enough that Louis almost answered, but she had not finished. "And since I would not have married, the French—or I should say Madame la Grande—would have had no excuse to make war upon my duchy. So I would not be fleeing secretly from my own lands, risking my soul by disobeying Holy Church to make a marriage I hate, to King Charles. You see, all different." Agitated by Anne's intensity, her palfrey sidled and Anne stopped speaking to lean over, pat her mount's mane and murmur in her ear.

Louis itched to pat Anne's hand. She looked so young and brave and troubled. Impulsively, he spoke. "It is not only girls who are forced to marry where they would not, nor have their rights stolen from them by the ruthless rulers of France."

Anne turned to gaze at him and he read contrition in her eyes.

"Shall I tell you?" he asked. "We have a long ride ahead." When she nodded, he told her about how King Charles's father, Louis XI, had forced him to marry the king's crippled, barren daughter, Jeanne, when he was only twelve so that the d'Orléans branch of the Valois line would become extinct. And why? Because the greedy king wanted the d'Orléans' lands. King Louis even joked about it. "It will not cost much to raise the children of that union," he chortled to his cronies. Instead of leaving him as regent, which was his role by right as First Prince of the Blood, the king had named his daughter—his *daughter!* —as regent—

Anne drew a sharp breath and Louis realized his faux pas. "I- I mean we are speaking of France." He stumbled over his words. "In France, the Salic Law applies. Women are *not allowed* to rule. Not like in Brittany."

Anne gave him a sardonic glance. "I understand, Duke."

"Anyway, Madame la Grande hates me. That is why I ended up fighting for your father in Brittany. And why I spent three years in her prison, still married to her ugly, barren sister." He spat into the oak trees on the side of the path.

Then he added. "There was one thing she could not take from me. Until Charles has a son, I am closest prince to the throne, so I am dauphin." He gave a humourless laugh. "Will not Madame la Grande be pleased when you take that position from me!"

The rhythm of their horses' hooves, muted by the leaf mould that lay thick along the wide path through the oak trees, filled the silence between them.

Finally, Anne replied, her voice flat, "As I said, Cousin Louis. Boys."

1 Prime—the first hour of daylight, traditionally 6:00 a.m.

2 Sext—noon, traditionally 12:00 p.m.

3 Landsknecht— a member of a class of mercenary soldiers in the German and other continental armies in the 16th and 17th centuries.

CHAPTER 2

A Secret Royal Marriage

Château de Langeais, France, 6 December 1491

Countess Louise d'Angoulême stood beside her husband, Carlo, and his cousin, Duke Louis d'Orléans, close to the entrance into the great hall of the Château. She assumed the appearance of listening while Duke Louis described the flight from Brittany with Duchess Anne. Instead, she compared her finery to the attire of the other ladies and preened. In her opinion, her gown was the most stylish, although others glittered with finer materials and more jewels. She warmed with satisfaction.

It had taken ingenuity to design it to disguise her growing belly. Since the week previously when Carlo had announced this rushed journey to Langeais, she, her mother-in-law, and her ladies had been busy. Louise had designed her ensemble while her ladies cut, sewed, and embroidered, taking apart worn gowns and reusing fine fabric. Her gown's decorative forepart[1], made of salvaged cloth of silver embroidered with her pearl and gold swan emblem contrasted with the pale blue brocade of the overgown. The upper sleeves, saved from another cloth of silver gown, had matching swan embroidery. They were attached to long, hanging lower sleeves in matching blue trimmed with rabbit fur. To complete her attire, a long-sleeved shift trimmed in fine lace peeked out at her wrists.

Louise doubted that her rivals could guess that she had pieced its parts together to refresh her gown. She and her mother-in-law had agreed it was essential they hide the family's straitened circumstances from inquisitive eyes. Nor did she want to display her hopes for an heir until she was certain she would not lose the baby. She could not bear people knowing of her failures.

When Carlo said she could bring only one lady-in-waiting to the secret wedding, she had almost refused to attend. It added to Louise's conviction that she and the new Queen Anne would be enemies before they ever met. First, of course, Anne was a de Montfort, traditional enemies of the de Rohan family. Maman Marguerite, a de Rohan by birth, and sister to the Viscount who was the head of the family, insisted that the ducal coronet of Brittany should sit on her brother's head. The so-called Duchess Anne de Montfort was nothing but a usurper.

Taking a swig of the mug of cider that was never far from her side, Maman Marguerite had said, "*Si la fillette*, the girl, she 'ad done as she should and married my nephew, she would 'ave saved herself and all of us this *tragédie*. Look what she 'as done! *La Bretagne,* she should never be part of France. *Petite Folle.*"

Louise had many other reasons, and any of them would have been sufficient. At her husband's sudden crack of laughter, Louise glanced at him. He resembled his cousin Louis, with his light brown hair and long Valois nose, and still lithe, athletic body. Unlike Louis, he took pride in dressing well. She wondered if he, too, resented that their penury resulted directly from his loyalty to Anne's father. Because of it, both he and his cousin Louis had fought on the wrong side in the *Guerre Folle*, the Mad War. He had been luckier than Louis for he escaped prison, but Louise and he were *still* paying the fines Madame la Grande had levied against his lands. And what had *she* ever done that Madame la Grande should punish *her* by marrying *her* to a penny-pinched ancient, so that now *she* had to scrimp day-in, day-out to present a proper appearance on a meagre income?

But then, Madame la Grande was heartless. Louise would never forget what it had been like to arrive at Madame la Grande's court as a lonely seven-year-old after her mother had died. The only person who had been unfailingly kind was little Marguerite, *Mme la Petite Dauphine*, as everyone called her. Louise was furious that Madame had tossed Marguerite aside like a worn-out shoe when she found a more *useful* bride for her brother.

Still, it was only at the instant that she saw Duchess Anne in the entryway to the great hall that Louise hated her. The feeling came over her in a molten flood, starting in her heart and burning outward through her veins until she could feel the heat flowing through the soles of her shoes and out the tips of her fingers. She was glad to curtsey so she could lower her head, for her face felt flushed.

Her eyes followed Anne after she passed. It was not only that the girl, who was obviously younger than she, was as tiny and delicate as a Breton faery. Nor was it simply that her clothing—her costly jewelled headdress, and the cloth-of gold wedding gown lined with sable—was as elegant as Louise's own, besides being as costly as a Turk's. Neither was it the beauty of Anne's enormous hazel eyes, chestnut hair and golden rose skin, for Louise knew that her own tall willowy elegance, fair hair and skin, and large stormy grey eyes drew men like helpless flies. It was none of those things, infuriating as they all were. No. It was her insufferable air of arrogance.

~

STIFFENING HER SPINE, Anne slid her hands down the skirt of her cloth of gold wedding gown until she clutched the jewelled rosary that hung from her waist. The parting gift from her dying mother, it contained a thorn from the crown of Christ's martyrdom and was her most precious possession. As she touched it, she sent a silent prayer heavenward.

A voice announced, "Anne, Duchess de Bretagne, Countess d'Étampes . . ." and continued to recite her titles. Anne glided forward into the light-filled room before her. Large circular candelabra hung from the high ceiling and marched down the centre of the large chamber, each blazing with wax candles. A fireplace burned bright at the far end. Someone had decorated the white-washed walls with boughs of pine tied with red ribbons and tiny silver bells. Their spicy scent added some warmth to the chill that had invaded Anne as she surveyed the scene. With this touch of the festive, she felt a dash of hope that this marriage might bring more pleasure than she had expected.

She glanced around as the courtiers rose from their obeisances. There were no more than thirty, most of them known to her, and she resented the scanty numbers and paltry display. As Duchess of Brittany, she deserved a grand ceremonial event with all her and her husband's vassals and teeming crowds outside a great cathedral cheering the future of the bride and groom and diving for largesse. Worse, this was her second meagre wedding within a year.

Her hands tightened around the rosary once more as she glanced toward the makeshift altar set up at the far end of the room in front of the fireplace. The two bishops who awaited her had promised that the dispensations they had signed were sufficient to annul her first marriage to King Maximilian and sanctify this one to King Charles. She slowed her already funereal pace toward them. It was bad enough that *her* marriage should be dissolved. Although her flesh had touched that of the Count de Polhaim in front of her court when he served as King Maximilian's proxy, she had never met Maximilian himself. He was a grown man who had promised to come to her rescue and had not. He deserved no better.

But Madame la Grande, deciding that Brittany was the greater prize, forced Charles to dissolve his marriage to young Marguerite d'Autriche even though they had been married for eight years. Even though he was king. The Regent herself had brought the little princess—who was King Maximilian's daughter to add insult to his injury—to France when she was only three years old and married her to Charles the day she arrived. She had been treated as the queen all her life. Anne tried to imagine how she would feel in Queen Marguerite's shoes. Probably she would loathe both King Charles and Madame la Grande. And likely she would blame the other woman, too.

That is me. What an unsettling feeling. I will have to do something to show her how sorry I am for my part in this.

Anne forced her mind back to her imminent wedding. A gold monstrance shone among the vessels sitting on the embroidered altar cloth that covered the temporary altar. Beside the altar, clad in gold and white copes and stiff mitres, two bishops lent their authority to the ceremony. Young King Charles, whom she had not seen since their brief stolen meeting in a small chapel outside Rennes almost two months previously, waited for her beside them. Anne relaxed a trifle. With proper modesty, she kept her eyes lowered and concentrated on moving gracefully on her uneven shoes, especially designed to conceal her one short leg and awkward limp. She would have no one remember that her body was imperfect. She reached his side without mishap. Although he was not tall, the top of her head came only to his shoulder, even with the lift in her shoe. In the chapel, he had been happy to discover that he was taller than she.

The Cardinal began the short service. The words of the marriage vows as they made them were uncomfortably familiar. "Charles, do you take Anne, here present, for your lawful wife according to the rite of our holy mother, the Church?"

Charles said, "I do."

They were the first words Anne had heard him say since she had last met him in Rennes. As Charles made his vows, it astonished her once again that words so weighty they bound a couple for life in the eyes of God and Holy Church should take so little time to utter.

"Anne, do you take Charles, here present, for your lawful husband according to the rite of our holy mother, the Church?"

Anne replied, "I do," her voice no louder than a whisper, so reluctant was she to remarry without the papal dispensations. Until the documents blessing their marriage arrived from Rome, she feared they were both legally wed to others. But she had spoken the vows now. Was she committing adultery? Would she burn in hell? Only her years of training kept her from wringing her hands. She wanted to turn and run from the room.

Before she could give way to panic, the Cardinal joined their right hands and married them, saying, "*Ego conjúngo vos in matrimónium. In nómine Patris, et Fílii, et Spíritus Sancti. Amen.*"[2]

After he pronounced them man and wife, Anne raised her eyes to the king's. Charles smiled down at her, the corners of his dark eyes crinkling, as he held her freezing hand in his. It was warm and she felt reassured. He was not handsome, for his nose was long and fleshy above his large, loose lips. But his eyes were large and fringed with thick, dark lashes and his hair looked as soft as her favourite puppy's ears. She felt a sudden longing to cuddle Fanchon, who was waiting for her in a room upstairs.

She accepted her new husband's arm and moved with him to the small nearby table where everything lay in readiness to sign the marriage contract, pleased that their cloth of gold wedding outfits with their sable-lined sleeves matched, as was traditional in France. It made their marriage feel less hasty. He had promised her he would see it done after she accepted his suit. When he made his proposal in the small candle-lit chapel, he had gone down on one knee. And when she agreed, he said she had made him the happiest man on earth. They both knew neither of them had a choice, but it was chivalrous of him to treat her as if she were his heart's desire. She had warmed to him then. It was a relief to feel the ice within her melting again.

As the contract signing dragged on, the courtiers' voices buzzed in her ears like the drone of lazy bees. Although the guests were few, each had an interest in the marriage. Madame la Grande and her husband were ensuring that none of the highest nobility in France and Brittany could deny their part so she insisted each must sign the marriage contract to demonstrate they had accepted its terms.

A flurry of activity caught Anne's attention at the far end of the great hall. A quartet of servants in the king's livery emerged carrying boards, trestles, and benches. They placed one table across the width of the hall and two more perpendicular to it. Anne watched the movements of soft-shoed butlers and pages from the corner of her eye while she conversed with the guests who had completed signing clustering near the fireplace.

Pages covered the tables with white linens that fell to the floor and placed a gilded salt boat on each table. Behind the centre table, two wooden armchairs raised higher than the benches on either side of them occupied the central position. A cloth of estate3 embroidered with the combined devices of Brittany and France hung above them. The position and prominence of the cloth of estate sent the message that her capitulation, and the attachment of her duchy to France, was the sole significance of her wedding. The king and Madame la Grande were boasting that they had gained what they wanted—her duchy of Brittany—by flaunting her under that emblem. They were presenting her like a prize won at a tournament, not a ruler of an independent state.

She tightened her lips to keep herself from glaring when the thin, sharp-nosed regent approached them with her husband and sketched a curtsey. She wore a gown that rivalled Anne's in magnificence. A jewelled black and white headdress hid her hair but could not disguise her prominent forehead, washed-out brown eyes, pale lashes and eyebrows, and thin nose. Her honour insulted by the table decorations, Anne comforted herself that her magnificence outdid her enemy's as noticeably as a peacock outshone a peahen.

"Madame la Grande," she said, "you have been busy. That is an elaborate cloth of estate you have prepared." A hint of scorn sounded in her voice

"As befits the King and Queen of France and Duke and Duchess of Brittany." Madame la Grande's eyes snapped, but her voice was smooth. "And may I present to you my husband, Duke Pierre de Bourbon. I do not believe you have yet met him. He is your new brother-in-law."

"How rapidly my family grows." It was true, Anne thought, and inoffensive. That Madame la Grande was now her sister grated like chalk on slate. Anne had adored her own sister, now an angel in Heaven. That she should be replaced by this. . . this. . . viper was just another painful sting of fate.

Well, the regent had held the position of first lady in France for far too long. She would soon discover that France had a queen now and she would have to accept she was no longer the first lady in the country.

1 Forepart–Placket and matching forepart—a separate piece of expensive and highly decorated material inserted into the opening of the overdress to cover the kirtle, often with matching lower sleeves.

2 *Ego conjúngo vos in matrimónium. In nómine Patris, et Fílii, et Spíritus Sancti. Amen."*—the traditional Latin marriage vow, translated as —By the authority of the Church I ratify and bless the bond of marriage you have contracted. In the name of the Father, and of the Son, and of the Holy Spirit.

3 Cloth of estate—a canopy-like arrangement of precious fabric above and behind a throne or dais.

CHAPTER 3

Celebrating the Marriage

Château de Langeais, France, 6 December 1491

Charles leaned close to Anne and murmured, "Wife, it is time for the dancing to begin. Since you are the bride, today I invite you to signal our intention to rise."

Anne was so accustomed to being the one who decided and signalled her intention to act that it took her a moment to understand the implication, that *Charles* now had the right to decide because he held a higher rank than she, that because he was her husband, she must obey him. In her confusion, she would have risen, but her husband held her back and half-whispered, "Signal my Grand Maître d'hôtel." Flushing, she obeyed.

The musicians blew a fanfare and the Grand Maître d'hôtel called, "All rise for the King and Queen of France, the Duke and Duchess of Brittany."

Anne fisted her hands. The most hateful clause in her marriage contract had been the one that gave her new husband the power to rule Brittany in her name. The sudden use of Charles's new ducal title sent a stab of pain through Anne's heart.

Her father was the last man she had heard addressed as Duke of Brittany. The memory unleashed a wash of grief at his unexpected loss four years previously. Anne blamed Madame la Grande for the deliberate choice of this moment to use the title to underscore her defeat.

As Anne and Charles descended from the raised dais, she turned her back to the room to hide her rush of tears, adding this insult to the tally of injuries done to her by the second lady in France. Beneath her pleasant smile she seethed as she walked arm in arm with her new husband accepting the congratulations of the wedding guests while they waited for the room to be cleared for dancing.

When they approached Duke Louis, he bowed. "M. le Roi," he said to the king, "will you release Madame la Reine to me so I may have the pleasure of introducing my new sister to my cousin, Count Charles?"

"Do you wish to make me jealous, Brother Louis? You have already accompanied her for two weeks!" King Charles laughed heartily, gave his cousin's arm a friendly squeeze to make it clear he was jesting, turned away, and was swallowed by the courtiers who surrounded them.

It sounded odd to hear herself addressed by her new title, as if it should belong to someone else, Anne thought, placing her arm along the top of Duke Louis's, keeping a wide distance between them. Her husband's comment might have been a quip, but there were several here who would not forget that Louis had once tried to annul his marriage to marry her. As he led her towards a window embrasure, she resisted for a moment, but gave way, for she longed for time to recover her equanimity. Louis pushed the heavy curtains aside, and they were half-hidden. She gazed out to the inky courtyard. Pinpricks of light reflecting from the torches glittered here and there in the barren gravelled square, hinting that treacherous ice lay beneath the surface.

"That announcement must have come as an unwelcome surprise," Duke Louis said. "I know it did to me."

"It stated the simple facts." Anne struggled and kept her voice steady. She was not willing to trust him with her pain. His had been the principal hand that had negotiated the agreement that had brought her to this place.

Instead, she said, "I had expected to meet Duchess Jeanne tonight. Did not the king and Madame la Grande want their sister here for the wedding?"

"The king invited her, but I sent her a messenger suggesting that to travel from Orléans during winter when the weather was uncertain would be dangerous for her health and she would please me best by remaining at home." The smile he gave her was impish.

Anne raised her eyebrows. "You did not fear irritating them so soon after Charles released you from Madame la Grande's prison?" The new queen kept her voice low, trusting the melody played by the musicians in the gallery to mask their conversation.

He gave a small smile. "Not after I had been so helpful in negotiating the treaty that brought him your exquisite self as his bride."

She crumpled a handful of her cloth of gold wedding gown and said, "Yes, when I sold myself for thirty pieces of silver."

"Madame la Reine, you judge yourself by a hard measure. You signed to bring peace to your duchy and to allow it to prosper again."

She wondered whether he was trying to convince himself or her. It was too late to repine, so she said, "It was better than to permit more war and destruction. But it still was losing."

"Madame la Reine, I say you made the right choice for Brittany. Its people can expect a lasting peace, a prosperous future and a queen of France who will protect their rights. For the rest, the future can alter its face as swiftly as the flip of a coin, as any man who has led a battle can attest. Only the Lord knows our fate."

She looked up at him and said, "Only if the Lord allows my duchy to recover its independence will I believe I did not fail my ancestors and my people." She turned away. "Let us meet this cousin of yours."

Anne guessed who he was before they were introduced, recognizing him from his long, hooked nose and fleshy lips, marks of the Valois family. He looked much older than the tall, slender girl with wide grey eyes who stood beside him.

"My cousin, Count Charles d'Angoulême, and his wife, Countess Louise." He kissed Louise's hand and clapped his cousin on the back. "How do you go on, Cousin Carlo?"

Anne gave her hand to the count. "I understand you were well known to my father. If you are cousin to Brother Louis, we must share family ties?" They began the obligatory tracing of their ancestry, searching for common threads. As they spoke, Anne became aware of a certain antagonism emanating from the unblinking eyes and unsmiling lips of the count's wife.

Turning to the countess, whom she guessed was little older than herself, she said, "Which part of the country are you from, Countess Louise?"

"My father, Count Philippe de Bresse, is uncle to Madame la Grande, so when my mother died when I was seven, he made me her ward. I grew up at Amboise with King Charles." Louise thrust her chin forward and added, "*and* Queen Marguerite. She is my cousin, for her mother and mine were sisters." Although the countess spoke as if simply conveying family information, she did not hide the barb in her voice when she mentioned the divorced queen.

During the three years Anne had ruled Brittany, many had sought to discountenance her. She had learned to display an unruffled demeanour. Often, a direct response was the most unexpected. "You must dislike this marriage then, for it injures your cousin. I regret it. It was not my desire to displace her."

The countess reddened and dropped her eyes. "I did not mean to imply you did, Madame la Reine. As women, we must marry where our duty lies." Realizing that this response slighted her husband, who stood beside her, her colour deepened.

Anne nodded, satisfied that the countess would be more careful with her words in future. She and Duke Louis walked on.

"She is another who holds a grudge against our sister-in-law," Duke Louis kept his voice so low only Anne could hear him. "Louise is not only beautiful, but very able. When her mother died, her feckless father sent her to Madame la Grande's opulent court almost penniless and without a dower. It wounded her pride. Then the regent married Louise to my cousin, who may be Second Prince of the Blood but is as poor as the fifth son of a country squire."

"You are exaggerating, Brother."

"Yes, but not by much."

The introductory music for the dancing struck up, and the lines began to form. As Louis walked Anne back toward her husband, with whom she would open the wedding ball, she continued to puzzle over the countess's enmity.

"Why should that make her want to offend me? I am the new queen. I could improve her position if I chose." Anne shook her head. It seemed foolish to her to affront the person in the best position to assist one.

"If I had to guess, I would say it is envy, Madame la Reine. You have everything she wants. Position, wealth, and power." Louis sounded as dispassionate as a general assessing the disposition of enemy lines.

Anne gave a bitter laugh. "I have lost the position I want; my duchy is drowning in debt; and Charles wields the power that should be mine. She resents someone who does not exist."

CHAPTER 4

The Marriage Night

Château de Langeais, France, 6 December 1491

When the musicians took a break, Madame la Grande came up to Anne and said, "Madame la Reine, is it not time that you excused yourself and retired. Let me lead you to your dressing chamber."

Anne was relieved for she felt exhausted. After signalling to the three ladies who had accompanied her from Rennes, she left the hall. She had not slept well last night in the strange chamber full of moving shadows and unfamiliar sounds and she had been on display since she rose. The wedding and reception had distressed her, and she looked forward to confiding in her principal lady-in-waiting, Lady Pernette de Montauban, after the draining day.

When she entered her room, it was crowded with most of the ladies who had attended her wedding. She resented them, for to reach the far end of the room where she could disrobe, she must thread her way through their ranks. They removed all her hopes for privacy.

Anne's eyes wandered to the silky night rail[1], sewn for the bedding ceremony, that lay on the coverlet of the canopied bed while Mme Pernette untied the laces of her jewelled hood, unpinned the heavy object, and lifted it from her head. Her maid released the nets that held Anne's hair, allowing it to tumble down her back.

Then Anne stepped behind the embroidered screen, held out her arms, and stood with them stretched out as Mme Pernette and her maid, who had served her since she was born, unpinned and untied the many layers of wedding finery that weighed her down. She sighed with relief once they had disrobed her to her feather-light linen shift.

Putting a warning finger to her lips, she sank onto a cushioned stool and whispered, "Two weddings in less than one year. I fear *this* marriage is not licit in the sight of God. When I said so to Cousin Louis, he told me I must go ahead since by now, King Maximillian will have been informed of my flight." Mme Pernette's eyes widened, and she drew in a whistling breath.

Anne nodded. "For a certainty, he will be enraged for himself and his daughter." She waved her arm towards women at the far end of the room. "Everyone insists it is necessary we consummate this marriage before his denunciation of the double adultery reaches Pope Innocent."

Her hovering maid said, "Stop fretting, Duchess, and lift your arms. You are safe." When Anne obeyed with a slight smile, her maid stripped off her charge's shift and washed Anne with scented soap and water. Once her faithful maid dropped the soft silk night rail over her head and placed the matching open-backed slippers on her feet, Anne squeezed her hand, thanked her and sent her away. Then she turned to her oldest friend. "Tell me, Pernette, what should I do tonight?"

"What do you mean? You have no choice! The bedchamber is prepared, and your Breton witnesses wait behind screens."

Anne put a finger to her lips. "Shush. That reflection was for you alone. I understand my duty." No one else seemed to share her concerns. . . but their eternal souls were not at risk.

Pernette prodded her in the ribs. "I promise you after tonight this will be a duty you will be happy to perform." She winked at her friend, who turned bright pink.

"It is a holy obligation," she said.

"Holy Church does not say we cannot take pleasure in our obligations."

Anne wanted no more of this talk. She rose and reached for her fur-lined dressing-gown. Pernette took it from her and helped her to don it.

When they emerged from behind the screen, Madame la Grande, officious as ever, came forward, took Anne's arm and led her past the line of ladies who were rising from the stools, chests, and cushions at the far end of her chamber. Among them Anne noticed Countess Louise who pushed her way to stand directly behind Anne and Madame la Grande as the procession formed by rank to walk to the official bedchamber.

Anne stared at the grand state bed, part of her dowry, adorned with magnificent hangings that combined the emblems of France and Brittany. Her Breton workers had unearthed them from coffers in her château in Nantes. They must have celebrated some previous union, and she had decided they would serve equally well for hers and ordered them refurbished. She surveyed the room that would end her girlhood and seal her marriage. Close to the head of the bed, on the side with windows looking onto the courtyard, she noticed a table with a carafe of wine, two glasses, and a ceramic biscuit jar. Beside it, two high-backed armchairs with padded seats faced the dancing flames in the huge fireplace. The arrangement appeared private but did not deceive her. She twisted her neck to peer deeper into the room. There, in the far reaches, hidden by shadows, stood painted screens. Well, it was as she had expected. Crossing to one of the chairs, she sat and clasped her hands in her lap.

~

CHARLES AND ANNE leaned against the pillows as the bishops blessed them and sprinkled their bed with holy water. Then they and the courtiers sauntered out, and Charles's valets of the bedchamber drew their bed curtains closed and Anne nerved herself to the coming ordeal. They lay motionless, side by side in a cocoon as dark as a starless night under the embroidered coverlet until the sound of the heavy door thudding closed signalled that they were as alone as they would be that night.

Anne heard a slight huff of amusement. The mattress and coverlet shifted, and she felt Charles turn. She turned her head towards him. As her eyes adjusted, she saw he had lifted himself on one elbow, facing her.

"Finally, we are private, wife. Are you as nervous as I am?" He lowered his voice and nodded his head in direction of the screens they knew were there. His teeth gleamed, and she felt his other arm reach over to touch hers.

She did not respond. A little breathlessly, she said, "Husband, I have something I would ask of you." Her tone sounded like a child's pleading for a favour, which did not please her, but she could not undo it, so she plowed on. "The papal dispensation has not yet arrived. . . ." She paused, hoping he would share her reservations and finish the sentence for her. He did not. After he let the silence lengthen uncomfortably, she drew a deep breath. "So, I hoped you would agree that we should postpone the consummation until it does."

Her new husband released his elbow and dropped onto his back, so he no longer looked at her. When he finally spoke, his voice sounded as cold as the ice in the courtyard. "I do not think that would satisfy your Breton witnesses. . . or my sister."

Anne rose on her elbow and leaned toward him, her voice eager. "I am sorry, Charles. I did not explain myself well. It would be a secret between us. I would not shame us or them. There would be blood. Of course, I brought a tiny knife with me. I could make a slight cut under my arm or on my thigh and use that. I am sure it would work."

Charles surprised her by rising to his knees and taking her shoulders. "Anne, you astonish me." He kissed the top of her head. "That is a brave offer, but do you truly believe there is a need for such an action? Two bishops have signed our dispensations and blessed our marriage. Undoubtedly, by now the Holy Father has signed it, too. I do not doubt that my messengers are hastening it to us. We have not received it because of distance alone. But it is done, I assure you. My Cardinal has received signs. Did not your confessor reassure you also?"

Anne fingered her rosary. "Ye-es." She hesitated. "But what if he does not? Then we shall both burn in hell. I fear for my soul and yours."

Charles frowned and tapped a finger on his lips. "Would it not also be a sin to deceive our lieges who will return to our Estates in Brittany to swear we have done our duty? When we confess, as we must once we receive the dispensation and consummate our marriage, will we not have to admit the deception to them?"

Anne blanched at the thought. "We could do a penance instead, perhaps." She felt herself weakening.

"But perhaps not. It would damage our authority. I could not do it." Anne could hear the decision in his voice. She did not think she could do so either. Her most powerful vassals were already too insolent.

"Besides, we need an heir. Until I have an heir, France and Brittany are both in danger. So, the sooner we make one, the safer our lands shall be." He removed the rosary, put his arms around her back, and nuzzled her neck. Anne abandoned her arguments.

~

When she opened her eyes again, velvety dark still surrounded her. She was not sure it was morning, but the air on her face and hands felt chilly, a sure sign that hours had passed. The rustle of sheets from the other side of the bed, coupled with the ache between her legs, sent memories rushing. She was no longer a maiden. It was too late to turn back from the path she had chosen less than a month previously. Pernette had been correct. Her deflowering had been much more agreeable than she had expected. Charles had told her she was beautiful, caressed her gently and taken his time. She thought she could learn to like this duty.

She reached out and touched the arm of the man lying beside her. His arm was much warmer than her hand, and it comforted her. Under her touch, he rolled toward her, yawning. Then he stroked her cheek. It was a soothing sensation. His voice whispered from the dark, "Beautiful Anne, my queen, you have delighted me. You are the perfect wife. I am certain we shall be the happiest couple in France."

Anne's heart felt as if it was melting inside her breast. At that moment, she discovered she loved him. Passionately. Tears popped into her eyes, and she snapped them shut. She waited until she could control her voice before answering. "Husband, I am pleased you say so."

He lifted himself onto one elbow and gazed deeply into her eyes.

"Yesterday," he murmured, "I kept watching your eyes. I could not decide whether they were green or gold. They kept changing colour. You have such glorious eyes. I feel as if I am sinking into them."

The thought flashed that he was feigning, but she pushed it away as they gazed into each other's eyes until she let herself believe she could see deep within him. She could trust him. He would take care of her.

He lowered his head towards her, and their lips touched. She relaxed and let the sensations take her.

. . .

1 Night rail—the former term for nightgown.

CHAPTER 5

Louise Receives a Shock

Château de Langeais, France, 10 December 1491

As the first streaks of dawn lit the horizon, the d'Angoulême rose early to get a good start on their return journey to their home in Cognac. In the frost-covered courtyard, Carlo oversaw the final arrangements for their baggage convoy, then gathered his armed guard and signalled they were ready to leave. Wrapped in a fur-lined cloak and leather boots, Louise minced across the slippery cobblestones to the enclosed litter, heaving a great sigh of relief. Five days of keeping up appearances in front of the haughty little queen and her overbearing former guardian was more than enough. Besides, the king's Maître d'hôtel had assigned them only one chamber plus two tiny sleeping closets for their attendants, so she had been forced to live in close quarters with her lady-in-waiting. Carlo had sworn he had ended his affair with Mme Antoinette de Polignac as soon as Louise was old enough to take up her marital duties the previous September, but her presence rankled.

Louise's lady-in-waiting trailed after her, carrying her book sack, traveling writing case, and precious hand mirror. After climbing inside, Louise settled herself with Mme Antoinette's competent assistance. Charles' former mistress had proved a blessing, Louise admitted to herself, generally respectful and helpful in teaching her to run the household as Carlo liked it.

Once on the cobbled road toward Tours, her mood lightened. The king had given them permission to stop at Plessis-lez-Tours for a blessing from Friar Francis de Paule on her coming child and Carlo had bowed reluctantly to her insistence upon doing so.

"It is dangerous to lengthen our journey in the dead of winter," he said. "I wish to get home before Christmas, especially now because of your condition."

She widened her large grey eyes at him, looking frightened. "My mother died in childbirth. As my confinement approaches, I find myself consumed with fear." She fell to her knees. "Please, Carlo. I trust the Friar and need him to intercede with the Lord on our behalf. We are fortunate to have this saintly man living so close. I must see him."

Carlo pondered. "It is true that King Charles reveres him, and that is important, too."

The Friar's otherworldliness was a mystery to Louise. He had not wished to come to France when King Louis XI asked and had only agreed when ordered to by Pope Innocent, which she thought was simply foolish. Still, God spoke to him, and *that* was worth cultivating for he had cured the plague in Provence as he passed through.

Louise went on, "To waste God's gift by passing by without asking for his blessing is to reject an offering from the Lord. He will turn his face against us if we are so impious." She widened her eyes and brought her hands together in a gesture of prayer.

Carlo glanced at the overcast sky. "Winter travel is risky. A storm can blow up out of nowhere and force us to impose upon an acquaintance until the route is passable again."

"I made a vow." He dared not force her to break a solemn vow.

He subsided, muttering.

When they trotted across the bridge that guarded the entrance to Château de Plessis, Carlo informed her he had sent a courier ahead to advise the friar that she would arrive that morning.

She reached out and squeezed his hand. "Dearest Carlo. You are the best of husbands."

She could see him swell with pride. He reminded her of a rooster about to crow.

SHIVERING inside her woollen mantle from the damp, Louise tramped along the slippery path followed closely by Mme Antoinette. It wasn't simply the cold. The dank smell of mouldering leaves surrounded her, and the wind moaned through the leafless branches like a lost soul. Finally, Louise and her lady-in-waiting came to an opening at the end of the sodden path. The friar's humble thatched cottage faced her. She had heard that when miserly King Louis had offered to build the friar a fine home on the grounds of this, his favourite Château, the saintly man had said it would serve Louis's soul better to build a monastery for the new Minim order and that for himself he wanted a simple hut in the woods near a stream far from people.

That is what she saw. Within the leafless glade a short distance from his cottage, she spied a simple stone chapel. The whole area looked deserted. Not an animal or chicken moved. But then, he ate no flesh, not even fish. Not so much as an egg from a chicken or cream from a cow. She wondered how he survived.

She wondered even more when he stepped from his austere home, for he was as thin as a starving child. He wore only a rough robe with a rope belt and well-used sandals, even on this windy winter day. Yet the smile he beamed upon them exuded a sense of peace. With a warm gesture, he invited them to step inside the cottage and seat themselves on the hard wooden bench near the open hearth. The fire was small, the room smoky and chilly. Mme

Antoinette stayed near the door. Brother Francis shot a sharp glance from one to the other before seating himself on the opposite side of the hearth from Louise.

The countess's drab woollen cloak covered a penitential-grey woollen gown high at the neck. She fell to her knees and clasped her hands. "Friar Francis, I come for your blessing on the new life I carry. Like every woman in my condition, I worry for my health and that of the babe during this perilous time." She risked a glance at him through her lashes, pleased her eyes had watered from the smoke in the room.

Like Saint Francis, he sat as still as a bird on a branch. The silence extended among them, broken only by the hiss of the wood coals in the hearth, the creaks in the cottage and the gusts soughing in the leafless branches outside. Louise's mind wandered. She startled when he began the Pater Noster, but she joined in after the first few words. When he completed the prayer, he drew a cross in the air and rose.

"Come with me, daughter," he said, walking toward the door. As Mme Antoinette rose, he touched her arm gently and drew a cross on her brow. "Remain here, daughter. I must speak to Mme Louise alone."

He glanced at her fine leather boots as his sandals flapped along the frozen cobblestone path between his cottage and the small chapel.

"A gift from the late king," he said. "Although I told him he was wrong; that we served the Lord no better, and perhaps worse, inside a building than in the world that God provides us as his cathedral. For your comfort, Madame," he added, "we shall sit inside."

When they entered, he genuflected, crossed himself, walked to the altar, and knelt before it in prayer. Louise followed his example, grimacing because the stone floor chilled her knees even through her woollen gown, kirtle and shift. She had adjusted her expression to a more pious one by the time he crossed himself and turned to face her.

Taking her hands between his, he said, "Madame, the Lord has sent me a revelation and informed me I must warn you of it. I begged to carry this burden in your stead, but He said I must tell you if you came to me."

Louise's heart began to race. Was she carrying a monster? Was she about to die?

His low, steady voice continued. "The world knows you as a faithful, Christian woman who carries out her duties humbly. Yet our new queen is also pious, generous and deeply faithful. I grieve for both of you." He stopped once again.

Louise itched for him to say more. As the silence lengthened, the wool of her dress prickled until her need to scratch became almost unbearable. She forced herself to overcome the urge as an offering to God for the blessing of a hopeful prophecy. When the friar gave a profound sigh, her spirits plummeted.

"The Lord's ways are beyond human understanding. Many times, He has sent me messages that remind me this life is a vale of tears, and my path as His messenger is thorny." He straightened his shoulders. "So be it. The Lord knows His instruments. You will have the fortitude to carry out the labour He has chosen for you. He has assured me of this. But are you certain you are ready to hear this burden?"

Louise could no more refuse to learn the secret than she could avoid listening at doors. It mystified her that the holy man could know the will of God yet not see into her heart. She pretended to hesitate. Her voice low, she said, "Friar Francis, your words strike such fear in me that I must hear this warning. I will bear the burden as I must."

The saintly man put a finger under her chin, raised her head and gazed into her eyes. "I fear that this revelation will lead you into the sin of desire when it should impose upon you a solemn duty and constant anxiety."

Louise wanted to shake the secret from him. She veiled her thoughts behind the bland countenance that she had trained herself to adopt, like that of a Virgin Mary in a painting of the Holy Family.

He asked again. "You are determined?"

"I must . . . to protect my unborn child."

"Be it so." He tightened his jaw. "You will bear a child who is to be King of France one day."

Her jaw dropped. Before she could speak, he said, "This will trouble the lives of every member of your family in the years to come. I advise you to guard this knowledge, revealing it to no one. The Lord required me to take you into His confidence, because your son must be trained as a king, although his future may appear unlikely for many years."

Louise felt stunned, not sure what to ask first, yet elated. "Tell me-"

"I may say no more. Now that you carry this knowledge, yours will be a lonely path. It is not your place to bring about this destiny. Indeed, you must not. For it will not be a kind one for your son and he will suffer, and you will suffer for him. Remember our Holy Mother, the Queen of Heaven, and hold her in your prayers, for her troubles will be yours. You must have faith."

This speech gave Louise the time to swallow the triumph that flooded her. The ache in her knees forgotten, she schooled her expression to a suitable dismay. "You speak wisely, Friar Francis. I will keep my counsel. Will you give me your blessing so that I and my child may bear this burden with the submissiveness it demands? For my companion and I must return to my husband to continue our journey before the winter weather prevents us from travelling."

She thought the saintly man sighed and stopped himself from saying more. He drew a cross on her forehead and helped her rise.

He stood on the doorstep of his cottage as she and Mme Antoinette departed. She turned and bowed at the edge of the clearing. Then they retraced their steps along the wooded path. This time Louise heard whispers of wings as if hosts of angels escorted them. As soon as they were no longer within hearing of the cottage, her companion said, "Your spirits are much lighter. What did the friar say?"

"I must not tell." Realizing her answer could only provoke curiosity, she added, "Until I have spoken to my husband."

Even that was not a wise reply. Mme Antoinette had been Carlo's mistress until Louise and Carlo had begun cohabiting the year previously. He had promised her that it was no longer so, but her mother-in-law doubted he spoke the truth, especially now that Louise was increasing.

"Unfortunately, ma chérie," Maman Marguerite had confided in Louise, tossing back a mug of her favourite cider, "men, they are not like us. They cannot control their desires. Carlo is so used to that strumpet, he would see no reason to deprive himself when you are not available. And he would tell you he was chaste, to spare you ze pain."

Well, this was one confidence Louise would ensure he kept. She would not tell him. If she told anyone, it would be the only person she trusted completely—her mother-in-law.

CHAPTER 6
Messengers

Château de Cognac, 10 January 1492

Carlo entered his wife's solar without knocking and snapped the door closed. Louise and his mother, embroidering before the crackling fire, flinched. After one glance at his frown, Louise dismissed their ladies and demoiselles to enjoy their private pursuits, although the Vespers bells had not yet rung. Then she rose and took him by the arm to lead him to the seat she had vacated.

"Let me bring you a goblet of wine," she said, and poured it from the carafe on the sturdy oak chest against the near wall. Her fur-lined overdress of fine wool swished across the tiled floor as she carried it back to him.

"My love, it does my heart good to welcome you." She pulled a stool close to his knees and sank gracefully upon it. "Although I sense that something troubles you."

Already the warmth, the sweet scent of applewood and the homey smell of beeswax appeared to be working their magic, for her husband's expression was softening.

"My chamberlain tells me you have told him to prepare lodgings for a Breton almoner to stay here. Who is he? What does he want?" The aggrieved note in his voice was unmistakable.

"Son, 'e brings me news of our family." Dowager Countess Marguerite placed the altar cloth she was embroidering on her lap and gazed steadily at her son. She continued. "He is almoner to the Marshal—I speak of my nephew, Jean de Rieux. Would you 'ave me turn him away?"

Carlo looked sulky. "I would have you send him on his way to the monastery in the village. That is where men of the cloth are best welcomed. You know, Maman, that I cannot be seen to encourage enemies of the king and queen."

"By offering a room for a few nights to an almoner?" she scoffed. "Son, you become more fearful than a rabbit." Colour rose in his cheeks, but his mother kept right on. "Our new queen ees a most pious lady, as well as a noted patron of scholars and illuminators. Père de Pennec ees collecting those new printed books for my nephew, for they fascinate him. He travels to Paris, stopping where he finds printers. He stops here on his way to Tours, for 'e carries a letter from my brother. Would you have me refuse him shelter after 'e does me a favour?" She took a gulp of cider from the mug beside her as she eyed him steadily.

Carlo played with the narrow ruffles at his wrist. "It would be awkward," he conceded. "Just don't encourage him to make a long stay. Both the Marshal and your brother, Jean, are *persona non grata* at court. We do not need Madame la Grande turning her suspicious eyes our way." He drained the glass Louise had given him and stood. "But I will have the Maître d'hôtel set him a place beside me tonight. I am curious to hear about these new books and those who are printing them."

Louise rose with him and walked him to the door. Neither lady spoke until Carlo closed the door quietly behind him and his footsteps faded down the stone steps.

"Well managed, Maman Marguerite."

The old lady smiled, her bright brown eyes almost disappearing into the wrinkles that surrounded them. "We both know my son's soft spots. Unlike his father, he ees sweet-tempered and so not terribly difficult most of the time."

~

A KNOCK SOUNDED. A young page opened the door and bowed awkwardly. "Père de Pennec begs the honour of speaking with you."

Once again, Louise gave up her seat to the guest. Only by his tonsure, silver cross and soutane did he reveal his calling, for otherwise he was a jovial, rotund gentleman with apple-red cheeks and wide smile, wearing comfortable boots.

When he asked if the Dowager Countess had received the letter he had brought from her brother, she nodded but did not pursue the topic. Instead, she inquired about his literary quest, and he spoke with enthusiasm about his finds, but his sharp eyes belied his breezy manner. With a gusty sigh, he said, "It is a disappointment that so many printers have fled the duchy since the troubles."

"The troubles? Surely with the peace the troubles are over... or the end is in sight?" Louise was curious.

"They are... for those who supported the duchess, but anyone suspected of being less than fervent, even if merely neutral, is finding it hard. Being replaced in their positions, their taxes rising, having trouble getting the supplies they need. Not that I say anything against the queen. Such is the way of the victors and the vanquished." He cocked his head. "What is the opinion in this area? Or has the change made any mark?"

"You will have to ask my husband." Louise was cautious. "From what I observe, no."

Turning to the Dowager Countess, he asked, "Do you believe there will be resistance because King Charles replaced the Viscount, your brother, with Queen Anne's uncle as Lieutenant-Governor of Brittany without the approval of the Estates?" Père de Pennec shot that flaming arrow of news as if it were only a twig. When both women gasped, the almoner said, "You had not heard. Forgive me for being the unfortunate bearer of this news." His eyes snapped, belying his regretful tone.

"No one objects?" Spots of colour flamed in Louise's cheeks; she could feel their heat.

"Many object, Mme Countess. King Henry of England for one. He was already furious about the marriages and has been sending messengers to all the courts of Europe denouncing the French marriage as a double adultery. He sees these appointments as an incitement to war."

"How do you know?" Both women were leaning forward now, their voices barely above a whisper.

Père de Pennec bent forward himself until the buttons on his soutane strained over his belly. "When King Henry was still in exile, just Duke of Richmond, I knew him well. Since he became king, our friendship has continued. He trusts me with his secrets." Putting a finger beside his nose, he nodded and leaned back, which eased the pull on his black gown. Louise felt relieved to discover this friendship with the king of England.

"But will he do anything? He is reputed to be as miserly as old King Louis." Louise was skeptical.

His eyes flitted from one to the other. He turned to the dowager. "I have spoken to your brother, the Viscount. The king offers support to the legitimate ducal line if they decide to fight for their rights. He will send his forces to join Viscount Jean when he has prepared everything for an uprising. And the king will pay for all the costs of the campaign. Viscount Jean instructed me to inform you of this personally."

The two women looked at each other, then back at the priest. The silence lengthened. "Why? Why would King Henry do this?" The dowager's voice was dagger sharp.

"A French Brittany on his doorstep is a great danger to him. Brittany has always been an English ally. And he believes they will win, for King Maximillian is eager to take up arms. Both he and his daughter have been grievously insulted."

Both women nodded. Maximillian took his honour seriously, even if King Henry did not.

"Why would my uncle want us to know this? The more who know the more dangerous it becomes." In Louise's experience, no one gave away secrets, especially treasonous secrets, unless they wanted something in return. She saw him take a deep breath. *So, now they were at the nub*, she thought.

"You and your family have much to gain when we succeed, Mesdames. Not only will your brother gain his rightful title and holdings as Duke of Brittany and you will receive the lands to which you are entitled as sister to the reigning duke, but King Henry will reward you for your loyalty to his cause. Mme Louise, your husband will be revenged for the humiliation he suffered at the hands of the Regent of France." His eyes moved from her to her mother-in-law and back.

She wondered if he was nervous. They could take him prisoner right now and receive great rewards from King Charles and Queen Anne. Of that, she had no doubt. "What would you require of us?"

His shoulders dropped, as if he believed he had caught her. Do not be so certain, she thought. You have given me a weapon. I must decide which path offers a better investment.

"You will not find it difficult or dangerous," he reassured them. "We need information. You, Mme Louise, are a member of the royal court, the queen's court. When you are there, you will have conversations with the men of the king's court and with their wives, daughters, sisters, and aunts. So, if we send you questions, or lists of information we need, you should be able to gather it. You can also spread rumours that would be useful to us, were it believed. What do you think? Is that possible?"

Louise nodded. "Those things are possible. But what would I do with it? How would I share it?" She smiled humourlessly. "I shall not slip out for midnight meetings or keep carrier pigeons in the mews."

He gave a jovial laugh and slapped his knee. "I was told you have a pretty wit. Nothing so dangerous. You shall write delightful gossipy letters to your mother-in-law. She shall write charming gossipy letters to her sister-in-law. After all, is that not what ladies do? Gossip, gossip, gossip. We have a code. And secret ink. But most of the time, it will all just look like family gossip. What could be easier? And the rewards are great."

The Vespers bells sounded. Both the Dowager Countess and Louise rose immediately and moved to the door.

Louise said, "Père de Pennec, you have given us much food for thought. After Vespers, my husband invites you to join us at our evening meal. He is a passionate collector of books and eagerly awaits your presence. Madame Maman and I will consult and inform you of our decision."

~

24 January 1492

EAGER TO LEARN the reason for their summons, Louise and the dowager countess joined Carlo in his library. Their shoes tapped across the glazed floor tiles to the fireplace whose chimney hood featured the Angoulême emblem. Carlo seated his wife beside the fire first, obviously proud of her delicate condition. She breathed in the scents of luxury—polished wood, expensive leather, and beeswax—as she gazed around the room, the loveliest in the Château.

Carlo spent their every spare *livre* adorning the room. In front of her, on either side of the fireplace hung Flemish tapestries in warm reds and blues. A high-beamed ceiling added to the magnificence. Mullioned windows sparkled with panes of glass that allowed the library's occupants a view of the manicured garden beyond. Oak bookcases lined the walls. The books themselves, enclosed in precious jewelled boxes, stood or lay, stacked and chained, on wide shelves. Louise felt the familiar stab of envy as she observed a book she had not seen before lying open on the carved oak table that occupied the centre of the room.

Carlos turned to a messenger standing discretely in the background. "Repeat your message."

He came from the king, Louise deduced from his colours of scarlet and yellow and his device of a golden sun.

"King Charles announces the coronation of his wife, Anna, Queen of France, on the eighth of February at the Basilica of Saint Denis and requests the presence of all Princes and Princesses of the Blood to pay homage to her as their sovereign Princess."

Louise kept her temper until their chamberlain had escorted him from the chamber. Then she burst out, "Why? Why should she be crowned now? She has not given France an heir. She has been queen only two months. There are many questions about the legality of this marriage. Why such haste?" Unable to keep still, she pushed herself to her feet. Although she was well into her sixth month, she barely showed the life within her, but it was slowing her down.

Carlo rose and took her arm. "Calm yourself, Louise. You will harm our heir. And you are speaking treason or close to it! Do you wish the entire household to hear you?" He forced her to slow her steps.

His mother patted the armchair beside her. "*Ma fille*, come, sit down again. There is much to examine in this news. You observe *correctement* that the King—and his sister I surmise—hasten this coronation. Why? To place the seal of legality upon it by anointing it with the blessing of Holy Church. This must mean that the threats against them rise to a dangerous degree." She rested her chin on her cane, her tone thoughtful.

Caught by her reflective tone, Louise stared at Maman Marguerite. She made an interesting point. Could the king have learned of the plot in Brittany? Or did the threat come from the East? Louise doubted King Maximilian would fight while King

Charles held Archduchess Marguerite hostage in France, for that is what they were now instructed to call her cousin and his former wife. Contemplating these questions, she seated herself again.

Carlo, whose mind had obviously been on a different topic, caught her off-guard. He said, "You must not travel to Paris during the winter, for it is a dangerous journey in your present condition. I shall go alone. The king and queen will understand and forgive your absence."

Returned to the issue, she resisted his reasoning for a moment. Then she relaxed. How she would resent seeing Queen Anne preen, the object of adulation by fawning courtiers, the centre of days of ostentatious spectacle! Besides, she had nothing to wear.

"I am relieved."

She saw his shoulders drop. *So, he had been anticipating an argument.*

He leaned back against the table and gave her a sunny smile. "How pleasant that we agree."

As they rose, Louise said, "If you depart promptly, mayhap you can travel with the king's messenger. It is a lengthy journey, and safer made in company. If you travel together, he will have the king's authority to requisition teams and stay at all the royal demesnes along the route."

~

6 March 1492

MME ANTOINETTE BUSTLED into the solar, beaming. "Count Carlo has this minute ridden into the courtyard, Mme Louise." Her dark eyes glowed.

"Well, it will delight him you are so pleased at his return," Louise snapped. Her lady-in-waiting tightened her lips but did not reply.

Louise recognized she had been gratuitously rude to the

woman who had treated her graciously when she had arrived as a young, unwanted bride in a household managed by this very woman. She should apologize. Yet she did not, for she felt ungainly and uncomfortable with only a month to go before her time.

It would not be she who celebrated his homecoming with her husband tonight. Not that she regretted his absence from her bed. To her, at sixteen, he was an old man at thirty-four. She was grateful that he was considerate and had no taste for very young girls. To her relief, he had waited until her monthly flowers began the previous year to exercise his conjugal obligations.

She was eager to welcome him, however. When she heard his footfall thudding on the stone steps, she pushed on the arms of her chair, struggling to rise. The young demoiselle serving her helped her stand as he paused in the doorway, bring a draft of fresh air with him.

"You have blossomed since last I saw you," he said. "I worried about your health during my absence."

Louise grimaced. "You need not remind me. I waddle like a duck these days."

As she took a step toward him, he strode across the solar and stopped her with a kiss on each cheek. "You must stay where you were, with your feet up, wife." He turned to the valet who had trailed him into the room and took a package from him. "I have brought you gifts and fairings."

Inside the cloth wrapping lay a golden necklace set with pale, balas rubies and pearls of a matching size. Beside it sat an enamelled pomander ball that exuded the rich scents of cinnamon and cloves. Delighted, she gave him her hand to kiss. "How well you know my tastes. You could not have brought me anything to please me more,"

"I could do no less than bring you offerings as exquisite as yourself."

"You are sweet. Fasten this for me." She fluttered her lashes and bent her neck, so he nibbled it as he completed his task.

She patted the chair beside her. "Now we must send for Maman Marguerite. She will want to know about your journey as much as I do."

"Go fetch the dowager," she said to her the young demoiselle.

While they waited, he assured her that the king, queen and Madame la Grande had understood their reason for her absence. "They send best wishes for the birth of a healthy child."

He opened the bag that depended from his belt and offered her another cloth-wrapped package. "From the queen."

Before opening it, she fingered it suspiciously. Inside lay a hinged, golden amulet engraved with an image of Saint Anne on one side and Saint Elizabeth on the other. Opening the clasp, she unfolded the paper, as thin as a butterfly's wing. It contained a prayer for a safe delivery. Refolding the paper, she closed the precious object, prey to conflicting emotions. It was the most thoughtful gift one woman could send another. Yet it was the last thing she wished to receive from the queen, and she remained suspicious of Anne's intentions. Still, she said aloud, "It will be a comfort in the days ahead."

She heard his mother's cane tapping along the stone corridor. Before the gentleman usher could knock, Carlo was at the door to offer her his arm. As she settled beside Louise in front of the fire, Louise caught the whiff of the scent of apple cider that always accompanied her.

Carlo said, "Cousin Louis told me that Madame la Grande was behind the hasty coronation. She persuaded Charles that King Maximillian was doing everything in his power to undo the marriage and Anne must be crowned to prevent it. God's anointed and all. The Papal dispensation arrived just days before the coronation and Madame la Grande was so relieved she had convinced Charles to have heralds cry it aloud throughout Paris for days. So, you ladies were half-right about the reasons for the haste, although I heard no rumours about the likelihood of war."

"Well, it was not that hard to deduce." Louise was tart. "What were they like—the coronation and *Grande Entrée?*"

"Really? All about Charles as ruler of Brittany. He flew banners with the combined devices of Brittany and France everywhere. At the coronation it looked as if every cardinal, archbishop, and bishop who could hobble was there, and I was almost smothered from the smoke from the incense. My eyes watered so much I feared Charles and Madame la Grande would imagine I mourned Brittany's lost independence." He laughed.

Pausing, as if recreating the scene in his mind, he said, "Queen Anne did not look as if she was enjoying the day. Her face was as waxy as the tapers the choirboys carried to light her way. At the banquet we learned the reason." His eyes danced, and he made them beg before he would reveal the secret. "She is increasing! Yes! We are to have an heir for France. After the king announced it, the rest of the festivities were rollicking."

Louise stopped listening. The birth token in her hand burned as she seethed. It was so unfair. With child already! How dare her rival fulfil her royal duty so promptly? Calculating quickly, she concluded Anne would give birth in September or October. She prayed it would be a girl. A boy would outrank the son she was carrying. It would be too much to bear. Surely Friar Francis could not be wrong? He was reputed to converse with God.

CHAPTER 7

Louise's Promised Child

Château de Cognac, 11 April 1492

Louise compressed her lips and forced one last push as she gripped the queen's amulet, her fingernails cutting into the flesh of her palms. The pain was so intense she was aware of nothing but the deep pulsing ache tearing her apart. She felt as if her hips were splitting open. Then blessedly the pressure eased. Sweat pouring from her face, she leaned back, her linen shift bunched up at her waist and clinging to her sweaty body. Behind her, her mother-in-law wiped her face with a cool cloth and crooned, "God be praised, ma chère fille, you have given us a grandchild."

Louise heard the wail of an infant. She struggled to sit upright, croaking, "Give him to me. Give me my son."

The midwife took her time to finish swaddling the newborn in a soft cloth before holding out the babe. "You have a perfect daughter, Mme Louise."

Louise stared at the woman uncomprehendingly, her arms

slackening. As the meaning of the midwife's words trickled into her brain, Louise corrected her. "Son," she repeated.

The midwife shook her head without releasing the infant. "Madame, you have a daughter."

"Let me see!" Louise's voice rose, and she scrabbled to unwrap the baby's binding.

"Daughter, be calm." Dowager Countess Marguerite moved forward deftly and took the infant into her arms as it continued to wail. "Allow the midwife to continue your care. You must expel the afterbirth and retire to your bed."

"But my son—"

"Hush. I will show her to you." As she jiggled the infant and cooed to her, Dowager Countess Marguerite untucked the cloth that bound her and uncovered her tiny chest and nether parts. Lifting the tiny one in front of Louise's eyes, she said, "The midwife spoke true. You have a perfect petite fille, Louise."

"Noooo. . ." Wailing and tossing her head back and forth as if she had just learned she had given birth to the devil himself, Louise began to rock. Opening her right hand, she threw the amulet from her with all her force before clutching her arms across her breasts to hug herself. As the precious object clattered against a plastered wall and Louise's wails rose hysterically, every woman in the birthing chamber froze, then turned to stare at her, mouths agape.

A nurse scurried toward Louise, but Dowager Countess Marguerite thrust the infant into her arms. Stepping forward, she slapped her daughter-in-law's tear-stained face hard.

"Stop that right now!" Her cider-sour breath spilled over Louise's face.

Wrinkling her nose, Louise popped her eyes open, hiccupped, and drew a few shaky breaths.

The dowager spoke to the midwife. "Give her a cloth to wipe her face and get on with the job."

She turned away, lifted the baby girl into her arms, and walked to the far end of the birthing chamber crooning, "You are your grandmaman's perfect little girl, ma chérie, oui, you are."

~

By the time Louise had been washed, dressed in a fresh shift, and tucked into her bed with a bed warmer at her feet, she had regained her composure. *How could she have shamed herself by such an intemperate display?* But she had been so certain. Friar Francis had said she would bear the next king of France and he communed with God. Everyone knew that his prophesies *always* came to pass. She gave a small shake of her head to dislodge her spinning thoughts.

When Dowager Countess Marguerite approached her again with the baby, Louise held out her arms. "I do not know what came over me," she apologized. "Let me hold my daughter."

The infant was asleep. When Louise cradled her in her arms, looking down on her, eyes squeezed shut, tiny arched eyebrows and a little rosebud mouth that she mumbled in and out, Louise felt a surge of fierce, protective love sweep through her. She fumbled to open the swaddling. "Is she so perfect everywhere? Her fingers? Her toes?"

"Every finger and toe." Dowager Countess Marguerite's voice softened. "But you should not disturb her. She has just nursed. Mme Antoinette will take her to her nursery so she can sleep. You must rest too. I shall go to Carlo. When we return, you can show him how well you have done."

Mme Antoinette came to her side and curtsied. "It is an honour that you have chosen me gouvernante to your daughter."

Louise kept her expression pleasant as she released her precious infant to the woman with whom she shared Carlo's bed. She did not say that economy more than preference had ruled her choice. Besides, the woman was mother to two of Carlo's children, so lowering her status to that of household officer, even if it was one of the great offices, satisfied something within Louise.

Two of the women who had stayed with her drew the hangings around her bed, and then withdrew to the far end of the large chamber, though Louise insisted that the curtains at the head of her bed remain open to let in some light. Once she was alone, Louise became aware of her aches. She could feel liquid, probably blood, trickling and sometimes flooding into the moss that packed her bruised lower parts, which worried her. She had heard too many terrifying tales of women who had survived the birth, only to die a few hours later, weltering in pools of their own blood. In the days ahead, milk fever could strike, and mothers often died of it, babbling incoherently.

She had gone to Friar Francis for reassurance that she would survive this birth. He had promised. Or at least he had promised she would birth the next king of France and care for him. That was the same as promising she would survive the birth. But she had given birth to a daughter. So. . . Her mind teased out the implications. Could it mean that she would have another child? The next one a son? Or many? By Our Lady what a frightening thought. Her hands slipped down to the tight wrapping around her belly. When she had seen vertical, angry, red streaks appear a few weeks past, she had rushed to the doctor, terrified. He reassured her they were normal and would fade to silver, but she knew then her body would never return to its slim, girlish shape. She should have known just from observing the wide hips and drooping breasts of the matrons surrounding her. It would happen to her too. Despite herself, tears trickled down her cheeks. She scrubbed them away.

Perhaps Friar Francis had not believed her humble enough. Or, even worse, perhaps God had seen her pride. What should she do to ensure that the next child—her whole body cringed at the thought of a second time—would be the promised son? They could never afford to endow the foundation of a Minim monastery or even a friary or chantry, nor would Carlo support the alienation of any of their lands to do so, but perhaps she could persuade him to allow her to make a large donation, say 20 *écus*, for perpetual prayers for his father's soul to a nearby Minim foundation? She could ask it as a gift for their daughter's safe birth. It would please God, it would please Friar Francis, and it would please her mother-in-law. It might help her forget Louise's unfortunate reaction to the infant's gender. Perhaps she could suggest they name her Marguerite as well. Both Carlo and the Dowager Countess would be flattered.

~

12 April 1492

BY THE NEXT AFTERNOON, Louise felt much stronger. To her relief, the bloody emissions from her body were now no heavier than her usual monthly flowers.[1] She had always been active, and her need to move overwhelmed her. Even her ladies' dire warnings of the fatal results of rising too soon could not keep her abed, although she promised to go no further than her favourite chair to play a quiet game of chess in front of the fire with her feet up.

She greeted Carlo with a lovely smile when he visited. After they had cooed over their newborn daughter and praised each other for their perfect, healthy, beautiful baby, Louise suggested they should name her Marguerite.

Carlo beamed. "You are the perfect wife and daughter-in-law," he said as he leaned in to kiss her. "I did not dare suggest a girl's name, for you were so certain she would be a boy. You have chosen as I would." He stroked tiny Marguerite's cheek. "I shall call her Margot. She is too tiny to bear such a big name." She whimpered. He lifted her from Louise's lap, stood, and walked back and forth rocking his daughter in his arms. He was not allowed to continue for long. Her wet nurse came to take her for her feeding.

Carlo returned to his seat beside Louise. "I must send to the court to announce her birth. I would invite the king and queen to stand as her godparents."

Louise was ready to combat this unwelcome idea. As she lay awake in the night, her thoughts circled back to the amulet Queen Anne had pressed upon her. These amulets were potent magic. Anne had said Friar Francis had blessed it. Who was to say whether the queen had ill-wished the token first, setting it with prayers that Louise give birth to a girl? She was Breton, and they were known to consort with faeries and other creatures. It would explain how she could have used the Friar's power against him.

"What about asking Madame la Grande and Duke Pierre to be her godparents, instead?" Louise suggested. "It would bind her to us and resolve the enmity between you and her. Now that Duke Pierre has inherited all the Bourbon lands, he and his wife are the richest family in France, except for the king, *and* he is my uncle." She watched her husband under lowered eyelashes. He looked thoughtful, so she added her cleverest argument. "And since they had a daughter last year, it is possible they may have a son, too, for until now everyone believed Madame was barren."

Carlo's eyes twinkled. "You are suggesting that this hypothetical son would be a suitable husband for our little Margot? You are an excellent planner, but are you not getting a little ahead of yourself, sweeting?"

She flushed. "Well, it *is* possible."

He patted her hand. "It is. Let me consider your suggestion. I must send the messenger today so we can hold the baptism next Sunday."

~

Saturday 16 April 1492

UNLIKE HER USUAL LANGUID MANNER, Dowager Countess Marguerite hastened about Louise's lying-in chamber, ordering her ladies-in-waiting and servants about. In the time it took for the bells to ring for Angelus, one of her gentlemen ran off to the kitchen to fetch wine and biscuits, while other servants set up screens around Louise's bed, and placed two stools, two braziers and two standing candelabra within the newly defined space. The dowager shooed the ladies to the far end of the room with their embroidery and ordered one to play the harp.

Louise watched the transformation bemused, without the energy to resist. Besides, she was curious to discover the reason behind this remarkable assertion of authority.

When her mother-in-law rounded the corner of the screens, Louise was ready. "Why all this fuss, Maman Marguerite?"

Dowager Countess Marguerite pulled a stool close to the head of the bed and murmured, "My brother, viscount Jean, has arrived for the *baptême* with Père de Pennec. After what he has told me, I knew you and he must speak privately, but it is so awkward with you in seclusion." She waved her hand around the area and said, "This is the best I can arrange. Even so, it will cause talk. Still, he brings *sa fille*, Lady Anne de Rohan, as your new *demoiselle*, so that is some justification for his presence in your rooms."

"Is it so urgent? Can you not relay the news?"

"Best you hear it yourself and ask *les questions* that occur to you. "

A short time later, the burly, bearded viscount arrived with Louise's mother-in-law. A small, thin girl trailed behind them, pale and retiring, but clearly Anne de Rohan from the large dark eyes set beneath thick eyebrows that met over her hooked nose. Rising from a doublet of scarlet set with the yellow and red diamonds of the de Rohan crest, her father sported the same features. *They look distinguished on a man*, Louise thought. *Poor child. On a girl, they are positively homely.*

"Here is Anne," the viscount said, pulling the girl forward by the shoulder. "She is twelve already and old to be joining a noble household for the first time. Curtsey to the Countess, child. It is good of you, Mme Niece, to take her in hand."

Louise produced her sweetest smile and reached out to give the girl her hand. "Lady Anne, it is a pleasure to welcome you to my household. We are family and that makes you especially welcome. I regret I cannot rise to bring you to my ladies. Maman Marguerite, do you present Lady Anne to them?"

In Dowager Countess Marguerite's nod, she read approval of her stratagem to speak with her uncle alone.

He looked doubtfully at the stool beside her bed. "That thing doesn't look up to my weight. I'm a heavy-set man, Mme Niece."

Louise smiled. "It is sturdier than it appears, Uncle. It is carved from ironwood."

He lowered himself to the seat gingerly. "My sister has arranged the matter well," he observed. When he had first spoken, his deep voice had carried, and Louise had wondered how they would conduct a private conversation. Now he dropped his volume to an almost inaudible rumble. It reminded her of her favourite cat's purr.

"The Duke and Madame la Grande arrive today?" When Louise nodded, he asked if the Duke d'Orléans or the Prince d'Orange would be in their entourage.

"Are they important?"

"The longer we can keep the king's allies out of Brittany, the better it is for us. The king and his advisors are arrogant, as the French always are." He screwed his mouth up as if he would spit, then remembered where he was. "He puts his people in charge and believes they have gained control. After all the intrigue during the Duchess's reign, you would think they would be more suspicious. But as we say, 'None so blind as those who will not see!' *Grâce à Dieu* the Lord is on our side." Both he and Louise crossed themselves.

"What would you have me do?" Louise restrained herself from demanding what was so urgent he had insisted on talking privately. Doing so had increased the risk. Men did not seek women for innocent reasons. To come to a woman lying-in after childbirth was like shouting from a tower that you had a secret to share.

"King Henry has committed to us. With funds, not simply

promises, moreover. Already he raids the coast from Normandy to Poitou. We have men in key positions ready to join us when the signal is given." He tapped the fingers of his sword hand on his right knee.

"Something agitates you, Uncle? You still have not said what you would have me do." She rubbed her eyes. The acrid smoke from the charcoal in the braziers reeked in the small area now enclosed by screens. She wished he would get on with it.

Viscount Jean craned his neck to peer over each shoulder and then leaned closer to her. "De Pennec has been successful in recruiting men to our cause." He stopped, pushing his lips in and out. "I worry that perhaps he has been too successful. The greater the number involved, the greater the risk. The Marshal assures me that de Pennec is entirely loyal, and I believe him." He snorted. "But like all priests, he is too fond of his wine. He didn't get that red nose of his from riding about in winter weather, no matter what he says."

"Yes, yes." Louise could not contain the impatience in her voice.

He gave her a sharp glance. "I tire you, Mme Niece. Let me come to the point. I fear that our plans are known and we will fall into an ambush. I need you to discover what you can—rumours, increased activity in Brittany, or from Bretons, letters or orders being sent, troop movements, anything out of the ordinary. When will you go to court?"

Louise's heart sank. A month ago, she would have welcomed this sort of opportunity. But she had not expected to become attached to her child. Yet it was so. "I cannot think of anything before I am churched."[2]

"But by the beginning of June? Surely you go by then?" Her uncle's voice was urgent.

So, the attack would come in June. Louise felt a prickle of excitement. It would be delightful to watch the queen's face when the news arrived that her duchy had been conquered. "I will do my best to convince my husband," she said. "Do your part to persuade him as well. For I am only a woman"

1 Monthly flowers—menses or menstrual period.

2 Churched— 'Churching' refers to purification of the mother in the church and her blessing from the priest one month to 40 days after giving birth after which the woman was permitted to reappear in the world.

CHAPTER 8

Anne Encounters Troubles

Château d'Amboise, 11 June 1492

Anne and her ladies had just returned from morning mass, her puppy Fanchon trailing at her skirts. It was the runt of the litter and Charles had given it to her saying it would never grow large enough to make a good hunter. As she settled, her gentleman usher knocked on the presence chamber door.

"The Countess Louise d'Angoulême and Lady Anne de Rohan," he announced, standing aside as they entered. Louise led the way as they approached the queen and curtsied deeply.

Queen Anne said, "It is a pleasure to welcome you to our court, Mme Louise." She signalled a maid to bring more cushions for the new arrivals and invited them to sit. "Congratulations on your new daughter, Mme Louise. You must be happy to have a healthy child and to have recovered well yourself." Turning to Mme de Vesc and Lady Pernette, she said, "The countess is mother to the infant Lady Marguerite. How old is she now, Mme Louise?"

Soon the women were deep into talk about babies, a subject

dear to every young mother's heart. Anne felt her baby move, a feathery sensation. She envied Louise for having already given birth. Every mass she prayed that her first would be a son. It would be a relief to achieve her duty to France immediately and would prove—to her as much as to the world—that God approved of their marriage and her choices.

Countess Louise interrupted Anne's musings. Holding something hidden in her palm, Louise said, "You were so kind as to send me this to help me through my travails. I return it to you, hoping it serves you as it served me." Opening her hand, she dropped the amulet Anne had sent her into the queen's lap.

Anne received the blessed object with gratitude. It had proven its worth, taking a young woman through her first childbearing with flawless results from all Anne had heard—for the infant had been perfect in body and health, and the mother had suffered no injuries or illnesses afterwards. Yet the countess's tone did not match her words. It had an edge to it, as if Louise intended another message. Why? Anne's attention sharpened, although she gave no sign of it.

"You bring Lady Anne de Rohan with you. Is she family?" The reminder of the countess's links to the de Rohan family, her family's traditional rivals, set off warning bells for the queen.

"Yes, her father is my mother-in-law's brother," Louise answered. "She is their elder daughter and has come to learn court ways as my demoiselle."

Lady Pernette spoke up. "Mme Anne and I have known each other for many years, Mme la Reine. She is the daughter of Viscount Jean, and we met often as children at their home in Pontivy, did we not Mme Anne?"

"We did, Mme Pernette." The girl spoke barely above a whisper, and everyone had to lean forward to hear her. As the silence lengthened, she added, her voice fading, "I did not expect to meet you here."

Queen Anne took pity on her. "The king and I agree that it is my duty, and my pleasure, to increase my court. You see here Mme de Vesc, the wife of the king's close friend. It is much happier for them to be together at court than for her to live nine-tenths of the year without him at his lands near Avignon and livelier for me to have her to keep me company. And I invite the wives and daughters of my Breton va-" she stumbled, choked back the word, and switched, "friends to join me to remind me of home."

She saw Louise's eyes widen and a knowing look flash across her face. It disappeared so quickly Anne could have imagined it, but she knew she had not. Had the countess guessed that her husband forbade her to manage her Breton estates herself? As ruling Duchess of Brittany, she had developed a sixth sense about people she could trust and those she couldn't. In these few minutes she had learned that Countess Louise was her enemy.

~

17 July 1492

ANNE FOUND herself wilting in the heat although it was not yet midday. Sighing, she decided to retire to her chambers. She left the newly laid-out herb gardens that were taking shape to the South side of the Château, her tiny spaniel following in her shadow. Gardens were her passion, and Charles had no objection to her desire to create them. They reminded her of home and her happiest hours spent with her mother choosing the plants that called bees to make honey for sweets and to heal wounds, plants to make medicines for the household, herbs to flavour their foods, and aromatics to sweeten the rushes spread on their floors. Everything should serve at least one purpose. It was God's plan. Then she insisted they be placed to form patterns and colours pleasing to the eye and to have colours and sweet scents during the entire growing season, from earliest spring to latest autumn.

Accompanied by Lady Pernette, Anne passed the rest of her ladies who preferred to sit under trees with their embroidery, listening to stories or gossiping among themselves. She did not mind, as long as they occupied themselves with productive work and behaved with propriety, for she wished the women at her court to be happy in her service. They had seemed happy enough, that is until Countess Louise and Lady Anne de Rohan had arrived a month previously. But recently, Anne had noticed that her ladies no longer sat together but splintered into smaller groups.

Today when she walked by, some ladies fell silent and then began talking louder and their laughter sounded brittle to her ears. Once again Mme de Vesc was to be found in the group surrounding the countess, her mouth in motion. It astonished Anne that the countess, with her sharp mind and tongue, could endure the lady's inane conversation, for she herself could only listen for so long to stories about her marvellous children, or how to make cheese, or the myriad things that could cause it to spoil, or the hundreds of different embroidery stitches, or other equally spellbinding topics.

When she entered her presence chamber, her chamberlain handed her a letter. "It arrived by messenger from your aunt Mme Philibert d'Orange."

Anne settled herself at her writing desk, and Fanchon jumped into her lap and curled up. Anne felt secure in this space with its high back, padded seat, stable rest for her left arm, and writing supplies at hand. Here she could sit at ease for hours, even with her uncomfortably large belly. It made it easy to keep up her extensive correspondence. After stroking the puppy's soft fur, Anne broke the letter's seal.

She lay it flat on her desk to read. Her aunt's family news soon turned to talk about her husband, the Prince d'Orange. She was worried about his extensive travels in Brittany for each time he returned to Nantes he was more worried, snapping at her and the children. The number of messengers kept increasing and now several arrived every day. Her aunt's letter continued in the same vein, covering both sides of the page. Folding it slowly, resealing it, and placing it within a locked letter box inside the desk, Anne leaned back and considered what to do.

After a time, she rose and handed Fanchon to Pernette. Two of her ladies who had returned from the garden, including Countess Louise, stood. Anne signalled them to sit again.

"I would be alone to rest."

Inside her room, she leaned against the door a moment, and said to the maid, "You may leave. I wish to rest after I return from-" she pointed to the inner staircase leading to the garderobe.[1] The staircase also led to the king's private chambers above.

When she opened the door, she discovered her husband's favourite gentleman of the bedchamber, Sire Etienne de Vesc, lounging in the king's armchair. His startled expression as he rose in a fluid motion told her that he had not expected to see anyone. She had certainly not expected to see him.

"Charles is not here?" Anne emphasized her use of the king's Christian name.

"Madame la Reine, I regret he is not. I await him."

At that moment, they both heard the king's voice issue from behind the door to his inner chamber.

"Ah, there he is." Anne picked up her skirt and moved toward the door, her hand outstretched to open it.

Before she could reach it, Sire de Vesc barred it with his body. Although he looked uncomfortable, he said, "I am sorry, the king has left me with instructions that no one is to enter."

Anne was speechless. When she regained her voice, she said, "I am his *wife*. He did not mean *me*. I insist you let me pass."

The Sire de Vesc hung his head, his face a deep red, but said, "I am sorry, Madame la Reine. I may not."

All noises had stilled behind the door. Anne was certain her husband could hear all that passed. She raised her voice. "I am the Queen of France. I order you to stand aside and let me pass."

The man facing her shook his head and did not move.

Anne felt her heart race and the heat rise from her breast to the top of her head as the Sire de Vesc disobeyed her direct order. Lifting her chin, she said, "I will remember this, M. de Vesc."

She turned on her heel. Her footsteps sounded like whiplashes to her own ears as she retreated.

~

SHE WAS glad the staircase led to her private chamber, and that she had insisted on privacy. As she climbed onto her bed breathing hard, it did not take her long to conclude there was only one reason that her husband's favourite would disobey her. Her husband was with a woman.

Her lips quivered. It should not surprise her. Now that she was so large, he refused to cohabit with her saying his doctors told him he jeopardized their baby in doing so. She had demanded the truth from her doctors and midwives, and they had said the same. But surely, if she could be continent, so could he. Is not that what they had promised when they married? *Forsaking all others cleaving only unto her, until death do them part.* She turned onto her side, squeezing her eyes tight, but her tears trickled out despite her best efforts.

~

ANNE WOKE to her husband's angry voice repeating her name.

"Anne. Anne! ANNE!"

She opened her eyes. He leaned over her, glaring. It made her want to cry again. She knew she would not be able to control her voice, so she said nothing.

"What do you think you were doing? When I give an order, I mean it to be obeyed. Do not humiliate yourself—or me—again with such. . . such. . . *childish* behaviour. You are fortunate that it was Etienne. He will not repeat to anyone what happened ." He crossed himself. "There are few in this court we can trust to be so discrete."

As he railed at her, Anne's quick temper rose. Pulling herself to a sitting position, she said, "And what were you doing that I, your wife, was not welcome? Am I not queen of this realm and responsible with you for its wellbeing?"

He looked astonished. "No, you are not. I mean, yes, you are queen. Your duty is to produce us heirs. *I* am responsible for France." He looked at her large belly, now quivering from her intense emotion, and his voice changed. "As you are doing so well. You must stay calm and rest. And I stormed in here and disturbed you with intemperate words. That was not the act of a loyal knight."

He dropped to one knee, so his eyes were just above the level of the mattress, and she found herself looking down at him. "Please forgive my intemperance. I did not take account that your delicate state makes you prey to odd fancies and an uncertain temper. Forgive me, dearest wife." He rose, took one hand, raised it to his lips, and kissed it while looking deep into her eyes.

Anne could not resist him in this mood. "I forgive you. Will you listen to me now? For I wish to be a good wife to you, and I insisted upon seeing you for a reason."

He tightened his lips again but held his tongue. Pulling up a stool, he said, "Tell me then."

She hesitated a moment, choosing her words. "I received a letter earlier from my aunt, Mme d'Orange. From what she said, there is trouble brewing in Brittany. I suspect a conspiracy." She saw that he was shaking his head and rushed on. "I promise you I am not interfering as I swore I would not, but I have much family and many correspondents. I hear things. I know my people. I could help you if you would allow me."

He reached out and took her hand. "Dear wife, ruling is not for women. It breeds rebellion. Is that not why Brittany fell—because you could not hold it? I can. Now, you have a son to bear. That is your work." He rose and kissed her. "Leave the ruling to me."

He walked towards the stairs, only turning at the sound of her words.

"What if they *are* right and the conspiracy succeeds? I will have sacrificed my patrimony for nothing!

~

18 July 1492

DAWN WAS JUST BREAKING when Anne pulled open the curtains around her bed. Recently she could no longer sleep through the night without rising for a call of nature. Careful not to disturb either her lady or her maid sleeping on pallets in her chamber, she opened the door to the private stairs and slipped up to the garderobe. About to return, she stopped when she heard subdued sounds from Charles's bedchamber and then its door slam shut. She hesitated, but after the contretemps of the day before, decided not to go up. Yet she was restless after their distressing conversation of the previous day, and she could not return to her bed.

Slipping into the small dressing chamber off her bedroom, she found a kirtle and dropped it over her shift. Since she could not lace it herself, she pulled a cape over her shoulders and stuck her feet into low, backless shoes. Then she stole from her room as discretely as a shadow at sunset.

At the door onto the gallery, she knocked sharply but kept her voice low as she ordered, "Open the door for the queen!"

She heard noises on the other side that informed her she had been heard. A glowering guard, fully armed and halberd at the ready, pushed the door inward. His expression cleared and he would have spoken but Anne put a finger to her lips. After she exited and he closed the door behind her, she said. "Thank you for your discretion. I did not want to wake anyone for they need their sleep, and I am risen early."

At first, she intended to go to the chapel but as she walked along the gallery towards it, she heard laughter, voices, and the echoes of leather-soled boots hurrying along a stone corridor. Following her ears, she turned towards the short hall that led to the stables' courtyard. The clatter of horse hooves, the snorting of horses, the call of hunting horns and yammer of barking dogs floated through the double doors that stood open at the end of the passage.

Stepping onto the portico, Anne saw her husband and his favourites, join his *Grand Veneur*, the huntsmen and dogs. He had said nothing to her at dinner the day before about a hunt today. She thought it odd, for hunting was one of his favourite sports and hers too. He glanced her way and she waved to him. His hesitation was obvious, so she walked towards the steps. It seemed to decide him for he jogged up to meet her, running up the steps as lithe as a young buck.

Giving him her hand, she said, "Where will you be hunting today?"

He dropped his eyes. "It is not yet decided. But what are you doing here? It is too early. . . er . . . you do not normally rise so early."

"I could not sleep. . . and then I heard the sounds of a hunt." She looked longingly at the men and women mounting their hunters and milling about in the courtyard. "If you could wait a short time. . . or better, say where you are going, and I could join you."

He looked horrified. "You must think of no such thing, Anne. What of our child? Do not be foolish! It is much too dangerous."

For the second time in as many days, Anne's temper rose as Charles gave her an order. She was unaccustomed to such treatment, and she did not like it. "My mother went hunting when she was increasing," she snapped, and lifted her chin.

"Your mother was not carrying the heir to France. Besides," he added, twisting a knife into her heart, "did she not die in childbirth?"

Anne winced as if he had struck her. Tears she could not

control sprang to her eyes, but she refused to let them fall. At the sound of her in-drawn breath, Charles seemed to recognize how cruel his words had been. He looked chagrined, but did not apologize, though his voice was noticeably gentler when he spoke again. "Dear wife, you must care for yourself and our unborn child as much as I care for both of you. Return to your rooms and do not think of riding or other such dangerous activities. When I return, I shall bring you a trophy from the hunt."

"As you require, Sire." She dropped a slight curtsey, wondering if he understood that she was mocking him. "When shall you return?"

Charles had already turned away and was descending the steps. "I cannot be sure. I expect I shall return this evening if the hunt does not take us too far afield." He gave a casual wave goodbye, not turning to see her off.

Torn between fury and heartbreak Anne muttered under her breath, "Is this a hunt for game? Or are you expecting to capture some of the two-legged variety to keep you company for the night?" She did not wait for them to depart but fled to the chapel where she could brood in peace.

During early mass Anne made up her mind that she would go riding after their morning meal. She said as much to Lady Pernette and asked her to send a page to order their horses saddled. Lady Pernette protested the entire time they walked to the great dining hall. Her remonstrances only made Anne more stubborn.

After being robed in her riding habit, Anne returned to her bedroom from her dressing room. Madame la Grande was waiting for her, seated in Anne's preferred armchair.

Anne greeted her without taking a seat. "Sister, how unexpected. Tell me, is there something I can do for you? I am happy to oblige. As you see I have plans to go riding, but when I return?"

Her voice sharp, Madame la Grande said, "Madame la Reine, it pains me to interrupt you, but my errand cannot wait. I beg a few moments of your time."

To Anne, her words sounded like a command not a request. She hesitated. Although she had been brought up to be courteous, she would not take orders. She was the queen.

Her sister-in-law was reminding her more and more of her detested gouvernante every day. It made it hard to trust her. Anne said, "I would be happy to oblige, but I find that my business is too urgent to permit delay."

Madame la Grande did not move. She lowered her voice until no one but Anne could hear her and said, "Please do not force me to report to my brother that you refused to listen to his elder sister and went riding. Especially after he instructed you not to do so."

Anne felt her face flame from the rush of anger that shot through her. "Who says so?"

Madame la Grande remained irritatingly placid and did not raise her voice. "You know, dear sister, there are no secrets at court." She waved her hand toward the chair beside her. "Sit by me."

Anne gestured to her maid. "Fetch us wine and biscuits, if you please." It gave her time to take a deep breath. Then she sat. "And your urgent errand, Madame?"

Madame la Grande sighed. "Madame la Reine, it is not my intention to criticize or irritate you. I do not ever wish to bring tales to my brother. But I must stop you from flouting him, for it would cause a serious rift between you. He is extremely sensitive about disobedience, especially in a woman." She reached out and took Anne's hands in hers. "I know this better than anyone. As his regent since our father died nine years ago, I have had to learn how to manage him." When Anne tried to pull her hands free, Madame la Grande tightened her grip. "My purpose is to help you, for I am delighted with how well you have managed with Charles."

Anne did not soften, although she said, "Thank you, Sister, I am pleased to have pleased you."

At that moment, after a soft knock, one of her ladies-in-waiting entered with their refreshments. Anne used the diversion to consider how best to respond. Continuing with her hauteur would be counterproductive. It would be useful to build a better relationship with her sister-in-law, who had ruled France despite opposition from the French noblemen who did not believe a woman capable of ruling. It had been she who masterminded the war on Brittany, Anne's defeat, and her marriage. Besides, Anne did need to know how better to manage Charles and if anyone knew how, it was she. So, after Anne dismissed her lady-in-waiting, she hung her head and said, almost choking on the words, "Forgive my pertness, Madame. I am unused to criticism."

Without looking up, she could sense Madame la Grande eye her sharply before she relaxed and lifted her goblet of hippocras. "You have done well to keep Charles so satisfied, but I recognize that it is difficult now that you are so far along, since you must not endanger your child. I, too, wish Charles womanized less. It is risky for his health and can lead to unfortunate entanglements." She paused as if considering her next words carefully and Anne wished she would measure her words less. "But berating him, particularly in public, makes him more intransigent and disobeying him is equally ineffective. In my experience, distraction and diversion with his favourite pastimes succeed." She sighed again. "It is unfortunate that M. de Vesc introduced him to carnal pleasures so early." Then she brightened. "However, he also enjoys other rough exercise. . . though you cannot join him in that, either. But I shall advise his household to encourage it. Masques, billiards, music and dancing, tennis and bowls, and games of chance and cards entertain him too. Let me help you organize court entertainments such as these each evening." Rubbing her hands together, she said, "The *Grand Maître de Menus Plaisirs*[2] will be sure to have countless ideas and all the right accoutrements."

Although Anne liked the suggestion, she felt suffocated by her sister-in-law. As Duchess of Brittany, she had been managing a court for years. How could she rid herself of this meddlesome nuisance? Madame la Grande and Countess Louise were like thorns in her court, and they pricked at her comfort like poorly placed pins in her Breton hood.

1 Garderobe—most commonly a toilet in a medieval building; also, a wardrobe or small storeroom in a medieval building.

2 Grand Maître de Menu Plaisirs—The Controller of the Menus Plaisirs heard directly from the king what the plans for the king's personal entertainment were to be set in motion; by long-standing convention, he was a duke; although he was not a professional, it was up to him to determine how to carry out these plans. The Duke in charge of the Menus and Pleasures of the King was an important official of the court.

CHAPTER 9
Blessings

Château d'Amboise, 20 July 1492

Louise slipped through the queen's bedchamber, and up the private stairs that gave directly onto the king's bedchamber above. Behind it lay his private cabinets. Here he held his most secret meetings. Her heart raced as she slid into place behind the tapestry, thanking God it touched the floor. *Did none of his closest gentlemen know of the spy hole in the wall that made it the perfect listening spot?* she wondered. She could not believe they did not. Yet no one had ever caught her. She planned to move in the opposite direction if she heard anyone else steal behind the covering and to slink out the far side, but it was risky. She stood with her back to the wall, her ear beside the peephole, filled with a rush of elation. Taking chances always made her feel alive, and she trusted her ability to find an escape.

Excitement coursed through her when she heard voices. She had guessed the location of this meeting correctly. The king and de Vesc greeted a third, whose voice she didn't recognize.

"Are you acquainted with the contents of the message, Chancellor?" It was the king who spoke.

"No, Sire."

"The messenger came from the Prince d'Orange. As Lieutenant-Governor of Brittany he has a network of spies so I trust his lists of names and details of meetings, but the gist is simple. King Henry is plotting with the de Rohan and the de Rieux to invade Brittany. They have conspirators in the major ports of Brest, Morlaix, Nantes, and Saint Malo who are ready to open our harbours to the English."

The Chancellor and de Vesc spoke over each other, but King Charles's voice quelled them. "These are the main ports of Brittany. The conspirators must be at least Captains of the Port if they hope to succeed! It is outrageous. How has it happened that my councillors appointed traitors to me?" Louise smirked at the silence that followed.

"There is more," the king spoke again, "as soon as the signal is given, the nobles in the conspiracy will declare for the English king and invade all their neighbours who refuse to surrender."

Both the Chancellor and de Vesc interrupted again, but Louise, rigid with shock, was no longer listening. *By Our Lady!* The whole of her uncle's plot—even more than she had been privy to—was discovered. She could not decide whether to flee from her hiding spot or stay to hear what the king would do.

"What steps has d'Orange taken?" De Vesc spoke.

"Aside from apprising me immediately? He sent the military protected by cavalry units to replace the captains and men guarding the ports who were named as traitors. They were to arrest every man involved, throw them in the most secure dungeons in the cities and guard them closely. He sends to ask what more I want done.

"He knows the names of certain of the nobility—like Admiral Louis de Rohan and the Governor of Auxerre—and is willing to bet his lands on many of the others. Viscount Jean de Rohan and Marshal Jean de Rieux are the most important."

Louise's eyes widened as she heard their names.

"Let us take in the army, Sire. We crushed them once, we shall do so again." Louise recognized de Vesc's voice.

"I confess, Etienne, it would do me good to plunge my sword into their traitorous hearts. But the duchy is mine already. Let us not destroy its value when we have a crusade to fight. I would rather bleed them of their riches."

"May I make a proposal, Sire?" It was the Chancellor's voice. "As I see it, this would solve two problems at once. It would increase your power to raise revenues in Brittany and turn the principal men of the duchy against the conspirators."

"Get on with it, then. Tell us."

"As they have conspired against you, eliminate their right to have an Estates General[1] and Parlement[2] of their own."

"Yes."

"That is brilliant."

Louise heard two different voices speak at once. Her heart sank. People would blame her family for this loss of the liberties the Bretons had fought hard to maintain in the peace treaty so recently signed with France. She must report this dire news immediately, so she slunk from her hiding place.

An hour later, she called Anne de Rohan to her chamber. "I have a letter you must send to your father now. Here is some parchment. Write a cover saying you send this at my request . . . That's right. . . Now fold mine inside. . . And seal it with your seal. . . Good."

Louise handed Anne a small leather drawstring bag that fit into her palm. "Now take the letter to the stables and have a messenger take it to your father in Pontivy."

Anne took the sealed missive Louise thrust at her but hung her head and did not leave.

"Well?"

"I-I do not know how to do that." The girl sounded as if she might burst into tears.

Louise tutted impatiently. "Do you know where the stables are? Where the messengers arrive and leave?"

The girl gave a small, reluctant nod.

"Take it there."

Lady Anne de Rohan, still looking at her like a frightened fawn, did not move.

"The squire in charge will ask you what you want. Tell him your Papa has ordered you to send him a reply. Give him a gold écu." Louise tapped the bag. "He will arrange it while you wait. Give this bag and the letter to the messenger. Do you understand?" When the girl nodded, looking more cheerful, Louise said, "One more thing. Promise him your papa will reward him *well* when he arrives."

~

30 August 1492

ANNE COULD NOT REMEMBER a time when she had not known and loved Queen Joanne of Naples, so it had delighted her when Charles suggested her as their unborn child's godmother. He invited her to write on their behalf to request that she accept the charge. Gripping the queen's reply in her hand, Anne led her ladies to the shady garden to enjoy the river breezes and the late summer flowers. In two days, she would enter her lying-in chamber, and would not emerge until her churching, forty days after the birth of her child. Always active and with a passion for outdoor activities, she wondered how she would endure the time sequestered in two darkened rooms without going mad. Coming to a halt under a lofty oak, she instructed the porter to place her chair in its shade. While her ladies spread themselves about on cushions, she settled Fanchon on her lap and broke the seal on the letter. For a moment she hesitated, remembering.

Queen Joanne was a Breton from the de Laval family, so she returned to Brittany when her husband, King René, died. A close friend of Anne's mother, she came often to the ducal court. Thus, she had become the closest to a grandmother Anne had ever known, for she never met her Maman's parents who had lived in far away Navarre or her Papa's parents, dead before her birth. Queen Joanne made a perfect grandmaman, too, for she was kind, and generous with her love, attention and praise.

To shake off the gloomy memories that threatened to engulf her, Anne snapped the seal with her nail. Queen Joanne accepted the holy responsibility of godmother eagerly, which cheered Anne's spirits. And she begged to attend Anne during her confinement and at the birth.

Although to my regret I have no children of my own, I have two score years of experience in birthing chambers. Besides, having familiar faces at your side will do you good, darling child, and sadly, you have few left.

Rumours fly that King Henry is going to invade, and he has help from within. People here grumble that because of this, you are punishing all of Brittany and that it is you who are responsible for the suppression of the Estates General, which I am certain is far from the truth, and I have much to tell you that I cannot write.

Shocked, Anne crumpled the letter into a ball. In their treaty, Charles had agreed that Brittany would retain all its ancient customs and liberties. Yet he had suppressed its fundamental institutions. How could he?

Immediately both Lady Pernette and Countess Louise leapt to her side, begging to know what had disturbed her. She tacked a smile on her face and waved them away. "Just a piece of family news. And no, I do not wish to share it."

She smoothed the letter as well as she could, busy considering the implications of the queen's revelation. From her words, Anne realized Queen Joanne and many others believed she had consented to Charles's shameful action. Worse, they blamed *her* for it. Yet this was the first she knew of it.

Her anger simmered. Charles's womanizing was bad enough, but this betrayal struck much deeper. She had married him to protect her duchy and her people. Yet only six months later, despite his solemn promises in front of the Parlement itself, he had broken his solemn oath. What meaning did their marriage contract have for him? How could she trust him if he could dismiss his vows so lightly? She considered confronting him about it. Then everything his sister had said about his resentment of women's domination flooded back.

She heaved herself to her feet and her ladies fluttered like hens disturbed by a fox.

"No," she said. "Stay where you are. I need to see the river. I will be shut away soon enough."

She plodded beside the ramparts parallel to the Loire River until her bulky body refused to go another step. Resting her arms on the edge of the wall, she gazed longingly up the river towards Nantes and Brittany. Who had advised Charles to suppress the Estates, and why? They were her antagonists—perhaps enemies. They did not care about Brittany's well being.

Yet what could she do now when she was about to be confined? Once she had assigned her powers to Charles, he had placed men loyal to him in every key administrative and military post. She no longer administered even her personal estates. As was her duty, she had come to love Charles. Why had he done this? How could she influence him to change?

1 Estates General—in France under the Ancien Regime the Estates General was a legislative and consultative assembly of the different classes (or estates) of French subjects. It had a separate assembly for each of the three estates (clergy, nobility and commoners), which were called and dismissed by the king. Some provinces had their own Estates General. Brittany as an independent duchy had one.

2 Parlement—a provincial appellate court of France, the **oldest and most important** of which was the **Parlement of Paris**. Parlements were judicial organizations consisting of a

dozen or more appellate judges. They were the courts of final appeal of the judicial system, and wielded power over many areas including taxation. Laws and edicts issued by the Crown were not official until the parlements assented by publishing them. Their members were aristocrats, called nobles of the robe, who had bought or inherited their offices.

CHAPTER 10

A Dauphin for France

Plessis-lez-Tours, 10 October 1492

"A boy! You have a son, Madame la Reine!" the midwife called out.

Tears sprang to Anne's eyes, and she laughed, so full of joy she felt she would burst apart, and then she found herself sobbing, unable to stop. Still straddling the birthing stool, she dropped the amulet she clutched in her hand and reached out her arms. "Give him to me."

As the infant let out a wail of indignation, the midwife held him in front of Anne's eyes, his genitals, engorged from the birth, evident to all, his tiny arms flailing.

"When he is cleaned up and so are you, you shall have him. But you must push once more to expel the afterbirth. And you are shaking too much to hold him."

This last effort passed unnoticed in Anne's euphoric state. As her maids and ladies raised her, washed down her sweat-soaked body with scented water, fitted her with rags tied in place and dropped a soft, clean shift over her head, she felt as if she was floating. But when Madame la Grande on one side and Queen Joanne on the other took her arms to walk her to her freshly made bed, every muscle in her body complained. Her legs felt like water, she was so exhausted. Yet through her pain, she heard around her the buzz of excited voices as the women who had shared her chambers for over two months echoed her delight.

Settled against the solid pillows, within fresh sheets topped by a coverlet embroidered in her arms of France and Brittany, she took a deep breath. Then a sharp yap from the floor beside her bed made her laugh. "Let Fanchon up. She has worried for me, and she is part of my family." Her faithful dog snuffled her face and then settled at her feet.

Throughout the last interminable months, incarcerated in these shrouded chambers as securely as if iron locks had bolted her inside, Anne had clung to the talisman blessed by the holy Friar Francis. She had been surprised and grateful that Countess Louise had returned it to her. The power of the good Friar's intercession with the Lord had accomplished its purpose. Today she had born a dauphin for France and had survived the birth.

"I dropped the amulet," she said to the maid smoothing her pillows, "will you bring it to me, please?" When the maid retrieved it, she tucked it under her pillow. It had brought her its blessing.

She had often wondered as she spent more time in the countess's company why Louise had given back the precious charm. The more she had learned about the failed rebellion in Brittany from Queen Joanne, Pernette, and the other Breton ladies she was slowly gathering to her court, the more evidence came to light that Viscount de Rohan and Marshal de Rieux had been at its centre. And her ladies whispered that spies within the court had provided them with information about the location of troops and naval vessels and where there were weaknesses. Even Mme de Vesc added to her knowledge, albeit unwittingly, for she dribbled on non-stop, talking about anything and everything that popped into her mind, and she was as observant as a blackbird spying shiny objects. Anne was observant too, and it did not take her long to notice that Countess Louise had taken Mme de Vesc under her wing. Yet whatever else one could say about the countess, she was both intelligent and witty and did not suffer fools gladly. Her sharp humour ensured that these kept their distance, so her patience with Mme de Vesc stood out like a thorn in a bouquet of daisies.

Madame la Grande, her face alight, carried her son to Anne. "He is perfect," she purred, placing the swaddled bundle in Anne's arms. "You have done well, Madame la Reine. We are grateful to you." Her voice trembled.

For the first time, Anne felt that the woman accepted her as a member of the family. As Anne examined her baby, marvelling over his tiny fingers, awestruck by the perfection of his minuscule fingernails, and charmed by his jaw-splitting yawns, her sister-in-law recounted her birth experience with her daughter Suzanne now just a year old and, to her, still as miraculous as the day she was born. Although she recognized she was being taken into Madame la Grande's confidence, Anne barely listened, caught up in the swell of maternal love that engulfed her.

Much too soon, Madame la Grande said, "He must nurse, and you must rest. I will bring him to show his father. Have you chosen a name for him yet?"

Anne shook her head. "We have talked about it, but we could not until we knew whether we had a son or daughter." *A son. Charles would be ecstatic.*

ANNE WAS NOT ASLEEP when Charles burst into her sleeping chamber. It was the first time he had entered her lying-in chambers since she had been sequestered.

"I could not hold myself back," he said, dropping kisses on her head, cheeks, arms and hands. "Thank you, thank you, my goddess, my beautiful and precious queen, for giving me such a perfect gift. A son! A dauphin for France!"

He was so exultant, so charming, so loving, that Anne's heart burst again with the passionate love that she had experienced in the first months of their marriage.

"I have a family now," she said. "It has been so long since I have had a family of my own. But with you and our son, I have a family again." She had not known until she said the words how lonely she had been since her sister had died. She had expected to have Isabeau beside her for years, and she had been only twelve, much too young to die. When she had a daughter, she would name her Isabeau, she promised herself. Even after the suffering of childbirth, she knew she wanted more children, more of this miraculous feeling of family. "What shall we name him?" she asked.

As he sat on the edge of her bed, one foot resting on the knee of the other leg, Charles dove into the discussion. His heroes were the great warriors of old: Alexander, Hercules, Charlemagne, Vercingetorix, Roland. But his choice was Roland. His eyes shining, Charles said, "Above everything, Roland held two values sacred: living an honourable life; and serving God and Christianity. And he died for his beliefs. He was devoted to duty—as a king must be."

Charles took Anne's hand, gazing far into the distance. "He is my ideal. You wonder sometimes why I act as I do. It is to live up to these ideals. And now that we have a son, I can act as I have sworn to do."

He was confiding in her as he never had before, and Anne knew she must support him, no matter what he said, for he was baring his soul to her.

"I am going to lead a crusade to take back the Holy Land from the infidel. The Turks grow bold and threaten us all over the Eastern Sea." He rose and paced up and down beside her bed, his voice passionate. "Pope Innocent has been calling upon the kings of our Christian nations to save the faith, yet none has answered the call. Well, I shall. I will lead this crusade. God has chosen me." Everything about him glowed.

Anne's heart sank. She had seen enough war to last a lifetime. Images of twisted, mouldering bodies lying outside the gates of Rennes, the sweet corrupt stink of their unclaimed corpses flooded her senses, numbing her joy. Wars left innocent people homeless and bereft—not only of their loved ones, but also of their homes and lands. They beggared a country and stole its wealth. And everywhere, death, death, death. Yes, she was a devout Christian, and she believed in obeying His Holiness, but could they not send mercenaries and gold? Pope Innocent did not need her husband as much as she did.

Yet she could say none of these things. From Charles's expression, she could tell he felt exalted, and no words of caution would reach him. They would only make him more stubborn and drive him from her. During the few short months of their marriage, she had learned he was intractable once he decided. So, she said, "That is a glorious and noble ambition. Please tell me more." She patted the spot where he had been sitting.

His shoulders relaxed, reassuring Anne she had responded correctly. For all his bluster, he wanted her approval. She gave him a sunny smile. "Your name will shine in our history, and you will have magnificent stories to tell our son. What do you plan?"

Sitting again, he told her about the alliances he was making with England, Spain, and Burgundy. "I got the idea from my sister and Duke Pierre," he said. "They paid your father's vassals regular pensions. Whenever they had a grievance, they came to the Regent, and she increased their pensions if they rebelled."

"How clever of them," Anne could not keep the sarcasm from her voice.

"It is the way wars are won."

Anne clamped her jaw shut. It would not improve their relations to give vent to her rage.

Charles chattered on. He was going to pay every one of Anne's debts to King Henry for his help during her resistance to obtain that alliance. And he had agreed to settle the French dispute over Cerdagne and Roussillon in Ferdinand's favour to buy his support. Anne's eyes widened as he added one concession after another to the costs of this expedition. And that was before he gathered an invading force, trained them, transported them, and fed them. Her own war had all but bankrupted her duchy. She understood France was the richest country in the world—she didn't know about the Turks, but still—yet how could he afford this?

"It is going to be expensive," she said. *Whisht, that sounded like a criticism.* "I am sure you have a plan to finance it," she added.

He looked at her sharply.

"I am thinking of my debts and your generosity in settling them," she explained. "You know well how much that war cost me, and that does not include what it cost France. Including, now paying my debts, for which I am eternally grateful, and so will be my people when they learn of it." She did not add, because it would bring them peace. Peace had always been her intention.

"I do have a plan. The so-called King of Naples stole my rightful heritage." He glowered. "When King René died, his claim to that kingdom reverted to the crown of France. So, my army will travel across Italy to reconquer what is rightfully mine." His face alight, he smiled at her. "It is a brilliant plan. My army will gain experience, which they will need. The Two Sicilies, particularly Naples, are enormously wealthy, and they will pay for the costs of my troops. Besides, the kingdom is the perfect site to launch the campaign against the Turk for the Holy Land. It has many harbours, and its wheat crop will supply my army with the provisions we need. And I have the rightful claim to the Kingdom of Jerusalem."

"It is brilliant, as you say," Anne agreed. "You have thought of everything. You are a worthy father of a Roland. We will raise him to emulate you."

But their choice did not go uncontested. The opposition was

so great among Charles's family and most important vassals, arriving in hordes to honour the glorious news and attend the baby's baptism, that Charles finally gave way. Madame la Grande brokered a compromise with him. The child would be named Charles-Orland. Anne stuck loyally by Charles's choice until he finally agreed to the change, and suffered for him when he finally conceded, tears in his eyes.

"God's wounds, what is the value of being king, when I cannot even choose my son's name?" he stormed to her. And she held him as he wept.

He did make them accept his decision that Friar Francis would conduct the baptismal service and that it would be as simple as possible. He discouraged his vassals from wearing colours or their robes of estate at the ceremony, although he said nothing about their coronets. In place of gifts, he required donations to his war chest.

Naturally, Anne did not attend the baptism, for she had not been churched. But Queen Joanne assured her that Charles-Orland had cried lustily when plunged into the baptismal font, and his two godfathers, Duke Pierre and Duke Louis, had performed their roles well. "Both of them must envy the king," she said, "for unlike them, he has a son. But even they must celebrate that the royal line is assured, and we can avoid another civil war over the throne."

~

Château de Plessis-lez-Tours, 14 October 1492

COUNTESS LOUISE FELT she must be the unhappiest person in all France. Glancing around to make sure she was unobserved, she left the gravelled path through the flower garden where it came closest to the woods, continuing to brood. Although there was no reason why it should be a secret, she did not want anyone to know about her visit to Friar Francis.

Her thoughts were dark. In each of her three tours of duty serving as the queen's lady-in-waiting at court since she had been released from her churching in May, it had ben harder to pretend a concern for Anne when she wished the queen would suffer a miscarriage.

This time, during Anne's seclusion, had been the worst. Although dissembling was second nature to Louise after growing up in Madame la Grande's court, watching Queen Anne glow with health and good humour had grated on her nerves. Anne's piety irritated her. Three times a day Anne had mass said at the door to her chambers. She did not require everyone to take part, but if one shirked, Anne inquired after one's health and the state of one's bowels. The message was clear, so Louise used the time to pray that Anne receive her just reward for her part in causing Louise to have a girl. She did not presume to tell the Lord what that should be, but at a minimum, Anne should have a daughter, too, in her opinion. Since the queen wore the amulet everywhere and had clung to it during the delivery of her child, Louise had held high hopes for she had placed a counter-charm on the talisman. So how could Anne have given birth to such a large, healthy son?

The Franciscan robe she carried caught on a bush, and she stopped to release it with care. It would never do to bring a flawed robe to the good friar. She had thought deeply about an offering. A simple robe should be acceptable, since when she had visited him last, his was tattered and filthy.

His disdain for the vanities of the world was well-know. Even yesterday in the baptismal service he condemned the gold and silver of the christening vessels, and the silk brocade altar cloths embroidered in gold and jewels, saying that their value would be better used feeding the needy. He had chosen as his text, "Be not deceived; God is not mocked: for whatsoever a man soweth, that shall he also reap.

"The Lord came to live among the poor and the humble," the friar preached, staring at the gauds the courtiers wore, "and warned you it was harder for a rich man to enter heaven than to pass through the eye of a needle. You are rich in goods, so struggle to grow rich in spirit in His devout and holy service, if you hope to enter eternal life."

She planned how to express what she wanted to say as she made her way to his cottage. How could he have been so wrong? she wanted to know. For the queen has a son and I have only a daughter. But if she used those words, he would accuse her of failing to trust in the Lord.

The holy man was sitting outside on a narrow wooden bench when she arrived. He looked like a skinny gnome.

"Daughter," he called to her, "come and sit beside me to enjoy this glorious day that our Father has sent us."

When she offered him the robe, he took it, saying, "It is kind of you to think of me. Gifts express generosity of spirit." Then he put it on the bench beside him, as if her care in its selection was of no importance.

He chatted away, more loquaciously than Louise had ever known him to be. The baptism had pleased him. She nodded as he spoke about the important message the king and queen had sent their courtiers by encouraging simple piety, rather than the display of wealth preferred by so many of the highest prelates who claimed to serve the Lord. "How little each of us needs of worldly goods," he concluded.

Louise murmured, "So true, so true," relieved she had chosen her simplest grey wool robe and boots tied with leather strings.

"In what way can I serve you, daughter?"

Taking a deep breath, Louise plunged in. "I came to give thanks for your spiritual care during the time of my travail, interceding for me with Saint Anne, mother of the Holy Virgin. My daughter is beautiful and healthy and every day I give thanks to the Lord and all the saints for the grace of her life." She paused, still struggling to find the right way to ask why Marguerite had not been a boy. No words came.

"Now that the Lord has blessed the country with a dauphin

and me with a daughter, I wish to show Him my gratitude. The count and I do not have the wealth to endow a foundation, so I come to ask your advice. Where can we donate twenty écus to best effect for the salvation of souls?"

Friar Francis seemed nonplused. "You are known for your generosity and good works. The Lord sees and blesses your deeds. There is no need for me to interfere."

"Nevertheless, I beg your guidance."

"Let me pray on it." He fell silent

She hung her head and adopted a prayerful pose.

After a time when he still did not speak, she broke the silence with a soft remark about the inspiration of the queen's faith, her trust in the talisman he had blessed, and France's joy now that it had a dauphin. She saw his face cloud and worried that he could read her heart.

Then he said, "The queen is a good woman of great faith. She will overcome all the tests of faith the Lord sends her." With that, Louise had to be satisfied.

CHAPTER 11
A Disaster for Anne

Château d'Amboise, 19 January 1493

Charles led Anne off the dance floor in the great hall of the Château as the music ended. Her faced was flushed, she panted slightly, and shone with happiness in the light from the great chandeliers. The candles high above them cast their flickering light on the painted ceiling. Their glow flattered the courtiers gathered below, attired in colourful gowns and doublets, their faces glistening, although the lively exercise soured the air with the stink of sweat. Anne was grateful that the rushes of dried roses and lavender from her gardens released their fragrance underfoot helping mask the odour.

The king stopped to greet his sister and brother-in-law. "You return to Moulins tomorrow?"

Madame la Grande answered first. "We must, Brother. We thank you for the pleasure of attending your Christmas court. You must be pleased with its success." She offered a dry smile. "The Italian ambassadors have gifted you enough paintings of the Madonna and Holy Child to furnish chapels in every royal residence, I would wager. Perhaps they should have consulted among themselves beforehand."

"Do you not admire the Italian style?" Anne inquired. "I hear your Master Painter has adopted it."

Before his sister could answer Charles intervened. "I will send the best artists from Italy back to France once I get there."

Anne thanked him, wondering if he thought this pledge would make her favour his war against the Kingdom of Naples. How little he understood her. She could support his crusade against the infidel, for that was a holy obligation. But a war for glory and territory? Never. Still, she smiled and nodded, certain he did not realize she had conferred with her Breton Cardinal Guibé about his plans.

The Cardinal had been a trusted supporter from the moment she became duchess at her father's death when she was still eleven. He had refused to let her gouverneurs force her into a marriage she opposed, and he crowned her despite their opposition. She trusted him as much as she trusted Baron Philippe, her former Chancellor.

The good bishop would persuade the Breton prelates in Rome to oppose the king's plans with Pope Alexander. She doubted the Pope would want France usurping his right to bestow the Neapolitan crown upon his chosen candidate. But Charles would not want to hear *her* opinion and judging from Madame la Grande's expression she was no happier about the Italian adventure than Anne.

"I hear you have signed a treaty with King Ferdinand," said Madame la Grande, her sharp nose quivering, "and agreed to give him the territories of Cerdagne and Roussillon."

Although she stated only facts, Charles bristled. "Do you have any objection? The territories were Aragonese. We captured them in the recent hostilities. They are not large and completely mountainous. It was a fair exchange for peace."

"Did I say otherwise, Brother? You are king and must decide."

She rested her hand on his arm. "Come, let us not part on a sour note." She curtsied.

Anne said, "Please accept my thanks. I benefited greatly from your experience in organizing court festivities," silently begging the Lord's forgiveness for her hypocrisy, for she had resented her sister-in-law's interference. "You stepped in when I was unavailable and managed the Christmas court as always."

Her three auditors smirked with pleasure. Anne accepted that this small deceit, a duty of her royal status, was worth the penance she would set herself.

After asking the king's permission, the Bourbon—Madame la Grande and Duke Pierre—left the great hall to prepare to depart before dawn the next morning. Watching them leave, Charles murmured to Anne, "I am glad to see their backs. My sister still wishes to rule. You would think she did not grasp why I settled with the Aragonese. Those lands in exchange for a free hand in Naples. Yet she opposes my right to regain my kingdoms although she favoured our conquests of Brittany and Burgundy." He seemed to be thinking aloud. "Do you think it is because she and the duke have inherited the Bourbon lands? A powerful central authority is not as appealing to her now, perhaps?"

Another lively dance tune filled the room. To distract him, Anne tapped a foot to the beat. Charles offered her his arm. When the dance ended, they continued their rounds, bidding adieu to the guests departing on the morrow.

Anne stiffened as they joined the Count and Countess d'Angoulême. Since Louise had joined her court, especially since Charles-Orland had been born, Anne had grown to dislike the countess more and more. It wasn't simply that she never curtsied quite deeply enough, or lowered her head or eyes when Anne passed, or made it obvious she was changing the subject when Anne approached any group Louise sat in—although these trifling affronts irritated her. Rather, Anne blamed her for the increased gossip and petty complaints among the ladies in her court. When Anne delved into the cause of the grievances or the source of rumours, too often the trail led back to one of Louise's close companions—Lady Anne de Rohan, Mme de Vesc, Mme Antoinette or another de Rohan minion—and went cold. At first, the queen thought it could be coincidence. But soon she detected a pattern. So, Anne was glad Louise and her ladies would leave the next day.

Countess Louise dipped a minimal bob in Anne's direction. *As usual*, thought Anne, contrasting it with the count's deep bow. He seemed sincerely respectful of the king and her and reminded Anne a great deal of his cousin, Louis, for they were both sociable and genuinely interested in others. Like Charles, they made themselves loved by their people, stopping to chat and to listen wherever they went.

This stroll among their guests was an example. It was one of the best things about Charles and it reminded her of her father, who had been equally genial. Louise on the other hand, sauntered about with her nose in the air, as if her Bourbon blood made her better than everyone around her until she wanted something, when she became as sweet as marzipan. Anne had watched her charming Mme de Vesc into becoming an acolyte, yet Anne was as certain as if she had overheard Louise saying it that she found the woman a bore.

Anne lingered with Lady Anne de Rohan. "You have a younger sister, do you not?" she asked, "What is her name?"

"Lady Marie, Madame la Reine." Her voice barely more than a whisper, the girl curtsied deeply, her face flushing crimson.

"Marie is it? Good." Now that she would have some free time, Anne decided to expand her court further. She would invite Marie. That way she could keep track of Louise's and the Count's activities, for her mother of maids[1] required the girls write to their families weekly.

She nodded to the group, and Charles and she continued their perambulation.

~

A clearing in the woods near Courcelles, 21 August 1493

WIPING his forehead with his sleeve, Charles rose from the folding chair placed beside Anne's, almost whacking his head on the tree branch above his head.

He gave a crack of laughter. "Good thing it did not knock me out. That would have put paid to the rest of the hunt," he said, raising an arm and swinging himself around to walk away from the cloth-covered trestle table. Immediately everyone in the party rose except Anne. Her belly swollen by her seven-month pregnancy she could not have done so even if she felt so inclined.

"To the horses," Charles cried. All those joining the hunt followed him, some grabbing meaty bones, pasties, or sweet pears from their trenchers as they trotted off. Only Anne's ladies stayed behind at the folding tables set up in the dappled shade of the grassy meadow.

The huntsmen, dogs, and horses had been resting under trees on the far side of the glade beside the shallow stream. As Anne watched, the peaceful scene shimmering in the heat haze flickered into motion. The still air erupted with barking, whinnying and the rattle of horse tack. Soon the confusion sorted itself into a lengthening train of horses and their riders trotting into the distance, the king and his cronies in the lead, the hunting hounds racing in front.

The fading hoofbeats and baying hounds gave way to the voices of her ladies and servants, all mingling with the flutter of leaves, the whistle of birds and the drone of bees. Behind her, the tinkle of water over stones reminded her how hot she was, even here in the shade of the trees. It would be wonderful to strip to her shift and cool in the stream.

Anne sighed. She had hoped that bringing her ladies and an elaborate picnic, along with the equipment for outdoor bowls and archery, would convince Charles and his courtiers to abbreviate their hunt and join her ladies for the afternoon. It had not worked. Charles had scowled when he found them at the meadow he had designated as their meal location when the hunt splashed in. He barely gave them time to set up the tables and put out the food before he insisted on eating. Then he was off again.

She winced as another pain, this one sharper, lanced her belly. It could not be her baby. He was not due for another two months. But she admitted to herself that she was uncomfortable. It was just as well that the hunt had ridden off. Rather than rest here, she would leave the servants to pack up. There was no need to spoil the outing for the rest of her court, though. She spoke in undertones to Mme Pernette and soon she climbed into her litter accompanied by just two ladies and a maid. A small armed guard escorted them.

The horses harnessed in front and behind the litter didn't stop it swaying. Anne lay back against the squabs, shifting every few moments, unable to find a comfortable position. Sweat soaked her gown. It was unbearable in all these clothes. She insisted that Pernette remove the sleeves and front panel and loosen the laces on her linen overdress. It helped, but not enough. She could no longer deceive herself. The pains were becoming worse, and she recognized them. Pains like these had preceded Charles-Orland's birth. But that could not be. It was much too early. She bit her lower lip to keep from moaning.

Pernette knew her too well. "Madame la Reine, what is it? You are pale and I see you are in pain."

Anne opened her lips to deny it. Then she felt a gush of liquid between her legs and a long slow ache. She could no longer restrain either a moan or her tears. As the distinct salty odour of a baby's waters accompanied the spreading stain on Anne's skirt, the faces of Anne's three women paled.

Pernette rapped imperiously on the front panel of the litter, and shouted, "Stop at once. The queen orders it."

On the instant, they jolted back and forth as their equipage rocked to a halt. A guard yanked the door open.

Pernette gave him no time to speak. "The queen's time is upon her. Find us shelter at once. We must have fire, water, and cloths. Send a rider back to her chamberlain to bring a midwife and a send a messenger after the king!" She saw indecision in his face. "Now, I tell you."

The queen groaned and the guard dithered no longer. As he slammed the door, he shouted an order to one of his companions to ride up and another to the coachman to follow him. The litter jerked and sped forward, tossing its occupants from side to side.

Anne remembered only snatches of the hours that ensued. At one point, the litter stopped, the door opened and raised voices argued. A man came—she thought it might be one of her guards—and lifted her from the litter. Later, she lay tossing on what felt like a plank inside a dark, stinking cave-like place. A woman she couldn't understand made her sit up and then removed her gown and kirtle. Someone wiped her face and arms and even her legs with cool water. Another person held her up as she walked and sagged and stumbled. Pains, and more pains, closer and closer together. Someone screamed. During it all, her head was so thick and her eyes so heavy she felt trapped in a nightmare she could not escape.

Orders. "Push."

"Wake up."

"Push."

Something hard shoved into her mouth. "Bite on this."

"Pray."

Through it all, Pernette's voice, talking, talking, talking.

Finally, a long, great shuddering, pressure, a blessed easing, and voices, "A boy . . . he lives."

Anne did not know how much time had passed or where she was when she opened her eyes again into a dim, low space that stank of smoke, yesterday's cooking, and too many bodies. Every part of her body ached, even her neck, when she rolled it to the right hoping to discover where she was. At her movement, the person beside her—a maid perhaps?—called, "She has opened her eyes."

After a quick shuffle, Charles appeared. Still in his hunting attire, he wore a frown. "I thank God you and our son are still alive. He is frail and tiny. I have had him baptized Charles. I feared there was no time to lose."

His ominous words sounded to Anne as if they came from a long distance away, perhaps across a wide field. She could understand their meaning, but they did not affect her as she thought they should. She was too tired and confused to ask about them.

She said, "Where am I?"

Her husband stared at her so long she began to wonder if she had spoken. His voice strained, he said, "We are in a peasant's cottage in the woods near Courcelles."

It did not tell her much. "Oh. What time is it?"

He made a whistling noise as he drew his breath in through his long nose. "We are approaching Lauds."

As her eyes adjusted, she said, "I do not know this place, but it seems-," she struggled to find the right word, "-primitive. Why am I here?" She shifted on the hard board under her.

Charles still looked annoyed. "Do you not remember?"

As the haze receded, a memory returned of the jolting trip and her labour pains. Then Charles's words registered, and astonishment swept through her. "We have another son. But it is too soon." Agitated, she tried to sit up. "I should not be here."

"No." Charles's tone was harsh.

"You are angry." Anne bit her lips, struggling to rise. "I cannot stay here. It is dirty and very small." Her legs gave way and she landed with a jolt on the hard surface under the bedsheet.

"No. You and my son cannot stay here. You must move back to Courcelles. A litter and the men to carry it should arrive soon. No, horses will not do," he answered, voice harsh, seeing the question in her eyes, "for you are both too weak for the jolting. Your three ladies, a nurse and a wet nurse the woman from this cottage has found, will stay with you and I will see you there."

He turned to leave, then turned back. "You were fortunate. You say this hovel is poor. There are many worse. I shall see them amply rewarded for their hospitality and care of you." He left without a backward glance.

~

THE TRIP to the summer Château was less painful than that from the glade to the cottage, but only because Anne slept most of the time dosed on poppy. Once back at the Château de Courcelles, she was confined to bed, but could not rest, shocked by her son's tiny size and the translucence of his skin. Unlike Charles-Orland, he did not wave his arms about or howl to be fed. His nurse and doctors would not allow him to stay with her. The doctor said it was because she needed to recover from the hard birth, but he refused to meet her eyes. She did not believe his excuses. Two days later, he came to tell her that her son had died.

After she recovered from her first shock and sorrow, she longed for Charles's arms, and to mourn together yet he did not come. It was then that her second wave of suffering began. She returned to Amboise where she spent hours in the chapel on her knees doing penance, convinced that her son's death and the loss of her husband's love were her own fault. She had kept her pregnancy from him for months. When he discovered it himself, her explanation that she did not want to give up their intimacy or the activities they both enjoyed did not placate him.

Her jealousy had driven him from her. "You hound me," he had said. "I can't breathe around you." And worst of all, her attempt to arrange a delightful picnic had ended in disaster. He blamed her for their son's death, and she could not deny it. She blamed herself. How long would it take him to forgive her?

She had sinned. Madame la Grande had warned her, yet she had disregarded her sister-in-law's advice. Was that not the sin of pride? And did not the church teach that it was her duty to obey her husband? She had not done so. She must accept this bitter loss as her penance. She deserved it for her many sins.

1 Mother of maids— a senior position in the queen's court held by a high ranking married woman with the responsibility for supervising the behaviour, education, and service roster of unmarried female courtiers.

CHAPTER 12

War Fever

Château d'Amboise, 14 September 1493

"It grieves me to see the queen on her knees in the chapel for hours every day. She mourns her loss so deeply." Mme Catherine de Brézé's voice wobbled as she confided in Mme Pernette. They sat together near the fireplace in the queen's presence chamber, working on their embroidery, the heavy blue and gold damask drapes of the window behind them held open with matching thick gold braid.

Seated behind the half-open drapes, her back against the stone wall, her feet up and her dress drawn down over her knees, Louise did not move or make a sound, although her ears perked. The book resting against her knees was excuse enough for her presence where she sat, and a reasonable claim that she had heard nothing. "Besides," she would ask, "why was it a problem? Were you saying things that should not be heard?" Attack was the best defence, she had learned long ago.

When she had first heard of Anne's disastrous delivery in a peasant's hut, Louise had imagined how awful it must have been and felt almost sorry for Anne. After learning she had given birth to another son, Louise had been bitter and then felt relieved, though guilty, when he had died. By now she was irritated that the queen mourned and mourned and mourned as if no-one else had ever suffered such a loss. Now, eyes on her *Chroniques de Roys de France Abreviees,* Louise waited for Mme Catherine to speak again.

A couple of years older than Louise, Catherine was still unmarried, although they said she was almost as beautiful as her grandmother, Agnes Sorel—the one they had called *La Dame de Beauté*. But scandal swirled around the family, and it had surprised all her ladies that Anne had invited Mme Catherine to court. But that was Anne. She was always saving fledgling birds that had fallen out of their nests and kittens whose mothers had disappeared. Even her spaniel, Fanchon, was the runt of the litter, who would have been drowned if she had not adopted her.

"I heard the other ladies say she was mourning more than the loss of her son. Many blows have prostrated her since she lost her duchy and married the king."

Louise recognized Mme Pernette's voice. "What have you heard?"

"Umm. Well. . .things like her husband's preparations for war in Italy, for she hates war. And who can blame her? And, and his infidelities . . . that they distress her, for she loves him. And it is a sin. And he has been so *cold* towards her since she lost their son." Catherine paused, her voice troubled. "And perhaps that is true, for she disobeyed him, and she was not careful. She should not have been—"

"It is not our place to judge, or ever to discuss, the queen." Mme Pernette's voice cracked like a whip across Catherine's voice, silencing it.

When Catherine spoke again, she sounded as if she might burst into tears. "But-but-but you asked me!"

"I tested you. You should have said you knew nothing because you should not listen to gossip. Whenever you hear anything, you must report the ladies and what they are saying to the mother of maids. That is what you should have done. Have you done so? I thought not. Well, you must. So, who were they?"

Behind her curtain, Louise tensed. She was sure she had been careful not to speak against the queen, but people did not always tell the truth when confronted. *Grâce à Dieu*, Catherine seemed to have taken Mme Pernette's words to heart.

"You are right, Mme Pernette. I have harmed the queen when she has been so g-g-good to me." Louise heard sniffling and someone, almost certainly Catherine, blowing her nose.

Mme Pernette was making hushing sounds to calm the woman, but she failed. Finally, she said, "I think you should retire. And when you cal yourself, speak to the mother of maids. You have a duty." Her tone was still stern.

There was some shuffling and sounds of footsteps, so Louise risked peeking around the curtain. The two women stood near the door. Catherine's head was bowed, and Mme Pernette held her hand to Catherine's back, as if pushing her to leave. Their embroidery lay abandoned in a heap on the floor.

Louise leaned back and deliberated. Mme Pernette would run to tattle to Queen Anne, that was certain. Catherine? She would not want to talk to the mother of maids, who supervised all the noble demoiselles of the queen's court, but she had no choice now. It was that or tell the queen herself. Possibly, the mother of maids would insist she tell the queen, anyway. Who would Catherine implicate? How could Louise learn what she had said?

~

Plessis-lez-Tours, 27 October 1493

"PÈRE LE BAUD, you are well come." Queen Anne beamed at her grizzled, grey-haired chaplain, who now served her after having served her father until his death. "Did you have any difficulty observing the sessions of the Council at Tours?"

"Not at all, Madame la Reine." The cleric, a red and gold dalmatic over his purple cassock, bowed and raised her hand to his lips. She waved him to take the armchair beside hers, a mark of high regard.

"When I told the Captain of the Guard that I was Historian to the Dukes of Brittany, there to chronicle the event for the Duke's issue, he ensured I had all I required." Père le Baud stroked his salt-and-pepper beard. But Anne saw his eyes crinkle and recognized that he intended her to share his delight at how well his ploy had succeeded.

"Was it as I thought? That the entire Council of State attended? Including the members of the king's special new council on the war in Italy?"

"Indeed, Madame la Reine. It opened as one would expect. The viper-tongued Chancellor called upon everyone present to swear an oath to serve the King and France and to uphold and make laws in the best interests of Holy Church. Archbishop de Saint Denis blessed the work they were to do, and all swore." Le Baud shook his head. "Even I, Madame la Reine, who have seen much controversy in my years of service, have rarely witnessed a session deteriorate as rapidly as this. Once Marshal d'Esquerdes finished presenting the war council, members were jumping from their seats, demanding recognition, and shouting objections over one another. Briçonnet—I mean Robert, not Guillaume—could not control the meeting. As soon as he announced the king had signed an alliance with Duke Ludovico Sforza of Milan, Duke Louis d'Orléans was on his feet, ranting that Milan was his by right. Then Archbishop de Saint Denis announced that Guillaume Briçonnet had been appointed Bishop de Saint Malo—" He stopped at Anne's sharp gasp.

"You did not know Madame la Reine? Nor did I. Neither did most of the members of the king's council, judging from the uproar."

Anne held up her hand to stop his flow of words. She had heard nothing about this appointment, yet it was one of only seven bishoprics in the Breton Church. Charles had *promised* that the Breton Church would maintain its independence, that the rules that regulated the French Church would not apply to it. It was another of her hard-fought inclusions in their marriage treaty. He and his negotiators had agreed finally, so it was impossible that he had done this in ignorance. And this was not the first treaty clause he had broken. He had suppressed the Breton Estates General! Did their marriage treaty mean nothing?

Under the Breton accords with the Holy See, no See could be filled without the approval of the Dukes of Brittany. She and Bishop Guibé had talked about it when he came to Charles-Orland's baptism, and he had kept her informed of all appointments, even quite lowly ones. Yet she had heard nothing of the See of Saint Malo. Could she no longer trust Bishop Guibé? If that were true. . . Her world rocked.

"Madame la Reine, how may I help you? Confide in me."

Anne lifted anguished eyes to his. "I knew nothing of this appointment."

"No more did I, Madame la Reine."

"Yet as duchess, they should have consulted me. I should have approved." She hesitated. Was she ready to admit her fear that she could not trust the one man within the whole Breton Church she relied upon most?

"Perhaps the duke decided himself."

Until Père le Baud said the words, that betrayal had not crossed Anne's mind. As soon as he said them, they rang true. Rage boiled within her and flooded her throat with bile. She had to clench her jaw to stay silent. *Just another of her rights ripped from her in the service of this shameful Italian war.* She did not speak until she knew she could keep her voice steady. "That must be it. I had not thought of it." She took another deep breath. "Continue."

"Many counsellors spoke against the war. Old Marshal de Crèvecoeur rose, supporting himself on two canes, his voice cracking with age. He said he understood why young men longed for glory and adventure. But when he was a young man, he had fought to recapture the Kingdom of Naples for King René. He could say from experience believing they could hold Naples was a dangerous illusion. Better to do as the Duke d'Orléans suggested and take Milan."

"And?"

"Boos and whistles, Madame." He shook his head. "The Duke de Bourbon rose and shouted to show respect, and that quieted them. But it was a shameful display. Bourbon spoke against the war, too, saying it was against France's interests, but it made no difference."

Le Baud said nothing for several minutes. Anne poured a goblet of wine and reflected on the war fever that was gripping the nobility. Had they forgotten so soon? Or was it not the same for them?

She shuddered. There was nothing about those years of war that she would want to repeat. It was not just the death or the poverty. Not even the suffering of her people, though that was one of the worst things about it. She remembered the constant fear, the worry every single day about what dreadful thing might happen and what terrible decision she would have to make. The worst was the relentless uncertainty; never able to sleep or eat or laugh without having to wonder what was coming . . . what dreadful news hoofbeats galloping down the cobblestones outside her residence presaged.

"At the end, the king himself came to speak to the council. He was passionate. He said that it was their Catholic duty to clear the Holy Land of the infidel. The Turks were a clear and imminent threat to all they held dear and true. It had been only months since the Turks had been dislodged from the toe of Italy. They were on the attack along the eastern border of Austria. How else could he call himself the eldest son of Holy Church unless he acted now?

"But to ensure a safe and expeditious conquest, he must ensure a safe route. The safest passage with adequate supplies was from the Kingdom of Naples. And he was the rightful heir to that kingdom. When King René died, he named the crown of France as his heir. Charles was only claiming his heritage. He was using it to serve Christ. Pope Innocent had blessed his undertaking, and their new Pope Alexander surely would, as well. Who would follow him? Who would not?" Père le Baud took a deep breath. "After that, who could say him nay? No-one dared."

What more was there to say? They both leaned back. After a silence, Anne sighed. She loved Charles too much to thwart him. Besides, she was learning the hard way she could not turn him from his purpose. "Thank you, Père, for giving your account. It is certain I shall not change the king's mind and that I must accept his decisions graciously."

The cleric nodded. "That is a wife's duty, Madame la Reine."

~

Château de Nantes, Brittany, 13 December 1493

IN THE GREAT hall in the Château de Nantes, Anne sat enthroned on the dais beside Charles under the white cloth of estate with its black ermine-tail emblems. It had been three years since her last visit to the greatest Château in Brittany, three years in which her life had changed completely. Then she had been duchess in her own right, sitting in the throne while her council sat around her, waiting for her to speak, for her to make the decisions, for her to approve every important action. She dipped her head, acknowledging the merry, jostling crowd of nobles, clergy and rich merchants, all attired in their bejewelled robes, most with their glittering wives and daughters beside them. They had risen to cheer her when she entered. Although the panoply of regal wealth and splendour surrounded her today, she had less power now than on her last visit.

Today, Charles came to claim his rights, not as King of France, but as sovereign Duke of Brittany, usurping her rights because he was her husband. Their welcome left a bitter taste in her mouth, although she bestowed serene smiles on her people. She had known this would be the consequence of the treaty she had signed over two years ago. But knowing something and feeling it were two different things entirely. It was as if the pain in her hip had invaded her entire body.

She had never felt so constantly tired before, so reluctant to rise from her bed, so careless of her appearance, so little interested in the events and people around her. It took all her training to keep from snapping at those who served her, and to answer their interminable questions. To choose was well-nigh impossible, yet she must make dozens of decisions each day.

She had developed a technique to keep her principal lady from hounding her. The first choice that came to mind she seized upon, and she refused to consider another. People called her obstinate, she knew, but she did not care. The method made life bearable. She also retreated for hours. The safest place was her prie-dieu or her chapel. When she heard mass, no one could interrupt her or demand anything, while the endless repetition of prayers hushed her racing, circular thoughts.

By making a determined effort, she returned her attention to the ceremony of vassalage unfolding before her, although it offended her. It should not even take place here. Its proper location was the cathedral in Brittany's capital of Rennes. But the foreign Bishop Guillaume Briçonnet whom Charles had imposed, giving a lengthy opening prayer, did not care.

Bishop Briçonnet called her Breton nobility to accept Duke Charles I as their sovereign duke and to come forward to swear allegiance to him. She watched as, one by one, they obeyed, forswearing themselves since they had made the same vow to her six years earlier. *Did any of them consider that by swearing to him while she lived, they were breaking their solemn oath to her?* She caught Baron Philippe de Montauban's eye as he came forward.

His expression was sorrowful. She knew he did, for his granddaughter, Mme Pernette, brought his sealed letter to her. He had begged her forgiveness. He wrote:

In this way, I hope to retain a modicum of impact. Otherwise, I shall lose all influence. Since I agreed to take the oath, I have learned that the king, your husband, has issued a proclamation to disband the Breton Chancellery that he will present at the ceremony of vassalage.

That news had been another shock—one more betrayal of the terms of their marriage treaty. It had sent her to bed, for it was hopeless to dispute with Charles and his French councillors. They were as slippery as the eels they loved so much whereas she was as genuine as the granite that made up the bedrock of her duchy.

It was harder to remain impassive when Marshal de Rieux, Viscount Jean de Rohan, and her former gouvernante took the oath of fealty. Traitors to her, and proven plotters against her husband, she doubted they would prove more faithful to this than to any other oath. But they would be judged at heaven's throne. Of that, she had no doubt. When she saw her cousin Prince Jean d'Orange, Lieutenant-Governor of Brittany, she nodded to him, grateful for his warning that had roused Charles to action when it had been almost too late. His level stare and unsmiling bow left her worried.

Finally, King Charles rose. She heaved a heartfelt but inaudible breath of relief. It meant this interminable ceremony was ending. He announced he had heard their concerns. In his role as dispenser of justice, his first act would take effect as of that day. Then he appointed Count Guy XV de Laval Lieutenant-Governor of Brittany. Anne put her hand over her mouth to hide her chagrin. Another perfidy. Without telling her, her husband was replacing Prince Jean d'Orange, *her* cousin *and* heir with the son of her *detested* former *gouvernante*. It explained her cousin's lack of warmth when he greeted her. Probably he thought she knew of this betrayal. Her spirits sank further, although she had not thought it possible.

Charles gave a brief speech, charming them with the sincerity of his gratitude for their loyalty to him and their gracious duchess. He called on her to rise. She felt a spurt of well-hidden spite when their cheers for her were louder than they had been for him and hugged the small victory to herself.

As she stood smiling beside him, Charles signalled his chamberlain. To Anne's surprise, Mme de Bussières entered from a side corridor. When the woman stepped onto the dais, Anne saw she held Charles-Orland in her arms! Waves of clapping and cheers rose through the hall as she handed the giggling 14-month-old dauphin to the king. Then a herald blew a fanfare, and the applause fell raggedly into silence.

Charles lifted young Charles-Orland high. "I present your future Duke of Brittany to you," he proclaimed.

Cheers burst forth once more, louder than ever. By their side, Anne burned with an even greater rage. There was only one case in which the dauphin would inherit Brittany—if they had no other living child. The treaty she had signed promised it. In every other case—if they had a second child, even if she were a girl, if he died before her—Brittany would pass elsewhere.

She had not yet fought Charles when he disregarded the terms of their treaty. But this one she would enforce, come what may.

CHAPTER 13

Louise's Secrets

Feast of the Conversion of Saint Paul, Apostle, 25 January 1494

For the past two days Louise had restrained herself, but today she could no longer contain her hope. Since her monthly flowers had started, she had been as regular as the cycle of the moon, except once. Then she had carried Margot, her gifted daughter, who at two could already repeat the whole of her Hail Mary. Today was the seventh day that her courses were late. As she knelt at mass with the rest of Anne's ladies, she prayed she carried the son Friar Francis had promised her three years ago. It was much too soon to tell Carlo or even mention her suspicions to a midwife, but she could pray—and ask the goddess of fertility to bless this son growing inside her.

As they returned to the queen's suite, Louise observed that the sun sparkled through the windows that lined the corridor at intervals. While the other ladies settled, she removed herself discretely and returned to the chambers she shared with two of the other attendants who waited on the queen that day. Opening the coffer that contained her belongings, she lifted the top tray and placed it on her bed. With the key she wore on a gold chain around her neck, she opened the small, elaborately painted box within. From it she took a linen bag and opened it to make sure it contained three wax candles, a few bay leaves and small a copper bowl, the size of a circle made of her thumbs and first fingers. Replacing everything but the bag inside her coffer, she got to her feet. Checking once again that she was alone, she fastened her woollen cloak, put on leather boots, hung the bag from her waist, and pulled her hood up to hide her face.

Leaving the central dressing room shared by all the ladies-in-waiting, she entered the long corridor. Without haste, as if exactly where she should be, she walked to the garden exit. There, she tugged on mittens and stepped into the fresh air. Looking around, she was pleased to see the entire garden area deserted, as she had expected it would be. She stood, inhaling the sharp winter scent. No snow covered the gravel garden paths, although a light layer sparkled on the lawns, flower beds and bushes arranged in geometric designs. For the past two summers, choosing the designs and plants for these grounds had been the queen's favourite pastime. Louise smirked, for she had benefitted from its bay shrubs that she had been using for her charms since she arrived in September for her stint as lady-in-waiting.

She started down a path toward the distant cluster of evergreens at the far end of the long grounds, as had become her monthly habit since she arrived. This was her second visit in January, an unusual event. But this time she was excited, hopeful —even grateful. And, as always, tingling with the spurt of energy that came when she courted danger.

In the enclosed opening within the embracing cover of pine trees, she inhaled the pines' fresh scent while she peeked through their shield. No one was about. She checked carefully on all sides before she began her ceremony. Crouching, she removed the paraphernalia from her bag. Gathering some snow, she mounded it into the small bowl. She set two candles down, one red and one green, and spaced them equidistant at the ends of the bowl on either side of it, placing them so they would not tumble. Taking the yellow candle now, she struck her flint and caught the spark on its wick. When it flared, she righted it and cupped it in her hand, until the flame was steady. Then she used it to melt the snow in the bowl and next dropped a couple of bay leaves onto the water. Finally, she set the yellow candle in front of the bowl, forming a triangle with the other two candles.

She admired the perfect arrangement for a time before moving on with the ceremony. She began by calling Mother Goddess and the Virgin Mary. Both, she believed, protected women while they were increasing—or so her mother-in-law had convinced her. How else would women have survived the dangers of childbirth before Our Lord came to save us, if there were no Mother Goddess? Maman Marguerite had said.

Then Louise chanted the incantation she had been using ever since she recognized she must bear another child if she were to fulfil Friar Francis's prophecy.

With one mind I call for thee
With one mind I long for thee
Son of Earth, Wind, Fire and Sea
Into my life I welcome thee
Virgin Mother send him to me

She repeated one decade of the rosary and repeated the incantation. And a third time she continued the ritual, after which she pinched out the candles and rose. Her knees ached from crouching, but she felt uplifted, convinced that she had been heard and blessed. With reverent care, she returned her implements to their protective bag and went back to the Château.

WHEN SHE ENTERED the ladies-in-waiting's common room, she was unpleasantly surprised to encounter Catherine de Brézé.

"What are you doing here?"

The young woman blanched. "Th-the mother of maids sent

me. Sh-she was worried when we noticed th-that you were not with us."

"How long have you been here?" Louise recognized her voice was sharp.

Mme Catherine answered, her voice hardly more than a whisper. "N-not l-long."

Louise realized that Catherine was terrified of her; it did not matter why. Good. She could use the woman to solve a problem that had been worrying her ever since she had learned that the court would go to Lyon. She would not go with it. Because both Anne and Marie de Rohan would come to Cognac with Louise, neither would be able to report on the queen for her, just when she had started being useful. Last month, Anne de Rohan had gone to Nantes when Louise stayed in Amboise and had told Louise all about the ceremony of vassalage when she returned.

Mme Catherine's fear was a blessing. Louise had learned the details of the twenty-year-old scandal that had rocked her family and the court from Carlo after he had encountered Mme Catherine's brother, Baron Louis de Brézé, at the Christmas court. Louise was certain the threat of exposure was just the thing to induce the girl to be her eyes in Anne's chambers. Her fear would keep her silent.

"I have been wanting to talk to you privately," Louise said, taking her by the arm. If it was possible to look more frightened, Louise could not imagine how. "My dear, you do not look well. Come with me. There is a spot in the library where no one will disturb us. You need a quiet place to recover."

Although Catherine resisted, she stopped as soon as Louise said, "I want to talk to you about your late mother. It must have been so distressing for you."

Louise said nothing more until they settled into a high-backed desk behind the shelves of precious books at the back of the library where they could not be seen.

Catherine turned a white, strained face to the countess.

Louise smiled. "I hear your Papa is living now with your

brother, Sire Louis? Do you visit him?" When Catherine shook her head wordlessly, Louise continued brightly, "I think I would be afraid of my papa if he had murdered my maman. Even if he had found her in bed with another man. And his milk brother, no less. What a betrayal."

"H-how do y-you know about that?"

"But my dear, it was the talk of the court at the time. My husband told me all about it. Your mother being royal and all. Even though she was a bastard, and old King Louis forced your father to marry her. But to murder royalty! They could have executed him. It is fortunate for him that Old Spider King Louis favoured him so. And that he ran to Louis and wept on his feet, begging forgiveness. And that Old Louis despised women so. But you wouldn't dream of repeating that, would you, my dear? No, I thought not."

Catherine fired up. "You make it sound as if . . . as if no other woman was ever unfaithful." Her voice trembled again. "My father was unfortunate. He found them together and lost his temper. It was a *crime passionnel*. And he has paid for it ever since. If he had not been so angry, if he had not . . . if he had discovered what she was doing some other way, he could have sent her to a convent for her whole life and it would have been justice." She stopped; her voice choked with tears.

"Well, let us say no more about it. King Charles—or should I say Madame la Grande, when she was regent—freed him. I wonder if the king has even heard the story, for he was just a toddler." Louise leaned back. "I imagine few at court these days know anything about it, for most are too young."

"Countess Louise, what do you want from me?" Catherine's voice hitched.

"Did you know I would return to Cognac when the court leaves for Lyon?" When Catherine looked relieved, Louise smiled. "Yes, I am disappointed, as well. But since I will be away, there is a small service you could perform for me if you would be so kind. I will no longer be present among the queen's ladies, able to keep abreast of events. If you could keep me informed, I would be so appreciative."

"Wh-what do you mean? Inform you how?"

"The usual way, my dear. Letters. Couriers, by word of mouth, if the content is too sensitive to put in writing."

"I-I could not. Queen Anne has been too . . . too good to me, and my family."

Louise gazed at her speculatively. She had not expected the mouse to show any spine. But she would buckle eventually. "Does the queen have terrible secrets to hide? I was not aware." Louise leaned forward, wearing an expression of keen interest.

"No. No. No, I did not mean that! I am not suggesting anything of the kind."

Louise sat back, looking puzzled. "Then what harm can come of doing as I ask? I am curious merely about comings and goings while I am from court. What is happening during this exciting time when the French army sets off to war in Italy? Who will be regent? Where will the court stay? These are not secrets, my dear. There is nothing shameful about them. Not like the secrets in your past."

Tears sprang to Catherine's eyes again. "As you say, Countess. Of course, I will keep you informed. Can I go now?"

"Let us leave together. I think you would do well to return to your room and rest. I will explain your absence to the mother of maids."

CHAPTER 14

On the Road

Château d'Amboise, 9 February 1494

Anne sat on a stool in Charles-Orland's dayroom, holding out her arms. "Come to Maman, my son."

Charles-Orland crouched on the far side of the room, a huge grin creasing his chubby cheeks. The embroidered linen gown he wore hid his sturdy limbs. He shook his blond head, grinning even more widely, if that were possible.

"I guess you do not know how. That must be why you refuse." Anne infused her voice with disappointment. "I think I must ask nurse to carry you."

She hid a smile at the look of consternation that crossed her son's face. He wobbled to his feet, crying, "Non, Maman," and toddled across the floor as fast as he could. When he reached her arms, he gave her an angelic smile. "Can."

"You can, too," she said, lifting him into her arms. As she fought back tears, she hugged him until he struggled. She loosened her grip but did not let him go.

Kissing his head and face, his arms and neck, she said,

"Maman loves you to bits and pieces. She hates to say goodbye and will come back as soon as she can. Until then, she will write you every day. Mme de Bussières will read her letters to you, so you will remember her. You must pray for her, and she will pray for you. Will you do that, my son?"

Charles-Orland seemed to understand that his mother was sad, for he ceased struggling, and patted his mother's face. He touched the tear that hung in the corner of her eye. "No cry, Maman."

She half-laughed, choking back a sob, and put him down. When he stayed by her side, patting the knee of her heavy travelling gown, she sniffled. "Will you bring me your horsey? He is very handsome."

"Lui?" he pointed to the wooden destrier he had been playing with before she had arrived.

"Yes."

When he hesitated, she said, "I am very fond of horses. Are you? Is he a good horse?"

He nodded.

"Is he a war horse?"

He nodded again.

"Show me his colours."

When he toddled off to get the toy, she gestured to Mme de Bussières. "Call a nurse to take him to eat. I know it is early, but he will not realize. I do not want him to see me leave. I will cry and he will become distressed."

She played with her son until Mme de Bussières returned with the nurse, who carried Charles-Orland away. He waved at his mother as if it were a normal day. She waved back and turned away, hiding her tears.

Regaining her control, she gave his *Gouvernante* her final orders. "You will write to me every day. Hide nothing from me. If he is ill, I wish to know. If there is illness in the town, report it to me. This illness that he has just recovered from worried me more than you can know. It distresses me that I will not be here if . . .

when . . . if he sickens again. . .and it will take days before I learn of it. Even though I cannot be here, I wish to be part of my son's life. I will write him every day."

She handed Mme de Bussières a handful of letters. "These are several I have written for those days when the courier is delayed, or a letter fails to arrive. If the numbers dwindle, write me and I will send more."

The nursery door opened and one of the king's chamberlains bowed. "Forgive me, Madame la Reine. The king requests your presence in the courtyard."

"Thank you." She moved toward the door, saying, "Walk with me, Mme de Bussières." As they hurried through the halls, Anne continued her instructions. "When you read my letters, show him my picture. Have him pray for me and his father at all his prayers." She thought a minute. "Oh yes, and make sure the court painter paints his picture on his birthday and sends it to me if I should be gone that long." They arrived at the main Château doors. Anne hesitated. Then she said, "Goodbye. Care for my son as I would."

Mme de Bussières curtsied and gave the queen her hands. "You may trust me, Madame la Reine. I love him too."

AS ANNE PASSED through the doors, the king ran up the stairs and took her arm. She smiled at him, trying to match his excitement. He had been itching to leave since January, but Charles-Orland's illness had delayed them. Charles had not resented the delay, for he feared for his son's life and would not leave until the child was declared fully recovered, but he was eager to join the army waiting for him in Lyon.

He walked her across the courtyard. Anne's ladies crowded in the courtyard—those who were joining her on the journey to Lyon, and those who departed now for their homes—sank into curtsies as they approached.

Countess Louise rose first and stepped towards her. Anne could not turn her back, much as she wished to. The countess seemed to glow. Perhaps she was as pleased to leave as Anne was to have her depart.

"Madame la Reine, before I return to Cognac with my ladies, we come to say our farewells and wish you a safe journey and a pleasant stay in Lyon. My husband will protect Guyenne with diligence. You should never doubt our allegiance to France and the king."

"You are good to say so," Anne said, startled. What had prompted the pledge? Should she worry about what the de Rohan were plotting now? Brushing the thought aside like an annoying fly, she turned away.

As Anne lifted a foot to climb into the litter she would share with two of her ladies, she caught a long look passing between Louise and Catherine de Brézé. Catherine's face whitened, and she dropped her eyes, looking guilty. Anne could do nothing about it now, but she vowed to find out why the quiet young woman appeared so frightened.

Queen Anne sighed as she thought of the long journey ahead swaying in the conveyance. Many of her ladies found it soothing, but it made Anne nauseated. But because it was winter, it was too dangerous to travel by boat up the Loire.

Pernette had been one of those who had loved travelling by litter. How she would miss her dear friend. She sighed again. Making advantageous matches for her ladies was one of her great pleasures and a task she considered a duty of her position. But when her dear friend Baron Philippe de Montauban had asked her to propose a splendid match for his granddaughter, it had been painful. Almost all the most powerful families with eligible men were her enemies, or unreliable allies at best. Even her half-brother, Count François d'Avaugour, had defected to the side of Marshal de Rieux when she had refused to marry the Sieur Alain d'Albret. Yet her father had enriched his only living son, who now proclaimed his abiding loyalty to her and King Charles. No matter what he said, she would never believe him.

But he was looking for a wife and had asked her to suggest

one. When she had asked Pernette, even before speaking to her grandfather, she had agreed, although François was fifteen years her senior, delighted to become Anne's sister-in-law. The marriage should be advantageous to both sides—and their close friendship should protect Pernette, should François prove a cruel husband. But now she had to leave Pernette behind for she was increasing already, and naturally she must give birth to her child on her husband's family lands. The journey would seem long without Pernette for company. As a footman put her little spaniel, Fanchon, on the seat beside her, she blinked back tears.

SEVERAL DAYS LATER, they arrived in at the Château de Moulins, the principal seat of Madame la Grande and Duke Pierre. This was Anne's first visit. The massive size and elegant decoration of the many buildings that made up the complex startled her. It was one thing to know that the premier Bourbon family was vastly rich; it was another to see their wealth displayed. She glanced at Charles, wondering how he reacted to this exhibition, but he did not seem even to notice. He must be accustomed to it, especially since the couple welcomed them with great pomp in recognition of Charles's position as king of France. The banners and decorated arches under which they entered the Château grounds flattered him as the next Charlemagne about to save the Holy Land, and crowds of Bourbon vassals cheered and bowed.

Charles pounded his brother-in-law cheerfully on the back as he strode through the great front doors of the Château, thrown wide to greet them, telling him all the latest news from the number of troops and strength of artillery gathering in the camps outside Lyon to the opportune death of King Ferrante of Naples on January 23. Madame la Grande, left to walk behind with Anne, gave a tiny, expressive shrug.

"Is he this exuberant always about his Italian venture?" she asked.

"He is. He had Bishop Briçonnet made a Cardinal and named him the financier-general for the expedition and will impose a new tax on families, towns and the clergy. They expect to raise two million *livres tournois* with it."

"Then we must ensure that the campaign is a resounding success and returns that much to France, do you not agree?"

Anne nodded. "And that *he* does not come to harm. For he intends to lead his troops himself." She shivered and crossed herself. Her sister-in-law followed suit.

Anne strove for a more cheerful direction to her thoughts. "How is your charming daughter, the little Suzanne?"

Madame la Grande relaxed, her face softening. She adored her only child, born after almost twenty years of marriage. "Two and a half already. Still small for her age, but so pretty. And clever. She adores her papa, and she has him completely in her thrall."

Her delight in her child sent a dagger of pain through Anne's heart. "It would give me great pleasure to visit her."

Madame la Grande swelled with gratification. "After our dinner, you shall accompany me if that is your desire. Let me show you to your suite to rest before you join us, for we shall dine in one turn of the hourglass."

THE NURSERY WAS EVEN BETTER APPOINTED than the one at Amboise, Anne observed, when they entered several hours later. As soon as the guard at the door announced them, the little girl, who had been sitting in her nurse's lap, demanded to be put down. She pattered toward her mother, rolling from side to side like a waddling duck. Madame la Grande crouched; her arms held wide. "Welcome, my sweet Suzanne. Come to greet Queen Anne."

A step behind her, Anne squeezed her hands together until

they hurt. As she watched the child wobble towards her mother, she recognized from her own childhood that Suzanne had a problem with her legs. Possibly one was shorter than the other. Possibly she had a club foot. Whatever the cause, there was no hiding the child's hitching gait, although her simple gown fell to the ground, covering her deformity.

When her sister-in-law took her little daughter by the hand and said, "Suzanne, this is our queen, Queen Anne. You must say, 'Welcome Madame la Reine.' Can you do that?"

The little girl put a finger in her mouth and raised large, worried eyes to Anne. She opened her mouth and then closed it again and shook her head.

Anne dropped to one knee before Madame la Grande had a chance to say more. "Do not worry, little one. You will learn all these rules soon." She hesitated. Would Madame la Grande take it as interference if she commented? She could not help herself. "Does your leg pain you very much?" She lifted her skirt, showing her sister-in-law and little Suzanne the shoe on her right foot. "See little niece, I have one short leg. The sole of my shoe is raised to make it easier to walk. I have worn shoes like this since I first started walking."

Suzanne crouched to examine her shoe. Then she laughed. "Funny shoe," she said.

Anne laughed too. "It is a funny shoe. Do you want to play catch with me? Let us ask your nurse for a ball." When the child turned to ask for one, Anne looked at Madame la Grande. "I hope I did not offend you."

"Although she is probably too young to understand, I think it very kind of you, Madame."

Anne thought her voice was softer than she had ever heard it before.

CHAPTER 15
Travelling to Lyon

Château de Moulins, 2 March 1494

At Charles's request, Madame la Grande and Duke Pierre dined privately that afternoon in the royal suite where the king and queen had lodged. Housed in its own wing of the great château, the queen's rooms lay along a corridor on the ground floor, as in Amboise. The king's luxurious suite, with its own private dining chamber, was housed above, on the first floor. Over the generations, the Bourbon had spared no cost on this wing; their trenchers lay on gold plates, they drank from Venetian glass goblets, and the meats presented to please their palettes had been encrusted with thin, gold foil. Even after two weeks of Bourbon luxury, Anne had not grown accustomed to the extravagant material display in the Bourbon home.

Charles's spirits were even higher than usual. "I watched the supply wagons depart today and, tomorrow, we set out. Now we are truly underway. Let us drink to it. I propose a toast. Next year in Jerusalem!"

They raised their goblets and chorused, "Next year in Jerusalem."

Anne wondered if anyone but Charles meant the words. She certainly did not. But Charles would set out on his crusade with her approval or without it. If she wished to keep his love and him in her bed, she must appear to support this adventure wholeheartedly. They had passed this visit in Moulins in great accord, and she would not spoil their last evening.

Duke Pierre said, "It is pleasant to pass this evening quietly together. It will be many weeks before we have such an opportunity again. But if there is no particular reason you wish my presence, Monsieur le Roi—"

"Ah, but there is," Charles replied before Duke Pierre could finish. "I have some appointments I wish to inform you of before announcing them publicly." He drew himself up, squared his shoulders, and eyed them one by one, challenging them to speak. From the thrust of his chin, Anne recognized he would hear no opposition. *He* was the king. "I am appointing Cousin Louis, Duke d'Orléans as Admiral of the Marine." He stared at his sister. "I know you do not trust him, Sister, but I do, and he is a great warrior. And as Admiral he will be on the sea not land, and far from Asti and Milan."

"Clever, Sire, clever," Duke Pierre agreed.

Anne admired her brother-in-law. His ability to put people at ease was a blessing and, as she watched, Charles's shoulders relaxed.

Madame la Grande did not argue with her brother, but her smile did not reach her eyes. Still, Anne thought, she was wise to keep silent.

"General Louis de la Trémoïlle and Marshal Pierre de Rohan shall lead the infantry and cavalry, respectively."

Anne dropped her eyes and focussed on the exquisite goblet she gripped between her hands. She kept the corners of her lips curled up in the simulacrum of a smile and concentrated on breathing deeply while the duke and duchess commented on the brilliance and great military experience of the two men. There were few men she despised more than these. De la Trémoïlle had claimed the French victory at Saint Aubin-de-Cormier, the defeat in which Duke Louis had been captured and that had broken her father's heart. Three years later, he had led the French troops who overran Brittany and defeated her. And Marshal Pierre de Gié, as well as being a traitorous de Rohan, had served France rather than Brittany his whole life. But she was queen of France now, and her duty and her hope of a successful marriage both required her to wish them well. She lifted her eyes to her husband's after her in-laws stopped speaking and said, "They have proven their abilities many times. They should serve us well."

"You please us. I leave the most important until last. I do not know how long our final preparations will take, so I shall announce this when we arrive in Lyon. During my absence I shall appoint you, Duke Pierre and Madame my sister, as Regents. I expect, Sister, that you will lead the Regency Council."

Anne stopped listening as she fought to maintain her outward composure despite her anger. *She* was queen. He should have appointed *her*. She knew how to rule. Had she not succeeded in keeping Brittany free for three years—despite civil war, betrayal, and an external war against the overwhelming power of France? And she had achieved it under dire conditions—coming into her inheritance when only eleven, receiving a bankrupt duchy, exhausted from years of external war and internal unrest. Did he not trust her to defend France as she had defended her duchy? How could he betray her love and loyalty so brutally? And publicly, without warning? She fought back tears of rage and humiliation as she smiled and nodded, lips frozen in place until her cheeks ached.

When he finally came to her bed that night, and after she had pretended pleasure in their coupling and he lay content beside her, she said, "I am sure you made the best decision to appoint your sister and brother-in-law as regents. I am surprised only that you did not add me to the Regency Council, since I am mother to the dauphin."

He yawned sleepily. "Well, I could not do that, my love, since you will not be in France. Or do you not wish to accompany me to Italy? You will not be in any danger. Duke Ludovico assures me that if any troubles arise, he will be delighted to host you in Milan."

A rush of guilt for her uncharitable anger flooded Anne. "Ah, what a wonderful surprise." She wrapped her arms around him as he turned from her to sleep on his side. Before she said more, she felt his breathing smooth into the steady rhythm of sleep.

Releasing him, she lay on her back, her eyes open staring into the darkness, prey to an uncomfortable mix of emotions. One part of her felt ashamed that she had jumped immediately to the belief that he mistrusted her ability to rule, but she was still angry that he had decided she would accompany him abroad without asking her if she wished to go. Another part of her was excited about the adventure. Yet she did not wish to leave Charles-Orland for the many months, perhaps more than a year, that the campaign would last. And their son could not join them. It would never be permitted for the king and his heir to depart France simultaneously. It was too great a risk. She shifted and tossed, unable to rid herself of the fretful thoughts that circled and returned in various forms. Annoyed with herself, she withdrew her mother's rosary from under her pillow where she put it every night and began to pray. The soothing repetitions calmed her and before she had finished one decade, she drifted into sleep.

By the time the two couples arrived in Lyon three weeks later, Anne was heartily sick of travelling, although this part of France, with its gentler climate, was new to her. Theirs was a vast cavalcade, for their four princely households travelled together. Over three thousand people moved slowly across the countryside. Wagons filled with every sort of household good and clothing; secure carts with leather and metal cases carrying state documents and gold coin; cages with falcons, hawks, and hunting dogs;

cooking and food carts; carriages carrying servants and litters filled with ladies; courtiers on horseback; and troops of men-at-arms in full armour to protect the vast array creaked along at walking pace, sometimes on cobbled roads but more often on rough wagon tracks. Everywhere, peasants tilling the fields and townsfolk in villages stared, bowed, curtsied and cheered as they passed. Charles and Anne waved and chatted with those along the wayside and stopped to meet the dignitaries of the towns and villages along their route. She was glad that the last few days she, the king and their immediate households finished their trip boating down to Lyon on the Saône River, situated at its confluence with the Rhône.

Lyon did not boast a royal palace, so they stayed in the Governor's Palace on the right bank of the Saône. As their first action, Charles insisted they attend mass at Saint Jean Cathedral to ask for a blessing on their crusade. He had gifted the new cathedral a remarkable astrological clock, and he wanted to view its marvels. Although exhausted, he then insisted on crossing the island between the two rivers to visit his enormous army, which was camped on the far bank of the Rhône. Anne did not see him again until the next day.

ON MARCH 15, the city honoured Charles and Anne with a Grande Entrée. As she rode through the city in an uncovered chariot, dressed in cloth of gold and bands of ermine, her horses caparisoned in white silk sewn with strips of jewels, her ladies-in-waiting and maids of honour, dressed in their best following her, occupying flower-bedecked chariots. Anne fell in love with the city and its people. It was lighter and gayer here than in the North. Citrus trees imbued the air with a light, tart scent. The city itself was bursting with gardens, its air rich with the aroma of roses, gardenias, lavender, and dozens more scents. The people flaunted their wealth, dressing in rich, colourful silks. Their well-rounded bodies and cheeks suggested they did not want for food and the city was renowned for its commerce—as a centre of finance, for its silk manufacture and trade and the new book publishing craft. Everything appeared so much brighter and clearer than she was accustomed to that her mood lightened. She waved to the crowd as she climbed from her open carriage to attend the celebratory mass at the abbatial church of Saint Nizier. At the guildhall dinner that evening, when the mayor and aldermen presented the keys to the city to Charles and her, she did not have to pretend enthusiasm.

ANNE'S buoyant mood did not endure. All too soon, Charles's cronies crowded the corridors of the small Palace that housed his and her courts. As protocol required, they came to pay their respects to her. She gave her hand and a false smile to his favourites: Baron Etienne de Vesc, Marshal Pierre de Rohan, and General Louis de la Trémoïlle among them.

Only when Duke Louis d'Orléans came to greet her did she feel any pleasure. When she invited him to sit with her, he appeared delighted and they spent the afternoon catching up and exchanging views on the latest court news, events of interest in the courts of their cousins across Europe and what they thought of the books and poetry they had been reading since last they met. But finally, they could no longer avoid speaking of the preparations for war that surrounded them. From him she learned that money was already running short. Louis had heard about their fiscal headaches from Cardinal Guillaume Briçonnet, in charge of Finances, and his brother, Archbishop Robert Briçonnet, who was Comptroller of Supplies. Yet the chiefs of artillery were demanding more artillery, better transport, and more gunners. Charles's aides-de-camps and advisors, all of whom came with their servants, their warhorses and their luxurious tents, were overcrowding the already congested camp, demanding space and accommodation fit for their rank, and quarrelling among themselves.

"What chaos," Anne said. "How will it ever come together? Really it is no better here. Charles's Principal Secretary—you know Père André de la Vigne?—and his Principal Equerry, Pierre d'Urfé, are becoming thinner and more agitated by the day. They scuttle between the court here and the military camp so often I think they have worn a path across the bridges." She tried to keep her voice light, but Louis knew her too well.

"What is worrying you, Madame la Reine? I would reassure you if I could." He stood and stretched, and Anne became aware of his lithe warrior's body. He wore a fine leather doublet over his white linen shirt, which displayed his broad shoulders and shapely, well-muscled arms, the result of a lifetime in heavy armour, fighting with swords, lances and daggers.

Anne hesitated. It was true, she was worried. Two months had passed, and the army seemed no closer to departing than when they had arrived. Charles spent less and less time in her company. As their courts grew, it had been impossible to keep both in the small Governor's Palace, and Charles left daily to use the buildings of the parlement to conduct court business. Ambassadors from every court and Italian state thronged the city, now convinced that Charles would go to war and determined to side with the winner.

Finally, she had moved her court into the Archbishop's Palace close by, but it had separated her further from her husband. Rumours abounded, and her ladies brought new ones to her daily. She did not doubt that some of her ladies passed rumours along to their families and people for whom they spied. People like Countess Louise.

Everything added to her difficulties with Charles. She was aware that his favourite, Sire Etienne, encouraged him to seek light women rather than return to her bed. He was not the only one. Count Galeazzo San Severini, Charles's Milan favourite, had arrived recently. A libertine himself, he had announced his intention to sample all the taverns and brothels in Lyon and he invited Charles to join him. Yes, of course she was jealous, but worse, she worried about disease. Not only the diseases he might bring to her and her bed, but the effect any disease could have on him. He had been a sickly child and he lived on his nerves. In the weeks since they had departed, he had become more and more exhilarated and now he vibrated like a drum most of the time. The longer they stayed in Lyon, which became daily more crowded with strangers come to profit from the courts and the army, the more likely it was that a dreadful contagion would spread like wildfire through the city.

"I do not like to speak of it," Anne admitted finally "Rumours start and fly too easily."

Louis looked concerned. "You know that nothing you tell me will pass my lips. But if there is a scandal brewing, allow me to scotch it before it causes serious harm."

She felt her colour rising, but she trusted him. "You must know that I am no supporter of this expedition." He nodded and she hurried on. "But it is too far advanced to withdraw now, for France and the king's reputation would be damaged. The risk of invasion would become serious, I believe."

Louis looked impressed. "Indeed, I agree. So?"

"One of my ladies has been tittering about Charles's new passion for astrology. Not to me, of course, but someone I trust has informed me. Apparently, this astrologer has a daughter—a strumpet—who is both beautiful and experienced at inflaming Charles's lust. My husband has gone so far as to hold council meetings at their house. It may not surprise you that Count Galeazzo San Severini encourages him in this outrageous behaviour."

As Anne spoke, Louis became more and more agitated. Soon he was pacing the room. She watched him for a time. Then she said, "Were you aware that Duke Ludovico has become much less enthusiastic about your march through Italy? Charles has suggested it may not be wise for me to stay in Milan when I accompany him and now says Florence might be a better choice. The Medici have always been friends to France."

"So." Louis's eyes rested on her face with an intensity she found disconcerting. "You think Count Galeazzo is under Milanese orders to persuade Charles to abandon the enterprise?"

Anne looked away, feeling her colour rising, "I cannot say. But holding council meetings in a whorehouse will make France a laughingstock. And consorting with ribalds every night is not good for his health."

CHAPTER 16

Anne's Mixed Blessings

Archbishop's Place, Lyon, 4 August 1494

Sitting at the small table in her bedchamber, Anne lifted the tankard of small beer. As she brought it to her mouth, she gagged at its malty odour. Her lips clamped tightly, she turned her head this way and that, searching frantically for a bowl. Her maid realized her need and grabbed an empty chamber pot. Just in time. By then Mme Catherine, her lady-in-waiting that morning, knelt beside her.

When Mme Catherine handed her a wet handkerchief, Anne wiped her face, and croaked, "Watered wine."

The maid offered a goblet, carafe, and a spitting bowl. After Anne had rinsed her mouth, she wiped her lips again.

"Might it be something you consumed?" Mme Catherine looked worried. "Should you stay abed?"

With a grimace, Anne glanced at her unfinished breakfast and pushed it away.

"To what end?" she asked. "I doubt this sickness will pass for many weeks. I shall hope it affects me only in the mornings. It is not the first time I have felt ill. It is simply the first morning I cannot control it."

When Anne saw comprehension flit across Mme Catherine's face, she nodded.

"Shall I bring your doctor? There has been whispering . . ."

Anne frowned. "There are no secrets at court." It irritated her that eyes watched everything, even her laundry, and then resigned herself, wondering if she could delay a few more days. Then she shuddered, recalling the disaster of the last time. If there was already gossip, her vomiting that morning would be common knowledge within one turn of the hourglass.

"Yes, fetch him. And the midwife."

She had known from the moment she realized she was increasing that Charles would never permit her to travel to Italy. It was the reason she had clung to her secret, hoping they would have begun the journey before she must reveal her condition. But preparations dragged on. Now she had missed two months of her courses. If she hid her situation longer, Charles would be furious and after losing her last child, she feared for herself, too.

When the doctor confirmed her suspicions, she asked him to allow her to inform Charles herself. He promised, but before her chamberlain had returned from the king's court with a reply from her husband to her request for a visit, she heard the rise and fall of voices and the muffled thud of many feet in her courtyard. The sounds grew louder as they approached her suite.

Her gentleman usher opened the door to her presence chamber and announced the king and his retinue. His entire body radiating delight, Charles entered beaming, followed by Madame la Grande and Duke Pierre, and his throng of courtiers.

He rushed to Anne and kissed her lips. "Madame Wife, you have given us our heart's desire. Another child." Charles pulled her to her feet and crushed her in his arms before his courtiers and hers. That he had interrupted his day to come to her when often she saw him only at meals—and many times not even then—told her how delighted he was.

He turned, holding her arm. "Sir Page, come forward."

A youth, son of one of his favourites, stepped forward carrying a purple pillow. From it, Charles lifted a jewelled rosary, one she knew was precious to him. He carried it with him always and hung it from his prie-dieu wherever he went. For a moment he held it, his eyes glistening. Blinking, he kissed the crystal reliquary that enclosed the toenail of Saint Joseph that depended from the delicate golden chain strung with pearls and sapphires.

"You know it was my mother's," he said, placing it between her hands, and lifting them to his lips to kiss them.

On an indrawn breath, Anne whispered, "That you gift it to me, makes it precious beyond words to me." She kissed his lips and then the crystal reliquary and its pearl-encrusted cross. "You could have given me nothing I would treasure more."

Tears clung to her eyelashes. Charles knew her tastes and the gifts that would best please her. But she wished he had come alone to celebrate this moment in private. They could have shared an intimate moment, and she might have become happy about the child, instead of dutiful. He might have immediately granted her the favour she hoped he would accord her to replace the lost happiness of accompanying him to Italy.

"Of course, you will not go to Italy now," he said, stopping to look her in the eye. How quick he was to ensure she had no illusions that he would permit anything so foolish! She was certain that it had been his second thought after praying she would bear a son.

"Of course not," she agreed, a smile glued to her lips. She had accepted it would be so from the moment the doctor confirmed her pregnancy, but the relief on his face hurt.

Since Charles forbade her to go to Italy, and gave the regency to his sister, Anne wanted to return to Amboise and her son. Each day when she wrote to him, she missed him more. The days that she did not receive a letter from Mme de Bussières, she imagined the worst. On days she learned he was ill, she must keep busy: visiting the poor, or ordering changes in the gardens, or debating new planting methods on her French estates, or giving advice to her ladies, for she could not keep still. A constant itch of worry prickled that she could not salve even with prayer the moment she stopped for she knew the outcome had already occurred, yet she did not know what it was. And her son had suffered, perhaps had died, calling for her, and she had not been there. The images squeezed her heart until she found it hard to breathe.

Yet when she thought to beg Charles to allow her to return to Amboise, she feared being far from him. What if he were to fall ill, be injured, or suffer some other harm? She would be just as far from such news at Amboise and felt pulled apart, like a prisoner tugged between two ropes. It would be best to leave only when Charles departed for Italy, she decided, for then he would be so far away that a few more days would make little difference to how much she worried and being with her son would bring her solace.

Despite the many demands on his time, she saw more of him now that she was increasing. He came to her bedchamber more often these nights, but many times he stayed only for a glass of wine. Each time she saw him, the circles under his eyes grew darker, and he had thinned. He was living on his nerves. She ordered bread, meat, and cheese brought to her rooms each evening and entertained him with stories about Fanchon's antics and the gossip in her court or asked him about his days. But what would she do when he left? He was a hopeless correspondent. How would she know how he was—and who was sharing his bed? The problem preyed on her.

~

ANNE STOPPED at the front doors of Saint Jean Cathedral after early morning mass, her ladies-in-waiting crowding behind her. Her Breton guards stood at the steps waiting to escort them around the block to the entrance to the archbishop's palace. She hesitated only a moment.

"No, I need some time alone to pray." She called to the Captain of the Guard standing nearby. "Captain, escort my ladies back to the palace. Then return. I shall remain."

When she spoke in that tone, no one argued. As they set off, she turned back and plodded down the left side-aisle ambulatory that led behind the high altar. There she entered the Lady Chapel to pray before the image of the Holy Virgin. The sacred space was illuminated softly by the candles placed before a painting of the Annunciation. Mary gazed upward at a white dove that glowed in golden light from the window, her blue eyes filled with wonder, fear and dawning hope as an angel knelt before her. Her golden halo glowed.

Anne stepped forward to kneel at the altar rail. It was then she noticed another penitent kneeling at the far end of the rail, anonymous in a dark cape and hood, head and shoulders bowed. Anne hesitated. She had hoped to be alone in this private space, for the hour was still early. Yet there was comfort in shared silent prayer, so she sank to her knees. The thick rich stillness, that was neither silence nor sound, but was the quality of the sacred inherent in the space, soothed her. Lifting the precious rosary that Charles had so recently bestowed upon her, she prayed. After a time, she noticed an irregular hitching sigh, with an added click, sometimes a gulp or squeak intermingled—a forlorn sound. She raised her head and looked about her.

Her eyes were accustomed to the dusky shadows now. Anne examined the heavily shrouded woman nearby. The robes over her shoulders shook and Anne was sure her unknown companion was smothering sobs. Undecided, Anne did not move from where she was. Many times, when she herself was grieving, she had not wanted consolation, but solitude. To find a private place and time was well-nigh impossible. This woman had probably sought this quiet sanctuary to be alone. Perhaps the kindest thing would be to tiptoe away, leaving her undisturbed.

Anne rose, preparing to leave. Instead, her feet took her to the woman's side. She placed a gentle hand on the woman's shaking shoulders.

"Your grief touches me," she said, her voice soft. "I would not impose upon your solitude, but a sorrow shared is a step toward healing. If you allow it, I would be honoured to hear your troubles."

At her first words, the woman froze. When Anne finished speaking, she lifted her face to Anne's, her eyes swollen almost shut and tears streaming down her face.

"Madame la Reine, I have been so wicked, and you are so good. I can never tell you and you will never be able to forgive me." She bent forward, crouching over her knees until her nose almost touched the floor, burying her face in her hands. Her sobs, now loud and wild, rose into the silence of the cathedral.

Of all the women she could imagine encountering, she had not once thought to discover Catherine de Brézé. She put an arm around the woman's shaking body as she adjusted her thoughts. "You must calm yourself, Mme Catherine, for you will make yourself ill," she said, pulling a cloth from inside her sleeve and handing it to the girl. "Mop you face and blow you nose and tell me your troubles. No matter what they are, I shall help you, for you are one of my ladies."

At these words, Catherine's wails, which had begun to calm, increased in volume again.

"Enough." Anne sharpened her voice. "If you keep up this clamour, I shall have to slap you. We are in a holy place. Now compose yourself. And breathe."

She rubbed the distraught woman's back until Catherine had managed a level of control, although her breath still hitched.

Anne said, "That is much better." She patted the young

women's shoulder. "You say you have injured me in some dreadful manner. Have you betrayed my trust?"

Catherine nodded, and another loud sob erupted.

"No more of that." Anne's voice was stern. She sighed. "You are not the first, nor will you be the last. Tell me what you have done and why. Then we shall repair the damage." She allowed a small smile to curve her lips, "For I see you are not happy about your part in it."

She winced as she moved a knee and added, "But before we say more, perhaps we could move from here. This floor is distinctly hard even with the layers of cloth under my knees."

Mme Catherine gasped and tried to leap to her feet to support the queen as she rose. But she, too, had been on her knees so long they had numbed and refused to obey her. They stumbled against each other like old ladies as they struggled to their feet. They could not help laughing, which breached Catherine's tragic mood. Moments later, when they found a narrow stone bench in the shadows, Catherine could speak without sobbing.

"Tell me now," Anne invited.

Catherine hung her head. "I-I have been spying . . . and writing about what happens in your court, but I do not want to any m-m-ore. I n-never wanted to. I am so s-s-orry, Madame la Reine." Catherine's pace speeded up. "But I was afraid n-not to, for she said she would tell everyone and—"

"Stop." Anne seized Catherine's arm.

Catherine jerked and obeyed.

"You have started well. Now, to whom have you been writing?"

"Mme the Countess d'Angoulême."

Anne took a deep breath. Somehow, the revelation did not surprise her, although she still could not fathom what the countess hoped to gain from it. "What kinds of information did she want?"

"Who came to see you? What was happening with the war? Who was being appointed to what positions? Who you wanted appointed and whether they were? How your health was and the health of the dauphin? If you were increasing and when you were due? The same about Madame la Grande and Mme the Duchess d'Orléans. In sooth, I had little knowledge about any of those things. So, I could not reveal much, although I felt terrible. You must believe me." The young woman grabbed Anne's hands, "Until today. . ." She shook her head and swallowed hard.

"But today?"

"Well, today we learned you are carrying a child. And I do not want to write to tell her. For I do not know why she wants to know. But I do know," Anne saw that Catherine's hands were shaking, "that she casts spells, for she did so when she hoped to fall with child herself. She talked of it."

For a moment Anne froze, if an icy hand clutched her heart and was squeezing it until she could hardly breathe. It was heretical to cast spells. If she had certain knowledge of it, she must inform her spiritual director, for it was a mortal sin. Did she dare allow Louise near her again? Could the countess harm a child of France from so far away? Would Louise dare to risk her immortal soul? Surely not. And why would she take such a risk as to speak about her sin?

Yet she *must* reassure Catherine that she had done right to confide in her. Gathering every bit of her determination, she forced herself to say, "You have done well to tell me these things, Mme Catherine. It is true that you did wrong to fall into this trap and hide Mme Louise's wicked demand. But unless you have done more than you have said—?" Her voice turned stern.

Catherine blanched. "No, no, Madame la Reine. I have not, I swear," she pulled up her rosary and kissed the cross, "I swear on the cross and my hope of salvation."

"Well, then. We shall turn this situation to our advantage. You shall write. But you shall write as we choose and inform her of what we decide she should learn. What do you say to that?"

Catherine did not look happy. "If you say I must, Madame la Reine."

Anne said, "Well, for the time being, I say you must. It shall be your penance. But you shall tell me how she intimidated you into this action that goes against your nature. For such is the case, is it not?"

Catherine told Anne the entire story of Louise's threat to shame her before the court with the story of her mother's adultery, her father's murder of her mother and his years in prison. "She said I would never marry after it became known," Catherine finished, close to tears.

As Catherine had recounted the sad tale, Anne's plans had solidified like clay drying in the hot sun. "We shall take care of several birds at once here," she said. "You shall continue writing to the countess, for it is better for you that she does not learn her plot is uncovered. Today you shall inform her that the king and I have announced we are having another child. Then you shall say I had been dreading the trip to Italy and am much relieved that I will remain in France and have not yet decided where I shall stay.

"Tell her the king has made a special donation of 50 écus d'or to the Grand Almoner for special prayers in my chapel and his at every office for the duration of my time, for my health and the wellbeing of the child I carry. That should stop her wasting her time on spells, do you not think?"

Catherine nodded, but she did not look reassured.

"This is not all, my dear. I will have no one threatening anyone under my protection. I promise I will arrange an excellent marriage for you far from the countess before she discovers you informed me of her threats." Poor Catherine would have to marry far from her family to place her outside the long reach of Louise's connections. Anne's animosity towards the countess deepened.

Catherine lifted Anne's hands to her lips, tears she could not hold back brimming over. "You are too good, Madame la Reine. I do not deserve that you should treat me so kindly when I merit dismissal for my betrayal."

Anne removed her hands. "No more tears, Mme Catherine.

You will find writing to Mme Louise punishment enough. Come, let us leave or the captain of my guard will come looking for me."

~

EACH DAY, as she sat to write to Charles-Orland, Anne brooded about how to persuade Charles to write to her when he was in Italy. Different ways to encourage him occurred to her, but she could think of nothing he would value enough to pick up a pen daily—or even every second or third day. Besides, he would never tell her about what she really wanted to know—how his health was, what he was eating, whether he had injured himself, and most important, what women he was dallying with and if he slept alone. Remembering her strategy with Charles-Orland, she thought about preparing letters herself, leaving places blank for him to add the information she most wanted to know. One day, when she received a letter from Mme de Bussières that included a scribble from Charles-Orland, she realized she had been thinking about her problem entirely the wrong way.

Why try to make Charles write to her? Really, he was no more capable of it than was his son. His father had not wanted him to "waste his time" with books and letters. Charles could read and write, but he had never learned to enjoy doing either. Rather than bemoan the fact, she would find someone to write to her for him. She turned the idea over in her mind for a couple of days. The more she thought about it, the more she liked it.

Naturally, she would have to choose the right person—someone she could trust to tell her the truth. Someone who would write daily. Someone Charles trusted to keep his secrets. Also, Charles would have to agree, otherwise, he might think she was spying on him and *that* would be a disaster. She had found exactly the right candidate, but she needed someone he trusted to suggest it. Although only eighteen, she had been married to Charles for three years, so she well understood his suspicious nature.

When the answer came to her in the middle of the night, it was blindingly obvious. Guillaume Briçonnet, Bishop de Saint Malo, and Charles's Chief of Finance for the Italian Expedition, would be perfect. He was both clever and obsequious. Lying awake, she pictured him: a man of middle height, as round as an egg and shaped like one too, with shoulders much narrower than his paunch. He had so many chins that he did not seem to have a neck. His head was fitted with a black cap that came down almost to his eyebrows. At the back of his neck, it reached to the top of the first roll of fat. It had ear flaps on either side that reminded her of mouse ears. Although she was still annoyed that he had been named Bishop of Saint Malo, she could be pragmatic when necessary. This was one of those times.

Since he was always flattered when she invited him to visit her, she expected to have little difficulty persuading him to accept her choice. She rose when he arrived. When he sat, she poured his goblet of wine with her own hands. Then she begged him to bless their wine and biscuits.

"Bishop, I am hoping you will be able to help me with a delicate matter. You are the only man I can trust."

He preened. "Anything to be of service, Madame la Reine."

"I know well that both you and my beloved husband will be occupied with the responsibilities of leadership for this expedition and will not have time to write me as often as I would wish. Yet you know how I rely on daily letters from someone in the king's confidence to know how he goes on. I have a cleric of great renown who is eager to accompany your glorious campaign to write its history. He would agree to write me daily, if you could persuade the king to bring him to write a history of this great undertaking."

Cardinal Briçonnet clapped his hands. "Madame la Reine, your proposal is inspired. And who is the cleric you propose?"

"He has been a member of my circle for some time. Père André de la Vigne."

Only Père André did she trust enough to explain what she

really wanted to know. But she told the bishop she wanted to experience the life that Charles lived daily; to know what and whom he saw, where he went, how he was received, what he ate, his health; the details of his progress day by day. These would be things Charles would not want to write, for he would think them dull or not fit for her ears. She wanted to hear it all, for ignorance of his experiences would separate them more than distance. "For we shall be apart for a long time. . ." she had ended.

Cardinal Briçonnet said, "Ah yes, Père André, a good man. I shall recommend him to the king as his personal secretary. He will work and ride beside your husband every day since it will be necessary so he can make notes and observations. He will be well placed to report daily on the king's health and . . . and so on. And I shall write myself when I can, Madame la Reine.

"You are too good," said Anne. She knelt and kissed his ring. When he rose to leave, she walked him to the door. After he left, she nodded to herself. There was no more she could do. God willing, it would be sufficient.

CHAPTER 17

King Charles Departs

Grenoble, Dauphiné, 28 August 1494

The day before the king and his enormous army were to march off to Italy, Charles arranged a final, private dinner in his apartments in the Governor's Palace. As if it were a formal dinner, he had disposed the seating in a single row at the table in the anti-chamber of his suite, Anne discovered when she arrived. She thought it odd when they were only four. Madame la Grande sat to her left, Anne sat to Charles's left, Charles sat in the centre, and Duke Pierre sat to Charles's right. It meant each person could converse easily with only the person on either side.

Butlers stood at the entrance handing the many dishes to the pages who passed before them at the table offering the dishes to each according to their rank while others kept their goblets filled with wine, well-watered for the ladies, to Anne's relief. The governor's chefs had insisted on preparing dozens of dishes. After the first remove, Charles ordered his Maître d'hôtel to place the dishes for the second remove on the table and leave them alone. Anne eyed the platters of savoury pasties, baskets of apples, grapes, and pears, plates of sticky-sweet dates, figs, Turkish delight and peppermint candies placed within easy reach. After all the wine Charles had consumed, he would leave Grenoble with a terrible headache if he ate many.

As soon as the door closed behind the servants, Charles pulled his chair past the two ladies to the end of the table, screeching its feet along the marble floor.

"That is better. Now I can see all of you at once." He frowned and pointed. "Still, it would be better if—Pierre, take your chair and move to this side beside me." He gestured to his left side. Now he sat between his sister and brother-in-law. Anne was left straggling at the end, or that was how it seemed to her.

He was not finished organizing. "Now hand me that plate of Turkish Delight and those pears. There, that is excellent. Now we can get on with it."

He took a deep breath. "First I must tell you about everything I have done." He stuffed a Turkish Delight into his mouth and chewed, then peeled a pear. "I have ordered all officers of government to bring their reports and the taxes they collect to you, Sister." He paused to gulp a mouthful of wine, "For the treasury will travel with you, of course."

Anne looked down. He was not an enjoyable sight, for he did not wait to finish his portions before speaking. After her exhausting Entrée and public reception by the city notables that day, Anne found her stomach sensitive. The heavy reek of boar still lingered in the room. Watching gobs of half-masticated fruit form lumps in his throat when he swallowed made her want to gag. She covered her mouth, spit the date she had started into her hand and dropped to the dogs crowding her feet, certain they would enjoy it more than she would. The dogs growled and wrestled for the treat but no one else noticed.

Charles carried on. "Of course, you will all return to Moulins. Duke Pierre, you issued the orders today that the court would leave by the end of the week, did you not?" He gave the Duke a wide smile as he rubbed his hands. "You must move fast if you are to arrive there by the time you hear we are across the Alps."

Despite her misgivings, Anne feared this was her last chance to demur. Circumstance had frustrated her every attempt to speak to Charles alone. His casual assumption that she would return to Moulins distressed her.

Leaning back to appear relaxed, she forced a tone of quiet confidence. "Yes, dear husband, let us speak of our living arrangements. I shall travel on to Amboise after resting a few days in Moulins. I am so looking forward to spending the time you are on campaign with our son." She picked up her goblet.

For the first time since the servants had left, Charles seemed to remember her presence. Looking astonished, he stared at her. "What can you be thinking about, Anne? You are aware of the arrangements I have made for the dauphin. A company of one hundred Scots Guards[1] under the direct authority of the Dauphin's Gouverneur guards the gates of the town and mans the ramparts, towers and gates of the Château. My son is living in the furthest wing at Amboise, and I permit no one, not even Friar Francis, to approach him. It has been so since we departed."

Anne took a sip and replaced her goblet on the table. With a soft smile, she said, her voice gentle. "Of course, my dear. Such wise orders. They protect our son well. But you cannot mean to exclude me, his mother? We do not wish him to grow up not knowing either of his parents. Do we?"

She reached out and held Madame la Grande's arm, saying, "You would not want to be separated from Suzanne for so long, would you, Sister? Is not to be with her an important part of the reason we return to Moulins? Is that not true, Duke Pierre?"

All three of her auditors squirmed and avoided one another's eyes. Finally, her husband replied, his voice conciliating.

"Dear wife, I understand it is difficult for you. It is for your safety and that of our beloved son that this is necessary." As Anne gazed at him, her eyes filling with tears, he floundered on. "He is the heir to France and his life is precious. What if he sickened from an infection you—or someone in your entourage—carried to Amboise?" when she raised her eyebrows, he became more rattled. "I did not mean your health is less important. You are my queen, and I must protect your health. You carry the next heir to France."

Teardrops trembling on Anne's eyelashes slipped down her cheeks. She dashed them away with the back of one hand. "I understand that to you I am important only as a vessel for your heirs," she said, her voice harsh. "But I love my son. His health is as important to me as it is to you. I am prepared to delay approaching him until Charles-Orland's Gouverneur is assured that I and my ladies are free of all infection, and he gives his permission."

"Please forgive me, Anne."

She persisted. "I will not go near Charles-Orland if there is the least chance that I or anyone close to me be ill. Or anyone in or near Amboise. What if I promise not to see him until after this baby is born, and I have been churched?" She wanted to fall to her knees and beg. In her hurry to plead her case, she lurched to her feet, bumping Madame la Grande's chair, and stumbled to his side where she clutched his arm.

Charles pushed his chair back and rose, forcing Anne to release her fingers. Then he took her hands in his. "Anne, I do not mean to be cruel. But I cannot agree. Both your lives are too precious. I cannot allow you both to be in the same place. What if one of my enemies captures the castle? I could not bear it." He ran his fingers through his hair, rumpling it into a tangle. "Please ask no more. I can never agree. You must wait until I return. Then we shall hurry to our son together."

Anne bowed her head to hide the slow anger that was building inside her. "Do not agitate yourself so, Charles. I shall say no more."

She doubted he believed her, but he chose to, for he heaved a sigh of relief, leaned over and kissed her cheek. Then he led her to her place and lifted one of her hands to his lips.

After seeing her seated, he spoke to Duke Pierre as he returned to his spot. "Have you ensured my wife will be housed in the royal wing of your Château at Moulins?" Anne knew he was trying to placate her. Although she smiled and nodded to appear to listen, she paid no further attention. As a burning rage more intense than any she had felt previously grew inside her, she needed all the self-discipline she had learned in her life to sit quietly and act as if all were well.

That night, consumed with rage at all his arbitrary decisions—his deceit over maintaining Breton rights, his incessant whoring, his insistence she come to Lyon although he rarely saw her, his refusal to allow her to administer her estates, his greater trust in his sister than her, and now his refusal to allow her to see her son—she sent her ladies from her room and alternately prayed and paced for hours. It did not help.

Late in the night, the rosary he had given her that hung on her wall caught her eye. She stood staring at it, breathing hard from her nose. Snatching it from the wall, she spit on it wishing it were a dagger she could use to stab Charles and all Frenchmen. It no longer represented love to her. It was nothing but a golden chain imprisoning her and Brittany just as he had imprisoned Duke Louis. She would throw it away in the worst place she could, just as he tossed away her love as if it was worth nothing. As she strode toward the garderobe, she paused. It *was* a holy object. It took but a moment to rip off the crystal reliquary and cross, which she flung toward her prie-dieu. Continuing across her room, she flung open the garderobe door, lifted the lid of the hole and flung Charles's jewelled gift down into the cesspit, waiting until she heard the faint splat. Stepping back, she felt no remorse.

Grenoble, Dauphiné, 29 August 1494

NEXT MORNING, the queen, the regents, the court and the high officials of the city celebrated mass to bless the army setting off to conquer Naples. While Grenoble's citizens crowded the narrow sidewalks to wave as the military band drummed past, followed by the king, his principal generals and then the soldiers, Anne watched from the balcony of the Governor's Palace.

Charles blew Anne a kiss as he rode past. He wore her ermine device on the breast of the gold-embroidered, white-satin tunic lined with silk that covered his golden half-armour. The tunic was bordered with scarlet cloth of gold and fringed with finger-length twisted gold threads. On his head, he wore a helmet adorned with twenty-four tall, white, bejewelled feathers. His sword, its hilt jewel-encrusted, hung from a silver link belt a hands-width across.

He is dressed as if he is setting off to a masquerade, not a deadly military endeavour that has already drained the treasury, Anne thought. Behind him rode his principal generals—Marshal de Gié, Marshal de Rieux, Viscount de Rohan, and General de la Trémoïlle among them. All of them her enemies, men who had fought against her in Brittany. Although they smiled and bowed to her now, as she was polite to them, she did not make the mistake of thinking that they were her friends. She resented that they were off to make their fortune at the expense of the innocent citizens of Italy and would have access to the king's ear.

As the endless procession of troops marched on, with its well-accoutred major-generals, lieutenant-generals, colonels, majors, captains and blaring bands, she wilted under the glaring sun. Nothing about the costly martial display cheered her. How many of these well-equipped, well-shod, fit and *healthy* men would return? It took all her training to stand and smile as she forced the memories of the moaning injured, the stench of death, and the pleas of hungry Breton women and children from her mind. She clutched her mother's rosary, hidden in the folds of her gown, concentrating on silently repeating the holy words of the decades over and over to hold herself together until the interminable parade finally passed from sight.

~

Notre Dame Cathedral, 29 August 1494

ONCE ANNE WOKE from a nap that afternoon, she could not sit idle. A restless energy invaded her body, filling her with dark emotions. Deciding she needed to take her troubles to the Holy Virgin, Anne returned to the cathedral despite Madame la Grande's objections.

Inside the building, recently embellished with an exquisite tabernacle created in Padua, she found a simple side chapel with an image of Mary gazing at her son with an expression of tender love. Anne lit all the votive candles and knelt, bathed in tears. The future looked as bleak to her as the battered Breton coast after a winter storm had destroyed her people's simple huts and fishing boats, drowning them and their scrawny chickens and goats. She did not know how long Charles would be gone. It could be years before he carried out his dream and sailed from Sicily to conquer Jerusalem. He wanted to emulate Sainted King Louis IX. But Jerusalem was notorious as the graveyard of Frenchmen.

Even if he did not go so far, who knew how long his campaign in the Italian peninsula would take. She knew that already the Duke of Milan regretted he had encouraged her husband. Even Florence, traditionally France's ally, was no longer reliable, since its influential leader, Lorenzo de Medici, had died earlier in the year. His son was proving himself not nearly as popular or effective. Besides, war was chancy. Even if the French proved wildly successful, a stray ball or an unlucky illness could take her husband from her before she knew he was ailing. And then, although she was still furious with him, what would happen to her?

Her grievances of the night before returned full force. Despite her experience and her right to the regency, Charles had not included her in the regency council. From her court ladies she had learned that his father had excluded Charles's mother when he chose Charles's regent. It was likely, therefore, that Charles would not include her in their son's regency council, if he were to die before their son came of age.

Madame la Grande had been regent for Charles. It was she who had pursued the war that had wrested Brittany from Anne and her father. She was the person who had forced Anne's marriage to Charles. Because of her, Anne was now alone in France without her husband, unable to live with her son, and condemned to live under the regent's rule until Charles returned —if ever.

What shall I do, Holy Mother? You love your son as I love mine. I wish to hold him as you hold yours. She focused her eyes on the compassionate gaze of the Virgin. *My thoughts leave me without hope.* Too bleak even to pray, she sank back until she rested her buttocks on her heels. In the background, she heard muffled sobs. They sounded so much the way she felt that for some time she was not aware of them as separate from her own grief. By and by, she recognized that the echoes of misery were not her own but came from nearby.

It was happening again. She scrambled to her feet, her legs burning with pins and needles, and limped from the chapel. Her eyes adjusting to the dim interior, she spied what resembled a large black cloak heaped on the stone bench beside the ambulatory wall. It was quivering as she drew near it, and the soft sounds of woe grew louder. Taking a seat on the bench, she placed a hand where she thought the head must be.

"Hush," she said. "You are no longer alone. How can I help you?" She felt a tremor pass through the unknown person's body.

"Who are you? What do you want?" The weeping stopped though the breath still hitched, and the wary voice was husky.

Anne was uncertain from the voice whether she spoke to a woman or a youth. "Will you not sit up, uncover your face and tell me to whom I speak? I wish to help you and you may be assured that I will do so."

Another sob wracked the form. "No one can help me, not

really. T-t-hat is why I came here. For s-s-solace from the Holy Mother."

Tears sprang to Anne's eyes. She brushed them away resolutely and gripped her hands together. "I, too, came for solace. If you tell me what troubles you, perchance it will ease you."

The person did not move or answer. Anne leaned back against the bench and waited.

"You sound kind," the voice sighed, finally. With a rustle, the person sat up and pushed back the hood of the thick, concealing cloak. The blotched face of a young woman appeared. Without looking at Anne, she rubbed her hands, which poked through her cape, over her still covered arms.

"What are you called, child?" Anne asked again, "and why are you alone here and so sad?"

She sighed again. "My name is Mme de Saubonne. I am here alone because. . ." her mouth quivered, and she pursed her lips, obviously to keep from crying.

"Cry if you need to, my dear," Anne said.

Still pressing her lips together, Madame shook her head. "I am a married woman and grown up. I must behave like one. It is just, just that . . . my husband left w-with the army today. So, I am alone." She sniffed. Then she sniffed again. And again.

Anne pulled the cloth she always carried from her sleeve and gave it to the stranger.

"How old are you? And when you say alone, where is your mother? Or who are you with?" She kept her voice calm, aiming for the same quiet, reassuring tone her confessor used.

Michelle leaned back against the bench. "I am a-almost fifteen. I had been staying with my husband at the king's c-court." She sighed again. "He has arranged for m-me to return to Lyon with a p-party of Cistercian sisters who t-travel in the royal entourage."

Anne could see young Mme de Saubonne's profile, her frown, her furrowed brow. Her shoulders hunched as she slumped over. Every curve of her body spoke of sorrow, yet nothing she had said so far matched the sense of tragedy she exuded.

"Will you remain in Lyon? With whom will you stay?" Anne was dissatisfied with her questions. She reached forward and took the girl's arm. "Tell me, my dear, why you are so very sorrowful."

The young woman dropped her head until it almost touched her chest. Anne could see tears dripping. Her voice was thick when she spoke. "My m-mother died in L-l-yon just before the army moved to Grenoble. W-w-we were going to stay in Lyon together at the convent there until my husband returned. Her sister—my aunt—is the Abbess there." She blew her nose, the blast like the honk of an angry goose.

The blare startled Anne, who barked a laugh, then cried, "I am so sorry! You surprised me is all."

Mme de Saubonne, waving her hands helplessly, fell into giggles. In the next moment, they were holding onto each other, tears of laughter pouring down their faces. It was not truly humorous, but it was the spark they each needed to lighten the tragedies weighing them down. When they finally gasped to a stop, they had formed a bond. It was a new experience for Anne, this sudden flare of recognition, the call of a kindred spirit. To find a true friend only four years younger than herself, in this unexpected place at this dark moment in both their lives lightened the heavy load that had been making her feel like a Methuselah. She said a short prayer of gratitude to the Holy Mother.

Before they finished, Anne pulled Mme Michelle's whole sad story from her. And she had a sad tale to tell. Russet-haired Mme Michelle and her young Breton husband, a close cousin, married in haste when King Charles announced levies for Breton brigades from Anne's lands. The Saubonne owed feudal service. As a younger son, he offered to go, believing he would make his fortune and her parents arranged their marriage. Immediately afterwards, her father, who had been ailing, died. Mme Michelle had not intended to join her new husband, but her mother wanted to travel, so she offered to accompany them and care for

Mme Michelle in Lyon. They would stay with her sister, the Abbess. It suited everyone. They had travelled with Anne's court, although it had grown so large, she did not remember them.

"Of course not, Madame la Reine," Mme Michelle said. "We were among dozens of Breton ladies travelling under your protection."

Once Anne realized she was Breton, it settled everything. Mme Michelle was orphaned and the wife of one of her Breton soldiers. Anne would not hear of her staying alone in a convent in Lyon. Both her duty and preference led Anne to decide that the young auburn-haired Mme Michelle must become one of her ladies with a court position and a small stipend. Then Anne would have someone who could become a friend like Pernette had been, someone she thought she could trust.

"Let us return to my chambers." Anne rose. "I shall send a page to your aunt, informing her of my decision." She took Mme Michelle's arm to hurry her along. "I will ask her to send your trunks and to attend me tomorrow to assure herself you are in my care. How is that?"

Mme Michelle said, "It is a like a dream, Madame la Reine. *Grâce à la Sainte Mère*, you have rescued me, when a few hours ago I saw no hope nor light."

Anne patted her arm. Mme Michelle was speaking for her, too.

1 Scots Guards—an elite Scottish military unit founded in 1418 to be personal bodyguards to the French monarchy. They were assimilated into the King's Household and later formed the first company of the Royal Bodyguard. They survived until the end of the Bourbon monarchy.

CHAPTER 18

Louise Gives Birth

Château de Cognac, 31 August 1494

"Maman Marguerite, can we please sit now?" Louise realized her voice sounded plaintive, but her mother-in-law drove her as hard as if she were an ox in a field. Small and spry, her mother-in-law, the scent of apple cider wafting from her kirtle, pulled Louise's arm to keep her walking.

"Chère fille, you will thank me in a few weeks. Despite what foolish doctors say, midwives and women who have helped at many births know that healthy women have easier births." Louise resisted, like a balky horse, and her mother-in-law relented. "But the sun grows hot, and you have done well enough for now."

Louise gestured to the bench under the spreading oak beside the Charente River. "Let us sit there."

She groaned as she lowered herself onto the iron bench, pressing her hands to her back. For a time, she and Countess Marguerite sat without speaking, watching the river flow by, silent between its low grassy banks. Despite the idyllic scene, Louise was not at peace.

"I received two letters yesterday."

"Oui? Did Carlo write?" Her mother-in-law's voice sounded lazy. "Who else?"

"No, neither came from him."

Mme Marguerite sat straighter. "Oh. Who then? You sound. . . . I am not sure . . . irritated? Tell me."

Louise shifted on the hard seat. "You know Catherine de Brézé? She writes to tell me what is happening at the queen's court. Supposedly." Louise huffed an angry breath. "The queen is increasing again. She does not travel with the king. Catherine says it is not yet known where she will stay, but the queen is *aux anges* that she will have another child. She believes she carries another son. King Charles is delighted, too, and showers her with jewels and lands. They are like newlyweds, Catherine writes."

The news annoyed Louise more than she wished to say. Even if her child were her longed-for son, she would be unable to relax, once again. The news was also proof the king and queen had reconciled. Apparently, the king was piling wealth and riches upon Queen Anne while he squeezed every penny from his nobles and even his clergy for his war.

"What is it precisely that concerns you, ma fille? It cannot be a shock that the queen should fall with child, for they are both young and hot, or so it is said." Maman Marguerite snorted.

Louise had no intention of confiding her dreams for her son —the son she was desperate for—even to her trusted mother-in-law. She said, "It is the letter from Mme de Vesc. She wrote, too, and it arrived along with Catherine's."

When Countess Marguerite looked mystified, Louise said, "My friend, the wife of Charles's favourite. She says that the queen is unhappy to be *enceinte* and has been pleading with the king to allow her to live with her son and is furious he will not allow it. Who am I to believe?" Putting her puzzlement about the conflicting information into words helped. One of them was wrong. It was unlikely to be Mme de Vesc, who was in her husband's confidence. By Our Lady, would Catherine dare mislead her? It was bold—and therefore unlike her.

She changed the subject, getting ready to rise. "There is much to do. I cannot sit idle here. Especially with Mme Antoinette unavailable and two squalling babies in the house."

Countess Marguerite put a hand on her arm. "No, Louise. Stay here and enjoy this peaceful moment. If we were to follow custom, as perchance I should insist, you would be lying-in now unable to do anything but rest."

When Louise did not relax, Countess Marguerite turned toward the younger woman. "I understand, ma fille. You are angry with my son, who is a philanderer. He insults you, foisting two bastards on your household just before you are to give birth. Worse, they are daughters who will require dowries if they live. But, ma fille, this is the way of the world." Her next words astonished Louise. "Even my late husband, who was so pious the Church thought to make him Pope, gave me a bastard to raise." She leaned back against the bench again and let a silence reign between them.

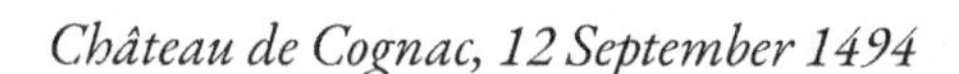

Château de Cognac, 12 September 1494

When she woke to sharp pains in the black of night, this time Louise understood what was happening. Before she opened the draperies surrounding her bed, before she called to her niece Anne and Antoinette, both of whom were sleeping on pallets in her bedchamber these nights, she clutched her rosary and sent up an impassioned prayer for the promised son to the Mother Goddess and the Virgin Mary. Remembering Margot's long-drawn-out birthing, she lay for a time counting the beats between pains. It did not take her long to realize that the interval between pains had gone from uncomfortable to intense.

Struggling to clamber to the side of her bed and sit, she reached for the opening in the curtains, calling, "Anne! Antoinette! Hurry!"

She panted, hugging her arms around the contraction that gripped her belly. Then she moaned. Edging her buttocks to the side of the mattress, she stretched her toes to the floor.

"Antoinette! Anne! Now! Come now!"

Warm liquid trickled down her legs. She had enough time to think *my waters have broken,* Grâce à Dieu *I was no longer in bed,* before the intensity of the pain redoubled, and she groaned, closed her eyes and bent over as far as her enormous belly would allow.

Once the pain eased, she became aware that comforting arms surrounded her back, supporting her. Someone removed her night rail and robed her in a rough cotton shift, one that she would not mind bloodying. Another maid helped her into a woollen dressing robe frayed at the wrists.

She saw that her bedchamber had become a beehive of activity. Maids built up the fire. Maman Marguerite bustled around in her night robe ordering servants to bring kettles of boiling water, put down clean cloths, place the birthing stool, set up a table for the birthing instruments, bring in the midwife, the milk nurse, call the priest and go to see if Carlo had arrived as he had promised.

"Walk, Louise, walk," she ordered.

"Maman Marguerite, I can barely stand!"

"If you walk, your baby will come quicker. If you have good fortune, you will be done within one turn of the hourglass. But move away from the bed. The maids must strip it and lay down straw before they cover it with rough cloth. We cannot have you ruining the mattress."

The door opened again to admit the midwife. Louise could not have been happier to see the beefy woman with muscular arms and a square face, her hair completely covered with a white kerchief. Glimpses of grey homespun poked from beneath the dark apron that covered her robe from her neck to the bottom of her skirt.

She exuded confidence in the way she stood observing the scene before she ordered changes. Her authority as she asked a maid to relocate the table with the birthing instruments and bring more towels, even her way of pushing her sleeves up her arms reassured Louise.

She ordered two of the maids to hold Louise's arms. "Keep Milady walking," she said, "But let her walk slow. She looks to be near her time."

That promise sounded like sweet music in Louise's ears.

Bathed in sweat, she struggled to free her arms from the women holding her. "I am too hot. Help me remove this robe."

Countess Marguerite shook her head. "It is dangerous to become chilled, ma fille."

"I will faint from the heat! I am melting!" Louise was getting angry. She leaned over again as another contraction took her and held her in its grip for what seemed forever.

The midwife came between them. "Mme Louise, time to sit in the birthing chair. I shall examine you. Countess Marguerite, will you oversee the final preparations of Mme Louise's bed? The baby is very close."

The mood changed immediately. Once the maid removed her dressing gown, another bathed her face and neck with lavender-scented water, a third held her shift up while the midwife plunged her arm inside Louise while pushing on her belly. She pressed her hand down as the next contraction came.

"Push," she ordered, her face intent, "puuush."

Once again, Louise felt that she was splitting into two.

She was panting, her breath dry in her throat.

"Breathe with the pains. Breathe with the pains." The midwife's voice rang in her ears. "Another big push. That is right!"

That same demanding voice! An enormous pain, the worst ever, surged through Louise's loins, followed by a strange, slithering sensation. She fell back drained, panting and only half-conscious.

She could hear the cheerful babble of voices around her. The midwife's face swanned into her still blurred vision, holding out the wrapped bundle. "You have a healthy, perfect son, Mme Louise."

"A. . . a son?" It was too good to be true. It must be a dream.

Maman Marguerite hung over her now. "We are ecstatic, chère Louise. A son for the house."

Tears rose from somewhere deep inside Louise and spurted from her eyes. She clung to the tiny body, unable to lift him to look at his face or open his swaddling to examine his tiny fingers and toes.

"Careful with him. He is still little." Her mother-in-law reached to take the infant. "Carlo has arrived. I shall take the boy to his father while the midwife finishes helping you. And then the maids shall clean you up, dress you in a fresh shift and you shall rest in your clean bed."

Louise wanted to resist, to clutch her son, the precious promised child who Friar Francis had promised. But she had sworn she would not shame herself as she had at Margot's birth. So, she gritted her teeth and opened her arms.

When the women around her fussed over her, she obeyed them, all the while wrapped in her own dreams. *I shall name him François for the friar*, she decided. *My little King of France. François I.* Immediately, her thoughts turned to the dauphin and from him to the infant growing in the queen's belly. She sent a prayer heavenward that Anne would have a girl.

CHAPTER 19
Life in Moulins

Château de Moulins, December 1494

Anne could not stop shivering as they rode into Moulins. Madame la Grande apologized, saying that from September until the end of January were the coldest, greyest months. The rosy stone of the main buildings in the bustling town and the magnificent Bourbon Château all glistened as their cavalcade crossed the magnificent bridge over the wide Allier River, that flowed placidly north to join the Loire, but the charming vista did not improve her spirits.

She must live at Moulins until Charles returned. She must adjust; she realized that. So, she must convince her sister- and brother-in-law she had submitted to their rules and would abide by them. More than that, she must persuade them that she saw the wisdom in them, that she was contented and happy. It became a game, coming up with strategies to get what she wanted by proposing them in ways that would gain Madame la Grande's approval. Most important, she decided, was to create the court she wanted, with the people she wanted to have in it.

As soon as her small entourage was settled, she invited the regents to the main meal in the wing they had given her. Only her chaplain, her Maître d'hôtel, and the widowed Queen Joanne of Naples, Anne's favourite grandmother substitute, joined the three of them at the high table on the dais, for there were no others sufficiently noble to sit with them. The voices of the members of her household who sat at tables arranged perpendicular to their own, echoed in the large, half-empty chamber. Only four musicians played in their empty gallery, so the music that accompanied their meal sounded thin.

For this meal, Anne had insisted that the service at the high table be rapid and elegant. It contrasted well with the slower service that resulted for the rest of the diners. Since the high table faced the others, it was impossible to ignore the situation.

As the servers carried out the remnants of the first remove and began the second, Anne turned to her sister-in-law. "I apologize for the lack of finesse at this meal, Sister. My household is adjusting to its new location." She nodded toward the awkward congestion at the doorways. "I will need to acquire a larger staff."

Madame la Grande was gracious. "Is not that always the way when moving into a different location? As soon as your Maître d'hôtel has had time to make the arrangements, it will all be smooth."

Anne said pensively, "Your ladies tell me that your court was the grandest ever known in France, with the most cultivated ladies and best entertainments."

Her sister smiled, looking gratified. "Ambassadors from the various courts extolled it. They compared it favourably to that of the court of Burgundy." She preened.

"A compliment indeed. I have a yen to achieve the same glory for the court of France once more when my husband returns. It is my thought to bring more ladies to my court now so they will be prepared when the army returns. How think you?"

"An excellent notion."

Anne took advantage of this approval to expand the range of

her influence. Little by little, with Queen Joanne as her guide and Mme de Saubonne, who had become her trusted private secretary, she took control over the management of her estates. When she corresponded with the members of her extended family, she invited them to send their daughters to her court. Then she encouraged her new ladies to draw her attention to authors, painters and musicians from their domains who needed patrons, making her beloved with both her court ladies and their protégés. Since she particularly favoured her Breton nobility, her popularity in her duchy grew. With so many of Brittany's greatest nobles away in Italy, she kept her increasing influence unobserved. In her own wing, with her own Maître d'hôtel, chamberlains, comptrollers and chaplains to manage her household, she carved out enough private space to create an independent private life.

This Christmas season the regents held the royal Christmas court at Moulins. The Bourbon always entertained largely, but this year they outdid themselves as they hosted a festivity that outshone Anne and Charles's Christmas court of the previous year. By now Anne was accustomed to Madame la Grande's need to demonstrate the importance of her family, so she shrugged to herself as she greeted the ambassadors from all their allies.

The day of the Twelfth Night celebration that marked the end of the Christmas season, Anne woke early. Dawn had not yet broken when she rose before the fires were freshened and she found a thin layer of ice in the jug of water. Shivering, she dragged a fur-lined robe over her fine wool long-sleeved shift and thrust her feet into fur-lined slippers. It was never this cold in Brittany even when it snowed. It rarely snowed here, but somehow the cold was more severe. It would be hours before the servants woke, so she stirred up the banked fire and added a couple of logs. Standing in front of it warming her hands until it blazed, she then pulled up a stool and snuggled into her robe.

Time was passing and she had not lost sight of her promise to Catherine de Brézé. Finding a suitable match for the young woman was not the easiest task she had set herself, but she was determined. Her timid lady-in-waiting deserved to be rewarded for telling her about Mme Louise's plotting. To keep Catherine safe from reprisals, she must find Catherine a marriage far from the countess. Although from all that Anne had heard Louise was wrapped up in her son, the countess was not one to forget a betrayal—or what she perceived to be one.

Anne shook her head to rid herself of her envious thoughts about Louise who now held her healthy son in her arms while Anne was separated from hers. Besides, Louise was done with carrying her child, while she still risked her life to bring another child into the world. She must settle Catherine before her time. Just to be sure.

The Bourbon hosted a magnificent Twelfth Night event with feasting, dancing, and spectacles that lasted the entire day and late into the evening. At the feast, Anne sat with the ambassador from the court of Hungary. His French was laboured, and they laughed together as they mixed snippets of Latin with their French. From him, she learned that their king, Vladislaus II, was searching for a suitable wife for his younger brother, Duke Sigismund.

After the feast, she sought out her good-natured, grizzle-haired, brother-in-law.

"Duke Pierre," she said, after they had chatted about his adored Suzanne and the latest news from Italy, "thank you for seating me beside the Hungarian Ambassador. I learned so much from him about his country. What a long history it has. So fascinating."

"You make a delightful ambassador for France, Madame la Reine," the duke said, "with you gift of charming the dourest of our visitors."

She gave him an arch look. "I take it as a great compliment coming from a man as affable as you, good brother. But I did not come to chat idly or exchange compliments. A comment he made brings me to you to make a proposal that will benefit our country and his."

"Excellent." Her brother-in-law's nose quivered like a hunting dog scenting game.

Anne noted his interest. "Allies are always useful. And I believe the king's wife is an Aragonese princess. Indeed, she is the widow of the former king of Naples, I believe. So, it would be advantageous if our own family married within the Hungarian court. Do you not agree?"

Duke Pierre nodded but, to Anne's eyes, cautiously.

"The ambassador mentioned that King Vladislaus is seeking a wife for his younger brother. Are you aware that Charles's unmarried aunt is serving as a lady in my court? Although she is your father-in-law's half-sister, she was much younger than he. She is just twenty-one and has never been married." As she described Catherine, Duke Pierre's expression warmed. Anne chose that moment to take the risk. "She is Mme Catherine de Brézé."

Duke Pierre's brown furrowed.

"Your wife was the person who pardoned her father."

"True." He chewed his bottom lip. "But to propose her for marriage into a royal line?"

"She comes from a royal line. There are reasons I wish this match if you agree that it is an excellent alliance for France." Anne sweetened the offer. "I am prepared to arrange a generous dowry, if you will negotiate the match."

"I will," he said. "If my wife agrees that it would be beneficial to our country."

As she reflected on her sister-in-law's good fortune in having a husband who considered her ideas, Anne thanked him for his courtesy. Although Madame la Grande could be charming on the surface, she rarely listened to advice once she had made up her mind, yet Anne was almost certain her sister-in-law would support the match.

Fleetingly, Anne recalled a comment that Madame la Grande had made one day—that Anne reminded her of herself when she had been Anne's age. Anne had not taken it as a compliment then. Now, watching her sister-in-law manage people to achieve her goals, she felt better about it.

~

March 1495

ANNE STROKED HER BELLY, pretending to listen to her ladies' cheerful conversation as it swirled around her. For the last three days, she had become increasingly anxious. Her baby was not moving. She was certain now. *What should she do?*

"Duke Pierre said there was—"

"Call Mistress Bouchard," Anne interrupted Queen Joanne, her voice sharp. She did not apologize. "I want the midwife *now*." She noticed that her three preferred ladies were looking at her anxiously. "Please."

The youngest, russet-haired Mme Michelle de Saubonne, jumped to her feet and ran off. Queen Joanne rose from her cushion beside the queen's chair and lifted one of the queen's hands to cradle it between her own.

"You are worried, Madame la Reine. What is the matter?"

"I need air."

She struggled to her feet and took her friend's arm. They donned hooded capes, and a chambermaid ran to open the door that opened onto a covered walkway. This time, Anne had insisted her confinement chambers be located on the ground floor with uncovered windows that opened to the outside. She also required they include a private inner courtyard. When pressed, she compromised on a small one with only a fountain, a sheltered portico on all sides, and space for Fanchon to run crazily in circles. But since it was winter, the space had been sufficient, for it provided the most important elements—fresh air and sunlight.

"Bring us braziers," Queen Joanne said as they stepped outside.

Fanchon yapped happily, racing to the centre of the courtyard.

"Look at her," Anne said. "She has no worries. As soon as she is outside, she runs like a puppy, yet when I bring her in, she settles and snoozes without complaints. At times, I wish we could trade places."

"What are your complaints? Please tell me. It is unlike you to snap."

"I miss my son. It has been a year since I saw Charles-Orland. Babies change so much in a year." She would not let her tears fall, but her throat hurt when she spoke.

"What have you done about that?"

"I write to him every day. I pray for him. I send him miniatures of me, and I receive images of him, send him toys, order him clothing. I have Mme de Bussières write to me daily so I can talk to him about what he is doing."

"In other words, you are doing everything you can to care for him and show him you love him and do not forget him. You are doing well." Queen Joanne was brisk.

Anne did not answer. When Catherine de Brézé told her that Louise had given birth to a boy and was raising her two children herself at Cognac, a worm of envy had started boring into her heart. Whenever Madame la Grande or Catherine spoke of Louise's children, the canker of envy grew. She had not told Queen Joanne that because she missed Charles-Orland, it exacerbated her resentment of Louise. Queen Joanne's voice disrupted the poison spreading in her veins.

"What does your Father Confessor say?"

"To love the Lord and trust him."

Jeanne's voice softened. "So, you must. You know you cannot travel to see him now for you must wait for your baby."

Anne shuddered. She did not want this reminder. She tightened her grasp on her friend's arm as they paced along flagged portico walkway.

Joanne worried away at her the same way Fanchon tormented

the stick he had seized. "I wonder whether this is the only reason you are so sorrowful today."

Anne searched for something else to say. She had so many anxieties. "The regents wish me to celebrate my husband's victorious conquest of Naples, especially since he captured it with practically no fighting or loss of French lives. He conquered it with as much ease as he and his army seized the other Italian states as they passed through." She twisted the cloth of her cloak between her hands and her voice trembled as if she were recounting a disaster. "Père de la Vigne wrote me that King Ferrandino and his heir abdicated and fled without a backward glance and the citizens lined the streets cheering as Charles and his army entered the city."

"Is this not a victory we should acclaim?" Queen Joanne sounded puzzled.

"I suppose so. But Charles has been ill several times along the way. Deathly ill, once." She caught her older friend's eye. "You have been Queen of Naples. How long do you think our armies can hold the kingdom? The ease of our triumphs worries me. Although Pope Alexander had promised the crown to my husband, he crowned King Ferrandino, and I heard from Duke Pierre that he only changed his mind from fear of the size of our armies. I do not think Charles should have threatened the Holy Father."

"The Holy Fornicator!"

"Queen Joanne, you should not speak so of the Pope. We must separate the imperfect man from his divine office where his judgment cannot err."

Queen Joanne raised her eyebrows, but answered, "It has been a week since we marked the victory with High Masses and processions throughout France. And the war prizes are so vast that he may enrich France with the booty. So, what else is it?"

Anne broke down. "Perchance, I worry for nothing, but I no longer feel my infant move. It has been three days now." Her hand tightened on Queen Joanne's arm. How much she hoped her friend would say something to reassure her, that she had heard many women say it had happened to them. As Queen Joanne's silence lengthened, Anne's heart raced.

"I feel dizzy. I need to sit."

"Madame la Reine, you must stay calm. Lean on me to walk to the bench over there," said Queen Joanne, leading her to the stone seat beside the door.

Anne breathed in and out through her nose to control her breathing. "It is not usual, is it?" she said finally.

Beside her, Queen Joanne sighed. "I would not think so. You are wise to call for Mme Bouchard."

THE MIDWIFE INSISTED that screens be placed around Anne's bed, put her ear to Anne's belly and rested her hands on it for what seemed like ages. Pressing her lips together to a thin line, she came to stand by Anne's head. Their eyes met.

"Madame la Reine, I may be wrong, yet I worry that I do not hear or feel movement."

When she said nothing more, Anne whispered, "Is there nothing you can do? Must I wait in fear?"

"How have you been feeling? What have you noticed?"

"I do not like to complain." Anne was reluctant to answer, but the woman waited, letting the silence lengthen. "My back. It has ached constantly in the past days. And. . . and. . . there has been some blood." She saw Mme Bouchard frown and added with a rush. "Not much. A few drops."

Mme Bouchard took a deep breath. "There are preparations that bring on contractions. I do not like to use them. They cannot be certain and may cause you to vomit and give you a flux. If we wait, the babe will come in the Lord's good time."

Anne's eyes filled with tears. "Until tomorrow then. I will speak with my good sister and my confessor." When the woman patted her hand, Anne saw compassion in her face.

"Please send my maid to me. I would stay abed."

~

NEITHER MADAME LA Grande nor her Father Confessor agreed she should take the raspberry tea leaf tisane or the castor bean oil.

"In another sennight," Madame la Grande finally agreed. "If you have not delivered by then, we shall see."

Two days later, the pains came hard and suddenly, with a flow of black blood. The birth happened fast, and Anne went through it in a daze. The saddest part of the whole awful birth, Anne thought, was the silence after her final push when she felt that sensation, as if a plug had popped from a blocked jar.

No thin infant wail rose to her ears. No cheerful voices rose in excitement to chatter in delight about the appearance of a beautiful, healthy baby.

Instead, the midwife said, "You have a girl. What is her name?"

Madame la Grande replied, "Anne," before Anne could say a word, before her frozen mind could comprehend the question.

Instantly, the midwife baptized her with the sign of the cross on her forehead and a quick blessing.

A nurse fussed over her baby, wrapping her, as Anne slumped in the birthing chair, tears running down her cheeks. Then Madame la Grande took the tiny bundle and came to Anne clasping her.

"Do you want to hold your daughter before I take her to the chapel?"

Her throat too tight to speak, Anne nodded and held out her arms. Her sister placed the infant gently into them. For the first few moments Anne could do nothing more than rock the tiny, almost weightless bundle, as sobs shock her. Then she opened the blanket to gaze on the perfect, pearly face. "She looks as if she is sleeping. She is so peaceful."

With a fingertip, she touched the blue-veined eyelids as delicate as butterfly wings and moved on to the white silk ribbon tied in her hair. "She has so much hair. It is soft as the silk. Her mouth —" She could not speak any more. Her tear drops fell onto her daughter's sweet face, and she wiped them away with her thumb.

Opening the cloth wider, to take her daughter's hand, she saw that baby Anne wore a long silk and lace robe that covered her completely. When she tried to unlace it, Madame la Grande gently pulled her hands away.

"Close her blanket again, dear sister. Say your goodbyes."

"So soon." Anne was moaning now. "Can I not keep her with me longer?"

"You know you cannot. It will only become harder. Kiss her and let her go."

Anne had never known her sister-in-law to be so understanding. She wished she could appreciate it more, but there was no room in her heart for anything but grief. Lifting her baby, she kissed her daughter on her forehead. Letting Madame la Grande take her was the hardest thing she had ever done.

CHAPTER 20
News from the Front

Château de Moulins, 31 July 1494

In the late afternoon, Anne and her ladies exited into her private gardens from her wing in the Bourbon's château. The fresh breeze rustled the vine leaves covering the walkway to the pergola and cooled her overheated skin. She savoured the mingled scents of lavender, rosemary, sweet thyme and roses that wafted in the air. She had made it her own private space, ordering the gardeners to plant the aromatic herbs she loved, for their scents reminded her of the herb gardens of her childhood, and the pleasure of making simples in stillrooms with her mother as they moved from one Château do anther. This had become her favourite retreat. It soothed her to bring dried herbs inside, to scatter on the floors, among her chests and in her bedding.

After a few steps, Anne took Catherine de Brézé's arm. "Let the others walk ahead. I wish to talk with you. No, no, do not be frightened. You are not in disgrace." She took a seat in the dappled shade. "Sit beside me, Mme Catherine."

Anne paused, reflecting on how best to break her news to the young woman. Two months earlier, when she had told the girl about the arrangements to marry Duke Sigismund of Hungary, Catherine had blanched. Yet although the marriage would take her far from home, where she would be surrounded by foreigners who spoke a language that she did not, she had agreed at once. Anne found her a teacher and she practiced diligently, but she had become thinner and more silent than ever. Yet when Anne probed, she insisted she wanted the marriage.

Anne took Catherine's arm. "This is good news. Or I hope it is." She smiled at her nervous demoiselle. "I believe you are anxious about your marriage to Duke Sigismund. Know that the Hungarian royal family is delighted with this matrimonial alliance. Through you, they are joined by blood to the French royal family. You bring them a rich dowry. You are beautiful and cultured and will shine in your new home."

Catherine's cheeks turned rosy. "You are too kind, Madame la Reine."

"All I say is true. Remember, I chose this match because it will serve you well. Mme Louise is a cruel woman who coerced you with threats of exposing family scandals. I do not trust her to mend her ways. You will be safe from her, for Hungary is beyond her reach. She has neither friends nor family there and your husband's rank will protect you."

"Thank you." Catherine's wisp of a smile was genuine.

"This is the news, then. The date of your marriage is now set. You will marry here by proxy in two weeks. Duke Pierre has received word that a Hungarian embassy will arrive next week with your new major-domo and principal ladies. They have requested that you set out on your journey the day after your wedding because your new husband and the Hungarian court are eager to welcome you."

When Catherine paled, Anne patted the girl's shoulder.

"What if they do not like me? I find the language very difficult, and I progress as slowly as. . . as an ant climbing a mountain."

"Yes. It is soon. It is better so. You will have no time to conjure nightmares. The seamstresses have been fitting you for your new wardrobe since the negotiations began. Your wedding gown is all but complete. Are you?"

Catherine firmed her chin. "Yes, Madame la Reine."

Anne could imagine how frightened Catherine must be at the prospect of leaving her family and country behind to venture across the vast distance from Moulins to Budapest, to a truly foreign court and strange, uncouth language. It was unlikely she would ever see her family again. When Anne had departed from Brittany to marry in France, she had despaired, yet she knew the French language and had grown up on stories of the gentle beauty of the Loire Valley.

"You are strong, dear Mme Catherine, you will have sons, and you will rule your own household. These gifts from God will make up for your many losses." Anne gripped her hands.

Catherine hung her head and a few hot teardrops fell onto Anne's hand where it lay over Catherine's. She sobbed once, pulled a hand away to scrub her eyes. "Forgive me, Madame la Reine. I know you speak true. Since it must be done, it is better done quickly—and I am grateful. It will be good to be so far from Mme Louise that I need no longer fear her, for it will not be worth her trouble. Only. . . what if my husband takes me into aversion?"

Anne took a deep breath. She would not offer false reassurances. This was the great fear of all noblewomen sent far away to marry foreigners. It could spell a rapid death. "I will send your dearest companion and your maid who has served you since childhood with you, so you are not alone. And I swear to you on this precious cross," she held her mother's reliquary to her lips, "that all I have said about the delight of Duke Sigismund and his family is true. He wants to please you. If you approach him in the same spirit, God will surely hear your prayers."

Catherine straightened her shoulders. "Dear Madame, please forgive me. After all you have done, I should be on my knees gabbling gratitudes, not moaning about my fears. It is the shock, nothing more. I am fortunate." She lifted Anne's hands and dropped kisses on them.

Pulling her hands away, Anne rose in haste. "None of that, Mme Catherine. I did my duty. If you are recovered, let us join the others. If you wish, you may tell them now."

~

TWO DAYS LATER, Anne and her ladies gathered in the pergola at the end of her private garden once again. For the entire week, the town of Moulins had been experiencing glorious weather. The sun smiled down from a cerulean sky and a light breeze kept the ladies from overheating. Within the pergola, the well-watered climbing vines, their roots covered with straw, provided Queen Anne and her ladies with a luxurious, leafy retreat.

Anne relaxed on the cushioned wooden bench that circled the lattice walls of the building. The juice of chilled melon dripped from her chin, and she wiped it away with the napkin Mme Michelle handed to her. Then she took a long swallow from the mug of small ale cooling in the bucket of ice well wrapped in layers of straw.

Although their setting was pleasant, the ladies' spirits were low. Foremost on everyone's mind was the French army's hasty withdrawal through Italy as it returned from its conquest of Naples. Each report from the front had been more worrisome than the last. Anne found the reversals hard to accept. The campaign had started with their army marching through the peninsula like a tornado, toppling what little resistance they encountered with ease, hailed as heroes, or so Père André's letters had claimed. He reported that their forces had conquered the few city states that resisted within days. She had evidence of its truth from the marvels that kept arriving at Moulins. The paintings, the books, the jewellery, fans, gloves, coffers, musical instruments—she could go on. And artists and artisans had arrived with them.

From Rome, Charles had sent her a rosary blessed by His Holiness himself, and a letter, written in his own hand, to report he had arrived there with his army in time to celebrate Christmas in the Holy City.

He conquered Naples so quickly that he had been crowned king of Naples and Sicily before she gave birth to their daughter in March. At that memory, she shied like a horse bolting from a collapsing bridge.

Shifting on the bench, she spoke almost at random. "Why is the return taking so long, when our army was so quick to win its way to Naples? It has been over four months since they left there. They moved rapidly when they wanted to ensure they were not trapped south of Rome, once all our fickle allies joined with the defeated Italian states in league against us. But once north of Rome they have inched forward, yet we have not heard of any large battles or any cities holding out against our advance."

The frightened expressions on her ladies' faces warned her she had revealed more than she should have.

"What have you learned from Duke Pierre, Madame la Reine?" Queen Joanne asked. "Or from Père André?"

Anne tried to repair her error. "Truly, the Regent does not confide in me. Père André writes only of the parades and grand entertainments that mark their passage along their return path." She forced a laugh. "Perhaps they dally for pleasure and booty, and I fuss because my husband has been gone too long. We learn more from Mme Michelle's letters than from mine."

It was the simple and frustrating truth. Because Michelle's husband lived in camp close to the front, he wrote to his wife about actual military actions. From the letters Michelle had shared with her, Anne learned about how vicious the French troops were, razing any Italian town that showed even minimal opposition.

When she glanced at her young secretary, Mme de Saubonne's pallor shocked Anne. *What have I said?* she wondered, worried her friend might faint.

"Are you ill, Mme Michelle? Perhaps you should retire. Mme Catherine, could you help her—"

"No, no, Madame la Reine. I am not ill."

Anne could not desist. Her friend was suffering. "You received another letter, did you not?"

When Mme Michelle's eyes filled with unshed tears, Anne said, "Is it worrying then?"

Mme Michelle hesitated.

"You look frightened. Is it personal?"

Mme Michelle shook her head.

Anne felt protective of this young woman who had already suffered too many losses. "Then I think you should read it to us or let one of us read it aloud. You should not suffer alone."

"It is not for myself that I fear. But it is too terrible. . ." Mme Michelle's voice trembled.

"Does it affect anyone else here?" Anne's voice became stern.

"No. . . Yes. . . Mayhap. . .I do not know. . ."

Michelle's confused answer decided Anne. "Unless we know the truth, how can we prepare for the return of our loved ones. For from your response, we will need courage."

The other ladies fell silent, every one of them looking anxious. Mme Michelle nodded and took a deep breath. "This letter was long delayed along the road. My husband wrote it before they left Naples."

Then she read his letter aloud.

Dear Wife,

The Italians could not conquer us by arms, but they are destroying us with disease. I am terrified, wife, as are we all. A terrible pustular disease races through our army like a new plague. None of us has ever seen or heard of anything like it. We call it the Italian disease.[1]

Men catch it from lying with the Neapolitan whores. Within one or two days, their pricks are covered with weeping pustules. These pass within a few days, and the man celebrates, thinking the disease has passed and gives thanks to the Lord. But he revels too soon. For once a man catches it, if he swives another doxy, even if it is before the pustules appear, it is certain he will pass it on.

Soon, suppurating, leaking boils form on men's faces and all over their bodies. You cannot imagine their suffering. Men who have had arrows yanked from their shoulders without moaning lie on their beds scratching bloody gouges into their arms and groin and screaming like the devil is dragging them into the pit of hell. Their agony is so great, and they appear so hideous, that I think they would rather suffer from leprosy. It is a curse!

None know of a cure, although the apothecaries, wise women and charlatans of every stripe offer ointments, salves and decoctions of unicorn horn and snake venom. Our soldiers will pay any amount and try anything, for their torment drives them mad. If they find the maud they suspect gave them the pox, they will kill her out of hand. The Neapolitans who welcomed us like heroes do not hesitate to knife us in the back if we venture alone in the streets at night. Leaving this plague-infested hellhole will be the happiest day of my life.

It should be a lesson to men to tie knots in the strings of their trews and use a hand for their dicks if they must, but most are too young and lusty. They believe this curse can never happen to them until God strikes them down for their sins. Trust me, dear wife, that I have never strayed from our marriage vows. This pestilence shows me how mightily God punishes those who have.

I do not write of this to frighten you, but to beg you to pray daily to our Father and Saviour to bring me and my companions home safe from this hotbed of evil. I regret that I ever wished to leave my peaceful home and your gentle arms. I long for you constantly and pray for your safety.

God keep you in his loving care.

MICHELLE LOOKED up to a horrified silence.

Anne, Queen Joanne, Catherine and the other ladies looked from one to the other, mouths agape. With one accord, they crossed themselves and fell to their knees.

"Why have I heard nothing of this plague?" Dazed, Anne rebelled against the magnitude of what she had just heard. "No one has whispered even a hint to me. Yet it is impossible that neither Madame la Grande nor Duke Pierre is unaware of it." Her thoughts fled to her husband. She knew him too well to believe he had been as continent as Mme Michelle's husband. *Had he caught this plague? Is he even now writhing in agony? Is he dead*? She gave a low moan.

Queen Joanne took her by the shoulders and shook her. "Do not leap to needless doubts about your husband! He is the king and surrounded by men who will not allow him to come to harm."

Anne swallowed, not daring to speak for fear her words would turn them into reality.

"Yes, yes, I understand." Queen Joanne shook Anne again. "He has many bed companions. But the women he takes to his bed are not street doxies. Only the best for our king. You know that."

Her bracing words recalled Anne to her duty. Despite her agitation, she must display fortitude. It would be terrifying if returning soldiers brought this plague, for it would spread throughout France like the Great Flood after God decided to destroy all flesh. But by showing her fear she would goad her ladies into panic, for they were already whispering among themselves.

She took a few deep breaths and said, "You are right. This is worrisome news and overset me for a moment, but I am calm now. I must discover more. My sister-in-law has a nose like a blood hound for ferreting out news. If anyone knows the truth, it will be she."

. . .

1 ITALIAN DISEASE—SYPHILIS, introduced into Europe in the late 15th century. Its source is unknown, but it became rampant in 1494/95 after the start of the French-Italian wars. Known by various names, in Italy it was called the French disease and in France it was called the Italian disease. There was no known cure, though it was treated with mercury, it raced through the infected individual causing great pain. It was usually fatal.

CHAPTER 21
Fleeting Joy

L'Hôtel-Fort, Lyon, 31 October 1495

In September, the Bourbon household and government administration crowded into Lyon from Moulins to wait for King Charles, the Duke d'Orléans and the returning army. The regents moved into the Governor's palace on the peninsula between the confluence of the Saône and Rhone rivers in the new part of the city, where the king always resided. With her enlarged court, Anne chose to occupy a large Hôtel-fort she had purchased. It stood beside the new convent of Les Trois Maries she had founded for the Breton Carmelite nuns who had come in her entourage the previous year. Both buildings were situated near the great Cathédral de Saint Jean in the medieval part of the city.

Two months later, everyone still waited for the king's return. On All Souls Eve, as Anne left her Hôtel's chapel, she had to bend double to fight the wind and heavy rain as she made her way around the covered walkway surrounding the courtyard to the entrance to her apartments. Even in that short distance, the downpour soaked her felted woollen cloak and pounded the cobblestones. Flashes of lightning and rolling bombards of thunder rattled her residence. The noise reminded Anne of the French cannonades during the siege of Rennes. Once inside, she fled to her inner chambers to escape the rage of the storm, but even here, muffled by thick stone walls, the tempest rumbled.

Her maids removed her dripping garments and wrapped her in a woollen shawl. Mme Michelle drew her to the bright fire in her bedchamber and threw on an apple log for its homey scent.

"Would you like me to read to you?" she asked.

"You are kind to offer, but no. When I have warmed, I shall write to Mme de Bussières."

Anne leaned back and wrapped her hands into the fur-lined shawl to warm them. Her trek had brought to mind her husband's victory at Fornovo after days of rain. Their men had been lucky. Despite the flooding of the Taro River, the sodden battleground and the overwhelming superiority in numbers of the Venetian League troops, their French had won through. Père André had written her about it, attributing their victory to God's grace, Charles's heroic leadership, and their dry powder. He also said the Venetian mercenaries had abandoned the battle to loot the French baggage train.

Anne twisted her lips in a sour smile. She had seen enough of war to recognize that unruly men bent on plunder could lose a battle even if superior in numbers. She would rather Charles lost his baggage if he saved their men to return home. That victory was one part of the reason she had gone to the chapel. The other was the news that Charles had recovered from the illness that had kept him in Grenoble since his arrival on French soil. At last, he was en route for Lyon and would arrive in a week. So Père André's last letter had promised.

Why did people whom she trusted to inform her try to hide the truth from her? They should know there were no secrets at court, for someone thought to benefit—perhaps to hurt her, perhaps for a reward, perhaps to win her favour by bringing her gossip. So, she knew Charles had brought his mistress. The

Countess Anna di Soleri had travelled with him all the way from Naples, and he had settled her in Grenoble.

Anne's informant had whispered that this Anna had stolen Charles's heart with her bravery in the saddle. "All along the return they hunted on days it did not rain; for the rest of the time they played other games," her informant told her. That festered like a poisoned wound for Anne was an intrepid horsewoman. It felt to her that this mistress had stolen *her* special place in Charles's life.

Anne was not grateful to the gossip, but she was annoyed with Père André and would tell him so when she saw him in person. He should have warned her, not let her learn it from one of Mme Louise's minions.

She ground her teeth. Mme Michelle said, "Is something bothering you Madame la Reine?"

"My thoughts annoy me. I am wasting my time. I shall write to Mme de Bussières."

"Does the measles outbreak lessen around Amboise? I worry about your son."

Anne's heart constricted. "In the letter I received this morning, Mme de Bussières said the disease was still rampant." Her hand tightened around the goose feather pen. "She said that Charles-Orland's doctors had written to the king that our son's court should move. She had just learned that Charles had refused, for the doctors travelling with him said Charles-Orland should stay where he is."

She bowed her head over the letter she had started, then turned toward Michelle, unable to restrain her frustration. "Why would he trust those men over the doctors who are with our son?"

~

WITH CHARLES ABOUT TO ARRIVE, another matter that had been troubling Anne since their soldiers had been trickling back to Lyon, now bothered her like a flea bite under her stays. She decided she could put it off no longer and promised herself she would confront her sister-in-law when she arrived for their regular afternoon visit.

Over the fourteen months they had lived under the same roof, Anne had observed her closely. Reluctantly, she came to admit that Madame la Grande knew how to manage men to get her own way. Anne often heard them complain she was masculine and bossy, but they thought her decisions astute, and often wily. As cunning as Old Louis, her father, they said, and they meant it as a compliment.

It still annoyed Anne that Charles had more confidence in his sister and her husband than in her. But she had discovered Charles did only what he wanted. Watching his sister, Anne learned that she was amazingly successful at persuading her brother that her ideas were really his.

But the thing that worried her now, was that no one was talking openly about the terrible pestilence the French soldiers were bringing back to France. Gossip was spreading but still there was no official acknowledgement. Both for her women and herself Anne wanted to know how much truth there was in the letter from Michelle's husband.

She asked her sister-in-law, "Have the camp followers who set out with the army returned to the permanent camp? And what about the husbands of your serving ladies?"

Madame la Grande said, "Some are slipping back, and they are reporting that many of their companions have died. I am attending to the many grieving widows in my household. I imagine it is the same with you."

"It has been becoming worse each month, Sister. I have promised to take in every Breton woman in Lyon whose husband died on this campaign. So many need help it keeps several of my secretaries busy." She raised the issue haunting her. "Some have died of battle wounds. But many more have died of a dreadful disease men are bringing back with them. They call it 'the Italian disease.' Yet you have said nothing more about it since I asked you earlier this summer. Is it true that it is a new plague?"

She observed Madame la Grande's reaction like a hawk as she spoke. Her sister-in-law dropped her eyes and thinned her lips. So, she *did* know.

A silence lengthened between them, until Madame la Grande sighed. "I have been hoping that it was not as bad as the first reports suggested, that it was a hysteria. But last week three doctors who travelled with the army arrived with a hospital wagon of men who are afflicted and brought two for Duke Pierre and me to see. Indeed, it is dreadful to look upon and the sufferers pitiable, although they are suffering from their own sins."

"I have been told it passes through sexual intimacy," Anne said. "What is the treatment? Is there a cure?" Her voice was sharper than she intended. What if Charles had contracted it?

Madame la Grande shook her head. "There is no known cure. Since it seems to pass only through sexual activities, the generals have banned all camp followers. They hang all—men and the doxies themselves—who disobey. But that leaves the infected women desperate and scattered along the road and they sell their bodies to any unsuspecting passerby, and so the plague spreads."

"But what about the infected men who come home? Wives are duty bound to submit to their husbands." When her sister-in-law looked pained but did not answer, Anne said bitterly, "Perhaps the widows are the fortunate women, after all."

~

Hôtel du Gouverneur, Lyon, 7 November 1495

DAWN HAD NOT YET BROKEN, yet Lyon was already stirring. An army of workers was sweeping the streets, throwing down fresh straw mixed with strong herbs, erecting city and royal banners, and cleaning city fountains of dead leaves and debris. Along the procession route, grand houses displayed tapestries from and flowers on their balconies, arrases from their windows, and clean steps to their entryways. As the light strengthened, the bells in the city churches began a continuous pealing and, in the streets, vendors wheeled their cars, touting their wares through the streams of citizens dressed in their best who arrived to line the route.

When the faint sounds of marching bands and choirs could be heard in the distance, Anne, Madame la Grande, their ladies, the Archbishop of Lyon and his acolytes came out onto the wide elegant balcony of the gouverneur's palace to join the celebration, waving to the crowd as they waited to cheer their victorious army.

Although the enthusiasm was infectious and the day sunny and cloudless, Anne felt distant from the excitement surrounding her. Tradition demanded that she see Charles for the first time in public, surrounded by his army and hundreds of celebrating citizens, all equally relieved to welcome their loved ones' home. He was France and a public figure first, as was she. This was their duty and destiny and she conformed, but she found it painful that her first sight of her husband would be in public.

People stood on tiptoe, leaned hands on the shoulders of those in front of them and strained their necks to see down the street. The approaching clamour of drums, bugles and singing mingled with the tramp of marching feet, and the clop clop of hooves but Anne did not move.

As the procession marched into view, the roars from the crowd, the showers of flower petals, blizzards of hats tossed into the air, and the marching band with blaring trumpets heralded the arrival of the victors. Then she saw them. The king and his most important generals and staff officers trotted along gleaming as brightly as their caparisoned horses. When she saw Charles, she thought perhaps he had grown—or mayhap his armour covered by a jewel-encrusted royal surcoat and golden helmet plumed with ostrich feathers made him appear so. Was this the triumph he had dreamed about when he was a boy, imagining himself a returning hero? Had this Italian adventure turned out to be the glorious quest he had imagined? From his jaunty carriage, she guessed he was in a wonderful mood, but it was impossible to know.

How would he have changed after all this time apart? Although she had written him, there had been much she could not safely say, for others read her letters. Worse, when she reread what she had written, how little the words conveyed of what she hoped to express. The letters she received from him were the words of others. She might know some small part of what he was doing, but nothing of what he thought or felt. Who had he become after all this time?

Later she sat beside Charles at the victory banquet in the Gubernatorial Palace, receiving his compliments along with those of the marshals and leaders of the expedition. She greeted the return of some—among them Duke Louis d'Orléans, Cardinal Briçonnet, Père André—with delight mingled with relief as she placed the gold chains that marked their service in the Neapolitan campaign upon their shoulders. When others came forward to receive their decorations, such as Marshal Pierre de Rohan, and Count Philippe de Bresse, Louise's father, she maintained the same decorum, but she was full of mistrust. *They certainly have no more love for me than I for them. De Gié, in particular, should watch himself. In his arrogance, he considers me harmless, like all women. One day, he will regret it.*

The banquet and dancing lasted well into the small hours as the Lyonnais celebrated, embodying all France's joy and relief that her men had returned.

But Anne did not look forward to the bedding that lay ahead.

CHAPTER 22

Lasting Sorrow

L'Hôtel Fort, 10 December 1495

Anne sat on a cushion playing *Primero*[1] with three of her ladies in her presence chamber. She could not concentrate on the cards, biting her nails and staring moodily out the windows during the pauses for betting. Since Charles had prevented her from leaving Lyon three days previously, she found these early afternoon hours between Sext[2] and Nones[3] the most difficult, for her son's health invaded her every thought.

About to play the card in her hand, she interrupted the game again when she heard booted feet in the corridor. When they stopped outside her apartments, she felt the blood drain from her face.

The sombre expressions on the faces of Charles and Madame la Grande when they entered sent her heart to her throat. Then Charles's face crumbled, his wails filled the room, and his shoulders shook as he staggered towards her, his blotched face swollen.

"It is Charles-Orland, is it not?" she whispered, rising awkwardly.

Madame la Grande stepped forward and took Anne's hands. "I am so sorry," she said. "He died on Saint Nicholas's Day."

Anne stared at her sister-in-law, unable to comprehend. Although she heard the words, at first, she could not take them in.

She repeated, "He is dead? He died on Saint Nicholas Day?"

As she said them, their meaning penetrated, and tears sprang to her eyes. Then Charles's arms enfolded her. She pulled away, unable to bear his touch. Turning her back to him, she wrapped her arms around her body as a great sob tore through her.

"Noooo." She sank to the ground as sobs deeper than any she had ever known ripped through her body. Her entire being gave itself over to grief and she rocked, hugging herself. From a great distance, she heard voices and from time to time she felt hands trying to lift her, but she shook them off. All she wanted was to be left alone.

Into the jumbled thoughts that had been plaguing her for months, she added a harsher refrain. *I should have been there. My son died without me. He did not know how much I love him. Some other woman held him, and he died without the comfort of his mother's arms. I should have been there. Other women had the joy of seeing him grow. Did he call for me when he lay ill? Did he suffer? No one could have cared for him as I would. I should have been there.* And the litany repeated.

After a time, she had to know more. *How had it happened? Was it the measles? Or had some other dire accident occurred? What had they done with his precious body?* Her sobs abated, and she struggled to get to her feet. At once, hands reached down, lifted her and led her to a chair. Through her burning eyes, she saw Mme Michelle, who handed her a cloth to dry her face and offered her a tankard of ale. Sniffling to control her tears, she glanced around. Michelle and the others stood nearby: Charles, Madame la Grande, Duke Pierre, and Queen Joanne.

"Tell me what happened." Her throat hurt to speak.

"Mme Bussières sent a letter. Shall I read it?" Madame la Grande answered.

Anne nodded.

Madame la Reine & Monsieur le Roi

I recommend myself most humbly to your majesties' good graces.

It is my most sorrowful duty to inform you that at sunset on Saint Nicholas Day, the 6th day of December, having received the last rites of Holy Church, your son and our dauphin, Charles-Orland, passed peacefully from this life.

As I had written to you, the dauphin had been ill with the measles for the past sennight. Despite all that his doctors and we, his nurses, could do for him; he steadily weakened. We obeyed the doctors' orders without question, but none of the bleedings, purging, or other remedies could prevent our beloved dauphin's decline. Throughout, he retained his sunny disposition, and we hoped for his recovery until the last day. Then the measles increased until they covered every part of his body, including the inside of his mouth, and his fever climbed higher and higher, although we bathed him in icy water.

At the end, he could no longer swallow any liquids. Then he found peace in the ministrations of his chaplain and the holy sacraments and sank into a peaceful, insentient state.

My husband, M. de Bussières, as his Gouverneur, has ensured he was embalmed and encoffined as his rank deserves and has interred him below the altar of Saint Florentin Chapel to await your return and decisions regarding his funeral and final disposition.

In the meantime, all those in the castle who have known and loved him will attend the funeral rites we shall hold on the third day after his death.

Sire and Madame, I offer you my deepest sympathy for your great loss and ours, and may God keep you in His holy care

Gouvernante de feu dauphin

Mme de Bussières

. . .

By the time her sister-in-law had finished reading the missive, tears again poured down Anne's face

"I felt his spirit come. . . to bid me farewell. . ." Anne choked and her voice broke, but she persisted. "I was praying to Saint Nicholas. . . to care for him. . . and my son's spirit came. The saint promised t-to care for him."

Tears still shook her, but she needed to act. "I must go to the chapel and order mourning masses."

Charles took her arm and this time, still paralyzed by the news of her son's passing, she did not reject him. When she patted his hand, his voice trembled. "Let me do this, Anne. I shall call my Great Almoner to discuss what the protocol should be, and then we shall come to you to make all the decisions together. Will that suit you, my love? For well I know I did not rush to Amboise as you wished and now. . . we shall never see our precious son alive again." Tears overflowed his eyes.

Anne bowed her head. It did not lessen her grief, but at least he acknowledged what he knew she believed. "Yes, that will be good. Now I shall go to the chapel. . . if you give me leave, milord."

She could not resist the jab; she wanted Charles to have no doubt that she would have been with their son if not for his orders. Staring at the door, she waited with her hands folded until he received her message and left with his sister and brother-in-law.

When they had gone, she buried her face in her hands for a moment. Taking a deep breath, she looked up at Mme Michelle and Queen Joanne.

"Thank you, my friends. I need to wash my face now. Queen Joanne, will you come with me to the chapel? I beg you, Mme Michelle, to inform my ladies of the details of our loss." She tightened her lips as tears rolled down her cheeks again. "I will need mourning attire. Can you arrange that? Any black cloth will do for the nonce, but they are to make up gowns in silks, brocades and fine wools for the year of mourning. If you could have a sempstress to fit me when I return to my rooms."

Queen Joanne walked by her side to the chapel. Anne took her arm. "You comfort me."

~

THE DAYS PASSED, but Anne's grieving did not lessen, although Charles recovered quickly. He came to her bed each night for comfort and seemed to find it in physical release. For her, their coupling was a duty that she submitted to as the Church required. True to his word, they made the funeral arrangements for the dauphin together with the Archbishop of Lyon. Anne wanted his obsequies to be as elaborate as those for every dauphin, with weeks of mourning masses throughout the kingdom before he was laid to rest, but she fought against his interment in the Basilica de Saint Denis as Charles wished, insisting she needed to visit her son's tomb frequently.

Charles also stipulated that the funeral services must be completed before the beginning of the twelve days of Christmas —by Christmas Eve at the latest. After Anne became so hysterical her doctors feared for her sanity, they compromised. Charles agreed to bury their son in the cathedral in Tours and she accepted that the interment would occur the day before Christmas Eve.

"It is not right that we fail to celebrate the birth of our Lord," he said. "As monarchs, it is our duty to our country. That must take precedence over our private sorrow. But we shall return to Amboise." He took her hands and smiled at her as if his paltry compromise were a recompense for the hasty burial of her beloved child.

He left to her the responsibility for resolving all the problems surrounding their rushed return to Amboise, as he resumed his obsessive involvement with Naples.

When she saw Charles next, he sat with his head in his hands, sunk in gloom. Thinking to share his anguish, she probed.

"It is another disaster," Charles grieved. "I have just learned that in Naples my cousin, Gilbert de Montpensier, has been captured *and* the *Castel Nuovo* has fallen to the Spanish. Worse, that usurper, Ferrandino, has been reinstated as king."

Anne inhaled through her nose, at a loss for words to express her rising fury at the desolation in his voice.

He bleated on, "Despite my *explicit* orders, my army in Naples was insufficiently reinforced and resupplied, or so the messenger—"

Anne broke in. "We have just lost our only son, whom we have not seen for over eighteen months! Who was the dauphin of France! And you are whining and moaning about the fall of a paltry Italian pile of rock? What is the *matter* with you?" With that, she stormed off.

1 Primero—a Renaissance card game that has many similarities to modern day poker.

2 Sext—noon, traditionally 12:00 p.m.

3 Nones—the ninth hour, traditionally 3:00 p.m.

CHAPTER 23

News Travels Fast

Château de Cognac, December 1495—January 1496

As the church bells in Cognac began tolling, the local priest came to tell Louise they announced the passing of the dauphin. Louise sought the Château chapel at once. Kneeling on the cold stone floor in front of the altar on which the priest had already placed lit candles to mark the grievous news, she bowed her head and offered a quick penitential prayer for having doubted Friar Francis.

Then she considered the effect of the dauphin's death on her family. As the holy friar had promised, the Lord had brought her son one step closer to the throne. She did not dare pray that the king and queen would have no more sons, but she did not regret that Charles-Orland had died. It was God's will, after all. One could not question God's will. Now Carlo's cousin, Duke Louis d'Orléans, was dauphin again. It was time to foster closer relations with him and his crippled wife.

On that thought, she rose and went to see Carlo. She found

him in his library. Soon they were discussing their arrangements to attend the funeral.

"I must attend but you need not. I shall set out as soon as I learn where it is to be held," Carlo said.

Louise contemplated the possibility. "But what about the Christmas court? Will you attend? I must serve my time as lady-in-waiting from Candlemas until Lady Day and how I hate the idea of leaving the children."

"If we attend the dauphin's funeral and Christmas court together, I will arrange with the king to postpone your court service until next year," Carlo said.

"Then let us do that." Louise kissed his cheek, grateful to avoid six weeks of subservience to the woman she detested.

Countess Marguerite sat before the fire in the solar, blowing on her fingers in their half gloves. "It is so unwise of you to depart in this weather." She hugged her shawl tighter, inched her stool closer to the flames and raised her voice. "Louise! Are you listening to me?"

"Maman Marguerite, I regret the necessity as much as you. I wish it were not so, but you know we must. King Charles—and Queen Anne especially—will never forgive us if we do not attend the dauphin's funeral." Louise perspired in her layers of travelling clothes—a long-sleeved linen shift, high-necked kirtle, and woollen overdress—topped by a felted wool cape lined with squirrel fur. "Carlo has placed heated bricks inside the carriage, and we will reheat them at each change." She pulled on fur mittens. "I promise we will travel only during daylight hours, which at this time of year will mean lengthening our trip by several days but will keep us and our horses safe."

Going to her mother-in-law's side, she kissed on her on the forehead. "You must know I do not want to leave you, my sweet daughter, or my precious César, especially at this Christmas season. We will return as soon as possible. But I must go."

"The king can do well enough without Carlo. I need my son more than he does and besides, he is not well. He wrote that he was abed with a catarrh for a fortnight after Michaelmas and his chest has always been weak." The Dowager Countess huddled closer to the fire, clutched a mug of hot cider, and shivered as a gust rattled the wooden shutters. "He should not travel in this cold. My old bones tell me it will snow before nightfall, for it is unseasonably cold even for December."

Hiding her impatience, Louise leaned down and hugged her. "I shall send Carlo up to say his farewells before we set off."

She was as good as her word. As she waited for him, she checked that their carriage contained the comforts to help pass the day. Then she took a brisk walk around the courtyard, for she did not relish being cooped up for the hours ahead. The heavy sky loomed, and she wondered if her mother-in-law might be right that it would snow. It looked dark enough.

Carlo reappeared, and they climbed into their iron-wheeled conveyance driven by three sturdy pairs. Their convoy made a din in the silent countryside. Louise had limited their company to a minimum for their first day's journey. Four carriages followed with their personal attendants, four additional wagons contained the clothing, household goods and furnishings they required along the way, and a guard of twenty-four travelled with them for protection on the journey.

The first few hours passed pleasantly enough. Because of his mother's comments, Carlo's hacking cough worried Louise, but it was dry, and he got cross when she mentioned it. Their feet resting on heated firebricks enclosed in cast-iron boxes swathed in thick felt, and themselves wrapped in blankets they played chess and cards, read to each other, picnicked on cold meats and bread, and napped.

Louise awoke abruptly, disoriented and shocked. Something

smothered her, blocking her sight. She shoved as hard as she could, trying to scream, but her mouth was full of fabric. Then she heard Carlo's voice and, as her senses returned; it came to her that Carlo was straddled half over her. She stopped struggling as he shifted. Some of his weight eased from her body, and she could breathe again. She still lay in a heap, her back against the seat of the carriage on which she had been sitting. The carriage front rose at a sharp angle above her and shuddered as if in a high wind. Outside, horses and men screamed. Feeling Carlo shift beside her, she turned her head toward him.

The yelling and shouting of men and the shrieking of terrified horses continued unabated outside.

"Louise, are you hurt?" Her husband's voice cracked.

"Carlo! You are bleeding!"

"Louise, do not move."

"What happened?"

The longer Carlo still leaned on Louise, the heavier he felt. Her back hurt as he pushed her against the base of the seat. Someone needed to take control of the frightful racquet outside and the jerky movements of their vehicle before it was too late.

"Can you move, Carlo?"

"I am trying." Most of the weight that had still been crushing her lightened. She could move her head enough to watch him claw himself upward to grab a leather strap.

"Grab my hand, Louise."

As they shifted their weight to the back, their carriage tilted forward with a jerk until it was almost level. They heard a cheer from outside and someone on Carlo's side tried to wrench the carriage door open. That was when Louise noticed its frame had twisted.

"Help me!" Louise recognized Jean de Saint Gelais's voice. The next moment, the door popped open, and several men grunted and fell backwards. Cheers mingled with sigh of relief.

"Thank the Blessed Virgin that She has averted a disaster," Louise said as she scrambled from the damaged carriage.

Their problems were far from over, though. The first few

planks of the bridge across the river had collapsed as the lead pair of horses stepped onto it. Some of the carters had scrambled down and now reported only they and a couple more were rotten. If they were replaced, the bridge would be usable.

They all gave thanks to their Saviour that the banks of the stream had not been steep, so the horses had survived, but the lead horses had bucked and sprained their tendons. They would need special care, and what Carlo would do with them was a decision for later. Right now, the grooms were calming the remaining horses. The skilled men among the entourage must repair the carriage sufficiently to make it usable, rearrange and hitch the horses into teams again, and the bedraggled convoy must make it to the closest village. To make matters worse, it started to snow.

Carlo handled the catastrophe with an aplomb that made Louise proud. Since they were still within his lands, he knew everyone and every hamlet, and he took charge with authority yet without arrogance. It took several hours to sort out their many problems, but he was methodical. He sent for men to salve and wrap the injured horses' legs and take them to the nearest stables. Carters arrived to take the carriage for repairs, and masons and carpenters came with tools and materials to fix the damaged bridge. By the time all was sorted, it was dark, and Carlo had been outside in the wet, cold weather for five hours. A nearby peasant offered them his family's smoky cottage for the night and crowded into his neighbour's. Louise did not complain aloud, for everyone else shivered inside the travel tents they set up swiftly and kept warm with fires built from whatever dry wood they could salvage.

By MORNING, Carlo's dry cough had turned phlegmy.

Shivering in her heavy, damp clothing reeking of smoke, Louise reluctantly suggested they return to Cognac. "When we learn that the court has arrived at Amboise, you can set out with a small company and ride fast. We will send a courier ahead to explain," she suggested, mindful of her mother-in-law's fears.

"My cousin would take it ill," Carlo replied after a bout of coughing. "Besides, if you attend the funeral and the Christmas Court, we will not lose you to the queen's service."

She was relieved to let him convince her for she hated leaving her children and only enjoyed the court for the gossip.

"Today I shall ride," he said. "Take Lady Anne in the carriage with you."

"But Carlo, your cough already sounds terrible. And look at the clouds. It will snow soon."

"Do not fuss me, Louise. I will not go through another day like yesterday. If I had been riding, I am sure the accident would never have occurred. I would have seen the bridge would not hold us."

When he spoke in that tone, Louise knew there was no point arguing. But she could not hide her relief when they arrived before the storm at their own manor in Chateauneuf-sur-Charente that evening.

Although people crowded every space in the manor—attics, outbuildings and stables—everyone found a warm place to sleep that night. The next morning, Carlo's cough was worse, and he was hot to the touch, but he insisted on rising. He spent the day tramping around with the seneschal discussing the repairs needed before winter set in for good, as well as law cases that he needed to review or rule upon.

By evening, he no longer had an appetite and did not argue when Louise insisted he retire to their bedchamber. She ordered a fire built up in the massive fireplace and called their doctor to him. After the physician permitted them to wait until the following day for a bloodletting, she prepared a mustard pack for his chest and gave him a draught of opium-laced cough syrup to send him into a deep sleep. He tossed and turned, moaning in his dream-induced slumber, and awoke heavy-eyed and hoarse. Nor did he object when she pointed out that the mix of snow and freezing rain made travel perilous and that another day of rest would benefit everyone in the party. The bloodletting weakened him, and his throat hurt, so he ate nothing more than broths and drank the herbal teas she persuaded him to swallow.

Louise nursed him day and night. He was necessary to her place in life, and she did everything in her power to restore him to health, sleeping on a pallet beside their bed, dozing when he did, bathing his burning body, adding layers of blankets as he shook and complained of cold, and applying her herbal skills to prepare remedies. Morning and evening, she and the physician consulted about his symptoms and treatments.

Nothing helped. Day by day he worsened, coughing up phlegm that went from greenish to murky yellow and then bright with blood. It pained her to watch him arch his back in pain as he coughed, and the shallow rise and fall of his chest, and laboured breathing. He fell more and more often into delirium. From a ruddy warrior, he melted into a yellow skeleton before her eyes.

As the days passed, Louise made the practical arrangements. One messenger she sent to his mother saying they were staying in Angoulême because Carlo was ill. She sent back half their entourage to ease the crowding in the manor and dispatched another messenger to Amboise to excuse them from attending the funeral and Christmas court because of Carlo's serious condition. She wondered if the queen believed her.

Carlo's steady wasting away despite her ever more desperate efforts brought back nightmare memories of the time when her mother lay dying, and she had been powerless to help. Shunted aside by the adults who took no notice of her, she had hidden in the dark corners of her mother's room as nurses, doctors, Maman's attendants, her Papa and finally the priest came and went whispering together, plying Maman with treatments that made her cry and moan and emit foul stenches. Although Maman begged them to let her die in peace, they pinched her nose until she opened her mouth and stroked her throat until she gagged. Louise stuffed her skirts into her mouth so no one could hear her sob as she hid. The memory of that helplessness surfaced as she dozed near her husband, powerless again. She needed him to protect her and her children from the men who would want to control her life when he was gone. Her own tears awoke her more than once. How she hated to show such weakness.

St. Sylvester's Eve, 31 December 1495, she could no longer deny the obvious. Her husband would not survive this attack. Calling his valet, she sent him to bring the priest and the sacraments to hear Carlo's last confession and administer the last rites. She would ask him to stay for the night, for Carlo would want him by his side.

After the valet left, she went to her husband's side. He was dozing but awoke when she touched his face.

"Louise." His voice was thick, and he had to stop to take a shallow breath. "You have blessed me with your care. I love you," He smiled at her. Lipless, and wheezing, he did not resemble the charming man she married.

Although she shuddered, she knew his words came from his heart. Blocking her nose against his stink, she bent and kissed his brow wanting to shout, *Don't leave us. We still need your protection.*

Instead, she said, "I love you too, dear Carlo. I have sent for the priest. Will you allow me to wash you and change your night shift?"

"It is time, then?" Tears sprang to his eyes. He tried to lift an arm but could not. "Thank you, yes." It was a whisper.

She left the room while the priest conducted Carlo's last confession. Her eyes adjusted to the dark of the corridor that was lit only by a single torch on the wall. Now she breathed the sharp, cold air outside the bedchamber for the first time in over a sennight, heard the creaks of the old building, and the faint murmurs of voices through the door. Everything felt strange, as if the world had become a different place while she had been incarcerated inside Carlo's chamber. She prepared herself to face it. It was a relief when the priest opened the door and called her back in.

"Say your final goodbyes," he instructed her, "and then I shall say a mass."

Louise took his last whispered messages for his mother, children, and even his mistresses. Then she sat by him and held his hand as the priest prayed.

She kept her mind rigidly on the words of the mass until she heard the death rattle from Carlo's congested lungs. For a time, she continued to hold his hand before crossing herself, rising, and gently pulling the sheet over Carlo's lifeless form. Then she thanked his chaplain, who had drawn a cross on Carlo's forehead the moment before she covered his lifeless eyes.

"I will have some of our men take his body to the chapel for embalming now," she said. "The carpenters have worked all night to ready a rough coffin. We will leave tomorrow to bring him back to Cognac. I must bring him to his mother. And I must dispatch another courier to the king informing him of his cousin's death."

The priest drew a cross on her forehead. "Daughter, you did everything a wife and nurse could do and more. Return home and grieve, as we shall here, for a kind and generous lord."

Louise focused her eyes on her husband's body, but her thoughts moved forward to the future. They came to rest on her son, the pivot of her universe. He was now Count d'Angoulême. She rolled the words in the mouth, savouring their richness: Count François d'Angoulême, Second Prince of the Blood. One step closer to his destiny. It was some comfort in this adversity. That led her to think about the queen who had just lost her little Charles-Orland.

She imagined that, like her, Anne would rather have lost her husband than her son. If that had happened, Anne would be regent at this moment. Louise thanked God for his mercy. To bow to Anne and her son when Friar Francis had promised that Anne would bow to François. . . it did not bear thinking of. Louise shuddered. Yet it could still happen.

CHAPTER 24

The Christmas Court

Château d'Amboise, December 1495

After Charles handed Anne into her carriage when they left Lyon, he told her he planned a lavish Christmas Court at Amboise. "I have informed my vassals I wish to thank them for their munificent support. It permitted us to conquer the Kingdom of Naples." Then he hurried away before she could turn, as if to escape her response.

She managed to restrain her anger until she had pulled closed the curtains inside the vehicle. December now stretched before her like a penitential season. She could not imagine presiding over twelve days and nights of festivities, that began the day after she buried her only child.

As each day drew them closer to her destination, Anne became more reclusive, retiring to the chamber assigned to her and her ladies and leaving it only to return to her jolting carriage the next morning. Propped in the darkened interior she alternately replayed her regrets about her failure to care for her departed son or dreaded the forthcoming festivities over which she must preside.

The journey took eight days, and by the time their unwieldy convoy arrived in Amboise, she felt more grief-stricken than when she had left. Girding herself, she comforted all those who had cared for Charles-Orland during his brief life and last days, then braced herself to visit his apartments. In a daze, she shuffled about his rooms as if in a shrine, touching the relics of his too-brief life, until she came to his bed. Then the dam she had constructed so carefully broke.

In floods of tears, she fled to her room and donned a hair shirt[1] next to her skin under her black mourning and knelt at her prie-dieu[2] as distraught as the first day she had learned of her son's death. In the days that followed, the depth of her desolation grew. Everything she saw offered a temptation to end her misery. Her dinner knife invited her to trip and fall with it upright in her hand to pierce her heart. Her Venetian glass goblet whispered she should sink into a faint, crushing it as she fell, to slash her wrists. As she walked on the battlements, she leaned as far out as she could through the crenels and looked down at the people, who looked as tiny as dolls. Then she imagined her feet slipping and herself falling. The urge to lean forward that little more almost overwhelmed her. Pulling herself back abruptly, she hastened to her apartments and did not leave them until the morning of the funeral except to attend every mass, day and night, in the chapel. Unwilling to be seen, she flitted like a wraith, hugging the corridor walls. Each day she became thinner until her ladies and physicians feared she would die of starvation.

~

24 December, Evening

On Christmas Eve, her confessor came to speak to her as she stole away after Matins.[3] "Dear daughter in Christ, you have attended every mass since your beloved son died. You must rest more! Promise me you will not return for Lauds,[4] for tomorrow is the day we honour our Lord's birth with feasting and celebratory masses." He spoke in a tone that she recognized brooked no refusal.

"How can I celebrate the birth of a baby when mine has just died?" She kept her head lowered, refusing to meet his eyes.

"Madame la Reine, you are not yourself. You have become maddened in your grief." Crossing himself, he knelt beside the queen and took her hands. "Dear daughter in Christ, you blaspheme against your Saviour in your grief. Do not open yourself to sin."

His reproof stung and Anne did not respond.

Raising his voice, he said, "If you do not answer, Madame la Reine, I shall go to the archbishop. I recognize your anguish. But you indulge yourself in obstinate despair, and it is a mortal sin."

Anne lifted her head to glare at him. "If the Lord is not to blame, then I am, for I did not go to my son when he needed me. I excused myself saying my husband forbade me, but I did not insist. I was a coward, Père. I failed him." Her frail body shook with wrenching sobs.

Her confessor hesitated a moment. Then he gathered her into his arms as a father would and patted her back as if she were an infant. She flinched and forced herself to stop sobbing so she could pull away.

"Enough," he said, once her tears ceased. "You must forgive the Lord and yourself, child. I am giving you a penance you will find hard. On your knees then."

After she obeyed, he drew a cross in the air.

"You will not attend the night hour masses but stay abed. Daily, when you arise, you will allow your maids to cleanse your body and attire you in fresh clothing. From the way you flinched, I suspect you wear a hair shirt?" When she nodded, he said, "You may no longer wear it. You may continue to wear mourning, but you must attire yourself as a queen, return to your regular schedule, and present yourself at the court's Yule festivities beside the king, as is your duty. You may attend only two masses a day. The king worries about you, as does everyone at court."

Anne shook her head. "I cannot. You ask too much."

He lay his hand on her head, saying nothing. The silence lengthened.

Anne had used the technique of silence herself and believed she could outlast anyone. She was wrong. "I am too weak," she whispered finally. "I will weep before everyone."

"If you do, your courtiers will forgive you. But it is time to return to your duties. Would you require less of them? Remember, this is a penance, Madame la Reine, not a choice. I impose it for three months."

Anne sighed and nodded her bowed head. A dutiful daughter of Holy Church, once her confessor imposed her penance, she obeyed.

The Christmas festivities tried her, but her court training and sense of duty permitted her to tolerate the endless hours of repetitive conversations, feasting, dancing, and sumptuous pageantry. She forced herself to concentrate on the meaning of Christ's miraculous story as she walked with the court in the processions that celebrated each event from the Annunciation to the Adoration of the Magi. In the evenings, she smiled through mock battles where brave knights saved damsels in distress; musical evenings; and endless poetry and story readings.

She forced down dozens of traditional delicacies: from enormous fish and minced meat pies to boar's head stuffed with layers of savouries and sweet fruits, to roasted peacocks in full plumage, and roast goose glazed with gold leaf. The marzipan and honeyed dates, figs stewed in sweet wine, and crystallized ginger, she downed with the wine brought from all regions of France, but all of it tasted like dust to her. These activities did not allow her to dwell on her grief, and slowly the dark cloud, under which she had lived, lightened. That black place within her, filled with evil voices that told her that her life possessed no value, had terrified her. It was a relief that her penance banished them.

~

4 January 1496

WRAPPED in a long ermine cape lined with white velvet, Anne stood with the ladies of the court on the long balcony overlooking the ancient *fosse*, the old dry moat that served now as the Amboise training fields. A rowdy game of pelote was underway between one team led by King Charles, and another by Duke Louis. Most of the ladies were cheering on their favourites on one or other of the opposing teams. Deafened by the cheers and laughter of the younger demoiselles, Anne rued her inability to share their delight in the event. Although she was but nineteen, and little older than most of them, she no longer counted herself young, for she felt as old as Sarah, mother of Saint John the Baptist.

Shouts from the playing field drew Anne's eyes and she observed the contest with displeasure. The players punched, kicked and whacked the moss-filled leather ball with a curved stick up and down the field as they assaulted one another in their drive to get the ball over the other team's goal line. They did not seem to care who or what they smacked with their sticks; anything was permitted, it was a vicious free-for-all. The contestants did not wear armour or carry arms, the game's only saving grace, in Anne's opinion. Was it not sufficient that these noblemen had done their best to kill themselves in Italy? Must they also destroy one another out on the slippery field?

Turning her head as little as possible, she checked to see who surrounded her. The mud on the bottom of her new cape caught her eye. It would be difficult to remove, and she felt irritated once again that she and her ladies had to walk through the slush to this old tumbledown part of the Château, scrabble through a dirty corridor littered with animal droppings, and freeze, all to watch men flaunting their love of violence.

Under cover of a sudden uproar, she took Mme Michelle's arm. "I will move towards the exit when the bells sound Nones," she murmured. "Follow me. Let no one stop me."

In a few minutes, they sidled towards the low doorway. Each woman whose eye she caught condoled with her until she felt as raw as the day of the funeral service. Had it been a fortnight already?

Her sister-in-law, Madame la Grande, poked her long nose into Anne's departure by stepping in front of her, as if she could read her thoughts and prevent her escape. She might have succeeded, but for Queen Catherine of Navarre, Anne's cousin. Her sudden shriek distracted Madame la Grande enough for Anne to slip away. She had almost made it to the doorway when Duchess Jeanne d'Orléans, Duke Louis's wife, spoke to her.

Without stopping, Anne clutched her sister-in-law's arm and drew her along. "I leave to attend mass," she said to Duchess Jeanne. "I doubt I will have another opportunity this day."

They limped together through the low doorway, both short enough they barely had to bend their necks to pass under it without hitting their heads into the smelly corridor beyond.

"If you do not object, I shall accompany you." Duchess Jeanne patted her arm. "My heart shares your sorrow, and I would share your prayers." Her musical voice was low and sweet. Tears sprang to Anne's eyes and she assented.

As they crossed to the chapel, Jeanne added, "My brother made it known to my lord husband that he wished my presence. I agreed so I could pray with you." She raised her eyes to Anne's before dropping them again. "Although I have never lost a child, I imagine often how the Virgin suffered while She waited with Her Son as He hung on the Cross. And I grieve for loss of my nephew, our dauphin, and the brave young boy who loved life. I have ordered a year of masses said at Blois for his soul." She swallowed; the sound harsh, as if trying to force down dry bread. "It is a sad season. I pray also for the soul of our cousin, Carlo. It will be a hard, lonely time for Cousin Louise and her two young children."

Sensing Anne stiffen, she withdrew her arm and went on, "I worry for Cousin Louise. It is a heavy burden to carry so young. A widow at twenty, with a mother-in-law to care for, two young children, and a son close to the throne. Many men will try to wrest control of the boy from her."

Anne had not expected this astute observation from her self-effacing sister-in-law. She considered Louise's loss. The death of her husband left her vulnerable, as Jeanne said. Since she was under legal age, it was almost certain she would be forced to cede the governorship of her children to another. *But at least Louise has children to comfort her*, the wicked voice of envy spoke in her heart. Why does the Lord bless that wicked woman and not me? Though Anne rebuked herself for her unchristian thought, the serpent of jealousy writhed in her belly. She ought to be more like Duchess Jeanne who did not bemoan her own difficult fate but concerned herself about Louise and her future.

"Who has become the countess's guardian?" Anne asked.

"My husband, as Carlo's closest male cousin. He is fond of Louise and her children and will probably invite them to live at Blois. It will please me if he does, for I will enjoy the children and what a delight it will be to have the company of Louise, for we share an interest in books and music."

Anne's heart went out to the lonely woman isolated at Blois by the animosity of her husband. It made her angry with Duke Louis. It was not Jeanne's fault that her father had forced the duke to marry her. Her father had also forced *her* to marry Duke Louis, who was an unkind and unfaithful husband.

"How do you keep yourself busy at Blois?" she asked. "Please forgive me for not asking sooner."

Jeanne laughed, the sound as true as a silver chime. "Do not apologize, Sister. We have spent little time in each other's company. I am content at Blois. Louis leaves the administration of our estates to me, a duty I enjoy. I have my ladies, my books, my music and my devotions." Her face shone. "The Lord is my shepherd, and Holy Mother Mary speaks to me. My solitude is precious, for I am with them."

Hearing the contentment in Jeanne's voice, envy consumed Anne, followed by shame that she should begrudge Louis's unloved, crippled wife her serenity and faith. Tears rose to her eyes at this latest sin. Would she ever rid herself of the evil thoughts that pursued her like swarms of angry bees, buzzing relentlessly in her head?

1 Hair shirt—a shirt or shift made of rough animal hair worn by ascetics and penitents next to the skin as a penance.

2 prie-dieu—a piece of furniture for use during prayer, consisting of a kneeling surface and a narrow upright front with a rest for the elbows or for books.

3 Matins—nighttime, traditionally 12:00 a.m.

4 Lauds—early morning, traditionally 3:00 a.m.

CHAPTER 25
Nothing to Celebrate

Château d'Amboise, 6 January 1496

It was Epiphany, the last day of Christmas, and Charles insisted Anne attend every Three Kings Day celebration. Her thoughts gave her no peace, but she complied with her husband's wishes. In a small act of rebellion, she wore a black French hood adorned with black pearls. Today, when the world celebrated the arrival of the kings who announced to the world the birth of its Saviour, she would not deny that she mourned. Charles could force her to attend the festivities, he could not make her enjoy them.

She joined him in the great council hall which today was being used for the morning meal. As she stood in the large stone entrance surrounded by her ladies, Charles caught sight of her and crossed the floor to take her arm, jauntiness in every step. As they made their way to their seats at the high table on the dais, he had cheerful greetings for everyone. Anne strained to keep a smile pasted to her lips, sourly reflecting that he lived up to his sobriquet of 'the affable.'

The room hummed with the same excitement that Anne felt crackling throughout the building. The great hall was closed to all but those who prepared the evening entertainment, but everywhere the Château bustled with preparations, and the enticing aromas of food and drink floated in the air.

Madame la Grande, Duke Pierre, and Duchess Jeanne joined them at the high table, and Charles jumped up to kiss his sisters.

"It was generous of Duke Louis to take upon himself the entire preparation of our celebration this evening," Charles said to his sister, Jeanne. "He begged the honour of organizing the Twelfth Night festivity."

Anne saw her sister-in-law answer, but her thoughts drowned out Jeanne's words. It was just Duke Louis's way to draw attention to his status as dauphin; the position he had finally regained. When he had conducted her to Langeais, Louis had boasted of being dauphin and sounded aggrieved that she would deprive him of his position. Now that Charles-Orland was dead, he had regained it and was mocking her and the king for failing to guard their heir. The gloom that had enveloped Anne since she woke thickened, until the words around her seemed muffled, to her relief.

Charles's voice broke into her thoughts, though he spoke to his sisters. "I believe this is his effort to cheer up the queen. I told him I was worried about Anne's health and the depth of her mourning." He took Anne's hand and gave her an arch look. "I have not forgotten nor have my sisters that he was a suitor for your hand when your father was still alive. He admires you, for he told me so and said you were as strong as the walls of Saint Malo and as loyal as a guard dog."

Anne gave him a strained smile. How tactless of Charles to bring up that time when Louis was a rebel against the crown trying to divorce Jeanne. Her mind scurried to a darker place. Or was he implying that she was being disloyal?

Charles was off again, reckoning up the scale of the duke's

provisioning for the festivity. "Twenty-four hogsheads each of wine and ale; five-hundred *livres* of wax candles, 50 *livres* of pepper, 2 *livres* of saffron, 100 *livres* of almonds and 300 *livres* of sugar in cones, and. . .and quantities of *other* spices." He tallied the supplies on his fingers.

"That is but the beginning: 10,000 salted eels in barrels, 200 live pigs, and 1,000 young hens." He turned to his sister again. "He must have stripped Blois bare, for my Maître d'hôtel told me he has also supplied hundreds of napkins, and dozens of linens brought from your home as well as your pastry chefs with all the supplies to prepare, fill and bake 500 galettes de roi."1

Jeanne smiled and nodded as the king rattled on. Madame la Grande gave her a sharp glance. When Charles turned to speak to her husband, she winked at Anne and asked her younger sister, "Did Louis really organize all that? I suspect he left it to you, did he not?"

Anne recalled Jeanne saying that Louis left the administration to her, as the Duchess put a finger to her lips, and said, "I would never take my husband's credit."

~

Twelfth Night Celebration, After Vespers

THE COURTIERS MILLING in the outer chamber opened a path to allow Anne and Charles to pass through to the entrance of the great hall where Duke Louis and Duchess Jeanne awaited them. Anne noticed that the duke had dressed richly for once, in velvets and silks—like a king. Over his fine linen shirt, he wore a tightly fitted, short doublet in embroidered silk with contrasting breeches of velvet slashed with silk that matched the doublet.

Obedient to her chaplain, Anne wore a white kirtle heavily embroidered with fleurs de lys[2] and ermines under her silk overdress, and her sleeves were slashed with white. A gold necklace strung with white pearls hung in the square neck, but her French hood was solid black. Nothing could hide the gaunt hollows in her cheeks and the dark shadows under her eyes. Madame la Grande and Duke Pierre followed the royal couple with Queen Catherine of Navarre between them.

A fanfare sounded and, with a flourish, the Grand Maître des Ceremonies threw open the double doors that had been firmly sealed since the night before. Wafts of spicy air greeted them as the royal party, led by the Duke and Duchess d'Orléans, stopped just inside the threshold to admire the pastoral paradise that had been created in the lofty chamber.

Even Anne, whose mood had not improved, approved of the transformation. Pine and cedar trees, their branch tips glittered with gold and silver, stood in pots and fresh greenery hung high on the walls brightening the hall. Colourful strings of holly berries in shades of red festooned their branches. The circular chandeliers, now twined with green-leafed holly and shiny berries cast a warm light from their thick wax candles. An entire tree trunk burned in the width of the massive fireplace, adding its pine fragrance to the pinecones, juniper berries and dried laurel leaves placed in pots around the chamber.

On either side of the great portals, pages stood ready to offer tankards of wassail[3] and portions of galette de roi[1] as each guest entered. When they served the royal party, the King teased Duke Pierre and Queen Catherine, warning them to eat carefully for they would not want to swallow the special porcelain miniatures that identified the king and queen for the evening and miss their chance to rule France. All but Anne joined in the raillery. Instead, she gazed around at the decorations, her expression vacant.

As they proceeded further into the vast room, minstrels entered from the sides and strolled about the hall singing and playing as courtiers flooded in. When she was close enough to view the seating arrangements for the feast, Anne felt irritated. At the far end of the hall, a dais had been raised in front of the fireplace and the head table placed on it facing the great doors through which they had entered. Placed perpendicular to it, long tables covered with tablecloths awaited the guests. In the centre of the dais, Charles's and her thrones sat under their cloths of estate. On royal purple cushions, in front of each throne lay a golden crown covered with paste jewels and a silver sceptre. No other thrones sat on the dais. To Anne, it was obvious; the evening's royal couple were to usurp their places.

A second fanfare sounded. The Grand Maître requested the lucky guests who had received the miniature king and queen in their galette to step forward. When Duke Louis stepped into the centre and bowed, laughter, clapping, and whistling broke out. Anne did not join in. She was convinced, and she imagined everyone agreed, that the recipients of the miniatures had been decided beforehand. *So, not satisfied with being dauphin, he is ready to take my husband's crown!*

She felt her husband's eyes on her unsmiling face as he applauded. *Why was he not annoyed? He should be.* The noise and clapping abated, then surged again as Queen Catherine de Navarre, blushing and laughing, stepped forward with the miniature queen in her outstretched hand.

Charles pulled Anne forward by the arm to congratulate the pair. Then he took Queen Catherine's arm and she had to take Duke Louis's. They led the evening's king and queen up onto the dais, to the royal thrones and invited them to seat themselves under the cloths of estate. A page stepped forward to hand first Anne, then Charles the regalia and they crowned the evening's king and queen. Anne made short work of plopping the crown on Louis's head and handing him the sceptre. Charles made quite a ceremony of it, laughing himself and inviting the crowd of courtiers to bow and curtsey to the new rulers. Then Charles seated himself beside Queen Catherine.

"Already dissatisfied with your rank as dauphin?" Anne sneered, as she took her place beside Louis. "You already crave my husband's place as king?"

Louis shot her a pained look. He hesitated a moment, then

replied, "Madame la Reine, the only pleasure I could hope for, were I so unfortunate as to find myself in the king's place, would be the good fortune of having his wife." His tone was light.

Anne felt herself turn hot. How dare he pretend this was all a jest. "You forget yourself."

He gripped her hand, and spoke low, "Sister Anne, I meant to offer you a compliment. If it sounded insulting to your ears, please believe no offence was intended."

This conversation must not continue. "I accept your apology." She pulled her hand away. How dare he take Charles's place upon his throne, pretending it was a nothing but a jape?

She became more and more annoyed as Duke Louis embraced his role as king for the evening. With a flick of the hand, he ordered the fanfare that heralded the first remove of the evening's banquet. An army of pages entered carrying enormous platters. Roast boar, richly glazed with gilded apples in their mouths, bowls of vegetables, soups, fruits, pasties and all manner of drinks circulated, and guests filled their plates and cups. In the minstrel gallery, an orchestra played lively Italian music.

After the first remove, Duke Louis rose and clapped his hands. In ran acrobats, tumblers, jugglers, and fire breathers, who performed breathtaking acts and received prizes from the Queen for the Day as they departed. Another wave of the Duke's hand, another fanfare, another parade of pages with the next remove. It was another excess: pies filled with eels, fish and venison; pies filled with small birds; pies of leeks and turnips; pies with medleys of spiced berries and fruits. As if that weren't enough, more pages brought platters of fresh oranges, peeled nuts, and vats of sweet, mulled wine. What did Duke Louis intend with this extravagant display?

From the dais, the duke ordered the lower tables removed and he returned to the centre of the hall to announce the evening's principal entertainment.

"Getting rid of us," Anne said to Charles, "so he can continue as the centre of attention."

"Really, Anne," Charles sounded exasperated. "Can you take no pleasure in it?" He frowned at her, looked ready to say something, stopped, and strolled away, leaving her to brood alone.

Louis announced they would receive a visit from the three Magi, who were following the star shining in the East, and invited applause for their appearance.

Anne saw a dais on the long wall, dark until this point, spring to life, illuminated by candelabra. At one end stood a rude wattle shelter with a thatch roof, inside of which sat an empty cradle. The platform floor was strewn with rushes and hay bales. A few tethered chickens and goats completed the scene. Joseph and Mary arrived with a sleeping infant Jesus, whom Mary placed into the cradle. Joseph and Mary then sat on the hay bales. At the unexpected appearance of the infant, tears Anne could not control sprang to her eyes.

From the surrounding dark, three men, dressed in magnificent wise men's robes, entered leading a costumed camel propelled by two sets of feet. Above, a Venetian glass star, probably threaded on an invisible metal wire began its journey towards the humble shed. After the wise men climbed the steps of the dais —followed by the camel who slipped and grabbed the closest wise man—Mary picked up the still sleeping infant and stepped out of the shed with Joseph. A very solid angel clambered onto the roof of their hut, shaking it ominously, and the star wobbled as it hung over the scene.

The three Kings thumped to their knees before Mary and the baby Jesus, and an unseen choir began to sing. Baby Jesus, already grizzly from being wrested from his cradle, decided it was all too much. He wailed, his voice so loud he out-roared the choir.

As the mystery play unraveled into a farce, Anne veered from repressing tears to suffocating hysterical laughter.

It became harder when the three Kings exchanged looks of horror, thrust their gifts at Joseph, leapt to their feet, and almost ran across the dais, pulling their stumbling camel. Mary, the squalling babe, and Joseph trailed them, Joseph juggling the precious gifts that looked in imminent danger of flying from his grasp.

Someone mercifully doused the candles before a disaster occurred and a fanfare drew attention to Duke Louis amid laughter and whistling.

"Time for dancing," he announced, cutting off the half-hearted applause and taking Queen Catherine's arm to lead her onto the floor. Charles led Anne behind them to form the next pair in the double line that formed at once, ladies and gentlemen facing each other.

"Well, that went badly," Anne said to Charles in a loud voice with a wide smile. He glared at her and spoke to the gentleman beside him.

At the first turn, when Louis partnered Anne, she said, "How unfortunate your playlet turned out so disastrously."

He laughed. "It turned droll, did it not. I did not plan it, but if it amused you, I could not wish for more." Flattery always irritated her, so his words reinstated her sour mood. Rarely had Anne been as relieved when a dance ended.

The evening wore on; servants circulated with wine and stronger intoxicants, biscuits and exotic sweets, and the dancing became more boisterous. On the dais, Duke Louis and Queen Catherine held court during their breaks from dancing. Charles spent his evening circulating among his guests flirting with the prettiest ladies, and Anne sat in the shadows with only one lady for company, refusing all offers to dance, and nursed her resentment.

As soon as she decently could, Anne sent a message to the king saying she planned to retire. Charles arrived and took her arm as she walked to the dais. Duke Louis and Queen Catherine rose to greet them.

Charles took the duke's hands and said, "Cousin Louis, the queen is tired and will retire. We wish to thank you for this splendid Twelfth Night celebration."

Bowing first to Charles and then to Anne, Louis replied, "It was my great pleasure, Sire." He hesitated, then added, his tone light, "If I have offended, Madame la Reine, it was not my intention."

Charles began, "How could—"

All evening Anne had been biting back her rage at the many insults he had offered to both her and Charles. She found his apology dismissive.

"Perhaps you did not intend to offend, Duke Louis, but you have. My son died one month ago." She half-turned, gestured to the courtiers crowding the dance floor, bumping into one another, laughing uproariously and shouting to make themselves heard. "Do you think this . . . this hilarity, for want of a better word, is appropriate? I do not."

Charles and Cousin Catherine looked horrified. Anne's voice shook. "You rejoice, Cousin Louis. That is what I see. My precious son is dead, and you rejoice. . . for now you are dauphin." Once started she could not stop the words that exploded from her like steam from a plugged kettle. "Not content with that, you cannot wait, but rush to step into my husband's shoes. You *have* offended me." With that, she hurried from the hall.

THE NEXT MORNING, Charles came to Anne's room wearing a thunderous expression. It got darker when he saw that every picture faced the wall, every ornament had been removed, every window was draped in black, and all the furniture covered in black cloth. So few candles lit the room it resembled a cave.

Charles gestured to her ladies to leave. They fled.

"I have spoken to my confessor. He requires me to forgive your uncharitable words to our brother because of your grief. I shall, but we must understand each other." He strode to the nearest window and tore down the black hangings. When Anne moaned, he scowled at her again.

"I am ordering your chamberlain to remove all this black drapery. I will tolerate it no more. I understand that you grieve, but your duty is to recover your spirits, not to allow yourself to wallow."

Anne had rarely heard him so curt. She felt aggrieved. She had been defending his honour as king. *Was he so blind that he recognized nothing of Louis's presumption the previous evening?* "Did you not see that he was taunting us—flaunting his role as next king of France? Why do you blame *me*?"

"Your anger does not move me, Anne, nor your ridiculous accusations. Last night you came close to causing an irreparable rupture between me and my dauphin. Do you know how harmful that could be? Whatever you fear, Louis has been loyal to me, and he is a great warrior and war leader. While we have no heir, we cannot afford to alienate him."

He strode across the room to loom over her and tightened his hands into fists. "If I were not a chivalrous man, I would shake you until your teeth shook. I spent hours trying to placate him, but he is still offended. He left this morning with my sister and his entourage. This quarrel you started will be all over Europe in no time at all."

He strode to the door. "Anne, you are not the only one who is mourning. I, too, grieve. Cousin Louise has lost her husband. It is time you thought of your duty to France."

1 Galette de roi—a large, circular cake made of puff pastry with its crisp, golden top and soft frangipane centre, each crowned with a golden paper crown.] One special galette de roi was set aside because it alone contained the miniature porcelain king and queen that would identify the rulers for the evening.

2 Fleur de lys—the fleur-de-lys, translated from French as 'lily flower' is a stylized design of either an iris or a lily that is now used

purely decoratively as well as symbolically, or it may be "at one and the same time political, dynastic, artistic, emblematic and symbolic", especially in heraldry. It is particularly associated with the ancient regime French monarchy.

3 Wassail—spiced ale or mulled wine drunk during celebrations for Twelfth Night and Christmas Eve.

CHAPTER 26

Troubles and Tribulations

Château de Cognac, 6 January 1496

As soon as they arrived in Cognac from Angoulême, Louise accompanied Carlo's coffin to the chapel. Immediately, Mme Antoinette flung herself at it, clutching its sides and wailing. Louise left her there on the cold floor as their chaplain arranged the chapel and lit the candles, preparing the coffin to lie in state for the count's tenants to mourn him. After several hours, during which his mistress continued her display of grief, while Louise prepared for his obsequies in Cognac, she returned to the chapel.

"Mme Antoinette, I understand that you grieve," she said, her voice neutral. "However, Carlo's children—including yours—need to be cared for."

Their gouvernante responded by covering her face with her hands and wailing more loudly.

Louise gazed down at her. Her voice sharper, she said, "Mme Antoinette, you are gouvernante to Carlo's children. It is a position of responsibility. This is a difficult time for all of us, and I require your assistance to supervise the care and education of all five children. I will leave you for a few minutes to calm yourself before you go to them." She left before she lost her temper, not waiting for a reply.

A turn of the hourglass later, she entered the garden from the back hall, to discover an agitated young Margot running after François.

"Here, François, catch the ball. See? I throwed it for you. No. François, don't chase Lion." There was a sob in her voice.

Louise caught François as he ran past her and swung him into her arms.

"Where is your nanny?" she asked Margot, who ran up.

"Don't know. François ran away. I ran after him."

"Good girl," Louise said. "He is too little to go off on his own."

"Am not, am not." François struggled in his mother's arms and Louise grappled with his wiggling body.

She smiled down at her sedate daughter. "How clever of you to protect him. Let's go back to your nursery together now."

Once she had resolved the crisis and discovered that their gouvernante had not returned, she sped to the chapel.

Mme Antoinette still knelt before the coffin, moaning.

Louise strode to her side and said, "Mme Antoinette, the nursery is in disarray, the nurses and servants need guidance, and the children require your care.

Mme Antoinette raised teary eyes to Louise's frigid ones. "Mme Louise, I cannot. My heart is too full of grief."

"A noblewoman does not abandon her duties. If you cannot perform them for love of the children, consider your responsibility to Carlo. Return to your duties at once."

Louise crossed her arms across her chest and waited. Until she began to tap her foot, the gouvernante stayed on her knees. Then she pushed herself reluctantly to her feet, sniffling loudly and shuffled from the chapel. Louise stood at its door watching until the other woman entered the Château.

Their conflict was not over. Mme Antoinette returned to the nursery but wept ceaselessly while performing her tasks. After a day of distressing her nurselings, their tutors and their nannies, Louise called her to Carlo's former library, now hers. She was sitting behind his desk when Mme Antoinette entered.

She immediately burst into tears. "This room holds many memories. My heart is breaking."

Louise glared at her. "Do you want to remain here?"

Tears staining her face, Mme Antoinette nodded.

"Then stop your tears. I will tolerate no more displays of grief. Next time I see or hear of any more outbursts or other problems with you, you will leave—without your daughters."

Mme Antoinette paled. Louise watched her freeze, lower her eyes, and swallow. She choked out, "Yes, Madame."

"Then we understand each other," Louise said. "You may leave."

From then on, she had no more trouble with any of Carlo's retainers.

~

Cathédrale Saint-Pierre d'Angoulême, 24 January 1496

BLACK CLOTH, dozens of funeral wreaths and hundreds of black candles enriched the interior of the splendid Saint-Pierre d'Angoulême Cathedral as befit the funeral of the First Prince of the Blood. Duke Louis d'Orléans followed the coffin of his cousin Carlo, leading the procession of mourners down the main aisle. Louise and her mother-in-law followed him, both draped in black brocade and long black veils. Their breath hung in clouds in the moist, chilly air.

As the enormous building filled with family, vassals, merchants and country folk, a mist formed. It created a hazy atmosphere that reminded Louise of Breton forests. When the priests paced down the aisle waving their censors, the spicy smoke added to the miasma. The shadow-filled setting matched her feeling of detachment as Carlo's protégé, Octavien de Saint Gelais, now Bishop d'Angoulême, led the service in his grand cathedral, read Carlo's eulogy and declaimed the ode he had penned for his former lord.

Louise looked down at the veil covering her mother-in-law from head to toe. The change in Maman Marguerite in the past month had been as distressing as Carlo's death. Louise had been counting on her strength to help her through the challenges confronting a young widow in a man's world, especially since her son was now First Prince of the Blood.

After she returned to Cognac, Louise had discovered that her mother-in-law was no longer a companion but had become a dependent. Yet she didn't know what was worse, Maman Marguerite's slipping into senility or her moments of lucidity; for when she regained her wits, she grieved the loss of her son extravagantly, blaming Louise for the trip that had taken him from Cognac for good.

After Carlo was buried beside his father in the vaults underneath the high altar, the bishop's brother, Sire Jean de Saint Gelais who had helped her organize the elaborate funeral, invited the noble guests to the Château to consume the funeral meats and condole with the grieving family. In the great hall, the dowager countess held the hand of her namesake, the little princess Marguerite. Beside her, the widowed Countess Louise, stoic and dry-eyed, held the hand of the young count. Outfitted in cloth of gold with a matching cap, complete with a long feather pinned to the brim with a ruby broach, perched jauntily over one ear, he made a charming sight with his dark curls and sturdy frame.

Louise intended to become known as an inconsolable widow and doting mother. To each guest she said, "You will want to make your bow to my son, Count François, First Prince of the Blood," presenting young François. Then she waited until her captive bowed, acknowledging the exalted status of her infant prince.

François was a friendly eighteen-month-old with a big smile who loved being the centre of attention. He was more than happy to grab a finger of any hand offered to him and gabble at his interlocutor. This usually drew a sincere compliment, for there were few who could resist the delightful baby. Louise was certain that as a beautiful woman of twenty-one, with two young children to support, she would generate sympathy in this role of bereaved yet dignified widow.

The Château d'Angoulême was not large. After one night, or at most two, her many guests departed rather than face another night sleeping on thin, straw pallets in a frigid stone hallway or crowded into the great hall. Louise's dearest wish was to wave her guests farewell and return to Cognac. She did not urge them to stay. But until Maman Marguerite's cousin, Marshal Pierre de Rohan and Duke Louis left, neither could she. De Rohan had King Charles's ear, both as one of his favourites and as Marshal of France. Duke Louis, the dauphin, as Carlo's closest male relative, was now the head of her family.

On the fourth morning of his stay, Duke Louis went to the late count's grand treasurer and requested him to invite the notary to read the late Count's will the following morning.

"Do not trouble yourself to inform the dowager countess," he said, as the man rose to go to Louise's apartments. "I will tell her myself."

When the duke entered Louise's black-draped solar, she was sitting near the fire beside her dozing mother-in-law, tatting black lace. He crossed the sombre room and lifted Countess Marguerite's hand, startling her awake.

"Madame, my condolences once again. May I return later to reminisce with you about our memories of Carlo?"

He turned to Louise and asked her to join him on the far side of the room. "My errand is unfortunate, but essential, Cousin Louise. The sooner we deal with these unavoidable matters, the sooner the formalities can be completed."

Dressed all in black, his fur lined black leather surcoat hanging open, exposing his swarthy neck and face, Louise found him faintly menacing. He tossed his hat onto a chest, and his long, black hair tumbled down over his shoulders. It looked as if he had not combed it in days.

Once they were seated, he said, "I have asked your grand treasurer to organize the reading of my cousin's will tomorrow morning."

His effrontery left Louise speechless. She pressed her lips tightly together to hold back sharp words. Then she said, "Should we not have discussed this before you gave the order?"

Louis threw up a hand. "Cousin Louise, I thought to take a burden from your shoulders, not to step on your toes. Forgive me."

Realizing that she had erred, she said, "No, no, it is I who must beg your pardon." How had she forgotten that Louis liked to be helpful?—even if the recipient did not find him so. Lowering her eyes, she fluttered her lashes. Since she needed his good will, she must tread carefully.

"I am overwrought. Thank you for taking this matter upon yourself. As you say, we must conclude these formalities before I can retire to Cognac to mourn with my children and mother-in-law."

The duke patted Louise's hand. "I told the Marshal that you would be reasonable."

"Ah, Marshal Pierre." Louise gave a tinkling laugh. "He cannot imagine that a woman can button her shoes without a man to tell her how. Such a dear, but old-fashioned." She held Louis's hands. "I count on you to assure him I can manage the affairs of my household—as I have the past year or more while Carlo was away guarding Guyenne."

"Carlo praised you whenever we met." Louis squeezed the hand she had placed in his. "Unfortunately, I did not see nearly enough of him recently for I have been off fighting in Italy and he was. . . ." Louis prattled on about his exploits while he turned her hand over and ran his index finger over her palm.

Solve one problem, encounter another, Louise thought. Why did men presume that all widows must be ready for a liaison? Briefly she considered whether there were benefits to encouraging Louis. Perhaps even to becoming his mistress? He was, after all, the dauphin.

Then she reckoned the disadvantages. When the relationship cooled, she had much more to lose than he did. If he ruined her reputation—and it was to his benefit to do so—she would lose custody of her children. Besides, he was not rich enough for her to take the risk. There was no guarantee—nor even a great likelihood—he would dower her with the wealth required to live in the style she thought necessary. So, no.

Therefore, she must reject his advances. . . but without injuring his masculine pride. She promised herself she would light a candle and pray for an extra hundred years in purgatory for that wicked Louis XI who had tied the duke to his barren daughter, Jeanne. Everyone knew Louis despised her; he made no secret of it.

Choosing grief as her escape, she forced a sob and tears, pulled her hands from his, clapped them over her face, and rose to her feet weeping and shaking her shoulders. She could sense Louis's shock. Wiping her eyes roughly on a sleeve to redden them, she turned her back to him.

"Forgive me, Cousin Louis, your talk of dear Carlo brought back a flood of sweet memories." She pressed a hand to her high-necked widow's robes. "I fear I must retire to compose myself. Perhaps you would share your memories with Countess Marguerite." Pulling a cloth from her sleeve, she touched it to her eyes, and hurried from the room without giving Duke Louis a chance to speak.

WHEN THE HOUR appointed for the reading of the will arrived, Louise waited until last to enter Carlo's large study. After the incident with Louis the previous afternoon, Louise had dressed in her severest black gown, a shade she decided to adopt until she was beyond marriageable age, to make her unavailability obvious.

The chairs formed a semi-circle around Carlo's desk, which his notary occupied. Duke Louis sat closest to the doorway, Marshal Pierre beside him. Maman Marguerite, her tankard of cider by her side, sat in the centre facing the notary with Mme Antoinette on her right. The last chair at the end of the semi circle was empty and Louise went to it. It provided her an excellent view of everyone.

Today Maman Marguerite appeared more alert than usual. When she saw Louise, she said, "I want to hear how Charles left things," so Louise hoped she understood the importance of what was happening. If only she remembered tomorrow.

Louise would have preferred not to permit Mme Antoinette to attend but she had no valid reason. Besides, she anticipated the others would find her presence presumptuous and Marshal Pierre's sour expression when his eyes rested on the woman confirmed Louise's prediction. Mme Antoinette was making herself no friends.

The dispositions in the will contained no surprises. After the birth of François, Carlo told her he had chosen her as his general legatee and guardian to all his children because she had proven well able to manage his household and estates. There had been only one caveat.

"Until François is of age," he had said, "because you are a woman, I am naming a council of eight to help you manage, but you shall be the one in charge. When François reaches his majority, the estate will pass to him, except for those lands assigned to your dower, and the council will disband."

Carlo had even sought her approval of the addendum that allocated small estates to Mme Antoinette and to Mme Jeanne Comte, the mother of his most recent bastard.

Then came the shock. "Until the dowager countess is twenty-five, if such occasion should arise," the notary read, "Duke Louis d'Orléans will be coequal to her in managing the council."

Rigid with anger, Louise glanced at Louis, grateful for the training that taught her never to show her naked thoughts or emotions. He did not seem to be surprised. How dare Carlo add such a stipulation without informing her?

CHAPTER 27
Pride & Humility

Château d'Amboise, January to April 1496

After Charles had scolded her, Anne retreated to her private inner chamber and curled up on a cushion in front of the fire, resting her chin on her knees. Although her husband's reprimand had enraged her, she admitted reluctantly that she had snapped back at him mostly because her conscience was troubling her.

Chewing her lower lip, she recalled her intemperate accusations against Louis and weighed them against his many acts of friendship. Some were important, like helping her negotiate a favourable marriage treaty despite Brittany's disastrous loss to France, whereas other were small acts of kindness, such as protecting her from Madame la Grande's sharp tongue at family gatherings. Louis had never been disloyal to Charles, and he had consoled her when she lost her second son.

She had been unjust to upbraid Louis—and worse, to do so in public. She must apologize. More urgently, she must beg Charles's pardon this very day, and convince him that she did so with a contrite heart. Being Anne, once she made the decision, she acted on it. On the surface they mended their breach.

Although she admitted it to no one, her loss of self-control frightened her. She tossed and turned several nights, hot with embarrassment and shame, reliving her intemperate accusations and hasty flight from the great hall. She repented her behaviour and confessed her sins of wrath and despair to her confessor and asked for a penance. When he told her that her penance was to behave with more moderation in the future, she objected that it was not harsh enough.

He smiled and said, "The Lord does not forget that you are but twenty and have recently buried your son."

By February, Anne was almost certain she had the best possible news for her husband. Still, she refused to call a physician; she had lost all faith in them. Their treatments did not work, they made every illness worse, and they would not keep her secrets.

Taking Mme Michelle, the one person she trusted, into her confidence, she whispered her suspicions.

Michelle said, "It is not something I tell many, but since we were not great landowners, my Maman was the one who cared for all who were injured or ill on our lands, She taught me much of healing and healing herbs."

Anne grasped her hands. "I was about to ask if you knew a wise-woman, or could locate one, who knew the tests that a woman was increasing."

"I know those tests, too," Michelle said.

With that, a deeper bond formed between them. Anne had always been fascinated by herbs and their lore. Now she had a friend and mentor. Together they could explore the secrets of plants. And she could answer her pressing question without a doctor.

Anne released a relieved breath. They agreed to meet in the castle stillroom and Michelle set off for the kitchens to collect salt, crushed sugar and white vinegar.

Before she left her bedchamber, Anne visited her garderobe. Although she gagged at the smell since her stomach was weak these days, she succeeded in collecting a clay jar of her urine.

Michelle bolted the door of the stillroom, and they gathered their tools.

"Three bowls? For three tests? Because three is the number of the Trinity?" Anne asked.

"That is the reason. Shall I conduct them now, Madame la Reine?"

"Yes. Look, I am shaking."

Michelle smiled at her. "You are overanxious."

She set up the tests. Into each bowl, she placed a measure of the urine. Into the first she added an equal measure of the salt and mixed them together. Both women held their breath.

The mixture formed clumps.

Michelle smiled at her. "Yes."

They clapped their hands. Almost immediately, though, Anne stopped. "It is bad luck to celebrate too soon." She touched the wooden table. "Try the next test."

Taking the lump of sugar, Mme Michelle first put it into a mortar and ground it until it was as fine as sand. Then she added an equal measure of it to the second bowl and mixed. As they watched, it, too, began to form clumps.

"Is that good?"

Michelle beamed. "Another positive!"

This time Anne allowed herself a little jig. Twice meant it was more than chance, especially given her tender breasts and morning nausea.

Before the third test, Anne crossed herself and sent a silent prayer heavenward. If it, too, proved positive, she would have joyful news for Charles tonight.

This time, before Mme Michelle poured twice the measure of

vinegar into the urine sample, she said, "If it changes colour and begins to fizz, it means you are with child."

It did.

Anne danced about the stillroom, laughing. She returned to Mme Michelle, who was removing the signs of their work.

"Is it magic?" Anne asked.

"No more magic than using willow bark tea to lower a fever or a smidgin of opium paste to induce sleep." Mme Michelle replied. "Someone discovered their uses in the past, and the knowledge is passed on. It is a gift of God. People call it magic because they do not understand it." She beamed at Anne. "Now you have wonderful news for the king."

As she knew he would be, Charles was beside himself with joy when he learned she was carrying another child. He insisted that his physicians confirm her condition and she obeyed him, relieved that he was treating her as his beloved once again.

In her happiness, Anne decided she must make amends to the other person she continued to sin against in her thoughts. After learning that Countess Louise's mother-in-law was ailing, Anne wrote to Louise, condoling on the lost of her husband and wishing Countess Marguerite a quick recovery. As a penance for her envy of Louise's two healthy children, since Anne knew that Louise loved books, she sent the exquisite primer that had belonged to Charles-Orland. It cost her dearly to part with the precious memento. That made it a suitable penitential act for the gravity of her sin. God would recognize the significance of her gesture.

Despite her disappointment, Anne did not complain when Charles told her he wanted to return to Lyon to restart preparations for his return to Italy to retake Naples now that she was with child. When they stopped at Moulins on their journey, she annoyed Madame la Grande by refusing to interfere when her sister-in-law begged her to discourage her brother's foolishness. Their reconciliation was too fragile.

When they arrived in Lyon at the end of February, Duke Louis was already ensconced in the military camp on the far bank of the Rhône. Although he came to greet the king, he did not visit her, sending a message with his regards. She deserved no better, she knew, but it hurt. He had always before treated her as a friend, visiting when in the vicinity, partnering her at cards and chess, and riding beside her in the hunt. To be treated with indifference was a new and disagreeable experience. She wanted to heal their rift, but he avoided her court.

The king, too, spent most of his time either at the military camp or in diplomatic and administrative pursuits. After over a month, when cold March turned into a grey, and rainy spring, Anne could bear it no longer.

"Dear Charles," she said when he came for one of his rare visits, "it is evident that you should remain in Lyon. You are needed. However, I am not."

When he stiffened, she rested a calming hand on his arm. "I mean no criticism. Rather, I am anxious about our project in Amboise. When we left, we knew that the construction underway would require our attention when spring came. Should I not return to ensure that the exquisite designs you have planned are executed as you wish?" She expected him to demur and was ready to point out that one could never trust builders to carry out the plans of visionaries like him.

He surprised her. After a moment's silence he said, "The rivers are now high enough that you can travel by water. It is the best way to return in your condition and the child should be born at Plessis."

Before she and her court left, she was determined to end the rift with Duke Louis, so she sent for him to attend her, knowing he could not refuse.

He arrived, in full court dress of cloth of silver and gold, his hair perfectly arranged—attired to meet a queen not a friend. When her gentleman usher announced him, he made a deep court bow as he entered and approached only half-way down her presence chamber. Anne walked forward to meet him, hands held out to take his. He dropped to one knee, took one hand and lifted it to his lips.

"Madame la Reine, your servant." His voice was chilly.

She kept a smile pinned to her face. "Rise, brother."

He took his time and she waited. Then she took his arm and walked by his side back to her seat.

"Please sit, brother," she said, indicating the chair placed near hers.

"It would be presumptuous, Madame."

She refused to let him goad her. "You are not going to make it easy for me, are you, Louis? Well, *I* prefer you sit beside me in this chair." She pointed again.

He complied but sat stiffly on its edge. On the table placed between their seats stood two goblets already filled with wine.

Anne dropped her eyes to her hands, clasped tightly in her lap. Reminding herself that she had been at fault, she took a deep breath. She would apologize whether he accepted it or not.

"Duke Louis, I owe you an apology for my unjust words and the disgraceful manner and unsuitable place in which I delivered them the last time we met." Anne's voice wobbled and tears sprang to her eyes.

She struggled on. "I beg your forgiveness and ask you to believe that I do not and have never meant them." She stopped and swallowed to hide the tears that choked her. Bowing her head, she let her French hood fall forward to hide her face.

Silence reigned and the duke did not respond.

Once Anne had regained her composure, she went on. "I

spoke in anger for I grieved—self-indulgently and excessively as I have come to recognize and regret. You were the victim of my lack of self-control." Pausing again, she took a deep breath. "I understand that words, once spoken, can never be erased. I simply ask you to forgive them if you can. . . and if you cannot, to weigh them against the years we have been friends. I was beside myself that night. I am deeply sorry to have offended you. . . and belittled your generosity."

There really was no more she could say. Would it be enough? As the months had passed, she had realized how much she valued their friendship. There were few people from her past whom she trusted. To have lost his regard forever would hurt. She ventured a glance at him from under her lashes.

Louis continued to sit stiff and unsmiling, allowing the silence to lengthen. He slumped, and he put a hand over his face. Then he sat back in the chair, one hand over his nose and mouth. With the other he pulled a cloth from his sleeve and wiped his face. Then he looked at her, a rueful smile twisting his lips.

"Of course, I forgive you, Madame la Reine." His voice was rough. "I forgave you long ago. I understand that it could seem to you that I was taking delight in my elevation and your loss . . . but it hurt that you would believe me so lacking in chivalry." He lowered his eyes at that admission and colour flushed his cheeks. "Thank you for your reassurances." He wiped his face once more, embarrassed, Anne suspected, at his display of emotion. "Let us say no more about it."

Smiling, Anne agreed. But it would not be so easy to mend what she had so carelessly damaged.

CHAPTER 28

Not as Single Spies

Château de Cognac, March to August 1496

The arrival at Cognac of the queen's letter and gift was unusual enough to provoke gossip among everyone from the stable boys to Mme Antoinette. She carried the packages to Mme Louise, who sat at the bedside of her dying mother-in-law.

Louise sent them away without opening them. What if the queen was asking her when she would perform her court duty? She did not want to think about it. Better to ask forgiveness later, saying she had been too preoccupied to deal with the package at the time.

"Put them on my desk in the library," she said. "I will get to them."

Throughout March, Maman Marguerite faded before her eyes. After they had returned from Carlo's funeral, Maman Marguerite had retired to her bedchamber, and she did not leave it again. For the first weeks, she smiled when the children ran around in her room. One day, when François was practising head-stands, she complained that 'the boy' was too boisterous," and banished him. She still delighted when little Margot—whose name she recalled—arrived, for her granddaughter climbed on the bed beside her and showed Grandmaman her picture books and told her Bible stories in her high-pitched voice.

By late March, Grandmaman could no longer receive little Margot's visits. She no longer recognized anyone, even Louise, and slept most of the time. Most of the time, too, she was gentle. Occasionally, she fell into a rage and lashed out at her nurse, her maid and Louise. Worried, for the dowager had never before been violent, Louise wondered if this happened to everyone when they became old.

In April, Maman Marguerite stopped eating. When the doctor said she would die within days, Louise grieved yet was relieved. The dowager had not been herself since Carlo died. When the priest performed the last rites, it was as if he gave them to an empty shell, though Louise did not say so aloud. She prayed she would die before she fell into such a state.

Viscount Jean de Rohan came to the funeral to represent the family, bringing news of Queen Anne's hopes for another heir. Although Louise tossed her head, pretending she already knew, her stomach tightened as it did each time she learned that Anne was increasing. It made her irritable. Then her uncle, who stayed until his sister's will was read, complained that Louise had warped Marguerite's loyalties, when the dowager left everything to her—though it was little enough, a few hogsheads of wine, a little silver plate and a few threadbare tapestries. Louise almost snapped at him. *Why should she not leave everything to her?* The countess had lived with the d'Angoulême since her marriage, and Louise was the one who carried the brunt of her care!

The Viscount even asked what had happened to the dowager's large dowry. It was none of his business that the dowager countess's properties had been incorporated into the Angoulême domain, but so seamlessly that no trace remained of the stitching. Nonetheless, Louise was grateful to Jean de Saint Gelais, who spent hours going through the documents in such detail that

Viscount Jean became overwhelmed. The explanations were so complex and diplomatic that her uncle was persuaded out of litigating although he left grumbling.

It was only after this, on a balmy day in early April, that Louise decided the time had come to open Anne's packages. Taking them outside into the sheltered courtyard with the children, their nurses and Mme Antoinette, Louise stopped to admire her sturdy, eighteen-month-old François. Taller and stronger than his two half-sisters born that same year of '94, he was also faster and better co-ordinated. He had walked early, and now ran everywhere. He could throw a ball and run to grab it faster than the two little girls. His language was developing quickly, too, and he spoke as well as they did. With his curly dark hair, twinkling black eyes and infectious laugh, he was always the centre of attention. It helped of course that he was the only boy. The only boy in the whole Valois family—unless Anne produced one.

Louise looked at the letter in her lap, reluctant to open it. When she did, Anne's wishes for the recovery of Maman Marguerite struck a raw nerve after her uncle's irritating visit, although at least she did not have to make an excuse for ignoring her court duty.

She was even less eager to open the heavy parcel enclosed in a wooden crate. She played with the children while they waited for a manservant to come and remove the sealed cover. The object it contained was wrapped in crimson velvet that she lifted out carefully for it was heavier than it looked. Unwrapping it, she found a tooled leather box, embossed with C-O and the late dauphin's crown and shield. The golden key was fitted into the clasp on its side. Turning the key, she opened the latch and lifted the lid.

She ran a finger over the exquisite cover of the book inside, lifted it gently from the velvet-lined box, and turned the pages. Each page was a work of art, and she had no doubt this was the late dauphin's primer.

It was an overwhelmingly generous gift, not only for its intrinsic value—that Louise immediately estimated based on the prices of the unpaid hand-illuminated manuscripts Carlo had left for her to pay—but also as one of the few treasures from the dauphin's personal estate. She doubted that she would be able to part with any of François's treasures if something were to happen to him.

Why had the queen sent her such a precious offering? It was both flawless and practical, a perfect tool to teach her children their letters. Remembering the amulet, her skin prickled. What did Anne want? What did she expect in return? Was she hoping this bribe would achieve what it almost had, to trick Louise into believing that all was well between them?

As she turned the pages, she pondered how to reply. She had put herself in the wrong by delaying so long. It took some time to find the right words for her letter.

Madame la Reine,

With this letter I recommend myself to your good grace.

It has always been my wish and pleasure to serve you humbly and I beg your forgiveness and understanding that I have failed to respond more timely to your gracious words and gift. Overwhelmed by the late Countess Marguerite's decline into senescence and her protracted illness, the result of her grief over her son's death, which occurred as we travelled to attend our beloved dauphin's obsequies, I have neglected my duty to you.

Your bequest of your precious son's exquisite primer moves me profoundly not only for its magnificence but also because it belonged to his cherished self and comes from your great generosity of heart. Madame, I pray God to give you a very good life and long.

As she scattered sand over her words, she reread the letter with satisfaction. Its grovelling, grateful tone, with just that little stab about Carlo dying in service to them, should appease Anne.

THE NEXT FEW months slipped by, filled with anxieties. The Saint Gelais brothers travelled around the estate settling debts and gathering all the legal documents necessary to prove her son's and her titles to every item. It was a tedious process. In late August, when she thought they were done, Jean de Saint Gelais, the chamberlain, received a notice from a royal notary, who was a cousin of Duke Louis d'Orléans.

The notary wrote that the Duke, as guardian to his cousin's son, had requested him to supervise an inventory to wind up the late count's Cognac estate on behalf of young Count François. He requested the names of Louise's representatives and a date for the inspection. A November date was agreed upon, but that was not what worried Louise. Why had Louis declared himself François's guardian? Her husband had named her, and *she* was the only guardian her son needed.

CHAPTER 29
Louise Does her Duty

Plessis-lez-Tours, September to November 1496

Anne's confinement chamber in Plessis-lez-Tours was crowded and stuffy. Louise stood behind the midwives encircling the queen's birthing chair, wrinkled her nose at the iron smell of blood, and listened to the midwives' hushed, frantic tones. Then she heard a baby's thin wail and her burgeoning hopes for a stillbirth perished. She did not join the rush of ladies eager to learn the results of the queen's long labour.

A woman's voice rang out, "You have a son, Madame! France has a dauphin!" The birthing chamber filled with a subdued buzz and the rustle of silk. Anne's five ladies crowded around the midwife, craning to glimpse the longed-for infant.

"Step back!" Madame la Grande's sharp voice pierced the bustle as she elbowed her way to the centre. Anne's ladies complied but continued to peer at the nurse and midwife, cooing and asking questions from a distance. The midwife ministered to the newborn while the king's sister observed her, eagle-eyed.

A son! God's toenails! In the deep shadows behind the queen,

Louise took a deep breath to recover her equanimity, unclenched her fists, and turned to face the room. Then she became aware of the anxious bustle surrounding the queen and slid forward.

"Another towel," one midwife ordered, dropping a blood-soaked cloth to the floor. Another midwife handed her fresh flannels from a stack on the nearby low table. The first placed it under Anne, and held out her free hand again, while the towel under Anne turned bright red with blood. The midwife replaced it with a new one as Louise watched.

Anne will die if they do not soon staunch her bleeding.

"Moss!" the midwife called, and the second midwife knelt to pack Anne's nether regions.

Obviously, I am not the only one to think so.

"Wrap her in a sheet. Now, you two, help us lie her on the floor. Lift her hips and hold them up." She shoved a pile of towels under Anne's hips and had each maid hold a leg elevated.

Unable to drag her eyes away, Louise watched as the women worked grimly to staunch the queen's heavy bleeding, sprinkling yarrow powder over the moss, and pressing towels down firmly. They waited.

"The bleeding's stopped. You can lower her legs." One midwife remove the stack of towels, smoothed one under her, and lifted the queen's knees as the other threaded a needle and stitched. Throughout, Anne moaned, long and low.

Finally, the midwife sat back on her haunches and wiped her forehead. "It is done. Poor woman. It's been a hard birth, and too early. Time to get her to her bed." They stood.

Louise saw an opportunity and stepped forward. Out of nowhere it seemed, Mme Michelle appeared. Ignoring her, Louise called, "Mesdames, over here. The queen has need of you."

Without arguing, Madame Michelle turned to the midwives and maids and said sweetly, "Can you help me raise the queen to her feet and walk her to her bed?"

The four sturdy women, who had nursed Anne through the crisis, knelt and gently raised her and helped her the few steps to her bed. It had been covered with a straw mattress wrapped in old sheets. Stepping in front of Louise, Mme Michelle stripped Anne of her blood-stained shift, asked a maid to dip a cloth in warm water, wiped the queen clean and dropped a fresh shift over her head.

Turning to Louise she said, "If I hold her head can you lift her feet so we can lie her down?"

"Of course." Louise smiled sweetly. She was ready to take charge again, but Michelle then said to the two maids on the other side of the bed, "Pull the sheet towards yourselves until the queen is well centred on the bed. Yes, that is good. Now lift her head and I will place this pillow under it."

All that remained was to pull up the coverlet.

Servant's work. Louise turned away. Well, anyway, the queen was too ill to notice that Mme Michelle had pushed her way to the front.

Anne lay still as a corpse, her face bleached of blood. As her ladies-in-waiting crept close to her bed, they murmured with concern. Louise thought Mme Michelle looked relieved when Madame la Grande returned to the room.

Here was another chance to take the lead. "Should we send for her chaplain to bring the viaticum?" Louise said.

A sigh like a breath of cold wind ran through the ladies at Anne's bedside.

"Not yet," replied Madame la Grande.

Louise raised her eyebrows.

Mme Michelle stared at the countess, unsmiling. "You seem in a hurry to send the queen out of this world, Mme Louise."

"Hush Mme Michelle," Madame la Grande said, patting the girl's hand. "You are overwrought. And you exaggerate, Countess. The queen is exhausted, not dying."

In the distance they heard church bells peal, announcing the joyous news of the dauphin's birth that would fly across France.

Louise glanced at Anne. *If she is not dead, she soon will be. Her eyelids do not so much as flutter. And where is the king?*

~

As the days passed, the queen failed to recover. She passed from the exhaustion caused by a long labour and loss of blood into a high fever and from there to delirium. Her ladies took turns sitting by her bed, bathing her forehead with cool, lavender-scented water, and reading from her Book of Hours.

The equally worrisome news of the tiny dauphin's lack of vitality and failure to gain weight flew through the Château and dulled everyone's spirits like a fog. Louise hid her hopes but paid a visit to the wet nurse.

"He does not seem eager to eat," Countess Louise observed as young Charles turned his head away from the girl's milky nipple.

She raised frightened eyes to Louise's and said, "I have plenty of milk, Madame, I swear it. See!" Moving the child to her other breast, she squeezed the breast he had refused. A stream of milk squirted in a high arc. "See. Is it not so?" Her eyes pleaded for Louise's support.

On October 2, the young dauphin passed into the arms of the Lord. Hiding her relief, Louise was quick to don black. Together with Mme Michelle, whose stony expression never warmed, she spent hours helping Madame la Grande with the arrangements for the young dauphin's obsequies.

It was a relief to return to Cognac as soon as young Charles joined his brother under the altar in Saint Gatien Cathedral in Tours.

~

20 November 1496

That cool, overcast morning, Anne stood beside Friar Francis at the top of the steps of the entrance to Plessis-lez-Tours, watching the last of Charles's cavalcade pass through the gates on its way to Lyon. As the clatter of hooves and wheels crunching on gravel diminished, the friar bowed his head to the queen and turned away. Before he could leave, Anne took his arm.

"Friar Francis, you have been of great comfort to me since the loss of my son. May I walk with you to your chapel and benefit from your spiritual guidance?"

She waited for his reply, her gaze lowered. From experience, she knew he would not hesitate to refuse if he doubted the petitioner's sincerity. Still, she had prepared with the hope he would agree, wearing a heavy cloak and warm boots and asking Mme Michelle to be ready to accompany her. Anne was ready to plead if necessary.

He hesitated only long enough to scrutinize her bearing. Then he leaned closer to murmur in her ear, "You are troubled, daughter?"

She nodded.

"Come with me then."

They walked down the three wide steps onto the wide gravel path, the friar's scuffed sandals smacking the pebbles. Anne glanced down at the sound and noticed his chapped hands and threadbare habit. "Allow me to send for a warm cloak for you, Friar."

"Unnecessary. Do not divert your attention from your concerns, daughter."

Chastened, Anne walked a few steps in silence. Glancing behind her, she was relieved to see Mme Michelle following them at a discrete distance. Anne did not speak until they had turned onto the narrow, wooded path that led to his sanctuary.

"Friar, was I wrong to resist travelling with the king to Lyon?"

"A wife should live with her husband. Why did you avoid your duty?"

"I am still weak from my accouchement—"

"If that were all, you would not seek my counsel. Only honesty will serve. Otherwise you waste both our time." His voice was stern.

Tears sprang to Anne's eyes. He was right. She forced herself to speak. "Charles claims he goes to Lyon to prepare for another military campaign, but he keeps his Italian mistress in Grenoble and often visits her there. When he stays at the military camp, he and his licentious officers revel with their whores. Aside from their immorality, I fear the Italian disease." When she paused, out of breath, the friar murmured, "Umhum?"

"This was our third son, and fourth child, who has died." Anne hesitated. Once she spoke the words aloud, she could not unsay them. Her lips felt stiff. "How could this be anything but a judgment from God? We broke two marriages to marry. . . and did not wait for the Pope's annulments to arrive before we consummated our own. I am afraid I have lost. . . my chance of salvation." Trying to swallow her sobs, she pulled a cloth from her sleeve and clamped it over her mouth.

Her whole body trembled like the leaves that rattled around them. They arrived at the clearing that held Friar Francis's cottage and chapel. Several stone benches nestled under the large trees in the clearing, but he led her toward the chapel.

Inside the small space, wax candles sitting on simple plates on the stone altar cast a warm glow on the image of a seated Christ with children and small animals. Friar Francis invited her to the stone seat under the window in the East wall.

"The Pope sent the dispensations, and the marriages were annulled, Madame la Reine. Perhaps you will spend time in purgatory for your hasty consummation, for on this matter, the Lord has not spoken to me. But your salvation is not in doubt." Friar Francis's voice rang with confidence and Anne's fear of hell vanished the way shadows disappear at night.

He tapped a finger on his lips for a moment before he spoke again. "As for Lyon, I advise you to pass the winter in Moulins with your sister- and brother-in-law. Your body requires time to heal before you return to your marital duties."

~

Château de Cognac, November to December 1496

IN THE FIRST week of November, Duke Louis's royal notary with his assistants arrived at Cognac to assess every storeroom, outbuilding, peasant's cottage, and outer field of the estate. After they completed the physical inventory, they thrust their eyes among the dusty documents so carefully locked into document boxes as they examined ledgers and leases. Louise's representatives, the de Saint Gelais brothers had prepared expertly, and few discrepancies came to light. Louise breathed easier once they had agreed upon the inventory and assembled in mid-December to sign the formal papers that would finalize Carlo's estate.

Once the notary folded away his documents, he said, "Now that we have settled all questions pertaining to the contents of the estate, we must finalize Duke Louis's guardianship of his late cousin's children."

Louise was caught off guard. "What can you mean? I am the children's guardian."

The notary looked pained. "Countess d'Angoulême, how can you suppose such a thing? You are only twenty-one, a minor yourself. Now that your mother-in-law has died, there is no close relation in your household over twenty-five and therefore of legal age to act as guardian. Surely that is evident!"

"No. No, I do not recognize that. My late husband appointed me guardian to all his children. He stated it clearly in his last testament."

"He must have expected to live longer." The notary's words felt harsh. "But I just report, I do not decide. The duke's case will advance in the courts. I am sorry if you do not agree with the law."

He left. Louise's eyes followed him. Her children were her life—especially François. No one would take him from her. He was going to be king. . . and she would be the king's mother. Friar Francis had said so.

CHAPTER 30
Easter Duties

Lyon, Easter, 1497

"Shall I play the lute?" Mme Michelle asked, as Anne pulled the curtains over the window opening to escape the rain that had started again. She agreed, to give Michelle something to do not because she wanted music. Leaning her head back against the hard headrest, she closed her eyes, hoping to sleep.

They were jolting along the wagon tracks on the route from Moulins to Lyon. Easter approached and since Charles remained in Lyon, Anne could no longer avoid going south to join him. Her spirits were low, and the journey already felt interminable.

On the fourth drizzly morning, Mme Michelle said, "Madame la Reine, perhaps you would prefer a different companion?"

About to enter the carriage, Anne stopped, her foot resting on the bottom step. "You have been perfectly satisfactory. But perhaps you wish a change?"

"You have been silent and refuse every diversion. If I have

bored you," her favourite lady replied, "another might entertain you better."

With a stab of contrition, Anne realized that her brooding could appear as if she were annoyed. How difficult it would be, enclosed with the queen, required to remain silent and do nothing unless she asked for something. "Not at all, Mme Michelle. I have been remiss and shall mend my ways. We shall play chess. How is that?"

"If that would please you, Madame la Reine."

Anne's spirits lifted at Mme Michelle's mischievous smile that signified she knew she had brightened the queen's mood.

After setting up the travelling chessboard with its circular holes designed to fit the bases of the short, round pieces, the women settled into the game. When Anne moved her queen to protect the king from check, she held it in her hand before setting it into place. "I never thought when I married Charles that Brittany could be free of France again. But until we have a son, so it is." She played the piece to block Michelle's attack. Yet even as she voiced the thought, she knew it for an illusion. Charles, or whoever the next king might be, would never permit Brittany's independence. Without their children to inherit, Brittany would suffer another destructive war.

"How is that, Madame?" Michelle's startled voice interrupted Anne's thoughts.

"The terms of our marriage treaty make it so. But I do not know why I voice the thought. It is lawyer's language covering every unlikely case, and Charles and I are still young. There is time for many children."

"Do not fear," Mme Michelle said. "Often, ladies lose several babes before birthing many healthy children. Trust in God." She signed the cross.

Anne squeezed Mme Michelle's hands, and said, "I pray that, like Friar Francis, you speak the Lord's voice."

~

Two days after they reached Lyon, on Palm Saturday, Anne joined Charles for the first important ceremony of the Easter calendar.

After the mass at Saint Jean Cathedral, while the congregation sat in silence, King Charles came to stand before the altar beside the archbishop. On Charles's other side, a curate waited with stamped golden coins strung on ribbons. Two young priests shepherded ten sad-faced men and women suffering from scrofula from a side chapel to stand before the king. His face serene, King Charles lay a hand on the swollen neck of each sufferer, touching their sores without showing either fear or revulsion, and leaned close to the diseased to murmur the sacred words of cure. As they received his touch, their grey faces brightened.

Anne forced herself to watch. When Charles leaned his face close to one skeletal mendicant, his hand over the man's suppurating sore, Anne shuddered. She doubted she could bring herself to lay a hand on the oozing growth.

After the king hung the blessed coin amulet over each sufferer's neck, the archbishop signed the cross over the recipient's head. Each one stood taller after the ceremony. Today, Anne too shared the aura of exaltation that intensified as the congregation watched the king replicate Christ's healing gift. As she witnessed her husband's divine gift, the sweet music of the choir singing psalms of praise lifted Anne's spirits into a shared moment of grace, and she repented her doubts about her marriage.

Anne's love for her husband blossomed. Charles never spared himself as he performed this holy but repellent duty, even when she resisted her duty to observe it.

When he joined her after the service ended, she whispered, "You were magnificent, Charles. You did not flinch when touching the oozing sores."

"But Anne," he said, "as king, it is my duty to give them succour. The Lord has given me the ability to heal this disease. Of course, it cannot harm me."

At his tone, her elevated spirits plummeted.

~

ON EACH OF the three days of the Triduum, Anne and Charles followed the archbishop and clergy of Lyon on foot in solemn, silent procession to Saint Jean Cathedral for the Tenebrae mass. After the solemnities on Holy Saturday, they washed the dirty, calloused feet of the parish poor. Performing the penitential duty, Anne's sense of closeness to Charles revived, and they held hands as they stepped through the great arched doors of the Cathedral carved with scenes from Christ's passion.

During their return to the governor's palace on foot, the skies opened in a sudden spring downpour. Their courtiers urged them to take shelter in one of the many covered *traboules*[1] in the area, but Charles and she agreed, with a complicit smile, that they would walk in the rain to honour their Lord's suffering. By the time they arrived home, they were soaked.

Anne looked down at the ruin of her brocaded silk. "It is nothing but cloth," she murmured in Charles's ear. "While we walked, I felt our souls join to adore our Saviour."

Charles squeezed her hand. "I also." He laughed and tossed his ruined cap with its bedraggled feather to one of his gentlemen.

Later that day, when Anne made her annual Easter confession, she divulged sins of anger about Charles's infidelities, lack of faith in the validity of her marriage and failure of obedience to her marriage vows. The penance her chaplain required took her several hours on her knees. Afterwards, she felt guiltily relieved she did not have to see Charles again that day and that he did not join her in bed that night.

~

Easter Monday, 27 March 1497

IN THE EARLY afternoon the following day, Anne's gentleman usher entered her presence chamber, followed closely by the king's principal gentleman, Sire Etienne de Vesc. He hurried forward without waiting to be announced. Bowing perfunctorily to Anne, he asked her to step to the far side of the room so he could deliver a private message. As Anne's ladies looked from one to another, she rose and led him to the window seat at the far end of the room.

"Madame la Reine," he lowered his voice, "the king's physician, M. Desmon, is with him. Since yestereve your husband has been ill with a fever and this morning he has started to cough. M. Desmon fears that the drenching he received has irritated his cold and moist humours."[2]

When Anne would have asked a question, de Vesc raised his palm. "He recommends the king stay abed without visitors. I come at his request to report his advice to you."

Although the man's gesture annoyed her, Anne overlooked his arrogance. De Vesc took pleasure in interfering between her and Charles. Besides, his news worried her more than she would admit. Charles had appeared well when last she had seen him. Why would his physician and his most trusted gentleman wish to prevent her visiting him? It must be serious. Could it be—surely it was not—the Italian disease?

"Thank you, Sire." Nodding coolly, she stood and walked towards her ladies, to make it clear their interview was at an end. She looked back over her shoulder and added, "When there is more information, please send M. Desmon himself."

As the hours went by, Anne became more anxious. After returning from Vespers[3], she decided to go to his chambers. She was about to set out with Mme Michelle when M. Desmon arrived. A small, thin man with a head too large for his body and eyes too large for his face, black robes swirling at his feet, he reminded her of a small bird always ready to fly away.

"Yes?" she said, not inviting him to sit.

"Madame la Reine, I have interrupted you."

"I am on my way to the king's apartments."

M Desmon clasped his hands together. "I do not advise it. The king is ill, very ill. He has a high fever, and his chest is congested despite our treatments. His melancholic and phlegmatic humours are seriously out of balance."

"Nonetheless, I shall attend him."

M Desmon fluttered his hands. "I fear there may be a contagion, Madame la Reine. I cannot advise it."

His opposition convinced Anne that he was hiding something more serious from her. "Thank you for your advice." She turned away.

M Desmon cleared his throat. She turned around and raised her eyebrows. "Yes, M. le Medecin?"

He hopped from one foot to the other, a frown wrinkling his brow. "The king is restless, Madame la Reine. He should not be disturbed. I strongly advise you not to go."

Anne stared at him, his obstruction solidifying her fears and her resolve. "Does the king suffer from an affliction so calamitous such as the pox or. . . or the plague that I will be in danger of my life?" Unconsciously, she pulled her skirts away from him as she awaited his answer.

Horror flashed across the doctor's face. "No, no, nothing like that," he raised his voice and flapped his hands in agitation.

"Then thank you again for your opinion. May I have my gentleman show you to the door?"

He clucked. "Then I shall accompany you, Queen Anne."

Anne paused and gave one more order to her gentleman usher as she left. "Send a messenger post haste to Plessis-lez-Tours. Beg Friar Francis to come at once. The king needs him."

For the next eight days and nights, while Anne remained at Charles's bedside, physicians and nurses spelled one another, treating the king and bathing him with ice water to reduce his fever. He passed from high fever into delirium and then into a coma. M. Desmon called it a brain fever and refused to predict Charles's state when he recovered—if he did.

When the king finally regained consciousness, he could not move the right side of his body, although his fever had passed. For the next sennight he lay in his bed, too weak to rise, his words too garbled to understand. By his side, Anne became more and more troubled watching while his doctors applied their remedies. They cupped and bled him, purged and sweated him and even pinched him with red-hot tweezers, and fed him a diet of soup laced with snake venom and dandelion tea until he was little more than a skeleton—all to no avail for although he did not die, neither did he recover, and his pain increased.

When the doctors admitted they had no more remedies and left, Anne and Mme Michelle treated Charles with soothing ointments and soporifics. Then he slept, eased for a time of his pain. They tossed sweet herbs on the braziers and burned applewood and cedar. But although Charles's sickroom smelled better, his wounds began to heal, and his appetite and colour improved, his paralysis and garbled speech remained.

~

14 April 1497

FINALLY, the man Anne had been praying for arrived. When Sire Etienne opened the door to admit Friar Francis, in his simple robes and sandals, Anne could not hold back tears. She led him to Charles's bedside and begged him to save her husband.

Charles was conscious. Half-paralyzed, unable to move his right side and weak as a baby, he rested against firm pillows that propped up his head and back. Cushions pushed under his arms on either side kept him upright. Servants had placed softer pillows under his knees, but he was a miserable sight. Sores and bruises covered his body from the doctor's treatments and from being bed-ridden so long. He could not walk, eat solid food, or speak.

Although they had done their best to cleanse the king's body and surroundings, the sour odour of illness hung in the stale air of the closed chamber and Charles's arms and chest were fragile as chicken bones poking through the thin linen of his bed shirt. The lightest of fine linen bedsheets covered his lower extremities.

Friar Francis stood at the end of the bed, facing Charles. He looked at the king for some time. Anne tiptoed away, thinking the friar would prefer to speak alone to his penitent.

"No, Madame la Reine," Friar Francis said. "You must stay and hear me and the prayers I shall offer to our Saviour."

"Son, can you see me clearly? Nod if you can?"

Charles gave a wobbling, lopsided nod and then winced.

"Good." Friar Francis sighed deeply. "Charles, I come to help you, but only you can heal yourself with God's help. I must speak frankly. The illness that struck you down came upon you for your sins. You suffer from the sins of pride and concupiscence. Though you call yourself a humble son of the Church, you have been leading a vile, licentious life. God is angry with you and has seen fit to punish you."

Anne had not thought it possible for Charles to look worse, but now he did. His colour, before a waxy yellow, had greyed.

"He does not want to punish you as you deserve, son, but to remind you that, although you be king, you are but a sinner. As king, you should set an example as shepherd for your flock. Instead, you lead a vicious, shameful life."

Tears flowed from both Charles's good and his swollen half-closed eyes. When the king tried to speak, the words came out as a strangled mumble from his paralyzed throat.

Anne put a crucifix into his good hand, and he lifted it to his twisted mouth. He was so weak it took all his strength.

"Do you promise to reform your way of life?"

Charles tried to nod and move the crucifix toward his

drooling mouth. He opened his lips to form the word, "Yes," but could only croak.

"Will you rid your court of libertines and end the costly and useless frivolity in which you waste your time?"

Charles's chin jerked as he tried to nod, but when Anne went to wipe his face, he struggled to push her hand away.

It was excruciating to watch. Yet Friar Francis was speaking the words she had never dared utter.

"Will you follow the prudent example set by your wife? She lives an upright, pious life, manages her court with decorum, and administers her domains through honest servants."

Anne blushed. Would Charles resent her for being held up to him as an example of exemplary behaviour contrasted to his own sins? Especially since she knew she too was sinful, even though her sins were quite different. She eyed Charles, but his palsy prevented her from guessing his thoughts.

Friar Francis had not finished. "It is never easy for a man to accept that his wife's behaviour is more admirable in the eyes of God than his own. For a king, surrounded by sycophants, treated from infancy as exceptional, and endowed with the right to demand obedience, it is even harder. Charles, the Lord has blessed you with a wife both wise and dutiful." He glanced her way, "Although she is not perfect, as I have often told her."

The hermit contemplated Charles. "You have made vows to change your way of life. This is what God, through His son and your Saviour, Jesus Christ, requires of you. Close your eyes. The queen and I will kneel, and I will pray. You will sleep. When you wake, you will have recovered the use of all parts of your body. With this gift, the Lord expects you to carry out every vow you have made today for the rest of your life."

"You will feel much better, but do not be in haste to rise from your bed. Equally, make the changes in your life with deliberation; do not rush to effect them in a single day. You are taking a direction for the rest of your life. Prepare each step as your body heals.

Count on your wife and keep her by your side. The Lord be with you."

Then he knelt, as did Anne. As he prayed, Charles fell into a profound sleep.

After they left his bedchamber, Anne asked the friar to remain until Charles recovered, but he refused. "Either he will fulfil his vows, or he will die. For the life he has been leading is killing him."

1 *Traboules*—from Latin transambulare via vulgar Latin trabulare, meaning "to cross", are a type of secret covered passageways primarily associated with the city of Lyon.

2 Humours—The humours were part of an ancient theory that held that health came from balance between the bodily liquids. These liquids were termed humours. The Four Humours were liquids within the body—blood, phlegm, yellow bile and black bile.

3 Vespers— sunset, evening, traditionally 6:00 p.m.

CHAPTER 31
Hope Renewed

Château d'Amboise, Yuletide, 1497

Anne stood arm in arm with Charles in the new courtyard admiring the elegant stone façade of the new wing they had ordered built at Amboise.

"Isn't it fine?" Charles beamed. "Now the entrance is sufficiently grand for the great hall. I was right to bring the Italians here to design it."

Anne gazed at the large plaster emblems of his crowned Jerusalem Cross and her crowned ermine tails displayed prominently above the pilastered entranceway. With the three shallow steps that rose to the wide platform and the wide double doors, it was grand but she did not like the symbolism of Brittany joined inextricably to France. Still, this was no time to quibble. When he gave her a wide smile that crinkled his eyes and invited her to pass through the handsome doors by his side, she smiled back.

The gallery they entered with its large windows and marble tiled floors smelled of new plaster and their footsteps echoed as they made their way toward the staircase at its end. Soon the sounds of awed voices filled the space as their courtiers followed them inside and craned their necks about them for their first look at the latest in royal architecture.

Anne and Charles parted on the first floor where his apartments were located. Before he left her, he kissed her cheek, and whispered, "Rest, my dearest wife. You carry my hopes and those of France."

"Certainly, *mon cher*."

She was panting by the time she and her ladies arrived at the landing on the second floor where her apartments were located immediately above his. This latest pregnancy was taking a greater toll on her than had any of the previous ones. She was no more than four months along, if that, and already she found herself tired and breathless after very little activity.

"Are you well?" Mme Michelle took her arm.

Irritably, Anne pulled it away. "I am fine. Do not fuss over me."

"How delightful it will be to see the new apartments," her friend said, as if Anne had not snapped and once again the queen sent a small blessing her way. How lovely it was to have a good-natured companion. Without touring her new suite, she sank into the armchair placed to give her a view over the gardens designed in the new Italian style, though now bereft of colour. What a relief it was to be back at Amboise with her husband.

In April, after Friar Francis had left, Charles had slept for twenty-four hours and had awoken restored in all his limbs, with his speech as clear as it had ever been. Naturally he had been as weak as a baby, but he had recovered his appetite and he was as good-humoured as ever. Moreover, he was humbled and grateful at the miracle the friar had performed. Dazzled by God's grace, he dismissed the whores and all those courtiers who did not reform, stopped all gambling in his court and took up his responsibilities for dispensing justice and conducting his council in person. Best of all, in July he dismissed his mistress and sent her back to Italy.

The rest of that summer was an idyll for Anne. The sun

shone, it was never too hot, and there was plenty of game to hunt in the woods around the city. Charles had recovered his health and energy and took delight in her company day and night. He invited her to stay when he sat in judgment on his court days and discussed with her the laws his councillors proposed at council. For the first time since they married, he invited her to accompany him on a progress through Brittany when they returned north in the fall.

"Are you certain?" she said, afraid to sound too eager.

"I think it is time for Brittany to receive a visit from its duchess again," he said. "They will see that together we are their good duke and duchess and that they benefit because we are also king and queen of France."

Even that remark did not tarnish her joy at the hope of seeing her beloved home.

But after Michaelmas[1] with the chill of autumn in the air, Charles's scattered generals returned from their great estates where they had been overseeing their own lands, and he lost interest in his reforms.

"I am eager to return to Amboise," Anne said, sliding a hand down his naked back one morning as Charles tried to slide from her bed before dawn. "Shall we choose a date so I can organize our departure?"

She heard him sigh as he rolled back towards her. "Dear Anne, you know very well that my military leaders have just returned to court, and the backbone of my army stays in camp here. Do not press for a date yet."

After that, they spent more time apart. He consorted with his military advisors, attended more feasts and hunted more often without her. One day in November, out hunting with his companions, he was caught in a downpour, and they stayed out overnight. Charles had a relapse.

Anne sent for Friar Francis. By the time the friar arrived a week later, Charles had recovered from the worst of his illness although his chest still rattled when he breathed. He acted delighted to see his spiritual advisor, nonetheless, and went with him to confess later that day. After Friar Francis told Anne that Charles was well, he took his leave of her, saying he preferred to stay at the Minim monastery nearby before returning directly to Plessis.

Anne did not see Charles the rest of the day. He sent to say he was unable to join her for the evening meal in the great hall, a level of consideration on his part that startled her. When he came to her bed that evening, his mood was subdued.

"Tell me frankly, wife," he said, "would you say that I am guilty of the sins of arrogance and pride?"

"Why would you think so?" Anne asked cautiously. "Has someone said so?"

Charles began to pace, fidgeting with the rosary he had brought with him. "Friar Francis imposed a strict penance on me and told me that my way of life had caused my relapse. He said that it was true I was living more simply and being more moderate and fulfilling my royal duties better, but. . . ."

He stopped and paced some more. Anne waited in silence, but he continued pacing, his expression gloomy.

"But. . . ." she prompted.

He sighed heavily. "He was very harsh. He called me arrogant and said that I was performing my good deeds in the wrong spirit. 'You are doing these things to honour yourself, not your Lord and Saviour,' he said and told me that I should examine my heart to do them as Jesus did, to serve my people for love of them. 'You should be as ready to die for them as He was for you.'"

Charles sighed again. "I feel ashamed. After he left, I thought about what he said, and I realized I had been neglecting you, too, since my generals returned. And I *have* been resenting my responsibilities."

Grateful he had answered his own question, Anne said no more.

~

Château d'Amboise, 6 January 1498

"How different my mood is tonight," Anne said, smiling up into Duke Louis's dark eyes. "Have I apologized sufficiently for my disgraceful conduct last year?" Dressed in a cloth of gold gown over a white satin underdress that hid her already swelling belly though she was only three months along, she rested her hand on his as they opened the Twelfth Night ball.

"It is I who was at fault, Cousin." Their steps matched as they danced. He shook his head. "I do not know what I was thinking. Knowing you as I do, I should have recognized that you could not forget your sorrow to join in a light-hearted celebration." A bemused expression crossed his face. "I did know it. But when the king said we should, and the doctors agreed, I believed they knew better than I."

Anne raised her eyebrows. "Hear my advice. Whatever a doctor says to you, do the opposite and quickly. Else you risk your recovery, if not you very life." Her eyes lit up, and she smiled wryly. "As you almost did when I fell into a rage."

"I would rather face your anger than the manipulation and pleas of my late cousin's wife." With his chin he gestured towards Countess Louise d'Angoulême, who sat among Anne's ladies, gowned in widow's weeds, looking soulful.

"She is blessed in her well-grown and healthy children," Anne said. It was difficult to keep the envy from her voice. Even the flutter of the life growing within her did not quell her jealousy.

"My prayers are with you daily, Cousin." Louis's thumb pressed the side of her finger in a gentle show of affection.

Anne refused to show her fear; it seemed like a bad omen. "What does Mme Louise want?"

"It is more what she does *not* want. I am guardian to her delightful children. For their good, I wish to supervise their upbringing. She fights me at every step. Even now she brings the case to the Parlement de Paris."

Anne's eyes widened. Since Countess Louise had arrived to

perform her service as lady-in-waiting, she had been surprisingly affable, sticking as close as a burr and agreeing with everything Anne said. Belatedly, she had waxed effusive over the precious gift of Charles-Orland's primer, offering excessive apologies for her delayed response.

"I think the Countess hopes to persuade me to support her against you," she said.

Duke Louis raised his eyebrows. "Will you defend her? I have heard you say women should have more rights in the care of their children."

Anne hesitated. Until Charles had forbidden her to see her son while he was away, she had not thought that a father could use his power to exclude the mother completely when she had done nothing wrong. She had understood that the father should be supreme when the mother had erred, but now she found herself skeptical about whether the woman's rights were ever justly represented. She had begun to take an interest in problems among her women whose husbands made it difficult to see or care for their children, especially when they married a second time. The ladies of her court reported that Louise was an attentive mother who adored her children. Justice demanded she assist the countess, yet she found it hard to credit that Louise had right on her side.

"Tell me more about the case," she said, "for you are correct. Too often, men remove mothers' access to their children to the harm of both, for harsh and mercenary reasons. Yet I judge each case on its merits."

Unfortunately for Louise, in her case Anne doubted that the duke was at fault, but she kept that to herself.

1 Michaelmas—September 29, one of the four quarter days, traditionally associated with the end of the harvest and beginning of the fall season.

CHAPTER 32
Spring Showers

Plessis-lez-Tours, 17 March 1498

It was early morning. Rather than wake a maid, Anne struggled to prop herself up against the pillows of her bed in her confinement chamber in Plessis. Even that effort left her gasping. A sharp pain seared from her eye through her head, and she tensed, fearing one of the headaches that left her as limp as a wilted flower. Looking down at her grotesquely swollen hands and belly, she felt sorry for herself. More than anything, she wanted to leave this bed in which she had lain for two months at her doctors' orders. They had not even allowed her to sit in a chair or walk in her room.

"Do you want to lose the child?" M. Desmon threatened.

"Is it true?" Anne asked Mme Michelle and the midwife.

Neither believed it. They gave her infusions of hawthorn berries and cramp bark, and salads of cress, chicory and sweet herbs. Yet they would not contradict the doctors when the life at risk was that of the heir to France. Anne did not believe M. Desmon, either.

Nothing helped, though. Anne felt sicker and sicker as her pregnancy advanced. Food nauseated her, and she vomited almost every morning. Seven months along and she still suffered morning sickness. It was unfair. Especially since no matter how little she ate, she inflated like a bladder. Her bowels were loose, too, and her headaches debilitating.

So here she lay. Two entire months! She felt desperate to go for a walk. Just a little walk. In truth, she wanted to ride like a wild thing, the way she had as a girl out on the wild coast of Brittany. Just then Fanchon, who had been asleep near her feet, wiggled himself up and licked her hand before snuggling in beside her, heaving a huge sigh and settling back to sleep.

Anne's thoughts shifted to Charles, and her resentment lay as heavy as an undigested meal in her belly. He had not been to see her since he sent her here after the Christmas court. Nor did he write. Madame la Grande, who had joined her during her confinement said that after she left, all his generals who had survived his first Italian campaign came to Amboise. Her sister-in-law complained that they encouraged his dreams of Italian conquest and added, "They say the Italians are laughing at us. And of course, Duke Louis never gives up on acquiring Milan."

Despite her fondness for the duke, Anne knew her sister-in-law was right. Louis wanted Milan as much as Charles wanted Naples. Louis was one of his most fervent supporters of the Italian adventure. They were off together now making a winter progress to the estates of Charles's richest nobles to garner support for another campaign this summer—if Anne's baby was a son. But no one matched Charles in his obsession with reconquering Naples.

Out of nowhere, Anne's heart started to thump wildly, sweat drenched her chemise, and she gasped for breath clutching one hand to her chest. Then without her volition, her body stiffened and her back arched. She groaned, jerked, and shuddered.

Fanchon leapt to his feet and barked hysterically until Anne's maids and ladies ran to her. Then, chaos erupted.

One person asked, "What is happening!"

Another said, "What should we do?"

She could see horror on their faces as tears she could not stop seared her cheeks.

I cannot speak. Anyway, I know no more than you. Grâce à Dieu, Mme Michelle, you have come.

When her lady-in-waiting pressed Anne's shoulders down against the bed, she felt calmer although she still could not control either her shaking or her tears. Then, just as quickly as they had begun, the convulsions stopped.

After ordering a maid to send for the doctors and then bring cool water, Mme Michelle stroked the queen's cheeks and forehead. "Do not worry, Madame Anne. You will be fine. We are going to turn you on your side." Michelle took Anne's hand.

To her great shame, as they were turning her, Anne lost control of her bladder and bowels. It was the ultimate indignity and she no longer tried to stop her tears.

"Run for the midwife. Start counting like this one . . . and . . . two . . . and. Keep counting until she stops moving." The urgency in Mme Michelle's voice frightened Anne and her tears turned to howls.

She felt no pain. So why call for the midwife? What was happening to her baby? Why was it so hard to breathe? Everything around her began to swim. Then she knew no more.

When Anne opened her eyes, she had no idea how much time had passed. People with long aprons surrounded her bed, she could smell blood and vinegar, and she ached all over. The only person she recognized was M. Desmon, who snapped his fingers close to her eyes. She blinked.

"Madame la Reine? Do you know who I am?"

What a silly question. "Yes, Monsieur."

His voice seemed far away and so did hers when she replied,

her words slow and far apart. She yawned, surprising herself. "I am so tired." As he continued talking, she closed her eyes again and fell asleep.

She woke because her whole belly tightened in the grip of a searing cramp.

"Noooo."

She was wailing as she scrambled to her knees. Hands reached out to grab her, but she fought them off. "It is too soon! It is too soon!"

"She is having contractions! Bring the midwife."

Arms reached around her shoulders, and a voice murmured close to her ear. "It is me, Mme Michelle, Madame Anne. Let me help you from the bed."

Anne struggled a moment longer. Then she slumped, sobs racking her body. "Why, Mme Michelle, why?"

Her friend rocked her as the next, longer contraction peaked.

Once they had readied Anne for the birthing chair, the midwife said, "Do not lose hope, Madame la Reine. Your baby wants to come now. It is early, yes. But he may be fine."

But when it was over, Anne brought forth a girl. And neither of them was fine.

~

Plessis-lez-Tours, 20 March 1498

Charles tiptoed to Anne's bedside, leaned over her and kissed her, his tears flowing when he saw her open eyes.

"Oh, my dear wife, I have been in tears since I learned of our loss. And you suffered without me, that is the worst. I have ridden non-stop to be with you." He took one of her hands and pressed it to his cheek as he sobbed.

Anne lay dry-eyed on her pillow, staring at their joined coat of arms on the cloth above her head. Once more, she had failed to give France an heir. She had no comfort to bring to her husband,

and his grief did not move her. She wished that it did, but it did not. For three days, she had nursed her loss, each day further sunk in melancholy, wondering what she had done to earn God's wrath.

His sister had held her in her first moments of grief. Madame la Grande shared her sorrow, spoke of the pain she still suffered at the loss of her first child almost twenty years previously. Where had Charles been when she needed him? Out drumming up support for a needless war over Naples that would bring suffering to innocent people who had done him no harm. As her people had done him no harm. Yet he robbed them to fund his prideful war despite his promises.

After he dried his tears, he raised his eyes to hers. "You do not weep?"

"I have been weeping for three days without cease."

"You are so pale. It frightens me. The doctors tell me you almost died." His voice shook. "You are precious to me, Anne. You must not die."

It would have been delightful to hear him say those words when they had first married. Or when he had returned from Italy before Charles-Orland died. She wished she cared whether she lived. But she knew her duty. "Dear husband, I do not intend to die. I have been ill, and I am recovering. I will be better in time."

Her tone was flat, and he looked uncertain, but he persisted. "My sister says you named our daughter Anne. It is a good name. For her beautiful mother, and for the mother of the Virgin."

Anne shook her head. "Your sister named her."

"Oh." Charles sounded nonplused. "Well, it is a good name."

Anne did not reply.

"Would you like to bury her with her brothers?"

"Whatever you think is fine."

Charles sat back and gazed at her silently. She did not return his gaze, nor did she break the silence. She understood he was worried, but she could not bring herself to care.

He said, finally, "I shall speak to the Bishop of Tours. It would comfort me if our little Anne joined her brothers so we can visit them together. I shall order it. Now, let me get a book and read to you. We both enjoy that."

She turned her head to him. "You are good, Charles. I would like that."

He did his best. She knew that. But in the end, her misery defeated him, for her rumination over God's reasons for taking all their children obsessed her. He stayed only until he had attended the funeral. At the end of March, he left Plessis, extracting a promise that she would travel to Amboise for Easter.

She rose from her bed to watch him depart. She had not yet been churched. Perhaps she could use that reason not to go.

CHAPTER 33

Return to Amboise

Plessis-lez-Tours, 5 April 1498

The king sent daily to Plessis to enquire how Anne went on. It was not hard to read his hidden message: *'When are you coming to Amboise?'* Still Anne tarried, reluctant to face the turmoil of the full Easter court.

Thursday, a breathless equerry arrived. When she entered her presence chamber to receive him, he knelt and said, "M Desmon sends this message."

"Tell me."

"The king requires you. It is urgent. The imbalance in his phlegmatic humour becomes severe, yet he refuses treatment, saying his Lenten vows prevent it."

A wave of panic hit Anne, remembering the near-fatal illness that had felled him the previous Easter. "I shall come at once." As she mentally listed the actions she must take, she half-turned away.

"Thank you for your service," she said, turning back. "Stop at the stables to have a courier return to say I will arrive tonight, before you rest."

Although her grand chamberlain argued, she chose to ride accompanied by three of her ladies and twenty of her Breton guard. "It is quickest. You and the rest of my court can follow with the baggage train."

Her guard set a moderate pace, and the party accomplished the trip in four hours. Even so, Anne ached as she slid from her mount. She had not ridden since January.

Before going to Charles, she demanded to see M. Desmon. She was relieved when he told her the king was considerably better already. Still, she said, "Then I need not have stirred my court into a tumult at my urgency? That was not well done, doctor. What am I to believe when you call me in the next crisis?"

M Desmon twisted his hands but persisted. "He has improved, Madame la Reine, but he still risks his life with his excesses. He must moderate his behaviour and you are the only one who can influence him. You and Friar Francis."

"Should I send for the friar?"

"No-o." The physician hesitated. "His behaviour does not warrant that yet."

"What behaviour?" She held her breath. Whatever he said, she must remain calm.

"The manner of the king's grieving for the loss of your daughter is weakening him. He wears only sackcloth with ashes on his head. No sandals, although the ground is cold. He has attended every mass since he arrived. After each, he prostrates himself before the altar for a lengthy prayer. To the usual Lenten prohibitions, he has added fish and wine, so he eats almost nothing."

When Anne would have interrupted, he continued, "That is why I sent to you. And there is more. He coughs and today he started wheezing, but he refused treatment, saying it is prohibited during Lent."

Although his immoderate grieving over the death of their

daughter and its effects on him worried her, Anne was somewhat reassured. The Lord would treat excessive observance with more compassion than debauchery. Had not Friar Francis said so?

Charles was overjoyed to see her until he learned she had hurried because she had heard about his devotions. She did not argue. At the next mass she arrived barefoot, in sackcloth and ashes. When she joined him at the altar and prostrated herself, he protested she was too weak.

"If you can suffer so for our daughter, I must, too."

When she refused to stop unless he did, he gave an exaggerated sigh, and rose.

"M Desmon should not have told you about my privations. Now you will worry, and you are not healthy yourself."

He stalked back to his rooms. At their evening meal, he accepted fish and wine with his dark Lenten bread and pease porridge when she placed on her trencher only what he did.

"We are both wretched," she soothed. "We have returned many children to God. But it is not yet time for us to join them. France needs us."

After the meal, they strolled in the gardens they had spent hours designing with his Italian expert. As they sauntered by a wooden bench, Anne said, "Shall we sit here? I find I am still weak. And the gardens are beautiful, even so early."

"M Desmon should not have worried you."

"I have eyes, husband. You have dark circles under yours, and you are thin as . . . as that stick over there." She pointed. "You will want to be fit Sunday for the King's Touch. Remember last year when we walked in the rain afterwards through the streets of Lyon? Everyone nagged at us to come in out of the rain."

He laughed and leaned in to kiss her, and she knew she had charmed him. It would be necessary to continue. And it would be good for her, too. Friar Francis was right. Service unto others was the best spiritual medicine. Too bad it did not yet come from her heart.

~

Château d'Amboise, 7 April 1498

Two days later, Charles had already regained much of his colour and good cheer. As Anne stepped onto the portico of the Château's new wing, followed by her ladies-in-waiting, he sprang up the steps.

"My lady queen, you look lovely today," he said, lifting her hands to his lips. She laughed lightly. Although she wore a new gown of figured green velvet, she still looked pale and plump, and she recognized he was practicing his charm. Curtsying, she played her part. "Thank you gallant sir."

"My gentlemen and I have arranged an entertainment for you and your ladies. Will you come to watch the best tennis players in my court compete?" He spoke so that his voice would carry, and her ladies clapped their hands, asking who would play and teasing the contestants as their courtiers mingled.

Anne hesitated. "Where will they play?" She remembered the last time she had watched games; they had been held in the old dry moat that ran the length of the old castle wall on the forest side.

"Where we always hold the games, in the dry moat," Charles answered.

Anne's heart sank. She had been there, standing on the long balcony overlooking the playing field, too soon after Charles-Orland had died.

As Charles led them across the rough ground towards the tower, she repressed a shudder at the troubling omen. Once again, they had recently lost a child, and she must pretend to enjoy another spectacle. This time she wanted to please Charles, who was eager to watch, so she smiled and clutched his arm as she stumbled on the uneven turf.

When they arrived at the low entryway, Anne wrinkled her nose as the reek of mouldy straw leaked out. "It is a good thing I am short," she said. Lifting her skirt and bending her neck to pass under the low lintel, she stepped over the doorsill.

Charles bent his head to follow and tripped on the crumbling, uneven stone. He struck the side of his head a sharp blow on the lintel and stumbled backwards. Flinging out his arms, he tried to save himself. Sire de Vesc, behind him, caught him before he fell.

"That was a nasty blow, Sire."

"It was nothing," Charles answered dismissively, shaking his head. This time, he stepped more carefully over the sill.

"Are you all right?" Anne said, clutching his arm.

"Of course, Anne. Don't fuss." He strode through the dark, filthy corridor that stank of urine.

When they reached the loggia that overlooked the playing field, the tennis players had already assembled. King Charles gave the signal to begin the game.

Anne checked the blow to Charles's head. Sure enough, a bright red lump had formed at the right side of his head near his eye. She did not speak of it though, knowing it would irritate him.

Servants jostled them, setting up braziers while the ladies and gentlemen who accompanied them chattered among themselves. The players were well matched, the game fast-paced, and soon Charles was shouting as loudly as his companions. Anne relaxed. Then Charles gave an odd moan. His legs buckled and he would have fallen but for the men around him who caught him. As he lay, a dead weight in their arms, his eyes rolled back in his head. For a long moment, a silence fell in the loggia.

As Anne stood in shock, Sire Etienne was the first to act. "The king has fainted. He must lie down. . . Lift his shoulders, you two. . . I will take this leg . . . You, take that one. We must carry him out of this cold wind. Into the corridor . . . Here. Stop. Now. Lie him down . . . Yes. I know it is filthy. But we must move him no further. Not until his physician has seen him . . . You there, go for the doctor. . .On the double. . .You! Fetch a litter."

For once, as Anne pushed her way through the shocked courtiers, she was grateful to the de Vesc for taking charge.

"Stand aside!" she ordered when they stood gawking. "Then, begone. Not you Mme Michelle."

Once she stood beside de Vesc, she looked around. "You and you. . . Bring the king's chamberlain and mine. We will need them to manage the physicians' needs." Then she sank to the floor beside her husband.

"Madame, you must not sit on the floor. It is filthy." She recognized de Vesc's imperious voice.

"My husband is lying here, Sire Etienne. This is where I must be. Now remove the rest of these hangers-on. And send for his chaplain."

She placed a hand on Charles's chest and felt its faint rise and fall. A rush of relief flooded her, and her voice shook when she said, "He breathes, *Grâce à Dieu*."

When Mme Michelle sank to her side, Anne said, "We must loosen his clothing." De Vesc, kneeling on the king's other side, did so.

"Cover him with your cloak," Mme Michelle suggested.

As de Vesc stripped his off, Anne pulled hers from her shoulders and placed it under the king's head.

As the minutes dragged by, Anne fretted. "What keeps them?" She rubbed Charles's inert hands. It was the only occupation she could devise that might help.

"Calm yourself, Madame la Reine. It only seems long because we fear for him." De Vesc spoke sharply.

They knelt in silence after that.

It was just a knock on his head. Yes, it was sharp, but he dismissed it lightly. It cannot be too serious. He will regain consciousness in a short while, and we shall tease him for giving us such a fright. But what if?. . what if?. . it is like last time when he could not speak or move. . . who will be regent then? What will happen to me? How selfish to be thinking of myself. I must pray. Hail Mary, full of grace. . .

"Look," Anne whispered.

Charles's eyelids quivered. After a moment, he opened his

eyes.

"Charles." Anne leaned over him, a jumble of emotions clogging her thoughts. "You collapsed. We are waiting for your physician."

He did not recognize me. Anne bit her lips together as his eyes rolled upwards under his eyelids until only a line of the white showed and he did not speak. *I must stay calm and show fortitude for him and everyone.*

After what seem an eternity, the welcome clatter of cartwheels and running feet filtered into the dark, noxious space. Leading the way and shouting instructions, M. Desmon slipped into the corridor, followed by servants carrying a palliasse.

The doctor sank to the floor, lifted the king's eyelids and placed his fingers on Charles's neck. His long face became longer as he felt the lump near Charles's right eye that was turning purple.

"We cannot move him from here. Lift him onto the palliasse. Carefully. Carefully. That is right. Remove the cloak and tuck the coverlet around him. Good."

He rose with some difficulty and turned to Anne; his expression guarded.

Before she could say a word, he held up a finger. "I need space to treat the king. I cannot yet tell you about his condition, which humours have become imbalanced to account for why he has failed at this time. My colleagues will arrive imminently. As soon as we have ascertained what is to be done, be assured you will be the first we shall inform. Until then, Madame la Reine, you must not and may not remain here, for your health and that of the king himself."

Anne would have protested, but Mme Michelle took Anne's arm, helped her to her feet and led her gently away. When they stepped into bright sunlight, Anne squinted and gazed around, dazed. "Where are we going?" she asked

"I am taking you to your apartments, Madame la Reine."

Anne nodded, mute.

CHAPTER 34

The Old Order Changes

Château d'Amboise, 7 April 1498

Throughout the day, messengers arrived every hour to report that the king had shown no change.

When her chaplain came to her rooms at Compline,[1] she ran to him. He told her he had received a message from the king's doctor. She demanded to see him.

Instead, her chaplain took her hands. "He asked me to inform you that when the king regained his senses, he asked for his priest. His chaplain gave him the last rites, which brought him peace. M. Desmon assured me that this was done as a precaution only."

His report terrified her. She returned with him to her prie-dieu, where she had knelt since returning to her rooms. Her chaplain knelt beside her.

"Will you say the prayers aloud?" she asked. "I have been here on my knees all day, but although I try, when I start, I keep seeing Charles lying on that dirty floor and I have to begin again and again." She stifled a sob.

~

IN THE DARK of the night, when the hour candle had burned down to its last inch, and her ladies had fallen asleep in their clothes on cushions, her bedchamber door opened. Alerted by the sound, Anne rose from her knees and hobbled from her oratory into the room, followed by her priest and Mme Michelle. Charles's chaplain and the Sire de Vesc entered, their faces drawn.

"Tell me." Her voice cracked.

The king's chaplain stepped forward.

At his sombre expression, her knees, already shaky from so long at prayer, would no longer hold her upright. She swayed and Mme Michelle, behind her, helped her to the closest chair.

"Please. . ." Her voice croaked. "My husband?"

The chaplain spoke. "The king gave up his soul to the Lord a few minutes past, Madame la Reine."

Although she had expected his words from the instant she saw his funereal expression, they did not resonate, but tears overflowed her lower lids and slid down her cheeks of their own volition.

The chaplain continued, crossing himself. "He died in a state of grace. He took the last rites in full consciousness. Only yesterday he made a full confession to prepare for the ceremonies tomorrow. At the last, he called upon the Virgin, Saint Claude, and Saint Blaise to carry his soul to heaven."

Although his confessor intended the words to comfort her, Anne felt numb. "Where is he now?" Her voice seemed to come from outside herself.

When Sire Etienne answered, Anne moved her eyes from the priest's to his. It took great effort. She noticed that his eyes were red, and his clothing crumpled and dirty.

"The king has been carried to the chapel to be prepared for his lying in state. Once it is ready, he will be taken to his apartments and laid out for the court to take its leave of him."

Anne's eyes did not move from de Vesc's face waiting for him to continue. When he fell silent, she said nothing. *There must be more. Charles could not have disappeared from her life and from France like a stone falling into a dark lake. How was it possible when just this morning he had been so full of life?*

Sire Etienne was talking again. "I took the liberty of sending the late king's grand chamberlain to Orléans to bring the news to Duke. . . I should say, King Louis."

King Louis. The words fell on Anne's ears like a sounding bell that startled her from a deep sleep.

"King Louis?" Her voice sounded uncertain to her own ears. Then she repeated, "King Louis." *So it is true. Charles is dead.* Questions formed in her mind. *How is it possible? What caused him to die? Why? Where is M. Desmon? But if Charles* is *dead, do the reasons matter?* Tears pressed hard against her eyelids.

"I give you leave." Her throat closed. *Go. Go. Go!* She dissolved into tears.

~

After Compline, 8 April 1498

TWENTY-FOUR HOURS LATER, Anne sat curled on a cushion in front of the fire in her bedchamber, a blanket wrapped around her, still crying. Although she had no more tears to shed, she could not stop, and her throat was so raw it hurt to sob. She could hear her ladies whispering behind her, but she would not allow anyone to touch her.

Michelle knelt beside her again with a tankard, begging her to drink. Anne pushed it away, suspecting it contained a soporific.

All she wanted was to be alone with her grief and her failures. It was so simple. Why did no one understand? The Lord had abandoned her. Everyone she loved died. Now Charles was dead, and she was more alone than ever. She had been angry with him for his absence when their last baby died. Angry that they had named her Anne, for after a time he would confuse their two lost little girls when he spoke of them. She should have forgiven him as her confessor had told her she must, as the saints did, as their Lord did. Turn the other cheek, He said, and she had not. Anne sobbed on.

Why had tiny Anne died? Why another dead baby? She *had* forgiven Charles all his transgressions before she fell with child again. Was she, too, filled with pride, as Friar Francis had accused Charles? Was she the hypocrite who had not cast out the beam from her own eye, yet was blaming Charles for not having cast out the mote in his?

Each thought brought more tears. She had lost everyone. All her babies. Her sister. Her father. Her mother. There was no one left. The nightmare thought that had been haunting her for years tapped insistently. No matter what her confessor said, this was the Lord's punishment. This was the reason all their children had died and now Charles himself was gone. God was punishing them for their sinful marriage. Unable to bear her thoughts, she clamped her hands over her ears and moaned, "Noooo."

Crouched into the smallest possible space, like a wounded animal, her arms locked around her knees and rocked from side to side. Even now Charles was descending to burn in the fires of hell for all eternity—and she would join him when she died.

The voices around her, the footsteps, the hands touching her were so many irritants, like mosquitoes buzzing around her. She slapped them away.

A HEAVY HAND rested on her shoulder. She tried to shrug it off. The hand did not move. Someone knelt beside her.

"Be gone."

"My daughter in Christ, you must rise." Anne recognized the voice. It was a voice that she should obey, that she was accustomed to obeying.

"Friar Francis?"

"Give me your hand, my daughter. I shall help you rise. You must get up."

The Friar helped her to her feet, although every part of her screamed 'no.' "Friar Francis, I cannot go on. I am as guilty as him. I am a sinner." Pins and needles burned up and down her legs, numbing them.

The friar put one arm around her. On her other side, Mme Michelle held her by the waist and they half-lifted her into a well-padded armchair.

Mme Michelle said, "She needs sustenance."

The friar nodded. "Something simple for the Duchess. Bread and cheese. Ale." He sat on a stool at Anne's knees and waited until she had swallowed a few mouthfuls.

Throughout all this, Anne had not lifted her eyes, although her sobs were now mere hiccups.

Friar Francis handed her the tankard of ale and wrapped her hands around it. "Drink." When she shook her head, he ordered, "Drink, Duchess. Now. I command it."

After she had finished and put down the cup, he said, "Look at me."

Reluctantly, she obeyed. When she did, the wizened old man in his ragged, undyed wool habit offered her a small, sweet smile.

Drawing a cross on her forehead he said, "Daughter, above all, the Lord loves you and wishes to succour you in your grief." When her eyes filled and she shook her head, his voice deepened. "You may be wrathful with your Saviour, you may shake your fist at Him and demand 'why,' but you must not doubt His love. He died on the cross for our sins. He understands our frailties. Believe in Him and repent your misgivings, and He will forgive." The friar kept his gaze fastened on hers until she inclined her head.

"Now, tell me what is causing this excessive outpouring of distress."

Once more she folded in upon herself and gave a sob.

Friar Francis commanded. "Stop. Do not speak. Say nothing until you can do so without tears." His voice softened. "I am in no hurry, daughter. Find the words, sentence by sentence. We talk under our Father's seal of confidentiality."

"Why?" Her lips quivered and she bit them and breathed through her nose. "They all died. All our children. . . and now Charles. I am afraid—" She had to stop, her teeth clamped down on her lips, as she swallowed her tears.

"You are afraid? Tell me."

She could only whisper it. "You said our marriage was licit, but I fear these are signs that it was not. We were both married. And we married anyway. And consummated. . . without waiting for. . . was it a sin? I have been afraid for so long."

Her words poured out like a bursting dam. The rage she had been swallowing since her first little Anne had died after Charles left her in Moulins flooded out. She drowned in her shame that she had abandoned little Charles-Orland to die without her. "And now this, Friar. I was angry with him, and he died for no reason. He just hit his head. It happens all the time."

She expelled a rush of breath and raised her eyes. "I confess to God and to you, Friar, that I have sinned, I have sinned, I have sinned greatly in my thoughts and words. I have sinned in failing to forgive Charles and my sister-in-law and for having accepted absolution when I should not have. I still fear that our marriage was not valid, and he and I will—" Her agitation built.

Friar Francis took her hands. "Your marriage was good and valid in the sight of God. When you spoke of this earlier, I prayed about it and wrote to the Consistory. There is no doubt that you carry neither blame nor sin. You may confess and ask absolution for lack of faith in me," a tiny smile flitted across his lips, "but rid yourself of this unfounded fear."

This time, his declaration, spoken with such conviction, lifted the weight, as heavy as the stone of Sisyphus, from her. Her heart was still leaden with sorrow. But overwhelming panic and guilt no longer held her in their grip.

"May I finish my confession?"

Afterwards, she said, "Friar Francis, you called me Duchess."

"Yes, my daughter."

"That is true, is it not? I am no longer Queen of France. But I *am* Duchess of Brittany."

"You are. And you will return to a Brittany stronger and more stable because of your sacrifices. The Lord has taken from you the comfort of your husband and children. In their place, He has returned your duchy to you as its sole ruler. And it needs you."

He stood to leave. "Before all else, you must eat, and then you must sleep. That is what I require of you."

Watching his departing back, she was amazed. How could she have forgotten Brittany? As God's messenger, he had reminded her of her purpose in the depths of her grief. She firmed her chin. She had a struggle ahead. The French were unlikely to surrender her duchy easily.

1 Compline—end of the day, traditionally 9:00 p.m.

CHAPTER 35

Where To From Here?

Château de Cognac, 8 April 1498, Morning

"The king is dead! Can you believe that Antoinette?" Out of breath from running, Louise pressed her hands on her cheeks to cool them as she tried to hide her excitement.

"King Charles? Are you sure?" The gouvernante, sitting in the children's day room, looked up from her embroidery. Her voice remained placid.

Even though she had doubted it herself, Antoinette's question and lack of interest irritated Louise. "Yes. I asked our priest. He said this pattern of ringing is used when a king dies. But Charles is so young. I wonder what happened?"

She stood at the back of the day nursery, brimming with anticipation, but undecided what to do. *It meant Duke Louis was King. And her son, her François, her César, was dauphin. Friar Francis's prophecy was coming true.*

~

EASTER CELEBRATIONS PREVENTED Louise from setting out immediately for Blois to visit King Louis. Once she had performed her essential duties, she passed several restless days wishing she had a friend or confident as close as her mother-in-law had been. After a week, she decided she could, with decorum, call her chamberlain, Sire Jean de Saint Gelais, back from Angoulême.

"Sire Jean," she said with delight when her maître d'hôtel opened the library door to announce him.

He bowed, took her hands, held them a moment too long, then kissed them and then both her cheeks. "Mme Countess, it is a pleasure, as always. How may I serve you?"

She gave him a slow smile and swung her hips as she returned to the chair behind the large desk. It pleased her that he treated her as a beautiful woman, for she had begun to notice he was a handsome man, only a few years older than herself, with a full head of chestnut hair and all his teeth.

"I am concerned about King Louis's intentions now that my son is dauphin." Louise plunged right in. "It was hard enough after Carlo died when he took the case of his guardianship to the Parlement de Paris."

Her chamberlain nodded. "We were fortunate the queen stepped in on your behalf. I believe he would have won all the rights over the young Count if not for her. She must suffer deep distress, having lost both her husband and her daughter so close one to the other."

"You are too soft about her." When Sire Jean looked pained, she said, "It is hard that she lost her husband and child, yes, but I hear she is busy gathering every last écu that Charles bestowed upon her, negotiating hard for her dower, and demanding all her Breton rights. As for helping me, Louis still won '*de jure*' guardianship, and the Parlement gave me only *de facto* rights to bring up my children day to day." She would have gone on, but saw her chamberlain's expression had stiffened. "Well, enough about that. She tried. I have a more important problem and I need your help. You are so clever with problems like this."

Before her eyes, Sire Jean's chest swelled like a cock preening before his flock. *Better.*

"You tell me that our finances have become increasingly tight since my dear Carlo died. Especially since we lost the income from the governorship of Guyenne."

He nodded, looking serious.

"Now that my son is dauphin, should not the king provide him with an income? I am sure you would know, and also what it should be."

"Yes, indeed, Mme Countess, he should and—"

"What about his own duchy of Orléans and its income?" she suggested.

When Sire Jean grimaced doubtfully, Louise went to work to persuade him, and to convince him it was his own idea.

~

Château d'Amboise, 9 April 1498

SEVERAL TIMES, Anne half-wakened, thinking she heard the ringing of bells, but the clamour ceased before she roused. The music of the bells wove its way into her dreams, lulling her back into the arms of Lethe. Fanchon's soft tongue licking her face finally forced her to open her eyes. She could have slept more, but Fanchon would have none of it. In her doggy opinion, it was time to rise, and she wiggled and whined until they both heard noises on the far side of the bed curtains. When her maid drew them back, Fanchon bounded down and raced for the door.

"She is not normally so eager to go out," Anne said as she stretched.

"It is rare that you lie abed this late," said her maid, as another maid hurried after Fanchon. "The bells for Sext rang sometime past. But we had orders not to disturb you."

As memory returned, Anne's momentary lightness faded. She prodded thoughts of Charles and baby Anne gently, as if putting her tongue on an aching tooth, to see if a shooting pain would sear through her heart. It did not. This ache she could endure.

"Bring me bread and small beer."

Yesterday, she had not addressed the question of mourning garb for herself or her household. That must be next.

"Send the wardrobe mistress to me, too."

The girl curtsied, "Yes, Madame la Reine."

Anne pursed her lips. That would have to change. From today onwards, she would be Mme la Duchesse, but it could wait until after she ordered court mourning. Those orders would cause enough stir for now.

It gave her no pleasure to be proven right, but it was not a surprise. Her wardrobe mistress, a good Frenchwoman, was at first unbelieving and then stiffly disapproving when Anne informed the lady that she would wear black for mourning.

Her wardrobe mistress sniffed. "But it is entirely against custom. The queen always wears white."

"French custom," Anne said. "Breton custom requires mourning in black. I am Duchess of Brittany now. Since I am wearing black mourning for my daughter, it will make it much easier on you and my court. Please have additional black chemises and sleeves made for me."

After her lady grumbled off, Anne considered the woman's reaction. She would certainly noise her complaints among the other ladies-in-waiting, and they would write to their families. That should spread the news about. Good. She wanted it known far and wide that she was asserting her Breton rights and that Brittany was an independent duchy once again.

ANNE WENT to mass with her ladies. It distressed her to hear the priest offer prayers for the health and long life of the king and queen, Louis and Jeanne. The shock focussed Anne's attention on her biggest problem: Louis and Brittany's independence. They were intricately entwined, like skeins of embroidery thread that had become badly entangled. She must separate them carefully or risk igniting another disastrous war. Yet she was determined to assert the rights inserted so skillfully into the treaty and marriage contract that had made her queen of France. Louis had helped her incorporate them. How would he feel now that he had to abide by them?

After mass, walking beside Mme Michelle in the gardens she loved, followed by several of her ladies, she pondered the question. Because she and Charles had produced no living children—she sniffed to hold back the tears that threatened—Brittany was wholly hers.

As its duchess, Anne forced herself to examine the situation cold-eyed. It should be simple, yet one issue remained. Her marriage contract stated that, impossible as it had seemed, if their matrimony ended without heirs, she must marry the next king of France or marry no one. But King Louis was married and had been for over twenty years. That should void the clause. Except he was married to a barren woman he detested.

She turned to Mme Michelle, whose shrewd political sense she valued. "Do you agree that the new king finds himself in a delicate situation?" she asked.

"Because he has no heir, and the new dauphin is but four years old?"

"Yes, you know Madame la Grande has always mistrusted him. She and Duke Pierre are his most powerful vassals and the Bourbon lands control central France. They could lead a rebellion, just as he led one against them after they were named regents instead of him," Anne said.

She weighed the possibility. Eleven years earlier, Madame la Grande, continuing her late father's policy of centralizing power in the king, had spearheaded the invasion of Brittany. Since then, her interests had changed. Her husband had inherited the huge Bourbonnais fief in central France from his brother and become the Duke de Bourbon. *Might the Bourbon now side with those who favoured greater independent power for feudal duchies, like Burgundy and Brittany?* "If they did, could I trust them as allies? We would have the same interests. I would find it hard."

"Why would they rebel? They are powerful within France and their duchies are appanages, they are not independent." Michelle sounded thoughtful as they continued their walk through the garden.

"I expect Louis will want heirs and his wife is barren. Madame la Grande has always opposed his divorce from Jeanne. If he tries, it could be a powerful inducement for the Bourbon to rebel. They could succeed, for they are the richest vassals in France; they have more allies; and are most experienced in governing. Or Madame la Grande could make it a condition of her support that Louis stay married to Jeanne." Anne became animated as she considered the hard choices that faced her in-laws. Her voice rose.

Her companion raised a finger to her lips and murmured, "Your ladies will hear you." She went on. "Louis is an astute negotiator. I wonder what they will want as their price for supporting him—and his divorce?"

"It will be high, perhaps the right to decide whom he will marry. Will he pay it? Madame la Grande kept him in her prisons for three years." Anne remembered his bitterness when he spoke about it as they rode towards France eight years ago. "Will he seek vengeance now he is king?"

"Not if he is wise. And he strikes me as a clever man." Mme Michelle replied.

"That is true." Anne smiled at her friend. "I see opportunities for Brittany in supporting Louis and persuading Madame la Grande to do so, too."

She rubbed her arms to warm them for a cool breeze had blown up. "You were not with the court when Brittany surrendered, but I was stubborn during the negotiations about my dower rights. Even then I was afraid Charles would betray his promises in the treaty. After a while, my councillors and the

French delegates gave way since they thought I would never gain sole control again. But I have, *Grâce à Dieu.*"

She stopped to admire the gardens that she had spent so much time designing. "I love these gardens but I would not miss them if I could return to Brittany to stay. So when I negotiate the treaty we must have, Louis will find me as stubborn as the Breton rock he said I was made from. Whatever I must give up, I am determined to restore the Breton rights and liberties that Charles revoked."

As Anne waited for her secretary, Père André de la Vigne, she called for her grand chamberlain to ready her apartments for her mourning. When he came, they agreed every wall and window, and all her public rooms must be draped with black. The rest of the chateau was King Louis's responsibility.

Père André arrived, looking nervous. "Please accept my condolences on the sudden, shocking loss of your husband, Madame la Reine." He bowed and backed away, as if expecting her to burst into tears.

She was not surprised. Undoubtedly whispers were circulating here and spreading throughout Europe that she was hysterical with grief. She knocked the thought away as she had learned to do. To concern herself over something she could do nothing about was pointless.

"Thank you, Père André. It is a sad time for France. Yet we must move forward. I would have you take notes."

He appeared relieved as he took out a slate and sat poised to write.

"I would have you circulate the following announcement to all courts within and without France.

Greetings, etc. My late husband, Charles King of France, having gone to God on the 7th April 1494, from this day forward, I wish to be addressed as Anne, Duchess of Brittany."

His eyebrows rose, and he hesitated.

She understood his doubts. "Yes. I have the right to use the title Queen of France. But once I have completed the forty days of official mourning, I shall return to Brittany, and I wish this to be known immediately. I will dictate the legal documents today."

Père André was Breton. He smiled and bowed again, this time more cheerfully. "I am your willing servant."

They shared a complicit smile.

"Let us begin with Baron Philippe de Montauban. He will be so pleased to hear that I am restoring the Chancellery that Charles suppressed and reappointing him Chancellor of Brittany—effective immediately."

Père André clapped his hands.

The corners of Anne's lips lifted. "Add that I require his presence at Amboise as soon as he receives this summons."

"That should toss the cobblestones into the millpond," Father Andre said.

"It should. And Père André, I need a new seal. Write up an order for me. It is to have my Breton arms only, with my motto: *No mudera*. For I do not change."

The next document took longer to shape. With Père André's words of advice, they crafted a proclamation addressed to the President of the Parlement de Paris, Guy de Rochefort, to announce the re-establishment of the chancellery and the appointment of its chancellor. She coupled it with a sharp demand for the return of the Great Seal of Brittany from the Parlement.

Anne sniffed. "Can you imagine? They removed it from Vannes when the king merged our chancellery into the general French accounts. I could have a new one made, but I want our original back. *And* I expect Baron Philippe to make a claim to the Parlement de Paris for the sums they misappropriated from our accounts."

Surprise is the best strategy, she remembered one of her

enemies saying. So, she had decided to launch her assault on all fronts simultaneously and without warning.

Although she was flagging, she pushed herself to finish. "Père André, please send a copy of both documents to the viscount de Rohan, as is correct since he is Lieutenant-Governor of Brittany. I want him to understand that now that I am back, his position is no longer powerful, for I shall rule. Send other copies to King Louis. This is a test. Will he honour my rights according to the clauses of my marriage contract?"

She had dulled the pain of the loss of her duchy by refusing to brood about it. When her enemies—Marshal de Rieux or Marshal de Gié or her former gouvernante—benefitted from the union with France or built their fortunes in Italy or made malicious remarks about her wealth as Queen of France, she filed them away as debts owed, with no certainty they would be repaid. Now she could consider what justice demanded. Know your enemies, she had learned, and don't mistake them for friends when they pretend to be.

The tasks she had accomplished had exhausted her. With her fatigue, her grief returned. She must lie down.

"King Louis will wish to see me when he arrives. I must rest before that, Père André."

He leapt to his feet as if she had berated him. "Of course, Madame la Duchesse."

CHAPTER 36
Surprises

Château d'Amboise, 9 April 1498

King Louis arrived at Duchess Anne's apartments without fanfare. Only when her gentlemen ushers bowed in a deep royal salute did she realize he had appeared. He came alone, dressed simply as always, this time entirely in black.

Anne, attired for the meeting in her richest black robes, made a deep court curtsey. He crossed quickly to her and lifted her to her feet.

"Let us have no ceremony, Cousin Anne."

"You are king, M. le Roi," Anne replied. How cleverly he avoided the entire issue of her title.

"Nor call me that. I am still your Cousin Louis. Please call me so. I come to offer my sincerest condolences on Charles's death. I loved him deeply and grieve for his loss." He took her hands and his voice intensified. "Cousin Anne, believe me, I am shocked, and have no words to tell you how distressed and saddened I am."

Leading her to a chair, he sat her down and pulled one up for himself. "I swear I never wanted or hoped or expected to be king.

This change is as shocking to me as I am sure it must have been to you. I would give anything to turn the days back."

She could not doubt his sincerity. Tears wet her eyes. "Thank you, Cousin Louis." She was grateful that he was addressing the doubts that had already seeped into her feelings towards him.

The crown was a rich prize. During those long hours when Charles had hovered between life and death, she had pictured how Louis would respond if Charles's chamberlain came to announce he was king. Would he truly grieve Charles's death when he benefitted so much? The emotion in his voice and the pain in his eyes persuaded her it was so. She felt comforted.

"You see I take my mourning in black, as is the Breton custom," she said.

He leaned back, eying her clothing. "Was your dispute with your wardrobe mistress lengthy? Did she call in reinforcements?" Anne caught the glimmer of a smile. *Really, it was not a matter for jest.*

"She informed me that tradition called for the queen to wear white. I observed it was French custom, but Duchesses of Brittany wore black." She chose to sound stern.

"Naturally, as Duchess of Brittany, as well as Queen of France, you follow the Breton custom. You do not surprise me. I have known you too long."

"You do not object?"

"I would not dare." This time he did grin.

Anne tried to frown, but a tiny smile crept to the corners of her mouth.

"There is another tradition," Louis said, "that the late king's closest male relative takes charge of his obsequies. Will you trust me to arrange the most splendid occasion I can contrive? Charles deserves it."

Her tentative smile vanished. It seemed so final. Each step made Charles's death more real, yet to her it was still hard to credit. This visit from Louis felt as painful as hammering a nail into her thumb. His kindness made it worse.

"I will take care of everything. Once he leaves the court mourning here, he shall go first to the Collegiate Church of Saint Florentin in the city, and from there the cortège will walk with him to Paris and on to Saint Denis. Naturally, he will rest in the basilica there."

"Is it. . . when will it be?" Anne asked

"I have discussed it with the marshals. To allow time to prepare the route and assemble the mourners, they propose April 28. The funeral service at Saint Denis will occur on May 1."

Anne nodded. "Thank you." There was another subject she must address. It was more intimate, and she blushed. "You will want to know when you can plan your coronation. To reassure you, I have *no* expectation that I am with child."

"Thank you for your reassurance. I do not wish to intrude on your sorrow, Cousin Anne. There are only a few other matters. Although you must stay sequestered until May 15, and I understand you have chosen to remain here, you are welcome to stay at Amboise as long as you wish. Have you made plans? Or will you inform me later?"

"Did you receive a copy of the proclamation I sent to the Parlement de Paris?"

"I did."

"Then you know I will return to Brittany. I have re-established the chancellery and now must restore the customs that my late husband changed during his tenure." It came out sounding like a criticism, although she had not intended it to. "But I still have not worked out the details. Then there are the arrangements to receive my dowry as Dowager Queen of France. Also, the repairs to the Hôtel d'Etampes outside Paris are not yet complete. So, I have several responsibilities before I can return to Brittany." She paused. "Of course, a new treaty will be required between Brittany and France." There. Louis must understand they had some serious negotiating to do.

Louis took his time to respond. "That *is* important. I will expect to meet you in Paris, after your mourning ends." He rose and kissed her hand. "Adieu, Cousin Anne."

~

Château de Blois, 17 April 1498

LOUISE ARRIVED at Louis's Château over a week after Easter, for even the death of the king of France must wait upon the death and resurrection of the Great King and Lord of all.

The Easter sermons had been serious and reflective that year, emphasizing the transience of mortal life, and the levelling power of death, be the victim king or pauper. Christ's sacrifice on the cross became a reminder that earthly life was short, and that Christ had saved the king and would save all. The message had grated on Louise, who wanted only to think of life and her family's future glory.

King Louis greeted the countess and her children when they arrived. She expected no less since she brought Dauphin François to make his vow of fealty for the first time since Louis became king. Young Count François was a clever active boy, tall for his age with a friendly smile and large dark eyes. His six-year-old sister, Margot, also tall for her age, and clever, looked pale in the severe mourning gown that did not flatter her dark Orléans colouring.

As Louis walked with Louise to his library, he said, "It is a pleasure to welcome you to my home. I beg you to make it yours and your family's from this moment forward."

Although Louise would have been enraged had he not suggested it, she said, "M le Roi, I had no expectation of such an honour."

She was irritated by his grimace.Then he said, "Please Cousin Louise, I beg you to address me as cousin. Let us restrict formality to public occasions. You honour me by bringing your family to live here so I will hear no more objections. But I hope you will forgive my lack of attention, for I am submerged under affairs of state these days."

"I have many important matters to discuss with you. I hope you will find a few minutes in your busy schedule for a poor widow, Cousin."

"Of course, Cousin," he said. "I shall send my secretary with an appointment."

Once she was settled, Louise called on Queen Jeanne, whose apartments were in another wing of the château. The queen interrupted her packing to welcome Louise and invited her in for wine and biscuits.

"I am moving to Paris at my husband's request to help with poor Charles's funeral and Louis's coronation," she said.

"When will you and the king be leaving Blois?" Louise asked. *Would they invite her to join their party*? she wanted to ask

"I must leave by the end of the week," the new queen said.

When Louise said, "And the king too?" Jeanne did not answer, instead pressing wine upon her and asking about her apartments.

Louise still found it an informative visit. Cardinal Georges d'Amboise arrived to pay his respects while Louise was with Jeanne. He told them he had just returned from a visit to Madame la Grande.

"Will the Duke and Duchess of Bourbon stay with King Louis when they attend the funeral of the late king?" Louise asked.

"They have their own Hôtel in Paris and bring a large entourage, so I doubt it, although he invited them," the cardinal replied. He added, "They make a long stay, since the king has promised that the Parlement de Paris will legislate inheritance rights for their daughter. She will inherit all lands, present and future that belong to the Duke *and* to the Duchess. The duchess inherited much from her father as a daughter of France that she wishes to incorporate into the Bourbon domains." He smiled blandly.

Louise raised her eyebrows, peering at Queen Jeanne. The queen must understand the implications as well as she did, although Jeanne smiled and nodded as if the information was nothing more than family gossip. Louise recognized it for the payment Madame la Grande had received as their support for Louis. It would infuriate the Montpensier heirs to the Bourbon estates, since, as a girl, Suzanne should not be able to inherit an appanage.[1]

After Cardinal Georges left, Louise said, "How generous of your husband to grant the appanage to his niece, although I imagine the Count Louis de Montpensier will be disappointed."

Louise thought Queen Jeanne would not reply, but finally she said quietly, "Please, Countess Louise, let us not pretend. Cardinal d'Amboise brought that information to let me know my husband has purchased my sister's support with the grant of the Bourbonnais to her daughter. He isolates me. Please forgive me but I have much to accomplish. You are dismissed."

Louise withdrew, unabashed. She suspected Jeanne would never be crowned queen.

WHEN THE COUNTESS met Louis the next day in his presence chamber, she expressed her delight at his ascension by giving him a long-coveted original manuscript of his grandfather's poetry from Carlo's library.

"This is a generous gift, Cousin Louise," he said, turning its pages as delicately as he would caress a lover's cheek.

"Your elevation to the throne is a momentous event, worthy of the greatest honour." She looked around at the symbols of office that he had adopted. "The porcupine?[2] Why have you chosen that as your device?"

"You bring me my grandfather's book. Did you know it was his emblem, too? I chose it because, like him, the porcupine is a fighter. It carries its own armour on its back." He bared his teeth at her as he took his seat, but did not invite her to sit.

"Forgive my hurry, Cousin Louise. You understand that I am overwhelmed with duties and new to them. What can I do for you?"

"François is the dauphin and will have greater needs in his new role. He should have companions of his own rank around him, as did the late king when he was young. Already he shows a talent for horsemanship and will need the most skilled—"

"Where is this leading, Cousin Louise?"

"The Dauphin should not be Count d'Angoulême. Now that you are king, your appanage of Orléans has fallen vacant. It would be a suitable grant to your heir, and its income sufficient to his needs."

"Dear Cousin Louise. Have you not thought I may produce a son of my own?"

"If you have not until now, it does not seem probable. Especially since you are sending your wife away." Louise was too annoyed to be careful.

"But Cousin Louise, it may be that God will perform a miracle."

"Another immaculate conception, since your wife is not here?"

Louis laughed. "You have an impudent wit, Cousin. The Lord can perform many kinds of miracle."

"Such as death or divorce as well as a miracle child?"

"Your banter veers to the perilous. I must see if my expectations come to pass," he countered.

"If they do, you may wish to choose a wife who has already proven she can birth healthy sons," she suggested. "One still young enough to produce more."

"You are wise. I will remember your suggestion if the occasion arises. Until then, you understand that I cannot alienate the duchy d'Orléans." His light answer and refusal to consider her justified claim to Orléans sent a flush of anger coursing through her.

He must have noticed her temper rising, for he said, "I would not have you leave entirely disappointed. To address the additional expenses of the young dauphin, I will grant you the domains of Saint Maixent, Givray and Usson. That will provide you with some. . . let me see, 8000 livres in additional income."

"Thank you, M. le Roi." She curtsied deeply. It muffled the anger in her voice at the paltry grant.

"Then I shall see you again at the funeral of the late king. Until then, be welcome here at your home."

Louise argued no more. It was a beginning. She would find a way to persuade him to be more generous.

1 Appanage — is the grant of an estate, title, office or other thing of value to a younger child of a sovereign, who would otherwise have no inheritance under the system of primogeniture. Typically, in France it passed through the male line and when the male line failed, it returned to the royal demesne.

2 At that time, they believed that the porcupine was a vicious fighter.

CHAPTER 37

Duchess of Brittany

Hôtel d'Étampes, south of Paris, 20 May 1498

Anne sat on the loggia fanning herself while she admired the gardens of her grand Hôtel. Her Italian garden designer had created arbored walks and trellises that met at an octagonal fountain in the centre, reminiscent of the much grander design he had created at Amboise. The highly scented plants, cedar, jasmine, pine, lavender, rosemary and lemon balm, released their perfumes in season and when dried, discouraged insects that could damage clothing.

Light filled her quarters in the new brick wing of her refurbished château. When she had sold it last in the summer of 1491, she never expected to recover it. King Charles—her eyes misted at the thought of him—bought it back for her soon after they married, but she had not lived in it until now.

Outside her quiet garden, the Hôtel was a hub of activity. She had chosen it as a suitable location to gather her possessions—the carved and decorated beds, coffers, benches, and wardrobes; the books, jewellery, dishes and plate, scattered among the royal chateaux where they awaited her visits—events that would no longer occur since Charles had died and the chateaux were no longer her homes. The stables and outbuilding were full to bursting with everything necessary to transport the goods she had acquired in France back to Brittany—the horses, donkeys, mules, and oxen; the carriages, coaches, litters, wagons, carts, and drays; the chests, trunks, boxes, coffers, closets, containers, and other packing cases. Then, she had engaged the new officers she would need for her expanded ducal household. Her purser had purchased printing presses, sets of the moveable type and the paper they used, and was still hiring the expert artisans to run them. All these people would need transport too.

Beautiful as it was here, she wanted to stay as short a time as possible while still freeing Brittany from the terms of the treaty she had signed in 1491. She and her new council had been working ceaselessly. After a month of feverish activity, they would meet King Louis and his new advisors tomorrow.

Choosing her council had been a labour of Hercules. She and Baron Philippe had debated for days before agreeing on its membership. She had learned enough from Madame la Grande to insist that the majority must be loyal to her for solid financial or family reasons. Baron Philippe was inclined to use membership to buy loyalty.

They agreed easily enough to include Bishop Michel Guibé and her cousin, Prince Jean d'Orange, as senior representatives of the Breton Church and the Montfort family. They argued about the Viscount de Rennes, who had stood by her until Rennes fell, until he understood her reasons and agreed. They added two of the minor nobility to represent the group loyal to the ducal family and who deeply distrusted the de Rohan and their allies.

Then Baron Philippe insisted, "You must include Viscount Jean de Rohan, Marshal Jean de Rieux, and your half-brother

Baron François d'Avaugour. They are your most powerful vassals. And the Viscount has become disenchanted with the French."

Anne pushed out her lower lip, ready to argue. They had been her enemies before Brittany fell, and she did not trust them any more now. Then she recalled her father's advice: *Keep your friends close and your enemies closer.* "If I agree, how will we control them?"

"As we always have, with a mixture of rewards and threats," de Montauban replied.

Remembering their many treasons, Anne said, "Can you promise me we will succeed?"

"No. But I can assure you if you do not appoint them, they will always plot against you and we will know nothing of their doings."

His point was so telling that Anne gave way. Besides, now that her dear friend Pernette was married to her half-brother, he had many more reasons to be loyal.

And her final choice, Seigneur Jacques de Beaune, the financial wizard she had discovered as Queen of France, now the trusted grand treasurer of her household, almost made her Chancellor clap his hands.

Her choices had proven fortunate so far. They were in surprising accord. While they might disagree on the means, to a man they wanted to reinstate Breton principles and laws as they had been before King Charles's changes.

~

21 May 1498

ANNE'S grand chamberlain led King Louis and his retinue to the council chamber in the new wing of the Hôtel d'Étampes. Robed as Duchess of Brittany, Anne greeted them and led King Louis to the throne on the dais and invited him to take the place of honour.

Then she knelt before him, placed her hands together in the formal gesture of vassalage and asked to swear fealty to him. She heard the astonished gasps behind her. King Louis maintained a neutral expression as he accepted her fealty with aplomb.

She was pleased with herself. It had been brilliant. In that one act, she removed the contentious issue of whether Brittany would recognize the King of France as suzerain, without arguing about it with her council. That should show them she intended to rely on her own judgment.

As she took her place of honour, she surveyed the room. When she judged that no one would dispute her action, she addressed Louis. "Your Majesty, the Council of Brittany has prepared a request to present to you, if you will receive it." From his imperturbable demeanour, she concluded he had expected this.

"With pleasure, Duchess Anne."

"Chancellor de Montauban, present our request."

He read their message. It was succinct.

Gracious Lord and Majesty, King Louis, XIIth of the name;

The Council of the Duchy of Brittany, constituted by Anne, Duchess of Brittany under the terms of the dissolution of her marriage in her marriage contract of Langeais, which came into effect on 7 April 1498, hereby proposes the following:

Whereas by the terms of treaty that concluded the war between the Kingdom of France and the Duchy of Brittany, the Kingdom of France contracted to withdraw its forces from the principal fortified towns and cities of Brittany that it had occupied;

And whereas this clause has not yet been fulfilled, although the war terminated on 6 December 1491 with the marriage of the said Duchess of Brittany to the late Charles King of France, VIIIth of the name;

And whereas the citizens and population of the Duchy of Brittany view these forces as an army of occupation, camped in its land and at its expense without justification;

Therefore, be it known that the Council of Brittany requests that you, Louis XII, King of France, order the removal of all garrisons that the Kingdom of France continues to quarter in any and all fortified towns and cities of Brittany, effective immediately.

Signed: Anne, Duchess of Brittany

The Baron de Montauban re-rolled the scroll, stepped to the dais, knelt, and handed the petition to the king.

The French Chancellor, Sire Guy de Rochefort, a member of the king's entourage, leapt to his feet, his face as crimson as the robes he wore.

Before he could speak, King Louis said, "Duchess Anne, Chancellor de Montauban, and members of the Council of Brittany, in the years since the 1491, Brittany and Bretons have proven loyal and stalwart. During the Italian expedition, many Bretons took part and gave their lives. Breton ships and mariners joined the naval expeditions against Genoa and Naples, and Breton seafaring skills played an exceptional part in our successes. It is past time that the garrisons be withdrawn from Breton territory, and I agree in principle with your request."

A buzz rose when Louis paused. Among the Breton Council, it rose as a pleased hum; the French contingent vibrated like angry hornets.

Louis raised a hand, and the noise abated. "I am assured that this is only one of several issues that France and Brittany must resolve before the duchess returns to Brittany. Therefore, I propose that the timing of the removal of the garrisons be an item included in the treaty between us before she leaves France this summer."

Since it was the king speaking, his retinue could not argue publicly, but from their nods, they appeared satisfied, as did the Bretons.

With that, the ceremonial meeting concluded. King Louis leaned his lips close to Anne's ear as he took Anne's arm.

"Are you satisfied, Cousin Anne?"

She smiled. "If you are, Cousin Louis." More, she would not say, but she was pleased. They would have a treaty that summer, and Louis understood what she wanted. She would soon learn what he wanted in return.

~

Hôtel d'Étampes, south of Paris, 5 July 1498

"YOU HAVE WORKED wonders with the redesign of this château," Madame la Grande said, as she met Duchess Anne in the gardens. "The new apartments are airy, and their large windows reflect the new Italian style." Anne had settled Madame la Grande and her ladies in the best apartments reserved for the most important visitors.

"It had been in our family for centuries but rarely used." Admiring the enhancements she had wrought, Anne said, "This serves as my Breton base in Paris for now. Besides designing the new buildings, the Italian architects have improved the donjon by knocking new rooms into the thickness of the walls on both sides of the tower and opening large windows into them that bring both light and cross drafts." She added, as courtesy demanded, "Most important, it offers me a home in which to welcome you."

She led Madame la Grande and her ladies to join hers under a leafy bower and invited her to sit on a shady bench.

"This is like the one I had at Moulins, and it reminds me of your kindness during a difficult time," she said. "Now, tell me about the coronation. I am sorry to learn of Queen Jeanne's troubles."

Anne had heard the gossip about Louis's refusal to permit Jeanne to be crowned with him both at his consecration in Reims and at his coronation at the Saint Denis Basilica four days previously. She had reflected on how to approach the sensitive issue. Because they knew each other well and had grown from enemies to trusted family, she had decided to be frank.

She chose her words carefully. "Our sister is a true saint and loves him more than he deserves. Yet although she must feel shamed, she cannot be surprised. To attend must have been painful for you and Duke Pierre, and Jeanne must feel you have abandoned her." Soon she would probably be in the same position and squirmed inside.

Madame la Grande looked sorrowful. "She does. I told her we could not in conscience foist a civil war upon France by opposing the divorce and annulment. She says she understands and forgives me. That made me feel worse."

"If it is any comfort, Cousin, I support your decision. We both know that civil war is terrible." The words brought a flood of memories. Awash in them, Anne put an arm around Madame la Grande's waist and gave her a quick hug. It surprised them both.

"Thank you." Madame la Grande's voice was warm.

This was the moment, Anne decided. She took a deep breath. "You negotiated the treaty that ended the war between France and Brittany, so you remember its terms. It requires me to marry the next king of France." She had said it often enough that her voice no longer trembled. "Louis has said nothing to me, but his repudiation of Queen Jeanne must mean he has approached the Curia and expects his petition for the divorce to succeed. Will you support our marriage if it comes about?"

Madame la Grande puckered her mouth as if tasting something sour. "I must, must I not?" She took Anne's hand. "Politics are cruel to women. You and my sister are paying the price. So did Archduchess Marguerite and Countess Louise. They both hate me for it. I hope you understand now and do not."

Anne probed her responses at the time and now. "This is hard to talk about. . . When I had to divorce Maximilian, and Charles had to divorce Marguerite and you forced us to marry each other as my only way to keep Brittany, I did hate you. As each of my children died, I have questioned whether my marriage was valid. Losing Charles has been. . . I loved. . . I grew to love Charles."

She stopped and sat in silence beside Madame la Grande. When she spoke again, her voice was stronger. "I also learned a great deal from you and came to admire you. It is never easy to rule. When I ruled as duchess before, I was so young. I did not fully understand hard choices until the treaty. It was easier to blame you than. . . I understand better now.

"I have not decided whether I shall marry Louis—if indeed he suggests I marry him. It will depend on the terms of the treaty that we arrange. If I am not satisfied, I shall not. After all, the treaty only says that if I marry, I must marry the next king of France. I may not marry. Or Louis may die, and I may marry Count François." At that, she gave Madame la Grande an impish smile.

"Since we are exchanging confidences, did you know," Madame La Grande said, "King Louis has started the process to guarantee Suzanne the rights of inheritance to all Pierre's and my lands through an act passed in the Parlement de Paris? It should be presented within the next month."

"No, I had not heard. That is excellent news for you," Anne said.

"King Louis is proving wise. He surprises me," Madame la Grande said. "Someone asked him about what he would do to those who had harmed him when he was Duke d'Orléans. He said it would be unfitting for the King of France to retaliate for the quarrels of the Duke d'Orléans."

"Fine words. I hear he is keeping the Marshal de Gié with him and will make him Gouverneur of the young Count François if he can wrest him from his dragon of a mother." Anne looked away to the West. "This time when he goes to the Parlement de Paris, he is king, so I expect when he asks for guardianship *de facto* as well as *de jure,* they will agree. Besides, I hear she is a trifle too intimate with her chamberlain."

Anne made sour moue and Madame la Grande said, "You would do better to learn to get along with de Gié. Louis has a high opinion of him."

"Well, as long as he stays with the French court when I return to Brittany, we may not cross paths," Anne countered.

~

IN THE HEAT OF MID-JULY, Louis came to conduct business in Paris and asked Anne if she would receive him.

When she asked Chancellor Philippe why, he suggested the king might have a personal request since treaty negotiations had advanced so amicably.

Louis came dressed for courtship in a silk brocade doublet over perfectly fitting knitted hose. Over this, he wore a sleeveless short cloak trimmed in shaved velvet. His matching brocade hat sported a peacock feather that swept down his back and he wore boots of soft black leather. His hair and clothing were well cut and well fitting, and he looked much younger than his thirty-six years. He left his four attendants with her ladies in the pergola, and together she and he strolled along the sweet-smelling pathways.

Anne, too, had dressed for a tryst in cool silks and fine lawn that flattered her creamy colouring and hazel eyes. The Breton hood she had made fashionable framed her flawless face and thick chestnut hair. As always, her skirts hid the shoe with one heel higher than the other that masked her limp.

She entertained him with a lively account of her visit with Madame la Grande, ending with his guarantee that little Suzanne would inherit the Bourbonnais. She would have gone on, but he interrupted her, blushing, and begged her to marry him.

She hesitated. "Ye-es. With conditions."

He looked nervous as a bird spied by a cat. "Tell me."

"Madame la Grande told me you declared yourself King of France, Naples, and Jerusalem, and Duke of Milan at your consecration."

"Is that a problem?" He sounded surprised.

"It depends. Truly, I will never understand this male desire to conquer other lands." When he opened his mouth, she put her hand over it, saying, "Do not explain. That is not my point."

She waited with a finger over his lips until he nodded. "First, when. . . if. . . the Lord gives us children, and you leave France, I will stay with them if I wish. Do you agree?"

"Charles-Orland?" he asked, his voice gentle.

She brushed the tears from her eyes. "Yes, or no?"

"Yes, my dear Anne."

"Second, these wars are costly. The new treaty reaffirms the independent Breton institutions as agreed at the time of the 1491 treaty. I have re-established the Breton Chancellery and Breton Church as they were. You agree that France will not interfere with either again?"

"You want France to support Brittany? I do not think my Frenchmen will agree."

"Not at all. Brittany will not provide financing for your Italian wars. In fact, my Chancellor will launch a suit to recover the overpayments that occurred after our Chancellery was integrated into that of France. He has been investigating the matter." Her chin jutted.

"You drive a hard bargain. I should know, as I was a member of your team then. You have not forgotten?"

She placed a hand on his arm and squeezed it. "Of course not. That is why I believe we shall agree. . . and that we shall suit."

He picked a sweetly scented red rose from a trellis and offered it to her. "You put it to shame."

She tucked it under the belt at her waist. As she was doing so, he sucked the drops of blood from his fingers.

"You hurt yourself."

"There were a few thorns. The pricks will heal and leave no scar. And the wounds are slight compared to the infinite value of the prize."

"You flatter me. I dislike flattery."

He laughed at that, raised her hand from his arm and kissed it. "That is one of the many qualities that makes you an infinitely valuable prize, Cousin Anne. I will be the most fortunate man in France if I win you."

"There is one other thing." She pointed to a bench, and they sat. She suddenly felt shy. This was something men expected women to tolerate, and the Church condoned, but Charles's promiscuity angered and worried her, especially after his army returned with the Italian disease. Louis was known as a womanizer, and he had a bastard whom he recognized. She did not want to suffer through that again.

"Everyone talks about all your women. . . Charles was like that. . ." She could feel her face burning.

Louis did not force her to continue. "Dear Cousin Anne, just as I value your love of honesty, I value your virtue, and the modesty of your court." He looked down at his hands.

When he gazed at her again, his eyes were blazing. "Old Louis, may he roast in hell forever, married me to his grotesque, barren daughter to end the Orléans line. I have suffered from his malevolence for over twenty years. Philandering was my revenge and the only reason I am pleased to be king is to spite him."

His expression softened as he gazed at her. "Charles's womanizing made no sense to me. Blessed with you, he fornicated like a stallion in rut. You were my sister-in-law, so I forced you from my mind, but I thought him a fool. If you agree to marry me, you will have no reason to doubt my fidelity."

"Then, yes."

"No more stipulations?" he asked, his tone teasing.

She gave him a sharp glance. "Just the usual things. A queen's dower rights. Regency, should you die before me. That sort of thing. Our negotiators can settle them unless *you* have something?"

He laughed again. "I knew there would be more. We can, of a certainty, leave them to the negotiators. We will read the final terms before we sign."

CHAPTER 38

The Importance of Sons

Château de Blois, 22 August 1498

Rain in August. Neither the tenant farmers nor their noble seigneurs would be happy, Anne thought, as she and her entourage trotted along the old Roman road that led to Blois, mud splashing onto her oiled leather cloak and boots. None of her travel companions were pleased about it, although they did not complain in her hearing. She was no more pleased than they, but it was God's will. She could see the town walls in the distance, and so she instructed her chamberlain to stop at the next large inn. Most of the company would wait for her there while she rode on with only a few of her retinue. The chatter among her party became more cheerful at once.

Within two turns of the hourglass, Anne and a small band of ten, now changed into dry clothes, left from the smoky inn outside Blois's town walls. The rain pattered steadily, sending runnels down the steep cobbled streets as she and her company trotted up to the castle gates. There, the guards recognized her ermine badge emblazoned with a crown and lifted the creaky portcullis without hesitation.

~

FOUR MENSERVANTS HELD a baldaquin[1] over Louise, her children, and Mme Antoinette to protect them from the rain as they crossed the inner courtyard toward the Saint Calais Chapel. Louise was irritable. How dare it rain at this time of year? Much as she adored François, having to keep his boisterous energy bottled up inside was tiresome. If they were lucky, the chapel would be empty, and he could run up and down the aisle for an hour with Marguerite.

The appearance of another baldaquin carried by four large officers caught her eye. Were they not wearing. . .? Yes, they wore the uniform of Anne's Breton Guard. The Dowager Queen—excuse *me*—Duchess Anne must be visiting. She had heard rumours that instead of returning to her duchy to stay, Anne would marry King Louis. Louise's first thought had been, Anne might have a living son this time. At the sight of her emblem, Louise's fists curled.

What was she doing here, anyway? This was the second time she was destroying an existing royal marriage to marry the King of France. To come and gloat over her discarded rival was sheer vindictiveness.

Louise changed direction so that her path would cross Anne's. When they met, she curtsied much less deeply than she had before. "Mme la Duchesse, what a surprise. Have you come to visit Queen Jeanne?"

AS SOON AS Anne saw Louise and her brood across the courtyard, she remembered Madame la Grande's gossip and had an urge to avoid her. Her sister-in-law, who rarely tattled, had been so outraged by Louise's behaviour, that she had told Anne the countess had rejoiced when she heard Charles had died, boasting that her son was certain to be king after Louis since Jeanne was barren and deformed.

Anne kept to her path solely because she would not give the Louise satisfaction of causing her to change direction. "Good morrow, Countess Louise," she said, when they met. "Yes, I come to bid her adieu before I depart for Brittany."

She dropped to a crouch. "Good morrow, Count François. Good morrow, Lady Margot. How do you go on?"

The two children made their obeisances, chattering about their planned visit to the chapel. They both liked Anne, who had always played with them when they visited the court with their mother.

"We live here now," Count François confided.

"Is that so? Do you enjoy living here?"

"Not much," François said.

Marguerite disagreed. "I like it. It has a big lib'ry. Queen Jeanne is nice."

"Queen Jeanne is ugly." François wrinkled his nose.

Anne said, shocked. "A prince never says anything like that about anyone. I thought you were a prince. Are you not?"

Count François put a finger in his mouth. He sounded defiant. "*Am* a prince."

"Then apologize and promise never to say that again."

The boy looked up to his mother and gouvernante, for support. Everyone stared at him disapprovingly. "Pardon," he said.

"Never again?"

"Never again."

The episode flustered Louise. The Duchess had reproved her son in public. Worse, he had misbehaved, so she could not take offence. "Please take the children to the chapel, Mme Antoinette," she said. When the gouvernante looked pointedly up toward their baldaquin, she said, "If you hurry you will not become very wet. Besides, the rain will not hurt you."

"I had not heard you resided at Blois," Anne said.

Louise had a sudden hope. The duchess was well known to dislike Marshal Pierre de Gié. Perhaps she could enlist Anne's help. "Now that Louis is king, he has claimed guardianship of the dauphin. He insisted on taking François from me, bringing him to Blois and appointing Marshal de Gié as François's Gouverneur."

"Yes, he mentioned it."

Displeased by Anne's unhelpful answer, Louise glowered. "Carlo's will named me the guardian of our children. I told the king that if he took François, he must bring me, Marguerite, and my court, too. Boys do not leave their mothers until they are seven. François is not yet four."

"It appears that he agreed."

"I gave him no choice." Louise stiffened.

Anne assessed the rich apparel the children were wearing and the fine black silk taffeta of Louise's widow's gown; the silk baldaquin embroidered with Louise's swans; and the four servants to carry it. She seemed to have found a soft bed to sleep in after all her complaints about her impecunious circumstances. "It seems you have negotiated an excellent compromise, Countess. I imagine the king pays all the costs of running Blois?"

Louise reddened and retaliated. "I hear you will marry the King of France."

Anne fingered her widow's robes. "My dear Mme Louise, unlike you, I am recently bereaved. I consider it too soon to discuss another marriage. The curse of courts is the circulation of gossip, and so much of it is false. I return to Brittany as its duchess and ruler. Brittany remains independent of France. You may repeat that, for it is and will remain true."

Suddenly tired of the pretence of courtesy between them, Anne said, "Another thing is true. You will do better to concern yourself less about me and mine and more about yourself and yours. Adieu, Countess."

The duchess stalked off, leaving Louise angry and puzzled.

Anne acted confident and cheerful, which was a bad sign. Louise's situation had seemed so hopeful when King Charles died without an heir, leaving an aging king with a barren wife. But as time passed, Louise had found her optimism dwindling. Her life of freedom, ruling in her own home, had been taken from her. The new king had taken control of her life and her children. Her premonitions seldom failed her, and they blared that, unlikely as it seemed, Anne would return as Queen of France and the future of her adored François as dauphin, and later king, no longer seemed as assured. Fewer than five months had passed. How had the sunshine faded so quickly, leaving storm clouds behind?

A GENTLEMAN USHER stood outside the door of Queen Jeanne's apartments when Duchess Anne and her small entourage arrived, accompanied by the queen's grand chamberlain.

He said, "Duchess Anne is here to pay her respects to the queen."

The gentleman usher replied, "She does not wish to be disturbed."

The grand chamberlain raised his eyebrows. "Nevertheless, Duchess Anne is here to see her. You *will* inform the queen."

Hesitating only long enough to show his disapproval, the young noble entered the queen's rooms. He returned after a brief delay and opened the door for Anne.

Queen Jeanne, dressed in her customary loose black robe and the floor length sleeveless vest she wore to mask her misshapen body, waited near the door.

"Sister," she said, "how kind of you to visit."

Anne curtsied deeply and said, "I regret disturbing you, Madame la Reine. I wish to bid you a formal *adieu* before leaving for my duchy and," she dropped her voice to keep their conversation private, "to talk to you about a personal matter."

Jeanne's eyes had filmed with tears when Anne addressed her

as queen. "Thank you, Sister, for your courtesy. Come to my private study."

She led Anne into an exquisite, whitewashed space. They faced a glowing window of the risen Christ, below which sat Jeanne's desk and stool and, beside them, a bookcase. Beside the door they entered through stood a prie-dieu upon which Jeanne's Book of Hours lay open. Above it hung a silver crucifix. On the wall to the left hung a moving Adoration of the Christ Child.[2] A white door that blended into the wall to the right led to her bedchamber. Jeanne opened it to fetch a low stool for Anne, who leapt to take it from her.

Jeanne refused her help. "I am your hostess. Please sit."

Anne sat and took a deep breath. As she did so, she scented the faint odour of roses that hung in the air. It calmed her, as did the peace that inhabited the small sanctuary.

"This is a holy place," she said. "It seems wrong to intrude the cares of the world into it."

"It is the cares and troubles of the world that draw us to our Saviour. Is that what brings you here?"

"I wish I did not need to come for this reason," Anne said. "Or to bring these troubles upon you. Yet I would prefer you hear them from me and know how much I regret my part in hurting you."

Jeanne looked at the crucifix on the wall. "Then I can guess what you will say, but tell me." She closed her eyes.

"King Louis has told me he has applied to Rome for a divorce and annulment, and there will be a commission of inquiry. If the annulment is granted, he has asked me to marry him, and I have agreed."

Before she visited, Anne had spent many hours in prayer. She came because she believed it would be crueller for Jeanne to hear her betrayal from another, and cowardly not to face the pain her decision would inflict on the sister-in-law she loved. She had asked the Holy Mother for help to form her words to the saintly Jeanne.

It had come to her to speak simply from her heart of her regret and apology.

Tears rolled silently down Jeanne's cheeks. Anne fell to her knees; her voice choking with her own tears and buried her head in Jeanne's lap. Jeanne patted her head until their sobs subsided. Then, in her gentle voice, thick with tears, she said, "Marriage is a holy union. Indissoluble. Explain to me why, dear Anne."

Anne lifted her head and took Jeanne's hands. "Mayhap I could have refused, although in the treaty I signed when I married your brother, I swore I would marry the next king of France if Charles died before me, and we had no son. Louis is a renowned warrior. If I refuse, yet marry elsewhere, I fear Brittany will face another war with France. Yet I must marry, for I have no heir."

When Anne had decided to speak to Jeanne herself, she had expected it to be hard. It was even more painful than she had foreseen because Jeanne was so blameless. Jeanne's anguish hurt to watch, yet Anne struggled to open her heart. "I am Duchess of Brittany and responsible for my people. I cannot bring another war upon them. If the divorce and annulment are granted, it will be the second time I cause this pain within your family. More than anything, I grieve for your pain, for I- I- love you, Jeanne."

Jeanne patted her hand, but still did not speak.

"If you only had sons," Anne cried. "I do not believe Louis would insist on this annulment if you had sons." The words hung in the air between them. Anne threw her arms around Jeanne. "I am so, so sorry. It sounds as if I am blaming you. . . as if this is your fault and I do not mean that at all. You are not to blame. Maybe the divorce will not be granted, and we both will be safe."

"There is no hope of that. I honour Alexander VI as Pope, but as a man he is corrupt." Jeanne's voice was steady now. She was twelve years older than Anne, and the saintly person her young sister-in-law recognized her to be. She took Anne in her arms, and they comforted each other.

After a time, she spoke again. "You are right. It is all about sons. I cannot give Louis a son. I pray you will. Every man wants an heir and France needs a peaceful transition."

She wiped her eyes. "I am a Princess of France. I understand. And you, Anne, are an honourable woman."

THE RAIN HAD CLEARED, and blue skies shone over the ancient city of Blois as Anne and her entourage rode out of the narrow gates of the Château and she paused to observe the view. As the sun rose, shining on the puddles on the grey-blue slate roofs and cobbled streets, a mist gave the scene a soft blurred quality that reminded her of the skies in Brittany. In the distance, sunlight sparkled on the Loire River, shallow and full of sandbars as it always was here this late in summer, where it flowed up through the countryside towards her duchy, her major city of Nantes and the coast.

She could look upon it again with pleasure as she used to do as a child when she watched the boats from their château windows or sat in their state barge as they were rowed along the mighty river. It was her highway again rather than a daily reminder of what she had lost. Her heart lifted.

After leaving Blois behind, they stayed on the North side of the Loire, following its course through the gentle countryside. It would take several weeks to return to Brittany, but she was on her way. She thought back to that hurried flight into France eight years ago during the cold grey days of November, thought of how she ran from Maximilian's landsknechts, facing a future she feared. From this distance of years, she realized how young, afraid, yet arrogant she had been. Then, she had faith that the treaty terms she had negotiated would secure Breton rights. After first meeting Charles, when he had been so chivalrous, she had imagined she could beguile him into letting her take back her rightful control of her duchy once she had provided a dauphin for France and a second son to become the next Duke of Brittany. That had not seemed an insurmountable challenge. How naïve, how innocent she had been.

The past eight years had been hard. Losing each son and daughter had left a scar in her heart that ached each time she unexpectedly caught sight of a mother cradling her infant in her arms. Although her confessor had said she must not blame herself or Charles but accept God's will, she would never forgive herself for her absence from Charles-Orland's sickbed at his last illness. Her lack of courage shamed her. Each time she thought of it, she renewed her vow never again to allow anyone to stand in the way of doing what she knew to be right. Yet she had also learned that she was not always right, and she benefitted by taking advice. Certainty should be hard-earned, not a childish stomping of her foot.

She thought again of Charles. He had not been a bad husband, but his infidelities had wounded not only her pride but also her feeling that she was desirable as a woman. Until Louis came to her in July, dressed in his best, not in his usual unkempt attire, and blushed when she admired him, she had forgotten how it felt to feel desirable. Throughout his visit, she had been aware of the way his colour rose, and how his eyes glistened when he looked at her; the way he held his breath when she opened the silken wrappings of the exquisite pearl and ruby necklace he had brought her; the way he moistened his lips when she exclaimed her delight; the way his breathing quickened when he held her close to kiss her cheeks and then her lips. She smiled to herself. He wanted her, Anne, as a woman, not just the duchess of Brittany, for Brittany. They had been friends for many years; they had quarrelled and repaired their friendship. They knew each other well. This marriage, if it came to pass, could bring them happiness.

Thinking of the obstacles, her mind turned to her conversation with Jeanne, and her pleasure dissipated. If only God had not demanded that she must cause her saintly sister-in-law to suffer. This was another of the stones He had cast onto the path of her duty towards her Breton people. Was it His way of teaching her that with responsibility came the sorrow of hard decisions with no good choices?

Her first test would come soon enough. Along their return route, she and her entourage would stop to meet her council. With them, she would send the order to the three estates—clergy, nobility, and bourgeoisie of Brittany—-calling their delegates to a meet as the Estates General in Rennes on September 15th. The meeting was her formal signal announcing Brittany's regained independence to both Bretons and Frenchmen. By doing this, she was reinstating the Estates General her late husband had suppressed. She would preside as its members undid the illegal changes wrought under his administration.

After Brittany had lost its war with France, she had accepted marriage to its king as the best way to salvage what she could of Breton customs and independence. Like the granite Breton coast battered by storms, she had endured her many trials with God's help to keep faith with her dream.

Although the treaty she had made then required that she must marry the next king of France if he wished, because of her marriage to Charles, Brittany had recovered its strength and much of its unity. When she and her council negotiated the treaty between their duchy and France this time, the terms agreed were much more favourable to Brittany. She was returning as the ruling duchess to her independent duchy.

She closed her eyes and Mme Michelle asked, "Is something wrong, Mme la Duchesse?"

Blinking, Anne looked around her at the sunny day and the shining river. "All is as well as it can be in this imperfect world," she said. Because it was imperfect. Once again, she needed to bear a son—two sons would be better—one as dauphin for France and one to become the next Duke of Brittany to make her dream secure. Her labours were not complete, but she had come a long way and learned a great deal. Smiling, she tossed her head and said, "Yet it is a beautiful day, we are young, and we are riding for home. It is as close to perfect as we can hope in this world."

. . .

1 Baldaquin—a ceremonial canopy of state made from the cloth hung above the seat of, or carried over, a personage of standing, as a symbol of authority.

2 Adoration of the Christ Child—a painting by Josse Lieferinxe, c. 1500, now hanging in the Louvre.

FINIS

Preview a Sample

For a preview of Keira Morgan's published book ***The Importance of Pawns*** in this series, ***Chronicles of the House of Valois***, read on. . . .

The Importance of Pawns

Chapter I

4 January 1514, Early afternoon, Château de Blois

Countess Louise d'Angoulême appraised her reflection in the fine Venetian mirror her son, her marvellous François, had given her for her holy days *étrenne*. Was it not just like him to give her the costliest gift he could find? And who would pay for it? Putting the problem aside, she turned her head this way and that. Were those grey hairs in among her glossy dark blond locks? Did she have crow's feet fanning from her wide grey eyes? The perfection of the image from this latest invention was perhaps not an advantage to an older woman. Impatiently she put it down.

When would that Agnez arrive? It was unsuitable that a woman of her rank should be kept waiting by a servant girl. She paced once more around the perimeter of her suite's presence chamber, pausing to stroke each thick Flemish tapestry that absorbed the chill from the stone walls. She reminded herself that she had done very well to parlay King Louis's favour into this suite of three rooms, despite the overcrowding at the Christmas court. It had taken some effort on her part, but despite Queen Anne's enmity, she had even charmed the king into furnishing the rooms. When she arrived early in December, she had come accompanied only by her bed and clothes chests.

Louise threw herself into a folding leather chair in front of the hissing fire. The crowned L & A for Louis and Anne emblazoned on the fireplace hood drew her eyes. How the emblem irritated her! When her son was king, she would order those initials replaced immediately.

A knock rattled the door of her presence chamber. Finally! When her gentleman usher pulled it open, the queen's maid, Agnez, sidled in. She bobbed a curtsey. "You send for me, Mme Comtesse?" She twisted her hands on her apron.

Louise did not rise. "The court is rife with rumours that the queen is sinking and will not last the month. Be it true?"

Agnez's chapped lips twitched into a knowing smile, and she gave a jerky nod. "Madame la Reine be mortal ill. She will pass soon, yes?"

Louise nodded. It was as she thought. Queen Anne was dying, and much sooner than anyone had expected — if Agnez's words proved true. Though there was no reason to doubt her. On past occasions she had earned her pay. But it was too irritating. Queen Anne's illness was just another difficulty! She still had not approved her daughter's marriage to Louise's son. They had been betrothed for years and would be married already, but for Queen Anne's unrelenting opposition. Not that plain, fat Princess Claude with her ugly limp and mousy hair was the match Louise would have chosen for her magnificent François, but what choice did she have? King Louis was her son's guardian, and he insisted upon the marriage. Too bad he couldn't control his stubborn wife — or did not choose to. At least Claude was wealthy, and soon would be richer since she was heiress to the duchy of Brittany when the queen died, and it was just one of Claude's dower lands.

"Baronne Michelle have been with Madame la Reine all the morning." Agnez brought a finger to her lips, muffling her words. "She will last but days, yes."

It took Louise a few seconds to understand Agnez's mumbled words. When they finally sank in, Louise barely concealed her worry. There would be no wedding if the court was in mourning. "You are certain?"

Agnez's chin bobbed. "Oh, *oui*. I scrub the floor, so I hear all." She frowned. "There was more, yes?"

"Yes?"

"She say—"

"Who said?"

"Madame la Reine say—" The girl fell silent.

"Tell me, child. I will not bite."

"She do not leave Bretagne to the Princesse Claude. Will leave it to the Princesse Renée."

"By the shoes of the Blessed Virgin!"

Agnez fell to her knees. "I be s-s-sorry."

The countess realized she was glaring at the girl. "There, there, wench, calm yourself, you surprised me. That is all. Stand up." Louise forced herself to speak coolly. She pointed to the ale, "Pour yourself a tankard. Now, what else did the queen say?"

After she took a swallow, Agnez snuffled through her nose. Hands gripping the mug, she said, "You be not angry, Mme Comtesse?"

"Not with you, girl. You have been useful and the more you tell me, the better I will reward you." That should open her lips. Hopefully, it did not encourage her to embellish her tale.

"You not like it, for sure."

Louise's grey eyes snapped. "I do not blame you for the words of others, girl."

Agnez pushed wisps of greasy hair back under her cap. She spoke in a singsong as if quoting: "Madame la Reine say, 'The Comtesse d'Angoulême is no more please about the marriage than me. She do not like my daughter and agree to it only to please the king since he powerful and rich... 'cause she greedy. Let 'er find out that Bretagne not go to Claude and see how fast she end the betrothal.'" Agnez slowed to a stop.

Louise did not doubt that Agnez had repeated the queen's words. Though Louise's face burned, she controlled herself. "Was there more?"

The girl shook her mob-capped head.

Louise stood. "You have done me good service, Agnez. Continue, and there will be more like this." She tossed her a bag of small coins.

Catching it, Agnez scrambled into a curtsey. "*Merci*, Mme Comtesse." She almost ran from the room.

Louise paced the parquet floor for some time before regaining her temper. That the queen was correct about her opinion of Claude and the marriage was irrelevant. That the Queen called Louise avaricious was insulting but unimportant — another example of a rich woman despising a clever one for her lesser means and greater talents. That the queen planned to disinherit Claude of Brittany was unacceptable.

As Louise moved about her rooms, she stopped to caress the soft Flemish tapestries, the glowing frames on the paintings by Botticelli and Raphael, and the tooled leather covers on the books she had taken from the great library. Was Claude worth marrying without Brittany? Her dowry also included Milan — the single richest state in the West. She was the best dowered heiress in Europe. But King Louis had lost Milan, and who knew if he would recover it — or be able to hold it. So, what was it worth? Yet her son valued it more than all Claude's other domains and was determined to regain her birthright. It was an obsession of his. To Louise it was a chimera, but she would do anything for her son. What made men so eager to fight, to become storied warriors, wasting their wealth and risking maiming and death?

Louise shook her head to rid it of these unwelcome thoughts. As she passed Botticelli's painting again, she paused to gaze at it. Venus floated to shore on a scallop shell while three Graces danced on the grass nearby. Its perfection usually restored her sense of order. Today it did not work its magic. Why could not the actual world be so orderly? Brittany was too great a prize to permit the queen to bequeath it away from Princess Claude.

* * *

Michelle de Soubise stood over the table cluttered with flasks and packets of remedies. When she opened the stoppered bottle of valerian, its woody odour penetrated the close air in Queen Anne's bedchamber. She measured a dose.

When Michelle put the cup to the queen's mouth, Anne wrinkled her nose. They eyed each other. She opened her lips and swallowed. "You know I do not like medicine."

"It is not a medicine, Milady. It is a restorative, to ease your pain." Michelle's voice was low and reassuring. Never would she admit to the queen that she gave her medicine. Queen Anne abhorred everything to do with doctors, blaming them for her children's deaths.

"You always have a pacifying answer." The queen smiled faintly, though pain lines creased her brow.

Michelle smiled back, repressing her sorrow. It was like pressing her tongue on a chancre to watch over the queen as she weakened and shrank. Although Queen Anne was only thirty-seven, she looked much older. Already her cheeks were sunken, her skin yellow and tight over her cheekbones and jaw. Only her enormous amber eyes fringed with long dark lashes hinted at her once great beauty.

Queen Anne should be in bed, but she would not stay there. A month ago, she had been bustling about, and still refused to admit how ill she was. So, she was resting fully clothed in her favourite armchair, her feet raised on a footstool. She shivered.

Michelle felt the queen's forehead. It was clammy, despite the heat radiating from the logs crackling in the fireplace of her vast bedchamber. Michelle crossed to the four-poster bed, the heavy canopy dressed in the queen's colours, to pluck up an ermine coverlet. At least this new part of the Château de Blois was well-sealed from winter's frigid draughts. The wainscoted walls insulated by the queen's favourite silk tapestries brightened the space.

Returning to her, Michelle draped the soft fur over the queen's knees. Queen Anne winced.

"Bring those braziers close, Agnez." When the chambermaid finished the sooty task, Michelle smiled a thank you.

"Stop bustling about, Mme Michelle. Your fussing disturbs me." The queen sounded querulous, a sign of her ill health.

Michelle sank to a stool beside the queen and smoothed her overskirt over her knees. "Would you like me to read aloud or to write a letter, Mme la Reine? Or...?"

"Not yet." Queen Anne leaned back and closed her eyes.

As the queen's *dame d'atour,* her highest-ranking lady and only real friend, probably even closer than her husband, she was privy to Queen Anne's deepest secrets. Perhaps only her confessor knew more. So, they both knew she was dying, although the queen had yet to admit it. But she had little time left and many hard decisions to make. Talking about them would help, Michelle thought.

The queen's voice disrupted Michelle's brooding. "The king keeps pressing me to agree to a date for Claude's marriage. Now that she's turned fifteen — and her monthly flowers have begun — he has become insistent. And after I am gone, I cannot prevent it. But what will I do about Brittany? How can I leave it to Claude when she is betrothed to Duke François?" She turned her head to Michelle, even that small movement sending a flash of pain across her face. "So, what do you advise, my wise friend?"

Michelle puffed out a breath of relief. Here was the opening she had been waiting for. Yet she was irritated, too. Brittany, always Brittany. "Dear friend, although I have waited to say so, it is time to turn your thoughts to your eternal life. Look at all you have already achieved for Brittany. Our homeland is now rich and peaceful. Please trust that our Saviour knows best. Turn your thoughts instead to final matters: the future of your daughter, Renée, the last dispositions you must make of your worldly goods, and your last confession."

"Do not rush me out of this world, Mme Michelle." Queen

Anne's voice cut sharp as a rapier. "You may not consider the future of Brittany one of my important final matters. I do." She straightened in her armchair, flinching again. Michelle guessed that her *renes* pained her much more than she would admit. "Listen to me."

Those were the last words she spoke. The next moment she was writhing in agony. Ordering Agnez to bring two men servants to carry her to her bed and send for Dr. Nichel, Michelle managed to get the queen to swallow a dose of willow bark tisane laced with opium.

* * *

After the queen's sudden relapse, Michelle sent a page flying to King Louis. By the time he arrived, Queen Anne was sleeping heavily from the dose of pain medicine.

King Louis, face lined with sorrow, stood at the foot of the queen's bed, staring at his wife's waxy face. She lay pale as a corpse under her embroidered coverlet.

Michelle touched her forehead. "She experienced an excruciating attack of the renal stone and is still fevered, but less so."

Queen Anne stirred and began a high-pitched mumble.

This was a worrying symptom. "Agnez, fetch a jug of the filtered, cold water." Michelle ordered. She poured a measure of clear water into a bowl, set two stoppered bottles on the worktable, added a measure from each to the bowl, and stirred. A fresh herbal aroma cleansed the stale air.

King Louis perched on the edge of the chair. "What are you preparing?" He leaned forward to sniff. "It smells of flowers."

"It is a mix of lavender oil, spirits of alcohol and pure water — to reduce her fever and freshen her. She will sleep more calmly."

"From what does she suffer?" King Louis insisted.

Knowing him, she believed he would prefer the truth, She said, "I can list her symptoms, but is not your question: will she recover?"

"I shrink from any hint that she will not, yet...." He squared his thin shoulders. "The unsugared pastille then." He stared at the floor.

"Her humours are imbalanced. For some time, I have suspected a bilious humour from the sour odours of her urine and breath, signs of a renal disorder. The agony she suffered today suggest stones have lodged in the renal passages. Only our Saviour can give a certain answer, but I know no remedy. My treatment today only served to reduce her pain."

"Why did you not send for my principal physician to attend her? Is Dr. Loysel not learned?" King Louis sounded like an inquisitor.

"You know Mme la Reine detests physicians. I have been ministering to her since she lost your last child two years past. She is resting quietly now, Sire, as you can see." Michelle strove not to sound defensive. "Dr. Loysel will bleed her, purge her, and prescribe stinking curatives of bats blood and snake excrement." She sniffed. "The queen has neither the strength nor the blood for such remedies. My treatment — willow bark tea mixed with a drop of opium — reduces her pain and allows her to sleep." She picked up her notes from the bedside table and offered him the note pad — leather-bound scraps of vellum held together by string. "I have recorded all my treatments."

King Louis swallowed and glanced at the notepad. "I must know she is receiving the best... the correct... treatment."

"To be sure, the queen must have the best care." Michelle hesitated. People could accuse even noblewomen of witchcraft these days and then torture and burn them at the stake for small acts. Whenever anything went wrong — a failed harvest, a sudden hailstorm, an outbreak of plague — the burnings started. With the queen so ill, Michelle would be safer if an infirmarian attended her. "Princess Renée's infirmarian, Dr. Nichel, has seen her. But perhaps your Dr. Loysel, should attend her instead."

King Louis considered. "It is true that my wife blames the doctors for our infants' deaths. And we both trust you...." He chewed his lower lip. "But I must be sure. She is precious to me."

He leaned over Anne and dabbed away a drop of sweat on her brow.

Michelle said: “Send for him, Sire. Let us hope he knows of cures of which I am unaware.” It was prudent to have him present. It should quell the inevitable rumours.

The king rose, still troubled. “I shall. Although I doubt he.... I have observed that my wife improves most in your care.”

“You are kind, Your Grace. In truth, the queen’s recovery lies in the Lord’s hands.”

~

If you enjoyed this sample of ***The Importance of Pawns*** and want to read it, go to Books2Read ***The Importance of Pawns*** **[https://books2read.com/u/3LRZ0X]**

Coming Soon

THE IMPORTANCE OF HEIRS

If you want to know about Keira's next books, Renaissance France, or the latest by similar authors, **sign up to get the latest about Keira's writing on her website.**

You will also get links to 36 FREE FRENCH RENAISSANCE NOVELS for you to download by authors like Alexander Dumas and Sir Walther Scott, all available on Project Gutenberg but hard to find.

Acknowledgments

This book has benefitted from the support of many.

Profound gratitude goes to five people.

First I thank my mentors and critique partners Roberta Rich, Rachel McMillen, and Emerson Nagel for their inspired advice and many lunches.

My editor, Claire Mulligan, through her encouragement and insightful comments has also helped me lift the level of my writing and to understand what a metaphor is.

And I thank Jenny Q from Historical Fiction Book Covers who stuck with me through many iterations to create another great cover.

These are only a few of many who have offered comments, feedback and corrections along the way. To each of you, I am truly grateful. Without you, this book would not exist.

It goes without saying, but I shall say it anyway, that every error of fact, imagination, grammar and orthography is mine alone.

Glossary

Adoration of the Christ Child—a painting by Josse Lieferinxe, c. 1500, now hanging in the Louvre.

Appanage—is the grant of an estate, title, office or other thing of value to a younger child of a sovereign, who would otherwise have no inheritance under the system of primogeniture. Typically, in France it passed through the male line and when the male line failed, it returned to the royal demesne.

Baldaquin—a ceremonial canopy of state made from the cloth hung above the seat of, or carried over, a personage of standing, as a symbol of authority.

Churched—'Churching' refers to purification of the mother in the church and her blessing from the priest one month to 40 days after giving birth after which the woman was permitted to reapppear in the world.

Cloth of estate—a canopy-like arrangement of precious fabric above and behind a throne or dais.

Ego conjúngo vos in matrimónium. In nómine Patris, et Fílii, et Spíritus Sancti. Amen."—the traditional Latin marriage vow, translated as —By the authority of the Church I ratify and bless the bond of marriage you have contracted. In the name of the Father, and of the Son, and of the Holy Spirit.

Estates General—in France under the Ancien Regime the Estates General was a legislative and consultative assembly of the different classes (or estates) of French subjects. It had a separate assembly for each of the three estates (clergy, nobility and commoners), which were called and dismissed by the king. Some provinces had their own Estates General. Brittany as an independent duchy was one.

Fleur de lys—the fleur-de-lys, translated from French as 'lily flower' is a stylized design of either an iris or a lily that is now used purely decoratively as well as symbolically, or it may be "at one and the same time political, dynastic, artistic, emblematic and symbolic", especially in heraldry. It is particularly associated with the ancient regime French monarchy.

Forepart—The placket and matching forepart are separate pieces of expensive and highly decorated material inserted into the opening of the overdress to cover the kirtle, often with matching lower sleeves.

Galette de roi—a large, circular cake made of puff pastry with its crisp, golden top and soft frangipane centre, each crowned with a golden paper crown.] One special galette de roi was set aside because it alone contained the miniature porcelain king and queen that would identify the rulers for the evening.

Garderobe—most commonly a toilet in a medieval building; also, a wardrobe or small storeroom in a medieval building.

Gouverneur/nante—the Governor/ness of the royal children, recruited from the high nobility, oversees the education of the children of the royal couple, including the Dauphin. He or she is sometimes assisted by deputy governors. While the girls remained attached to the Queen's House, it was customary for princes raised by female governors until they were seven to "pass to men" at that age (the age of reason at the time).

Grand Maître de Menus Plaisirs—The Controller of the Menus Plaisirs heard directly from the king what the plans for the king's personal entertainment were to be set in motion; by long-standing convention, he was a duke; although he was not a professional, it was up to him to determine how to carry out these plans. The Duke in charge of the Menus and Pleasures of the King was an important official of the court.

Hair shirt—a shirt or shift made of rough animal hair worn by ascetics and penitents next to the skin as a penance.

Humours—The humours were part of an ancient theory that held that health came from balance between the bodily liquids. These liquids were termed humours. The Four Humours were liquids within the body—blood, phlegm, yellow bile and black bile.

Italian disease—Syphilis, introduced into Europe in the late 15th century. Its source is unknown, but it became rampant in 1494/95 after the start of the French-Italian wars. Known by various names, in Italy it was called the French disease and in France it was called the Italian disease. There was no known cure, though it was treated with mercury, it raced through the infected individual causing great pain. It was usually fatal.

Landsknecht—a member of a class of mercenary soldiers in the German and other continental armies in the 16th and 17th centuries.

Lauds—early morning, traditionally 3:00 a.m.

Matins—nighttime, traditionally 12:00 a.m.

Michaelmas—September 29, one of the four traditional quarter days, traditionally associated with the end of the harvest and beginning of the fall season.

Monthly flowers—menses or menstrual period.

Mother of maids—a high ranking married woman with the responsibility of the unmarried female courtiers, their conduct and service.

Night rail—the former term for nightgown.

Nones—the ninth hour, traditionally 3:00 p.m.

Prie-dieu—a piece of furniture for use during prayer, consisting of a kneeling surface and a narrow upright front with a rest for the elbows or for books.

Parlement—a provincial_appellate court of France, the

oldest and most important of which was the **Parlement of Paris**. Parlements were judicial organizations consisting of a dozen or more appellate judges. They were the courts of final appeal of the judicial system, and wielded power over many areas including taxation. Laws and edicts issued by the Crown were not official until the parlements assented by publishing them. Their members were aristocrats, called nobles of the robe, who had bought or inherited their offices.

Prime—the first hour of daylight, traditionally 6:00 a.m.

Primero—a Renaissance card game that has many similarities to modern day poker.

Sext—noon, traditionally 12:00 p.m.

Scots Guards—was an elite Scottish military unit founded in 1418 to be personal bodyguards to the French monarchy. They were assimilated into the King's Household and later formed the first company of the Royal Bodyguard. They survived until the end of the Bourbon monarchy.

Terce—the third hour, traditionally 9:00 a.m.

Traboules—from Latin transambulare via vulgar Latin trabulare, meaning "to cross", are a type of secret covered passageways primarily associated with the city of Lyon.

Vespers—sunset, evening, traditionally 6:00 p.m.

Wassail—spiced ale or mulled wine drunk during celebrations for Twelfth Night and Christmas Eve.

Afterword

Appendix 1 — Information About Times

Liturgical [Canonical] Hours

Already well-established by the 9th century in the West, these canonical hours consisted of daily prayer (liturgies) that were also used to refer to the time of day. Though the times changed throughout the day since they followed the hours of sunlight, I have used the following times as a rough guide. Often Lauds and Matins were combined.

Lauds (early morning) 3:00 a.m.
Prime (first hour of daylight) 6:00 a.m.
Terce, (third hour)9:00 a.m.
Sext (noon)12:00 p.m.
Nones (ninth hour) 3:00 p.m.
Vespers (sunset evening) 6:00 p.m.
Compline (end of the day) 9:00 p.m.
Matins (nighttime)12:00 a.m.

Typical Mealtime Hours

In European courts at this time, it was typical that only two meals a day were served in the Great Dining Hall. They were provided to those who had the right to eat at the King's or Queen's table.

First meal, about 10: 00 a.m.

Second meal, about 4:00 p.m.

People at court often/usually went to mass before the first meal.

Quarter Days

Lady Day, March 25, the old New Years Day until 1582

Midsummer Day, June 24, Day of Saint John the Baptist

Michaelmas, September 29, Feast of Saint Michael Archangel

Christmas Day, December 25

Other Major Holy Days

Twelfth Night (6 January) Three Kings Day

Candlemas (2 February) Feast of the Purification of Mary

Ash Wednesday

Easter and Easter Week

Pentecost (Whitsunday) 50 days after Easter Sunday, The Descent of the Holy Spirit

Martinmas (11 November) Feast of Saint Martin of Tours

The Trouble with Dates

Until France adopted the Gregorian calendar in December 1582, introduced by Pope Gregory XIII in October 1582 (and which occurred at different dates in different countries) the new year started on April 1. That is why those events occurring between January 1 and March 31 are often recorded in different years in different documents. Thus, for example, Anne de Bretagne's birthday, which fell on January 25, is variously recorded as occurring in 1476 or 1477.

Facts and Fiction

This is a work of historical fiction. Although I have stayed close to the historical facts as I know them, I have made a few conscious deviations for the sake of my novel. However, everything about my character's motivations, opinions and words is fictional, even when grounded in fact. It is impossible to know how the real people thought or felt, except inasmuch as we are all human.

There is little known about Louise's life before she became King's Mother. Even less is recorded about her mother-in-law's life. Their relationship is fictionalized, although her mother-in-law did live with her and left all she owned to Louise and her children.

The enmity between the de Montfort and the de Rohan is fact as is the de Rohan conspiracy with England. I telescoped the time frame.

Louise's jealousy of Anne is well known. At its core was Louise's ambition for her son. Chroniclers of the time do not provide many details so the incidents in my story are mostly fictional, but they seek to capture their on-going and intensifying feud.

Louise's struggle after her husband's death to retain her right of guardianship against Louis d'Orléans is well recorded, and they compromised until Louis became king and insisted upon overseeing the upbringing of his dauphin.

Charles's infidelities, his illnesses and his sudden accidental death are historical. So is Anne's hysterical shock in reaction and her subsequent recovery and assertion of her rights in Brittany. So are the main events in her relationship with Duke Louis d'Orléans.

If you are curious about particular incidents, contact me.

Sources

I have studied this period for many years, and cannot give my exact sources. Here are several books I have used for the novels in this series. I also read regularly the many articles available on-line written by experts in the field.

Gaugain, Lucie, *Amboise: Un Château dans la Ville*, Presses universitaires François-Rabelais de Tours Presses universitaires de Rennes, 2014.

Le Boterf, Hervé, *Anne de Bretagne,* Editions France-Empire, Paris, 1976.

Matarasso, Pauline. *Queen's Mate: Three Women of Power in France on the Eve of the Renaissance*, Ashgate Publishing Ltd, 2001

Mayer, Dorothy Moulton, *The Great Regent: Louise of Savoy 1476 to 1531*, Funk & Wagnalls, 1966.

Tanguy, G. Morgane, *Anne de Bretagne: Jardins Secrets*, Editions Fernand Lanore, Paris, 1991.

For Discussion

TOPICS & QUESTIONS FOR DISCUSSION

1. Anne declares that everything would have been different if she had been a boy. As the story progresses, what do you learn about how it would have been different for her?

2. From the moment Louise saw Anne, she resented her. She said it was Anne's arrogance What do you think was the real reason?

3. All the women in the book had arranged marriages. Do you think the couples love their partners?

4. Did Anne and Louise have the same goals? What did they want?

5. Anne and Louise each had a weakness that caused them to suffer. What were their weaknesses and how were they different?

6. What kind of power did Charles wield over Anne and why? Did he abuse his power? How did she manage the situation?

7. Why was Brittany so important to Anne?

8. How did you feel about the various women — Anne, Louise, and Jeanne—by the end of the novel?

About the Author

The adventure and romance of Renaissance has fascinated Keira since she was young.

It isn't just the history. In her fiction, readers enter the world of the French court with its irresistible characters, and dangerous intrigues. The accurate historical details of food and clothing, chateaux and furnishings, coaches and litters, gardens and chapels, friends and children bring the world to life as her historical characters struggle with their real-life challenges.

She studied Renaissance and Reformation history in Canadian universities to the doctoral level. But her favourite reading was historical fiction, since in it authors explored the feelings and thoughts that motivated people rather than just the facts. When she recognized she would rather write fiction than history, she chose a career in the Canadian public service and wrote in her free time.

She now lives in Mexico with her husband, two dogs and two cats where she writes full time. *The Importance of Sons* is the second of her published novels. She is writing a four-part series in the Chronicles of the House of Valois. *The Importance of Pawns* is already available.

Keira welcomes comments and suggestions at her website Keira's Renaissance Fiction & History. If you have an article to share, ideas for content, or ideas on improvements, write to her. Her email is on her contact page.

Follow Keira on her social media sites, on her Goodreads, and Amazon Author pages.

Facebook.com/kjmorganwriter
Twitter.com/KJMMexico
Instagram.com/RenaissanceFictionLady
Goodreads Author
Draft2Digital

Made in the USA
Las Vegas, NV
30 September 2024

95969381R00225